Jeremy A. Freed

Cover and Illustrations by:

John "F" Fountain

To Kyle and Lucia, Tyler, Mylan, and Cassie. In a lot of ways, this story is me. So more than anyone else in the world, I wanted you to have it. You are real, my universe, and every other way I describe it in these pages. Thanks for being right there beside me.

-Dad

Contents

SERIES: Cobalt Laser
SEASON 2, EPISODE 10

"All's Well that Ends Well"
TIMESTAMP: 20:58

COBALT LASER STOOD BESIDE his brother and sister, admiring the spectacle that had nearly taken their lives before it changed its mind and saved them instead.

Standing at the edge of a gaping hole in their starship's cargo bay, three young robots held hands: One in blue armor, one with a dull bare metal finish, and a third, a head taller than her brothers, with red detailing and a simple knee-length dress to match—all on their own since the day they activated in an empty space station.

Cobalt, Silver, and Crimson Laser watched the looming asteroid drift off to join the other silent inhabitants of the cosmos. The massive rock continued its path until it hung a short distance from the *Teacup*. It kept pace with them for a moment, but as the *Teacup's* engines fought the pull of gravity, the asteroid gradually fell behind and joined the endless parade of debris marching toward the void at the center of the black hole, carrying the villains with it.

The now-peaceful panorama of unveiled space swept Cobalt's smile away. "We did it." He breathed the words softly, barely believing them himself. As reality sank in, his smile returned, but it didn't bring its usual cocky attitude with it. "We finally did it."

"And we have the tracking frequency," Silver said. "Nothing can stop us from finding the creator now!"

"We're going home!" Crimson folded her hands and hugged herself. "We're really going home!"

"What's next?" Silver asked.

"I don't know," Crimson said. "But I'm going to the galley right now to bake you a pie, Cobalt! You earned it." Pie. Everything in Crimson's universe revolved around it. All occasions called for pie, and there wasn't a problem in the galaxy it couldn't solve.

Cobalt chuckled. "Thanks, Crimson." He strained for one last glimpse at the asteroid, but it was gone, forever intermingled with the glow of millions of other celestial objects. "I don't know, either. I guess it's the end of this chapter of our lives. But whatever comes next..." He gathered Silver and Crimson to his side.

"...I'll be right there beside you," they said in unison.

After that, the whole world faded to black.

In retrospect, Cobalt should have been alarmed. But at the time, it seemed perfectly natural. He spoke, but he wasn't sure who he was addressing.

"I'm Cobalt Laser, and this is the end of my adventure for now. A lot of people call me a hero, and I suppose they're right, even if it doesn't always feel like it.

"The destiny I've pursued all my life is finally in my grasp, and I have my family to share it with.

"Thank you for joining me. Goodbye for now, but maybe I'll see you again in future adventures. Be strong. Defend and protect. Stand up for what's right. And maybe someday, you can be a hero too."

And then, though he had no way to perceive it, Cobalt's entire universe froze. And it stayed that way for a very long time.

CHAPTER 1

IT WAS HARD TO feel heroic when he couldn't sense his arms and legs.

A disembodied soul floated in silent darkness. He remembered nothing, except who he was: Cobalt Laser, teenage superhero—the most sophisticated robot in the galaxy!

Cobalt's main processor raced, commanding body parts that didn't exist. A memory flashed by—a face, but he couldn't quite place it. Then another. One more, and the floodgates opened. Sights and sounds from the past bombarded him in an overwhelming out-of-order mess.

Cobalt screamed into the mental prison. He might be a robot, but he was a robot with the mind of a fifteen-year-old. And unfortunately, the young superhero lacked the experience that any other fifteen-year-old in a 50-parsec radius would bring to the table. Namely, Cobalt had never been in a situation beyond his control. Neither had he ever been afraid. The rest of us earned those medals long before reaching fifteen. But Cobalt hadn't, and that made the darkness that much worse. More distressing, where were his brother and sister? They'd always been right there beside him. He fought his panicking brain, pulling it into focus.

He grabbed the most recent memory and hung on. He had to figure out what happened! Only seconds ago, the whole world faded to black. Then what?

Then he recited a message. Who was he talking to? That wasn't clear, but he remembered a feeling of confidence and hope. Hope? Here? Why?

A tingling sensation put that thought on hold. His feet! Something cold, hard, and flat bore his weight. He wasn't floating aimlessly in space after all! That made two new emotions for Cobalt today—first fear, now relief. Things weren't as bad as he originally thought. His processor slowed to a less chaotic rate, and his questions came back. How did he lose consciousness without falling over? How did he lose consciousness at all? He didn't breathe oxygen, so the holes riddling the *Teacup's* cargo bay wouldn't have caused...

The *Teacup*. He remembered his starship—home to him, Silver, and Crimson. They were with him. So were Hex Ten, Heinous, and Irk.

Soft humming and beeping rose in volume around him. Electronics. That was a good sign. He wished his eyes would just open and show him the control room of his ship. The tips of his fingers began to tingle. The sensation made its way up his arms and into his shoulders. The pressure from the solid floor climbed into his knees. As his senses returned the panic faded, allowing him to focus on the events just prior to the fade-out.

Hex Ten invaded the *Teacup*. Throughout all their encounters, Hex never had the determination to attack Cobalt in his home, but there he was. He said something about a black hole and a tracking signal. They fought. Then there was an asteroid. And then...

And then he won. Cobalt won, for good. This time, Hex Ten didn't escape to fight another day. He didn't shake his fist and bellow, "I'll get you next time, Cobalt Laser!" He was gone along with Heinous and Irk, never to bother Cobalt, Crimson, and Silver ever again.

What happened after that? He didn't recall blasting away from the black hole or following the tracking signal. Crimson said she was going to bake a pie, but he didn't remember eating it.

Cobalt's processor halted as brilliant white light flooded his field of vision. Finally! Shapes began to form.

This was not the *Teacup*.

It was some sort of laboratory. Static sloshed in Cobalt's skull as he took in the new surroundings. He noticed a delay between when he wanted his neck to turn and when it actually did, and another between his eyes pointing at something and his brain showing him what it was.

When the image stopped swimming, it resolved into Silver standing beside him. Seeing his younger brother calmed Cobalt's nerves. The duo looked very much alike aside from their height difference, and as their names implied, the color of their metal skin and armor. Cobalt wore several shades of blue in a pattern that looked like a permanent superhero costume, while Silver looked like brushed aluminum.

Silver gazed back at Cobalt, wide-eyed. Clearly, he was just as bewildered. Cobalt rolled his head in the other direction. It obeyed him better this time. There stood Crimson, his slightly older sister, staring ahead with a terrified look on her face. Her vision must have come online just then because she blinked and examined her surroundings. When she saw Cobalt and Silver, the fear in her eyes subsided, and she smiled at them.

Cobalt hadn't noticed his clenched fists and jaw until now. He released the tension in his shoulders and returned his sister's smile. *I'll always be right there beside you.* It was their special sibling promise, and they'd kept it.

Something was definitely out of place, though. Crimson's bright red knee-length dress seemed less vivid than Cobalt thought it should be. Come to think of it, all the colors around him were dimmer, yet deeper. He lifted his hands. They looked more... he didn't know how else to describe it... *real.* Everything he saw, from his siblings to the haphazard collection of lab equipment and electronics around him—even the texture of the concrete floor—held a rich level of detail that would've been beyond his imagination only seconds ago.

A click in his throat hinted that Cobalt's speech system was online. He gave it a try. "Where are we?"

"My laboratory." The response made Cobalt jump. He glanced around the room, looking for its source. A shuffling sound drew his focus to a shelf loaded with equipment. Someone emerged from behind it.

A human! A thin man, a bit taller than Cobalt and Silver, but not quite as tall as Crimson's slender frame. A generous mop of brown hair covered his head completely, but it stuck out in more directions than Silver's *Flashing Blades*. He kept his hands tucked in the pockets of his white lab coat. His eyes darted back and forth, making contact with the three of them in turns. A pleasant smile decorated his face. Devices beeped and fans whirred in the background.

The human opened his mouth. "Excuse me, I'm just a bit overcome. My name is Dr. Andrew Smalls." He swallowed and cleared his throat. "Welcome to the real world. I am your creator."

Creator.

It all came rushing back. Though they still seemed strangely distant, in less than a second all the events of the last several minutes found their holes in Cobalt's memory and snapped into place...

SERIES: Cobalt Laser SEASONS 1, 2

SEGMENT: Title Sequence
TIMESTAMP: 00:00

Every episode of *Cobalt Laser* began with the percussion-heavy, fast-paced orchestral theme song and this monologue:

"Hi, I'm Cobalt Laser, the most sophisticated robot in the galaxy! I can think, feel, and dream. How I got here and who made me, no one knows. That's what I'm trying to find out! With my brother Silver Laser and our sister Crimson Laser, we're searching the galaxy for our creator in our starship, the *Teacup*.

"But we're not alone! Constantly pursuing us is the villainous Hex Ten and his minions, Heinous and Irk. He wants our creator's blueprints for his own nefarious purposes: To build an unstoppable robot army! But with the weapon I call *Perfect Punch*, a powerful beam that shoots from my eyes, and Silver's *Flashing Blades*, we'll keep Hex and his schemes at bay!

"I'm Cobalt Laser, and these are my adventures!"

SERIES: Cobalt Laser SEASON 2, EPISODE 10

"All's Well that Ends Well"
TIMESTAMP: 16:47

WE'RE BACK! AND OUR hero is up to his optical receptors in trouble!

In the devastated cargo bay of the *Teacup*, Cobalt Laser squared off with his arch nemesis, Hex Ten. He gazed at exposed space through the hole in the bulkhead where Hex and his followers, Heinous and Irk, had broken in. Luckily, none of the six robots in the cargo bay breathed oxygen, or Cobalt might have felt a twinge of concern.

"You've thwarted me for the last time, Cobalt Laser!" Hex Ten pointed through the hole in the *Teacup's* hull at a swirling mass. "Once it's beyond the event horizon of this black hole, your pathetic little ship will take you and your obnoxious siblings beyond this dimension and out of my way for all of eternity!" The evil robot spread his arms and threw his head back in a villainous laugh. Already almost twice Cobalt's size, he looked even larger with his outstretched gorilla-like arms. Though still more than a million kilometers away, the glow of the material being pulled into the black hole cast a glare on Hex's reflective rock-like skin, making him look like a living sapphire.

Silver shook his fist at the villain. "Hey! Don't call the *Teacup* pathetic!" His famous *Flashing Blades* prickled from his body. Most of them radiated from a central point on his back, while a few more faced forward. Cobalt once made the mistake of comparing him to a porcupine, earning himself an impassioned lecture on why sea urchins are way cooler. Two more blades, the ones he used most, projected from his wrists like swords.

Silver struck a threatening pose. "And next time, use the door!" He spun his wrist blades to punctuate his words. "Whaddaya say, Cobalt? Let's knock them back through the way they came!"

Cobalt, as he always did in these sorts of situations, wore a confident smile. "Sounds like a good idea to me." He kept his eyes glued to the hulking Hex Ten on the other side of the *Teacup's* cargo bay. He braced himself and stared intently as he heroically announced the name of his signature weapon. "*Perfect Punch*!" Brilliant blue beams shot from his eyes. Hex leaped to one side as *Perfect Punch* ripped the flooring away from the spot where he had been standing. The two of them had played this game many, many times since their first encounter, and Hex knew his opponent's timing as well as Cobalt knew his.

"Cobalt! Be careful!" The plaintive voice came from behind Cobalt and Silver. Crimson Laser clung to a girder on the wall of the cargo bay. She shook her shoulder-length blonde hair in a futile effort to keep the curly artificial fibers out of her eyes. Unlike her brothers, she had no weapons or armor. Her usual contribution was to implore the boys to blow things up as carefully as possible. It was a contribution that went largely ignored.

Crimson never minded that. While plenty of fans felt uneasy about the show's unbalanced writing, which assigned so many disadvantages to the only girl character, no-one raised enough objection to change her circumstances. But of course, Crimson couldn't possibly know any of that, so she simply figured that dodging the occasional bit of shrapnel was part and parcel of being the responsible older sister.

"Yeah, be careful, Cobalt!" Silver scolded. "The *Teacup* already has enough holes in it, thanks to these clowns!"

This was enough to make Hex's right-hand man, Heinous, speak up. "The only clown around here is you." His raspy voice matched his cockroach-like appearance. "I have no patience for mockery. You know nothing of honorable combat!" Steadying himself on the two appendages he used as legs, he wove the upper four in a complex pattern, creating a hovering ball of energy.

Hex's eyes widened as he anticipated his general's next move. He held up his hand and shouted, "Heinous, no!"

But he was too late. Heinous threw the orb at the Laser siblings. Cobalt and Silver dove in opposite directions, narrowly missing the projectile as it passed between them and hit the wall a short distance from Crimson. It exploded in a blinding flash. When it dissipated, it left matching holes on either side of the cargo bay, providing a spectacular view of space.

Crimson found it difficult to appreciate the scenery. She was busy screaming in terror. If the shot landed just a couple meters closer, she would be on her way to the center of the black hole right now in a cloud of debris and space dust. Instead, the explosion sent her skirt fluttering around her.

Instinctively, she used one hand to hold the skirt down and protect it from the flying debris. Had the writers allowed her to realize she'd worn this same dress for the last 25 episodes of her life without ever tearing it, she might have used both arms to hang onto the girder instead.

"Heinous, you fool!" Hex said, his voice rumbling. "We cannot destroy this ship yet! I have no intention of joining these bickering children in an eternal void." Hex looked impatiently at the computer terminal beside the door to the *Teacup's* bridge. He yelled at the figure operating it. "Irk, have you found anything yet?"

If Cobalt, Silver, and Crimson were in their teens, Irk was a robotic representation of a grade schooler. Even after standing on the crate he had pushed over to the terminal, the little copper-plated robot had to stand on his toes and reach over his head to work the console. He spun and gave Hex an energetic smile. "Yep!" he chirped. His round face and diminutive body bore a stark contrast to the monstrous appearance of his associates. "No doubt about it. The tracking frequency they discovered will lead us straight to the creator!"

"Then it's decided." Hex turned toward Cobalt again and glowered. "It's the end of the line for you, Cobalt Laser. I thank you for your contribution to my cause."

"Not a chance!" Cobalt shouted back. "*Perfect Punch*!" The weapon fired again. Hex dodged again. A new hole appeared in the *Teacup's* hull. Again.

Silver clapped his hands to the sides of his head. "Cobalt! What part of this don't you understand? If you keep putting holes in a starship, at some point it stops being a starship!"

Cobalt hadn't stopped smiling since this all began. "Got any ideas?"

"You know I do!" Silver returned his brother's confident smile and nodded. He produced a small electronic device with a radar dish at one end.

"Pulse resonator!" Cobalt held up his hand.

Silver tossed it to him. "I modified it to give it significantly more oomph."

As the device sailed past, Crimson got a closer look at it. "Wait a minute," she said indignantly. "That's mine! Silver, have you been in my room again?" The looming danger suddenly became Crimson's second concern. If a black hole wanted to swallow her up, it would have to wait.

Cobalt effortlessly caught the resonator.

"Oh, excuse me." Silver rolled his eyes. "Mine had a low battery. Can you ever forgive me?"

"That's disgusting!" Crimson puckered her face at her younger brother. "Did you touch anything else?" The show's writers made up for Crimson's helplessness by giving her an overcompensating supply of pettiness. They thought it was funny and cute. As far as Crimson knew, her anger was justified.

Cobalt tossed the resonator, flipping it around. He didn't need to. He was just showing off. So now it was backwards. He cranked its power to maximum. At this level, it would do a lot more than clean corrosion out of a robot's hard-to-reach places. He flipped it again.

"Well," Silver said, putting his hands on his hips and wagging his head at Crimson. "It was on that shelf above your bed. So I had to stand on your bed. So I had to touch your bed." As with most arguments involving his big sister, Silver did his best to make things worse. He smiled broadly as he lifted one leg and wiggled its boot-shaped metal toe. "With my feet."

"Sillll-verrrr!"

The pulse resonator landed once more in Cobalt's hand, this time pointing in the right direction. He pushed a button. It hummed, and then throbbed. Then it pulsed. And resonated.

"Stay alert!" Heinous said as the space around them began to distort. The distortion spread past Hex, Heinous, and Irk. It hung there for a moment, then collapsed forcefully on a point behind them in space, just outside the ship. It cracked against an asteroid a few hundred meters away, knocking it off course.

Hex looked around him, counting himself, Heinous, and Irk. Then, to make sure he'd gotten the right number, he counted again. The distress fled from his expression, replaced by a vicious smile. He turned toward Cobalt. "You missed."

"Did I?" Cobalt laid flat on his back on the deck of the cargo bay, just as the errant asteroid passed through the hole behind Hex, Heinous, and Irk. The asteroid plowed into them and sent them flying through the hole in the opposite wall. Cobalt flashed the three of them a smile and waved goodbye as they passed over his head. The giant rock missed taking Cobalt with them by millimeters.

Silver sighed. "Cliché." He took Crimson by the hand and led her to safety beside Cobalt.

Crimson shook her finger at her younger brother. "That was too close, Cobalt Laser!"

Cobalt winked at her. "Don't worry about me! Taking risks is part of being a hero!"

Cobalt stood as close as he dared to the edge of what remained of the *Teacup's* cargo bay, peering into the infinite beyond…

CHAPTER 2

IT DIDN'T TAKE AN expert to realize the machine was broken. Sheet metal went in one end. That part worked fine. The problem was on the other end. It was supposed to come out looking like a turbine rotor, but instead the machine produced abstract sculptures inspired by the impression of a turbine rotor.

David picked up a piece of the accidental artwork and examined it. He let out an exhausted sigh and dragged his eyes wearily back to the offending machine. His arms fell to his sides, and he gave the botched part a lethargic toss onto the floor beside him. It emitted a sharp ring as it hit the concrete. The echo bounced across the expanse of the factory, joining the chorus of bangs, shouts, and general noise of the bustling facility before clattering into silence.

"Have we had even one successful batch, Tad?" he asked before turning his attention to the machine's operator.

"No, sir," Tad said. Tad was the only person who ever called David "sir," and that was only because he called everyone "sir." David did not look like a "sir." Even if he did look closer to his real age of 31, he'd still have a hard time convincing a stranger that he was anyone particularly respectable. His nerdy, unkempt appearance ensured that.

Tad shrugged. "The most we get out of it are five, sometimes eight, good ones before it starts doing this."

Resigned, David picked up a toolbox and opened a panel, exposing the machine's inner workings. "And this is what, the fifth time since we installed this thing that I thought I'd finally fixed it?"

"Seventh," Tad corrected him. A commotion on the far side of the factory caught his attention, approaching them like a homing torpedo. "Hey, boss," he said. "Things are about to get tense."

David looked up. He sighed again. Winding around the strips of yellow caution tape on the floor that marked the walkways through the factory came a figure with a very familiar and purposeful gait. Dan Epic, President and CEO of Epic Manufacturing, plotted the shortest path between himself and David, closing the distance with intent to intercept.

David gave a nervous chuckle as soon as Mr. Epic was within earshot. "Hey, Dad." He waved. The wrench in his hand accidentally banged against the shell of the errant contraption. He flinched as the noise reverberated.

"How are we doing here?" The CEO's words carried the tone of a statement more than a question. He folded his arms and waited for an answer. Dan Epic's stern face unmistakably shared the features of his son, but that's where the resemblance ended. Not a single one of Dan's swept-back silver hairs was out of place, in contrast to David's randomly assorted mop of black strands. Between that and his perfectly pressed slacks, unwrinkled button-down shirt, and perfectly polished loafers, all of which were the exact opposite of David's wardrobe, Dan Epic carried himself as the sort of person who was immediately a "sir" even to heads of state.

"It's um, it's... broken." David pursed his lips. "Again." He gave it a bit more thought and looked at the floor. "Still."

Dan Epic reached for the gold-colored silk handkerchief in his shirt pocket. As he rubbed it between his thumb and forefinger, his expression softened. "Look, David, I get it. You're trying as hard as you can. I appreciate it. And thank you too, Tad."

Tad nodded politely.

David leaned against the machine and pretended to take another serious look at it. His job was secure—his dad wouldn't fire him. But that bothered him all the more. What would he be today if he didn't have his dad propping him up? Would he have succeeded at all? Worse, was he dragging everyone else down? Would his dad have been better off today if he'd hired a real machinist instead of taking on his own kid, who declared himself an expert in the field after barely pulling through a couple semesters of community college? He came to his senses, realizing he'd been transfixed on a single, nondescript bolt on the machine's casing for far too long.

Mustering his courage, David dragged his gaze away from the bolt and forced himself to look his dad in the eye. "I just don't know what to do. This is impossible."

"We have to do something. The client is expecting a thousand of these by the end of the week, and we're still struggling to put out our first hundred."

David grunted and motioned at the machine. "Well, it's clear this isn't going to work. At least, not with the time we have left." David braced himself and took a breath. He didn't want to have this conversation, but he was out of options. "You know what my suggestion is."

Dan bristled immediately. "No." He spun on his heel and walked away. "No robots."

David chased after him. "Dad, the latest ones are amazing! I saw them at the manufacturing expo last month. You talk to them and show them what you want to make. You walk them through it, and they learn. After a couple hours of training, you leave them with a pile of sheet metal and come back to a crate full of perfect parts! No tweaking, configuring, or fine-tuning.”

David's father sputtered. “Robots with a mind of their own? That's supposed to make me feel better?”

“Come on! It's not like they're alive. Having a conversation with one feels artificial. It's the same as talking to a car. You don't have a problem with that.”

“I don't have a choice with that.”

“I don't think you have a choice left with this, either.”

Dan stopped abruptly. David almost ran into him. Without turning around, he drew a deep breath. He spoke calmly and firmly. “No.” He resumed his march off the production floor.

David groaned and continued his pursuit. “Dad, this is irrational. They weren't real robots. It was a cartoon.”

“It was the end of my career.”

“It was the start of a new career! It was twenty-four years ago.”

Dan reached the elevator at the end of the walkway and punched the call button with more force than necessary. “And for twenty-four years, the rule has been that we don't talk about this!”

David could not let this opportunity go to waste. He wouldn't let his dad walk away, not after he'd finally mustered the courage to bring the topic up. His heart pounded as his voice rose to the top of his throat. “Holding a grudge against ordinary everyday robots makes no sense!”

The elevator opened and Dan Epic left his son outside.

David raced against the closing doors, making his final appeal. “If you really expect me to take this place over, you need to start letting me make some of these decisions!” The doors closed. He shouted, hoping his dad could hear through them. “You need to trust me!”

SERIES: Cobalt Laser
SEASON 2, EPISODE 5
"The Heist" TIMESTAMP: 20:12

"CRACK THE SAFE, IRK!" Hex Ten pointed at the large metal box in Heinous's arms. Heinous set it in front of him.

Irk held up his left hand. "No problem, boss!" After a few seconds, it glowed red hot. He pressed it against the lock. While he waited for the heat to transfer, Irk prepared his right hand, which had already accumulated a layer of frost. He swapped hands. The lock pinged and popped as the rapid temperature change weakened the metal. Pleased with his work, he stepped aside to make room for Hex. His boss drove a heavy fist into the now-fragile lock, shattering it.

Irk pried the door open and reached inside. "We have it!" He showed the treasure to Hex and Heinous. "The crown jewel of the Ferusian Dynasty!"

The confused faces staring back were not what he expected. He followed their eyes to the object in his hand. Rather than a large cut diamond, Irk held a plain blue ball. The smile fled from his face. As Irk rolled the trinket between his fingers, he noted its rubbery texture. He barely had time to wonder what happened to the real jewel when he noticed some writing scrawled on the counterfeit. He read it aloud. "You've got this coming, Irk. Sincerely, Cobalt Laser."

Hex and Heinous exchanged panicked looks and dove for cover just as the fake gem popped, covering Irk and everything around him with a sticky blue goo.

Irk held his arms out and watched the slimy mess drip from him. The little robot groaned at the puddle spreading around his feet. When he finally decided to move again, he wiped his eyes as best he could, plopped on the floor, and wailed.

CHAPTER 3

"A cartoon?" Cobalt said. "So, you're trying to tell me I'm not real? That we're all just fictional characters?"

Cobalt sat beside his brother and sister. Dr. Smalls had found three chairs in his labyrinth of assorted junk and furniture and swept the clutter off them. After that, he'd hunted for a spot with enough working light fixtures. Finding that, he'd swept the area clear of expired chemicals and tangled cables and set the chairs in their place. Despite the scientist's urging to "make themselves comfortable," Cobalt felt anything but.

Cobalt struggled to process this new situation as Dr. Smalls paced in front of them. "Oh, you're as real as I am." He paused to shake a finger at Cobalt. "Your memories... Now, that will be an interesting question to explore. I suppose they're very real to you."

Silver clenched his fists and glared at the scientist. "I'm not someone's psychology experiment!"

Dr. Smalls drew back and raised an eyebrow at Silver. "Oh, you're far more than that!" He chuckled to himself and paced vigorously. His arms gesticulated wildly as he spoke. "You are my crowning achievement! My magnum opus! You three are the first unmodified incarnations of my Adaptive Personality technology!"

Cobalt exchanged glances with his siblings.

"Your personality just needs a seed. A backstory, if you will. You start with that history, but from there, you become your own person and write your own destiny!" The doctor clapped his hands and danced. "And it worked! You are Cobalt Laser, and you're standing right here talking to me as a person, not as a mindless artificial intelligence!"

Cobalt wrinkled his nose. "Artificial intelligence?" he echoed.

Dr. Smalls curled his lip and cocked his head to one side. "Did they never use that term in the show? That's kind of surprising." He shrugged. "Maybe not. It was quite a few years ago." He put his hands on his hips and paced slowly. "That's right. You used to call them 'ordinary robots.'"

Silver balled his fists and seethed. "Hey! Who are you calling an ordinary robot?"

A tired expression crossed the scientist's face. "Certainly not you, my boy," he said. "That's my whole point. You know you exist. An artificial intelligence doesn't. It's no more conscious than..." He scanned the room, humming impatiently and twirling his hands in circles. Finally, he pointed at something fuzzy and green sitting on a plate across the room. "...that sandwich. No, I thought about all the fictional characters I'd like to meet, chose you, and accomplished the impossible." He stopped pacing, smiled wryly, and pierced Cobalt's soul. "You are alive, Cobalt Laser."

Cobalt squirmed in his chair. Alive? What was he before? He remembered recovering the final piece of the Epsilon Crystal from Hex Ten, as if it happened yesterday. Was he not alive then? Other events from his past returned in vivid detail. Receiving the Medal of Dignified Enthusiasm from the Galactic Council. His vacation on Tezin Prime. The time he stuffed Irk in a shipping pod and sent him to

Klaxon IV, where the punishment for all crimes is two weeks without video games. If he wasn't alive before today, who did those things?

He caught Crimson's eye and returned her worried expression. Questions swirled in his mind, and one of them finally took shape. "Okay, so why me? Why choose Cobalt Laser?"

The scientist blushed, rolled his eyes, and shrugged. "Well, I'm a huge fan. Ever since your show premiered, I've been the head moderator of the Cobalt Laser Fanbase Wiki." He beamed. "And I still am to this day!"

These words were nonsense to Cobalt. Shifting uncomfortably, he pushed his palms into the seat of his chair and looked to Silver. Silver shook his head slightly and frowned. He looked past Cobalt, passing the silent question to Crimson. She pushed her mouth to one side and shrugged. All three turned their attention back to Dr. Smalls.

"When I first imagined the Adaptive Personality, I couldn't think of any better identity for it than…" He put on his best Cobalt Laser impersonation and recited, "The most sophisticated robot in the galaxy!" He clapped his hands again and squealed. "I can't believe it! I'm friends with Cobalt Laser! This is the best day of my life!"

This was all a bit much for Cobalt. He cast a pleading look at Silver, silently begging him to think of something.

Silver scrunched his face. After a moment's consideration, he addressed the scientist. "Uh, excuse me? Dr. Smalls?"

"Please. Call me Andrew."

"Andrew. You said we were the first unmodified incarnations? What does that mean?"

"Excellent question!" Andrew pointed at Silver and slapped the workbench beside him. "A significant amount of experimentation had to occur before I was confident enough to actualize you three. One

Adaptive Personality precedes you, and I think it will be beneficial if you have a chat with him."

Andrew turned and beckoned to someone on the other side of an equipment rack. Cobalt squinted, trying to see behind the disorganized mess of devices and debris piled on the shelves. A little metallic hand emerged and gripped the leg of the storage unit.

"Unlike you three, he was a prototype. His personality required my continual intervention to develop over the past year, but he has stabilized. And thanks to my perseverance with him, you won't face the same hurdles." Andrew stared at the hand. When it didn't move, he coughed. "Don't keep us waiting!"

Out from behind the rack stepped a familiar short robot with a copper sheen. Its cute round face peeked at them bashfully. "Hello."

Cobalt, Silver, and Crimson leaped off their seats. In his eagerness, Silver deployed *Flashing Blades* before he was fully on his feet. It caught his chair in the process and sent it flying behind him.

"Look out, it's Irk!" Cobalt braced his feet and stared hard at the villain. "*Perfect Punch*!" He focused on his target, standing like a statue.

Irk hid behind his hands and trembled. A few seconds later, he still had not vaporized. He opened one eye and peeked back at Cobalt.

Crimson brought her hands to her mouth. "Oh no, it didn't work! Cobalt, be careful!"

Andrew grabbed his hair. "No, no, no! I forbid you to fight!"

Cobalt rubbed his temples. What happened to *Perfect Punch*? Irk should've been blasted, leaving a charred little robot body with blinking cartoon eyes. *Perfect Punch* had never failed before, and he'd taken it for granted. It was as much a part of him as his fingers and toes. What kind of world could this be, if you couldn't rely on your signature weapon?

"I've got this!" Silver made a show of his spinning wrist blades and marched toward Irk.

The sight of *Flashing Blades* brought Cobalt hope. Maybe that meant *Perfect Punch* would come back. But then, did that mean *Flashing Blades* was unreliable here too? Cobalt wondered how Silver would react to that, but at least they'd have the same problem. Then they could be right there beside each other whenever either one had a need.

Alarmed, Irk squealed and started climbing the equipment rack to escape. "I told you this would happen, Andrew!"

Cobalt wondered what Irk's strategy was. Without Hex Ten and Heinous, his best bet was to run away, but why confront the siblings in the first place? Irk should know he'd never stand a chance on his own, and to expect some sort of comical punishment for his misdeeds. It wasn't even clear to Cobalt what type of mischief the villain might be up to, but one thing was certain: Villains are never up to any good and must always be thwarted.

Andrew repeated himself, more sternly this time. "I forbid you to fight!"

Silver flinched. He put his hand to his head and blinked hard. Refocusing on Irk, he rushed toward the equipment rack and slashed at its base. It tilted precariously, then toppled. Irk let out a shrill scream as he rode the top shelf of the rack all the way to the floor. Cables and scrap of varying shapes and sizes spilled off the shelves in a terrible crash and tangled around the rack and each other, ending in an indecipherable heap of wreckage.

Irk struggled against the mess of cables that entangled him in the fall. He fought to extricate himself while Silver approached menacingly.

Silver flexed his blades. "You've got this coming, Irk."

Andrew screamed desperately. "Silver Laser, I forbid you to fight!"

Silver froze in place, poised over Irk. The childish villain always dreaded receiving his comeuppance, but something about this encounter seemed to strike a measure of genuine terror in the little robot. Irk cowered behind his hands, whimpering and shielding himself from the ready blades. When Irk finally dared to peek, Silver's eyes glazed over. He folded his blades away, walked back to Andrew, and sat in one of the upright chairs. Irk collapsed into a heap and shivered. Then, jolting back into action, he sat up and focused on untangling the mass of cables that tied his knee to the wreckage, keeping a wary eye on Silver. Cobalt thought it odd that their normally irritating adversary wasn't gloating at his narrow escape.

"Okay. Okay," Andrew said, panting. "It's fine. We learned something. Surprises are bad, explanations are good." He took a cleansing breath and pointed across the laboratory. "Irk, go to your room and don't come out until I call you."

Irk eyed Andrew and grunted irritably. He tugged at his leg, but it wouldn't come loose. He held up the index finger of his left hand. After a few seconds, the tip of his finger glowed red hot. He touched it to the cable, melting it. He jerked his leg one more time and was finally free. He marched toward the door, looking over his shoulder with a sour expression.

Cobalt took his eyes off the spectacle and crept up beside Crimson. She looked back, wide-eyed. She returned her attention to Silver, who simply stared blankly into space. After a bit, she gave Cobalt's hand a little squeeze, picked up the chair Silver tossed earlier, and sat beside him. Cobalt took the remaining seat on Silver's other side.

Andrew took another cleansing breath. "Now, where did we leave off?"

No way would Cobalt let Andrew change the subject! He had more questions about the last two minutes than the rest of his life total. He pounded his fist on the side of his chair. "Why didn't *Perfect Punch* work?"

"Of course. There's a lot to unpack here." Andrew bounced on his heels and lectured. "This is not the cartoon world. Where you come from, science-y words are thrown around, but they're meaningless. Your world was more of a magical one than scientific. *Perfect Punch* is an arbitrarily powerful laser, or energy beam really, that can do as much destruction as the plot requires. In this world, I can't build that."

Cobalt gripped his seat again. The world spun around him.

"At least, not in a space the size of your skull. Your head would need to be roughly the size of this room to accommodate it."

Cobalt wasn't buying it. "But Silver has *Flashing Blades*. And Irk was able to use his hot hand."

Andrew sighed and nodded. "Those powers are within the realm of current engineering," Andrew said. "The system I developed to build you watched every episode of the show and analyzed each character individually. In addition to initializing your personalities, it also designed your bodies. If it could reproduce your capabilities with available technology, it did. If it couldn't, well..." He shrugged. "Think of it optimistically. You were too powerful for this world!"

Cobalt's main processor did the same racing thing as when he woke up in the empty darkness that morning. "So now I'm completely powerless!" he said, voice shaking. His eyes darted to Crimson's hand. He wished he could reach it, but Silver sat between them.

Andrew waved him off. "Don't worry about it. In this world, you won't find any use for something like *Perfect Punch*." He motioned toward Silver. "In fact, your brother will probably never use *Flashing*

Blades. And your sister..." Crimson fidgeted as he assessed her. "Well... She doesn't have to worry, either."

Andrew's eyes glimmered. "Let's try this." He headed over to a desk against the far wall and activated a computer terminal. "This is the Cobalt Laser Wiki. I'll leave the three of you to peruse it and read about yourselves and the world you came from, as well as this world's opinion of it." He beamed. "I don't think there's a single article here that I haven't either written or edited myself, so it's basically my own instruction manual to you!" He stepped out of the way and gestured to them. "This should answer most of your questions. We'll talk after that."

***

The late morning shone through the glass roof and walls, illuminating the laptops, briefcases, and other business implements scattered across the mahogany table in this, the most ornate conference room in the entire corporate complex of Epic Investments.

"After compiling the results of thousands of surveys of your clients and employees, we believe we've captured an image that truly represents the soul of your company to the people who depend on it most." The blue-suited young man paused to flip to the next slide in his presentation, displaying a bar graph.

Christine Epic took the last sip from her coffee mug. A tiny service robot, about the size of a housecat, patrolled the tabletop. It noticed the empty mug and dutifully darted over. Christine waited for it to fill her cup halfway and held up her hand. The robot emitted a cheerful bleep and backed away obediently. Christine's attention shifted to the woman who picked up her associate's train of thought.

"We have prepared a full set of marketing materials that evoke the emotions and attitude that Epic Investments embodies when the organization is at its best." Christine admired the young woman's business suit. It was, of course, only a fraction of the cost of her own black and white ensemble, but very similar to what she would've worn herself ten years ago, before she had become one of the top entrepreneurs in the world. Many more years before that, her hair was also curly, shoulder-length, and blonde, like this woman's. But she had long since shortened, straightened, and dyed hers brown. That had been her preferred look since fifteen years of age, and it was still the same now at 38. The woman smiled at her. "I'd like to introduce your new company logo."

At that cue, the man flipped to the next slide. The screen covering the far wall lit up with the image of a metallic red shield.

Christine took another sip of her coffee. She glanced at the shield, then glared across the table at her trusted assistant, Darlene. Darlene fidgeted and pushed her thick-rimmed glasses up the bridge of her nose. She avoided meeting her boss's gaze.

The marketing consultant coughed, and Christine noticed she'd stopped talking. Refusing to acknowledge the consultant, she kept her eyes trained on Darlene.

The woman spoke again. "I'd like to hear your thoughts."

Christine answered, still refusing to turn her head. "Did you receive a communication about possibly including a lightning bolt in the design?"

"We did," she answered.

Christine relieved Darlene of the intensity of her gaze and focused it on this new target.

The woman continued. "Please understand, Ms. Epic. This sort of thing happens all the time. You hired us for our expertise. Please trust us."

The man jumped in to help his associate bear Christine Epic's displeasure. "A lightning bolt is a very aggressive symbol. It's great for tech companies and caffeinated beverages, but not so much for an investment firm."

It was the woman's turn again. "A shield represents safety, stability, and defense. This is the impression you want to give someone who is trusting you with their life's savings."

Christine closed her eyes and exhaled. "I suppose I can understand that, but..." When she opened them, she was the Sphinx, and their answer to her next question would determine whether they left the room alive. "Why red?"

The man cleared his throat. "While we don't want to present an aggressive image, we do want a sense of urgency. A call to action."

Christine pressed her hands together and rested her chin on her thumbs. Darlene did not need to adjust her glasses again, but she did it anyway. She fidgeted too, for good measure.

"Red often expresses that," the woman said.

Christine took another sip of coffee. She let the room marinate in uncomfortable silence, then tossed her perfectly styled hair. "I don't like red."

The consultants exchanged glances. Christine waited. She wondered if all marketing people have a telepathic language, or if it was unique to these two.

The man raised his eyebrows and turned his attention back to Christine. His voice carried a hint of agitation. "If it makes you feel any better, this isn't red strictly speaking. This specific shade is called Crimson Aura."

Christine drew a wheezing breath and gripped the edge of the table.

"Uh-oh." Darlene toyed with her workspace, busily rearranging the items.

Christine exhaled slowly. "Crims..." She pushed away from the table.

Darlene nearly knocked her own chair over as she jumped to follow. "Ms. Epic will be out of town for a week." She dodged people, chairs, cables, and the refreshment table on her way to the other side of the conference room. "We'll touch base after that. Thank you for all your hard work. I mean that!" As she passed the bewildered marketing consultants, she leaned toward them and whispered in a voice she hoped Christine wouldn't hear, "I'll talk to her!"

She ran to catch up with Christine, who had already slammed the door behind her.

CHAPTER 4

Cobalt read the screen to the others. "*Cobalt Laser* is an animated television series created by Dan Epic. Season 1 spans 16 episodes and received critical acclaim." He turned in his chair to face the others. "Who's Dan Epic?"

Silver stood nearby with his arms folded. "It says he's the creator, but I thought that was Andrew?"

Irk perked up. Although he'd been allowed back into the room, he carefully kept his distance. He sat flat on a tabletop, with his feet stretched in front of him and hands behind, propping himself. "Mr. Epic made the cartoon show that gives us our memories. Dr. Smalls built our robot bodies and found a way to put those memories inside us."

Silver rolled his eyes. "I get that, but I mean really, which one do we call our creator? Or is our creator someone else? Maybe another fictional character in the cartoon world?"

Irk shrank. "It's confusing to me, too."

Cobalt continued reading. "The show was quickly approved for a second season, which proved to be a dismal failure. Season 2 episodes consisted of silly comedy vignettes and recycled themes from Season 1. It failed to retain the interest of fans or attract new viewers. Production on all unfinished episodes was abruptly halted, and the team hastily produced a finale to wrap up the series. This was released as Episode 10 of Season 2. No new media was produced after that.

"In a widely circulated email, Epic brutally criticized the management of Total Media before leaving the entertainment industry altogether. *Cobalt Laser* was his only professionally produced work. He used his royalty income to invest in a manufacturing firm and disappeared from the public eye. He refuses all interviews."

Cobalt paused to digest what he'd read so far. "This is a lot to take in," he said. Crimson sat nearby on the floor, facing the corner and hugging her knees to her chest. Cobalt drummed his fingers on the desk, working up the courage to address her. "What do you think, Crimson?"

She shrugged and wagged her head slowly. "What does it matter?" she said, almost whispering. "I'm useless, right?"

Cobalt clicked on the "Main Characters" section and scrolled to Crimson's bio for a second look. It read, "the stereotypical useless girl whose only contribution to the team was baking pies and shouting, 'Cobalt, be careful!'"

Cobalt scowled at the screen, then turned his attention on his sister. "That's not true!" he protested.

Crimson spun to face him, still sitting on the floor. "It's not?" she countered. "Then name one thing—one—that I did in my whole life that actually made a difference." She pursed her lips and held a single finger in the air.

Cobalt froze. His processor spun for several cycles, but he drew a blank. There had to be something! This was his sister, after all! What would his life be without her?

Silver groaned. "Snap out of it, Crimson!" he said. He snatched the computer mouse and hastily scrolled through the wiki. "You did plenty. Says here that estimates vary, but you baked somewhere between 1,028 and 1,579 pies."

Crimson trembled. She puckered her mouth as if ready to scream, but at the last moment curled into a ball and huddled in the corner.

Cobalt turned on his brother. "Silver!" Did he have any empathy at all?

Silver tossed the mouse across the desk. "What?" he said. "Look, can we just focus? We've got way more important things to figure out."

A tiny, pained voice interrupted their argument. "I understand." Irk stood a few steps away from Crimson, tapping his fingers together and looking very small. "I've been in this world for a while now."

Irk cleared the static from his vocal queue before continuing. "You were comic relief, Miss Crimson. I was too, for most of our show."

Crimson relaxed a little and turned an ear toward him.

"It was supposed to make people laugh. But if it makes you feel better, a lot of people said it was unfair. You were the only girl, and it wasn't right to make a joke out of that." He took another timid step. "It didn't get any better in Season 2, and some say that's one of the reasons they stopped watching."

Cobalt jumped as the door flew open and Andrew walked in.

Andrew carried a duffel bag, which he waved at the group. "So, any questions yet?"

Cobalt shifted in his chair as he recovered from the surprise. "What can you tell us about Dan Epic?" It took some effort to keep the annoyance out of his voice.

"Oh, a real piece of work, that guy." Andrew put the bag on a table and started stuffing pieces of lab equipment into it. "I met him at a convention once, before everything fell apart. Even then he was un-approachable. He didn't value his fans and made signing autographs look like a chore." He found a second carrying case and darted around the lab collecting machinery to cram into that as well. "I still loved his show, though." He winked at Cobalt. "And you guys!" He saw a tool on a shelf above Crimson's head. He went to get it and ruffled her hair as he passed. Crimson squeezed her eyes shut and hugged her knees tighter.

Cobalt pointed at the screen. "This says he's at a place called Epic Manufacturing. If we went there, do you think we could talk to him?"

"Oh, no, no," Andrew said, laughing. "Trust me, you don't want to do that."

Silver asserted himself. "I think we might."

Irk's eyes widened. He crawled down the other side of his table and hid behind the furthest leg.

Andrew's smile twitched, but he quickly restored it. He looked Silver in the eye. "Not now. Maybe later."

Cobalt's processor raced. He needed to defuse this. Arguing with the person who brought them into this world seemed like a very bad idea. "Andrew, please. We appreciate you and everything you've done for us. This just seems like a lead worth pursuing."

"Cobalt, you don't understand. You're going to need a lot more guidance before you're ready for something like that." Andrew showed his bag to Cobalt. "As you can see, I'm getting ready to go somewhere. I'd put it off if I could, but there are people following the progress of the Adaptive Personality very closely, and I need to tell them about our success. It'll only be overnight. I'll leave you here with Irk, and when I get back, I promise we'll talk about researching your roots."

Silver hit the table. "I've been across the galaxy in a starship I built myself, and I've never answered to anyone but Cobalt. I do not need your permission to go anywhere."

The commotion woke Crimson out of her thoughts. She hid behind Cobalt and put a hand on his shoulder.

Andrew smiled calmly at Silver, watching.

Silver glanced around the laboratory, eyes shifting. He stomped and motioned to his siblings. "Let's go." Andrew kept smiling. Silver started for the door. Cobalt followed him, with Crimson in tow.

Andrew spoke. "I forbid you to leave this laboratory without my express permission. All of you."

Silver cast a suspicious glance back at Andrew. He pressed his lips together and reached for the door. And stopped. His hand refused to touch the door control, no matter how much he strained. He whipped around. "What is this?" His voice trembled. "Some kind of mind control?"

"I'm sorry," Andrew said. "I really hoped it wouldn't be necessary, but the three of you have behavior inhibitors. Please understand. I only have your safety in mind."

The pain in Crimson's expression gave way to concern. "Behavior inhibitor?" She reached for the door controls. Her hand also stopped short. She strained, but it was no use.

"You got a taste of it when I prohibited you from fighting with Irk." Andrew stuffed his hands in his pockets. "You will be unable to do anything I forbid you to do."

Electricity tingled up Cobalt's spine. He glanced at Silver and Crimson, but they didn't notice him. Silver stood with clenched fists, fully focused on Andrew. Crimson stared at the hand she'd used to try the door.

Andrew threw up his arms, chuckling. "Okay, listen, we're getting too serious here." He boosted himself onto Irk's table and sat eyeing them with his hands in his lap. "There's nothing ominous about this. Really, it's just a matter of safety, and all of this will be open to discussion when I return." He looked over the tabletop to where Irk was hiding. "Irk, tell them how many prohibitions you currently have."

Irk stepped halfway out from behind the table leg. "1,087," he said. He smiled, not resting his eyes on anyone in particular.

Andrew shrugged. "See? And he's just fine. That number is only high because, as I mentioned before, he's the result of a lot of proto-typing. That, and he carried quite a few more bad habits over from the cartoon world than any of you will." He winked at Irk mischievously. "He's a villain, after all. You were a naughty little guy at first, weren't you, buddy?"

Irk grinned and kicked at the floor. "Yeah, it took some time for me to adjust."

Andrew slid off the table. "Then it's settled. We'll discuss this when I get back. Let me just arrange for some transportation." He went to his computer terminal and ordered a cab. "Five minutes. Can't beat that!"

Andrew grabbed his luggage and headed for the door. "I have a meeting to attend. The world has a lot of problems, and many sci-entists like me think robots are the solution. It's important work." Cobalt cringed when the door control worked effortlessly for him.

Andrew waved. "I'll be back soon. I love you guys! I really mean that."

And then he was gone.

***

Christine bolted through the hallway with Darlene in pursuit.

"Christine! Please!"

Christine kept marching. The pursuing footsteps stopped. She managed three more steps before her best friend's voice filled the hallway, sounding like a fed-up mom.

"Christine! You stop this right now!"

Christine stopped in her tracks and groaned. Darlene was right. She turned around and waited for Darlene to catch up to her, hobbling as she approached. Christine regretted making her run in high-heeled shoes.

Darlene continued with her you-listen-to-me-young-lady voice. "I hope you come back from this vacation rested and *calm*." She emphasized the last word.

"I doubt it," Christine said as the pair continued toward the building's atrium. "This is always one of the most stressful weeks of the year." She buried her face in her hands and groaned. "I didn't get around to packing."

Darlene smiled knowingly. "As always. Don't worry. I've got you covered." She swiped her badge to open the atrium door and let Christine go ahead of her. "As always."

"Thank you." Christine crept past Darlene as she held the door, unable to look her friend in the eye. Here she was, one of the most successful people in the business world and she couldn't even pack a suitcase. Well, she could pack a suitcase. She just didn't. Somehow, that felt worse.

Christine surveyed the bustling atrium. Employees of Epic Investments passed by in every direction like a colony of ants, doing everything from trading securities to stocking vending machines, along with every other task that kept the whole organism alive. An organism that Christine raised herself from its infancy. Her limo waited for her beyond the glass doors on the other side.

Darlene paused to remove her heels. "Oh, this room is huge!" she muttered. She walked behind Christine, talking as they went. "There's a whole new wardrobe packed and waiting for you in the limo." She gave Christine a gentle push toward the exit. "It's already tagged and checked. The driver will make sure it gets onto your flight."

"Thank you," Christine said again. For someone who was once described as "a force that keeps the world of finance and investment spinning on its axis," she was beginning to feel like a big baby.

Darlene continued. "And of course, everything is green, yellow, black, or white. All appropriate to the local climate, and nothing high power or high fashion." She took Christine by the shoulders and turned her toward herself. "You're not greeting the stars at a movie premiere. You're going to your parents' place for a week of pot roast and mashed potatoes."

Christine rolled her eyes. Darlene made it all sound so simple, but it wasn't only about family reunions and home-cooked meals. Christine reminded her, "And to close the books and plan next year's budget for my dad's and brother's little factory."

Darlene waved her hand dismissively. "Which you can do in your sleep the first couple days after arriving." She gave Christine a pat. "It's going to be great. I envy you. My mom doesn't cook like that." Christine rolled her eyes again as Darlene pushed her through the door.

A moment later, the limo pulled away. Darlene waved at her through the glass, and she returned the gesture half-heartedly. Darlene surely wasn't sorry to see her go, and honestly, Christine couldn't blame her. She trusted Darlene to clean up the mess she'd left with the marketing firm. Whatever Darlene chose to do, it would be okay. And it wouldn't be red.

SERIES: Cobalt Laser
SEASON 2, EPISODE 8

"Rocket-Propelled Grenade Run"
TIMESTAMP: 15:16

Crimson gripped her seat belt with both hands. She stared out the windshield of the race car as the road ahead became the road behind at an alarming rate. Once again, Silver held her life in his hands, being the only one of the siblings who could drive a land car. Had it been up to her, they'd be nowhere near this backward planet where ancient motor races were still popular, but the prize was a piece of the Epsilon Crystal, and they couldn't let Hex Ten win it.

"Are you sure you can drive this thing?" she said. She wished robots needed air. Then maybe she could do some breathing exercises.

Silver rolled his eyes. "I'm doing it, aren't I?" He hit the brake and leaned on the steering wheel. The siblings' vehicle drifted around a hairpin turn.

Crimson grimaced as the centrifugal force smashed her against her brother. "Oh, gross!" She pushed away from him until she was back in the passenger's seat.

"Hey, I'm trying to steer here!"

Cobalt stood in the back seat with his head poking through the roof, watching the car behind them. He turned and looked into the front seat. "Relax, Crimson!" He raised his voice over the car's engine. "Who built the *Teacup* and who pilots it?" His attention returned to the other car. Hex, Heinous, and Irk were steadily gaining.

Crimson sighed. "Silver," she admitted. She took in the scenery as it zipped by. This planet did have a lush green countryside, if nothing else.

"*Perfect Punch*!" Cobalt took a shot at the pursuing car with his eye beams, but the villains swerved out of the way. He looked back at his sister. "And who keeps all our machinery in working order and figures out all the alien technology we encounter?"

"Well, Silver, I guess," Crimson said. "But what does that have to do with it? Race car driving is a professional sport that takes an expert who..."

Silver interjected. "Bah, experts! I scoff at them, and you should, too!"

Cobalt aimed again. "*Perfect Punch*!" This time he took out one of Hex's wheels, forcing their opponents out of the race.

Silver watched the explosion in the rearview mirror and pumped his fist. "All right!"

Crimson braced one arm against the dashboard and pointed though the windshield with the other. "Silver! Keep your eyes on the road!"

Silver spun the wheel a moment too late. The car crashed through a fence and cut through an alien farmer's field before bouncing back onto the road.

Crimson groaned. A six-legged, three-eyed space chicken sat in her lap. She heaved it out the window. "I'm sorry I doubted you." She rolled her eyes at her little brother.

CHAPTER 5

SILVER FOCUSED AND RUBBED his temples. "Okay, so to activate our behavior inhibitors, Dr. Psycho has to say, 'I forbid you to… blah, blah, blah,' and then we can't *blah, blah, blah*. How do we make it so we can *blah, blah, blah* again?"

Irk giggled. "You're funny!" He kicked his legs, banging his heels against the plastic crate he was sitting on.

Silver rolled his eyes. "I'm serious! Did anyone notice any other patterns?" He turned his back on the annoying little villain and folded his arms, staring at Cobalt.

Crimson spoke in a subdued voice, catching Silver's attention out of the corner of his eye. "I remember when you were chasing Irk, he had to say it three times before you stopped." She sat on the edge of a table, watching her feet dangle. She looked at Silver and a little glimmer returned to her eye. "Were you just not listening?" The halfhearted smile disappeared and she clouded over again, seemingly lost in her brooding once more.

Silver put his hand to his chin. "I did hear him," he said. "But now that I think about it, I did feel a weird pull in my mind when he said it the first two times." It was the same feeling as when he reached for the door control. "I think the behavior inhibitor was trying to stop me."

Cobalt paced in front of Silver and pondered. "Maybe it didn't work at first because you were so stressed? The situation was really intense."

Silver pressed his hands to his head. "So being stressed makes it harder for a prohibition to take hold, but once it's set, it's there for good. I wonder…" He snapped his fingers. "Wait a minute!" He pounced on the chair in front of Dr. Smalls's computer terminal. He opened a panel on the side of his head, stretched a cable from the cavity, and plugged it into the console. Computer code scrolled across the display.

"Okay, there!" Silver pointed at the screen. "That method gets called when our emotional intensity exceeds a certain threshold. It increases our energy output to enable a fight or flight response."

Silver flashed a wide smile at Cobalt, very satisfied with himself. His brother cocked his head and wrinkled his eyes. Silver's enthusiasm drained. "Wait a minute," he said, confused as well. "How do I know all this?"

Irk jumped on top of his crate and bounced on his toes. "You're a technology expert! The fabrication system knew that when it built you, so it preloaded your mind with knowledge about this world's technology, including knowledge of how our bodies work." Silver groaned at the little robot's childish energy. Undeterred, Irk whirled around and pointed at Cobalt. "And you, even though you didn't get *Perfect Punch*, I'm sure you're a martial arts or boxing expert in this world. And Miss Crimson…"

Irk's voice trailed off as everyone looked at Crimson. She waited for Irk to continue, but he just froze. Crimson wilted and swung her feet.

Silver wanted to break the awkward silence, but saying nice things about his sister didn't come easy for him. Maybe Cobalt would come up with something. Crimson squirmed. Silver thought she was trying to shrink.

Irk regathered his thoughts, stammering as he built his energy back up. "Uh, anyway, I have the same knowledge because I was a tech expert in our world, just like you!"

"I'm nothing like you," Silver snapped. He glared at Irk.

Irk recoiled as the enthusiasm drained from him. Silver emitted a satisfied grunt. The little robot sank back onto his crate.

Silver looked at the screen again and submerged himself in concentration. He pointed at a line of code. "If I overload this counter, the code that checks prohibitions will always return false. It'll be effectively the same as having no prohibitions!" Silver slapped his hands together and set them to typing.

Cobalt stopped him. "Wait a minute. If this is such a good idea, why hasn't Irk tried it?"

Irk smiled back weakly. "I have a prohibition against modifying my own code. Number 153."

Silver hesitated. Could he be wrong? Impossible. He was a genius in the cartoon world, and he could trust himself in this one too. He nodded decisively. "I'm going through with it." He typed for a few seconds, hitting the final key with a flourish. He unplugged himself and marched toward the front door. He reached for the control and...

He still couldn't touch it. His hand hovered centimeters away from the button and refused to go further.

Silver seethed. "Aaaargh!" If he had hair, he'd be pulling it out. "What went wrong? I know that was the right code!" He was still struggling with the idea that his life and choices before today had been a script written by someone else. What good was this supposed "real world" if he still had no control over his own actions?

He wound up to kick the leg of the computer desk, but as he brought his foot forward, he froze like a statue. Time stopped.

Somehow Crimson's voice was suddenly in his ear. "Silver, are you okay?" It felt like he just woke up again. Crimson stood in front of him now, holding him by the shoulders to keep him from falling over. "You passed out for a few seconds!" she said.

"I... I think..." Silver broke free from his sister's grip and ran to the door. This time he hit the control without a moment's hesitation. He giggled maniacally as he jabbed the button repeatedly, causing the door to open and close half a dozen times.

He spun to face his siblings. "It works!" He laughed like Hex Ten. "I just needed a strong emotional response to activate the modification."

"This is all good for you," Cobalt said. "But what about us?"

Silver waved his hand. "Easy! I'll just pass the modification on to you." He stretched the cable from his head and handed the end to Cobalt. In no time, he finished the process with both siblings.

"Now we just need to invoke a strong emotional reaction." Silver stood in front of Cobalt. "I'm really sorry about this." He sucker-punched his brother in the gut. When Cobalt doubled over, Silver went around back and slapped him hard on the rear end. Cobalt yelped and leaped into the air.

Cobalt lunged for Silver, hissing through his teeth. "Are you crazy?" Before he could move very far, he seized up and collapsed.

Silver peered over Cobalt and waited. After a bit, Cobalt's joints unlocked and his eyes started moving again. "You're welcome," Silver said.

Cobalt winced as he rolled over. "You're a jerk."

Silver turned to face his sister. "Your turn!" he said eagerly, rubbing his hands together.

"Silver, don't you dare!" She backed away, guarding her backside with her hands. She, too, froze and collapsed.

Silver stood over her and met her disoriented gaze as she recovered. "That was no fun. I was going to recite my favorite entries from your diary."

Crimson seethed as she lifted herself onto her elbows. "Sillll-verrrr!"

She wrinkled her nose at Silver and prepared to tell him off, but uproarious giggling interrupted her tirade before it started. Irk almost fell off his crate. "This is even better than our show!" He struggled to keep his balance.

"Let's just get out of here and find Dan Epic," Cobalt said.

Silver nodded. "Good idea." He went to the computer terminal and looked up the address of Epic Manufacturing. "Now, what did he call that thing? A cab?" Ten minutes later, they were ready to go.

On their way out, Silver almost ran into Crimson as she hesitated at the door.

Cobalt frowned at her. "What's wrong?"

Crimson looked behind her. Silver followed her gaze to Irk.

"Shouldn't we bring him with us?" she asked.

Irk perked up, sitting taller on his crate.

Cobalt squinted at the copper-plated robot. "But he's a villain."

Irk wrung his hands. "That's not how it works in this world—it's not that simple! I can help you!"

Crimson squeezed Cobalt's arm. "Maybe we should listen to him," she said.

Silver shook his head. "Don't be gullible," he said. He shook a finger at Irk. "I may not know how this world works, but I know who you were before we came here, and I'm not about to start trusting you now!"

Cobalt shrugged out of Crimson's grip. "I agree," he said, narrowing his eyes at the little robot.

Crimson gave Irk an apologetic frown. Irk looked at the floor and turned his back to them. Cobalt went outside and Silver followed, pulling Crimson along by the hand.

CHAPTER 6

T HE TAXI HAD FOUR seats. Crimson sat beside Silver in the back. Cobalt had the front seat, directly ahead of her. The seat behind the steering wheel was empty. When Cobalt originally tried to sit there, the car's computer instructed him to "please leave the driver's seat unoccupied." When he demanded to know why, it launched into a cheerful lecture on the history of motorized transportation and vehicle safety law. The taxi was what the Lasers called "an ordinary robot" in their world.

That was forty-five minutes ago. Cobalt stared out the window. "How much longer?"

The taxi answered. "There are four hours, twenty-three minutes remaining in this journey."

Crimson smiled at Cobalt's reflection in the passenger window. She tried to catch his eye, but he just stared ahead, looking extremely bored. Giving up, she resumed looking through her window at the alien world. At first the scenery fascinated her, but after several minutes of nothing more than an endless stretch of freeway and cars whizzing by too fast for her to make out any detail, she lost interest.

She wanted to ignore Silver. He'd always got on her nerves in the cartoon world, but this was so much worse. The episodic nature of their previous life ensured he'd only get a quick jab in here and there, then they'd move on to another subject and she'd get a break. This was relentless. Surely, six hours of nonstop Silver was more than anyone could bear.

And couldn't he sit still, for even five minutes?

Silver tried to stretch his legs, but they banged against the back of the driver's seat. He complained to no one in particular, "I wish I'd brought something to read."

"Like my diary?" Crimson said. The words were out before she could stop them, and she wasn't sure whether she felt good or bad about it. Either way, the fight was on.

"Oh, please." Silver rolled his eyes. "I never read your stupid diary. I just needed to get a reaction from you."

Crimson turned to answer her little brother, but he hastily looked out of his window and mumbled to himself. "But apparently, that was a lot easier than I expected."

Crimson saw her own irritation in her reflection. She racked her brain for an appropriate comeback.

Of course, Silver spoke before she could think of anything. "Who wants to read about your crush on Prince Granite of Mineralis, anyway?"

Crimson jolted. "You did too read it!" She grabbed his shoulder. She'd make him look her in the eye and try to deny it!

Silver tensed as he faced his sister. His eyes immediately darted to the side after meeting her glare. "What? No!" His eyes stopped shifting and settled on the seat between them. "It was obvious! I... I bet you wrote about it in your diary!"

Crimson released her grip and let him slink away. "You're disgusting, Silver," she said. She huffed and curled into a ball, facing the window. If crushes were fair game, she knew just how to get back at him. "Hey, why don't we talk about Vanessa? The girl who defected from the Robot Ninja Clan?"

Silver twitched like he'd been hit. "Oh, now who's disgusting?" he wailed. "She burned up in the atmosphere of a white dwarf!"

Crimson sighed. "You're right. I'm sorry. I went too far." She didn't mean to hurt him. At least, not that much.

"That's right. And she actually liked me back! And we'd still be happily together now, if not for her selfless sacrifice! That's more than I can say for you and Prince Granite."

Not fair. She showed mercy, and he got another jab in? Crimson's face contorted. Her mouth was a blaster, charging up for its strongest shot. She fired. "Oh yeah? Well, I'd say she's better off!"

Silver barely noticed. "Oh, for you it was love at first sight, but when he saw you, he said..."

Crimson lunged across the back seat and clapped her hands over Silver's mouth. "Shut up! Shut up! Shut up!"

She jumped at the sound of Cobalt yelling. "Stop it now! Both of you!" The furious look on his face froze her. He lowered his voice to its normal volume and scolded both of them. "I'm not putting up with this for another four hours. Silver, switch places with me."

Crimson's stomach twisted. Cobalt never raised his voice to her before. Ever. Didn't he know how irritating Silver could be? Was anyone on this planet on her side? Still, she'd much rather sit by Cobalt for four hours. This instance aside, his sweet, doting attitude toward her seemed to have followed him to this reality, and sitting next to him might give her a bit of reassurance. She suspected he also wanted his big sister's presence. She reached for her seat belt, but the taxi intoned before she reached the button. "Please remain seated in compliance with the law."

Cobalt turned to face the dashboard again. "What do we do? We can't let those two sit together."

"Agreed," the taxi said. "In five minutes, we will encounter a rest stop. I will pull over there and you can adjust the seating arrangement. Please maintain composure in the meantime."

"See?" Cobalt turned his head as far as he could without leaving his seat. "Even the car can't handle you." He was mostly talking to Silver, but Crimson noted that he also took a brief glance at her.

"Please do not involve me," the taxi said. "This is not my business."

Crimson huffed and hugged her knees, facing her window. Five minutes; she didn't even want to see Silver until they were over.

Silver managed to behave for a whole ninety seconds before the silence was too much to bear. "I spy with my little eye something that is..." He paused as he scanned the alien landscape for anything he could identify.

Crimson finished for him. "Something that is stupid: your reflection."

***

Meanwhile in another world, wholly distinct from either of the universes the Lasers knew, a different scene unfolded. This world's protagonist never experienced anything so exciting as a starship battle. Truth be told, she had no concept at all of peril or suspense. Even so, she knew responsibility, and she treated her mission with the utmost importance.

Inspector Princess considered her options. She knew the right choice, of course, but to simply say so would defeat the purpose.

The children had to learn.

Before her stood a candy store, a post office, and a pharmacy. All of them, just like everything else in this world including Inspector Princess herself, resembled a child's crayon drawing.

"Where would we find a bottle of medicine, Ruffy?" Inspector Princess motioned with her magnifying glass toward her faithful dog companion. "The candy store, the post office, or the pharmacy?" She examined each building in turn through the glass.

Ruffy lifted one of the thick black crayon marks that served as his front legs and scratched his head. "Gee, Inspector Princess, I don't know. Maybe it's because I can't see these buildings too well. I wish the sun wasn't feeling sick."

Inspector Princess smiled. She knew the real reason was that Ruffy's three brain cells were made of crayon wax. But she would never say that.

It was time to ask the children. Inspector Princess never saw them, but she always instinctively knew where in the crayon sky to direct her appeal to them. "What do you think?"

On the other side of the television screen, unseen by Inspector Princess, Irk bounced with excitement. "Oh, I know this one! Medicine comes from a pharmacy!"

Ruffy licked his lips with his crayon tongue. "I think we should try the candy store. Yum!"

"I don't think so," Inspector Princess said with a giggle. "Try again."

Irk rolled his eyes. "The pharmacy."

"Aw, it was worth a shot." Ruffy swung his head, flapping his ears back and forth. "I know it's really the post office."

Irk groaned and held his head in his hands. "Why are you asking the dog? He never knows!"

Inspector Princess looked through the screen at Irk. "Do you know the answer?"

Irk jumped from his seat and approached the television. "The pharmacy, Inspector! Please!" He grabbed the edges of the screen and locked eyes with her. "Someone has scribbled out the sun! The sun! There's no time to waste! People are going to die if you don't get it together!"

"That's right!" Inspector Princess said cheerfully, waving her magnifying glass. "The pharmacy! Now let's help the sun feel better!"

Irk went back to his seat, ashamed. Of course Inspector Princess knew what she was doing. She was a professional. In dozens of episodes so far, she had never fumbled a case.

"Thanks for your help!" Inspector Princess's face filled the screen. "I'm glad I can always count on you!"

And she was the only person in any world who ever said anything kind to him.

***

The taxi came to a stop. "I will take this opportunity to recharge my power cell. Feel free to use the next few minutes to stretch your legs."

Cobalt stepped out of the car. This was the Lasers' first real opportunity to explore this world outside of the laboratory. Other vehicles filled the parking lot, and people walked to and from them to a nicely landscaped building less than thirty meters away.

Crimson stayed close behind him and asked, "What do we do?"

"Stretch our legs, I guess," Cobalt said. The planet's sun gave his metal skin a pleasant warmth. Refreshed, he took a closer look at his surroundings. A tree growing from an island of dirt in the parking lot caught his attention, and he couldn't resist touching it. The smoothness of its leaves and roughness of its bark teased the tactile sensors in his fingertips. While exploring, his hand uncovered a beetle, which unfolded its iridescent wings and flew away. These details were so fascinating! Why hadn't he noticed them in the cartoon world?

Crimson's voice yanked him out of the moment. "We're drawing attention," she said. He looked away from the landscaping, into her worried expression. He followed her gaze to a crowd of approaching humans.

One stranger waved at them. "Nice costumes. Is there a convention in town?"

"Costumes?" Cobalt said.

"Who are you supposed to be anyway?"

A middle-aged woman spoke up. "Don't you recognize them? That's Cobalt Laser! And Silver and Crimson."

A murmur rose from the crowd as it grew. The back of Cobalt's neck tingled. These people recognized them!

"Oh, wow, that's an old show."

"Not that old! You're just too young!"

"I'd almost forgotten."

"That's some amazing cosplay! They look just like real versions of the cartoon characters!"

Cobalt's excitement faded. That's right. He wasn't real to them. He wasn't quite sure who they thought he was, but they made him sound like some sort of impostor.

A member of the crowd got Cobalt's attention. "Can you do *Perfect Punch*?"

That touched a nerve, but Cobalt tried not to let it show. "No, not in this world."

Someone in a red cap laughed. "*Not in this world*! Way to stay in character!"

Cobalt noticed he'd clenched his jaw again. He slowed his processor. The crowd didn't know who he was, but at least they were friendly. If only he could prove to them he really was *The Most Sophisticated Robot in the Galaxy*, maybe they could help him.

He'd barely begun forming ideas when Silver jumped in front of him and announced, "No problem, though. I can do this!" He flexed. "*Flashing Blades*!"

The crowd gasped in awe as the reflective blades extended, making Silver resemble a metal peacock.

"That's incredible!"

"I wonder what it cost to put that together!"

"Yeah, why didn't they put a little more into Cobalt? They could've at least put flashing lights in its eyes or something."

What was Silver doing? He'd barely had time to think, and here was Silver, taking charge and changing up the whole situation before Cobalt could even react. Come to think of it, Silver had been making a lot of decisions without him lately. Cobalt never formally claimed to be head of the team, but he was used to everyone naturally following his lead. Maybe that shouldn't bother a real hero, but Cobalt couldn't help it. Everything was changing so fast.

Someone else in the crowd spoke up. "What does the girl do?"

A tight group in one corner erupted with laughter. "Absolutely nothing!" one of them blurted.

A lady in front, standing near Crimson, pursed her lips and craned her neck to see where the insult had come from. "Hey!" she shouted. "It wasn't funny then, and it isn't funny now!"

Crimson gave her a bashful smile.

Someone in the crowd gasped. "Check out those facial expressions!"

"It's cute," someone from the group of loudmouths answered. "But they should've invested the effort into the Cobalt costume. Instead, they wound up with two useless robots!"

Cobalt felt heat rising in his cheeks, and it wasn't coming from the sunshine. He glanced over at Crimson. She toyed miserably with her fingers. Cobalt pointed at the lady. "She's right!" he said. "Don't say that about my sister!"

"True to character again," Red Cap said. "The real Cobalt Laser would've stood up for Crimson!"

Someone countered, "She should've stood up for herself! That was the real problem with the show's writing."

"Well, sure," Red Cap stammered. "But that's not my point!"

"So, what is your point?"

A murmur spread throughout the crowd and increased in volume, and Cobalt lost track of which opinion went with which person. Electricity tingled up his spine. He saw a crowd get angry once before, on Petalox Orbital Station when an incoming supply of nacho cheese got hijacked. It wasn't pretty.

Silver shouted above the dissent. "Check this out!" He spun his wrist blades in opposite directions.

The crowd sent up a round of enthusiastic applause, and once again all eyes were on Silver. Although this particular interruption was timely, Cobalt began to understand why his sister snapped at their younger brother so often. Cobalt felt a fresh wave of regret. If he hadn't lost *Perfect Punch*, Silver wouldn't have needed to cover for him. Since that happened, Silver gradually took more ground from Cobalt.

Cobalt shivered. Silver was his brother—should he really look at it that way? Then again, didn't Silver owe him and Crimson a little respect? Back on the *Teacup*, everything was so simple. Cobalt set the course, Silver pushed the buttons, and Crimson kept fresh pie on the console. Here, Cobalt worried about his brother's next move—a concern he usually reserved for villains.

Lights blinked in the corner of Cobalt's eye. It was the taxi. He put his hand on Silver's shoulder. "Um, it's time to go," he said, thrusting his thumb over his shoulder.

Silver folded his blades away to another round of applause. "Thank you very much! This planet has some great people!"

That earned him more laughs. He blew them a kiss.

Cobalt tugged on his brother's arm. "Now," he insisted.

Silver waved a final goodbye as he followed his siblings.

Silver occupied the front seat of the taxi for the remainder of the ride. "That was awesome! I think I'm going to like this place."

The taxi turned on some music.

"Yeah," Silver mused, nodding, "I think we found a place where we all really belong."

The taxi turned up the music in the back seat until it drowned out Silver's voice. Cobalt appreciated the gesture, but he was too lost in his own thoughts to hear anything else anyway. He and Crimson spent the next four hours watching the scenery in silence.

***

The dishes were clean.

Melinda Epic ran through the rest of her mental checklist: carpets, bathrooms, sheets, towels, and the dining table. That was everything — and dinner was waiting in the oven. It would keep warm there until everyone was home. Then her whole family would be around the table again for the first time in a year.

Epic Manufacturing was a trifling enterprise in comparison to Epic Investments, but it got them this house. And even though the three-story ranch was a tenth the value of her daughter's penthouse suite, Melinda was glad to call this cozy place her home.

The doorbell rang. Melinda threw the door open and squealed with joy. She wrapped her arms around her daughter.

"Hi Mom, I love you too," Christine said. "Can I at least come in first?"

Melinda took one of the suitcases from her daughter and led her into the living room. "Did you have a nice trip?"

"Yes, thanks. They always take care of me. Are Dad and David home yet?"

Melinda shook her head. "No. They're working through some sort of problem at the factory. They promised not to be more than two hours late."

Christine shifted her shoulder bag to her other arm. "That's good, actually. It gives me a chance to settle in before I'm bombarded with questions."

"I made them promise to wait until they get you into the office tomorrow before discussing any business. And business talk stays at the factory this year. No bringing it home." Melinda held up the suitcase. "Now, let's get you settled in. Your old bedroom is ready if you want it."

She regretted making the suggestion while the words were still in her mouth.

Christine gave her a tired look. "You mean the museum? Mom, you know how hard I've worked to leave that little girl behind. I'll take the guest room."

Melinda blushed. Even though Christine and David were well into adulthood, as long as she drew breath they'd still be her children. It's just… sometimes she picked the wrong time to show it. It's something she'd done since they were teenagers, and she still hadn't figured out how to stop. There are some lessons love just won't let you learn. She turned away bashfully.

Christine's expression softened. "Hey, enough of that. I'm home and I'm happy to be here. I love you, and dinner smells great. I will go upstairs, get settled in, and then we will start over and speak only of happy things."

Melinda smiled pleasantly. "That's a good idea. I'll carry this up for you and leave you to it."

CHAPTER 7

David pulled another abstract sculpture out of the turbine-producing machine. The echo when he threw it on the floor was much louder now that he and his father were the only two people in the building. Everyone else had gone home twenty minutes earlier.

Dan Epic leaned against a tool bench. "We have a good relationship with this client. I think if we explain the problems we're having, they'll give us another week."

David shook his head and muttered, "That isn't even enough time." He stuck his hands into the machine and poked it in places that probably only made it grumpier. "Unless there's a breakthrough, like right now, I don't know what to tell you."

Dan reached for his gold silk handkerchief and rubbed it between his thumb and forefinger. David watched his dad's jaw loosen, just a little. Although he was too young to remember the details at the time, he knew that when his dad's show flopped, stress had gotten the better of him. Things got pretty bad, but his mom didn't give up. To help him through it, she gave him that handkerchief. Touching it was supposed to remind him that Melinda was still there, believing in him. And it worked. The handkerchief was never more than an arm's length away after that.

A chime sounded from Dan's pocket. "That's the security system. Someone's ringing at the front door." He pushed away from the bench and answered the call. "Hello. I'm sorry, but the office is closed. Please come back tomorrow."

A nervous voice came back from the phone. "Hi, is this Dan Epic? I mean, Mr. Epic?"

"It is, but I'm not taking visitors. I'm in the middle of something very important. Like I said, I have office staff who can help you in the morning."

"Oh, no. We came a really long way, and it's really important. Please, Mr. Epic, we need to talk to you."

Another voice interrupted the first one. "Our power cells won't last through the night. Tell him we need to recharge."

A feminine voice joined the conversation. "We can conserve enough power to last until morning if we go to sleep right here."

Dan Epic marched toward the elevator. "What are you talking about? No one is going to sleep in my parking lot! Can't you find a hotel?"

David considered staying with the machine, but on second thought, some entertainment might do him good right now. He followed.

"I'm sorry, I'm... I'm not from around here. What's a hotel?"

David barely managed to join his father in the elevator before the doors closed.

Dan drew a deep breath and blew it out slowly. "You are distracting me from something very, very important right now." His voice carried an edge, and his pointed attempt to blunt it only amplified its impatience.

"Well, it's nice to know we're not important."

"Shh! He can hear you! I'm very sorry, Mr. Epic!"

Dan stabbed his finger at his phone and cut off the conversation, scowling. "Those voices sound very familiar, but I can't place them." His whole body shook.

"Maybe someone's playing a joke," David said.

"They picked the wrong night for that." The elevator opened into the main lobby, and Dan made a beeline for the front door. The moment he saw through the glass, he stopped.

His jaw dropped.

David stopped short behind his dad. He recognized the faces peering back through the window, and his heart skipped a beat. He took a moment to catch his breath. "Awesome!" he whispered. He hit the release button on the front door.

Dan jumped back. "David, what have you done?" He stood frozen as the robots poured into the room in an enthusiastic bundle of gratitude. Cobalt headed toward Dan while Silver and Crimson took in the surroundings; Crimson looked, whilst Silver touched. The shorter aluminum robot dashed past his sister to investigate the furnishings on the reception desk.

David's heart swelled with nostalgia as the robots spread through the room. He hadn't seen these characters since he was a child, and here they were, as real as himself. He'd been seven years old when *Cobalt Laser* aired, so he had a fuzzy memory of its plot and episodes, but the images of its characters were firmly cemented in his mind.

The thing that immediately struck him was the contrast between his childhood memory and what he now saw with adult eyes. The Laser siblings he remembered were cool space heroes with powerful weapons. They traveled the galaxy, faced impossible challenges, and beat insurmountable odds. They upheld all that was good and right, and they were examples to aspire to. But while they still projected a heroic aura, something new became apparent to David.

They were kids. And they were absolutely adorable.

The cartoon versions of the Lasers kept their eyes behind protective visors. The visors on these robots were display screens, projecting a video image of those same big, expressive cartoon eyes, which gaped around the room in awe. Cobalt's fixed on David and flashed a look that said, *thank you.*

Their mouths, noses, and cheeks seemed more cosmetic than functional. Made of some sort of flexible polymer, the mechanisms behind them produced lifelike movements while retaining the cartoonish expressions and round shapes that defined the characters' original design. Their lips synchronized perfectly with their words, and David felt sure he caught Crimson wrinkling her nose at Silver.

Their knees and elbows were industrial grade servo joints. David couldn't tell which brand—they appeared to be custom made—but they had all the marks of high-quality engineering. Their hands moved with human dexterity. Cobalt's and Silver's were encased in close-fitting gauntlets, an extension of their permanent armor. Crimson had skin on hers, made of the same polymer as the robots' faces. She'd want gloves before she attempted any assembly work. He couldn't get a close look at their knuckles, but if they were anything like the other joints, these robots would be equally able to bend steel as well as delicate work like sorting eggs.

Cobalt let go of the door, closing himself and his siblings in the room with the two humans. At that, David was as sure as he ever was of anything. These robots were the answer to his problems.

He grabbed his dad by the shoulders. "Dad! Don't you see? This is exactly what we needed! Just this morning, I said how badly we needed robots, and here they are!" He swept his hand, encompassing the universe. "Something bigger than us is at work here."

"Bigger? Like a criminal organization plotting to rob the place?" Dan shrank away from the blue metal hand reaching out to him. "Doesn't this seem fishy to you?"

David stepped in front of his father and shook Cobalt's proffered hand. "Hi. I'm David Epic, and this is my father, Dan Epic. This is our factory."

"I'm Cobalt Laser," Cobalt said. "And this is my brother Silver and sister Crimson."

David crouched to Cobalt's eye level. "Yes, I know!" He faltered finding his next words. He was addressing a superhero, but noticed he'd been pitching his voice for a conversation with a child. He cleared his throat and tried to use a normal tone. "I only saw a few episodes of your show back when I was little, but believe me, I remember!"

"Sillll-verrrr!"

David spun to find the cause of the outburst. Silver knelt on top of the reception desk, having displaced most of its accessories, which now lay on the floor. His sister had caught him in the middle of one last experiment, which involved him dumping a potted plant out onto the surface of the desk.

Silver hopped off the table and scurried away as David approached. David tried to brush the dirt back into the upset pot. Crimson reached in with a helping hand, but they only succeeded in spreading the mess around.

Crimson muttered. "I'm sorry! I am so, so sorry!"

David gave up on the mess and set the pot upright. "It's okay," he said. "Someone will take care of it in the morning." He remembered Crimson as the self-appointed parent figure, making arbitrary rules to uphold her imaginary authority, but here he saw her in a different light. The almost-adult young lady fidgeting in front of him reminded him more of an underpaid babysitter, doing her best to sieve a speck of decorum out of a jumble of chaos.

She squirmed, pinching the fingers on one hand, unable to look away from the ruined plant. David gently touched her elbow and she recoiled before timidly facing him.

"It's okay," he repeated. "Thank you for trying to help."

Crimson's eyes wrinkled and her mouth gaped. She stood like that so long David wondered if her processor had frozen, but then she straightened up and smiled. She had a set of cartoon teeth—not individual ones, but a pair of solid white plates behind her lips that spanned the width of her mouth.

Dan stomped. "Enough!"

David jumped. Cobalt snapped to attention. Crimson's smile fled and she went back to pinching her fingers. Silver knelt on the floor, brushing the remaining dirt off his hands and onto the carpet.

Dan glared at them and lowered his voice to a rumble. "If this is a joke, it's not appreciated! Who sent you, and what's going on here?"

David couldn't believe his father was this angry. His brain buzzed, hunting for the most impudent way to let him know he was being a jerk.

Thankfully, Cobalt spoke up first. "Well, sir. I'm afraid we have more questions than answers. We were hoping you could help us."

"What do you mean?"

"Well, we know that we are, or were, cartoon characters. We still don't fully understand what that means. But we're robots now. I mean real robots, not cartoon robots. A scientist brought us to life and now we're just trying to figure out who we are and where we belong."

Dan dismissed Cobalt with a wave. "This all sounds like nonsense," he said. "If any of that is true, it sounds to me like you need to find this scientist you're talking about."

Silver spoke distractedly as he wiped his hands on the sheer curtains lining the picture window by the entryway. "One little problem," he said. He took a corner of the curtain, scrubbed the last dirty spot off his thumb, and tossed it aside. "We already met that guy and he's kind of a jerk. When he gets back and notices we're not there, I picture him being the kind of guy who clenches his fists and shouts, 'They've escaped!'" Silver used his best villain voice.

David laughed. This Silver was the same sassy goofball he looked up to as a seven-year-old.

Dan scowled and folded his arms. He clenched his jaw for a couple seconds before replying, "Great. It sounds like I'm in possession of someone else's missing property."

"Property!" Crimson shivered. "I hope not."

Dan stuck a finger in Cobalt's face. "Well, one thing's clear," he asserted. "You are not my problem. I want nothing to do with you."

Cobalt peeked out from behind the finger. "Please, Mr. Epic!" His video-animated eyes were a picture of desperation. "We've come so far. Just give us a chance."

David heard enough. Scattered throughout his vague memory of the show's details, a few key points stood out. One of them was the solemnity of the promise, "I'll be right there beside you." He made his decision. Here and now, these were his robots. Not like property—that thought made his mouth taste like acid. No, this went both ways. He'd be their human, too.

He started toward the elevator, purpose in his steps. "I like that idea!" he said over his shoulder. "You want a chance? Follow me."

Dan sliced the air with his hand. "David, no!" He pointed at the front door. "I want the three of you out of here."

David held the elevator open. "I'm telling you, Dad. This is no coincidence. You'll see." He beckoned to the robots.

The Lasers looked at each other. Silver shrugged and headed over. "I like that guy," he said.

As Silver walked past him, David fought an overwhelming urge to pat him on the head.

Cobalt took Crimson's hand. The two of them withered under Dan's disapproving glare. David waved, garnering their attention. He beckoned to them, prompting a couple bashful smiles in return, and they hurried to follow their brother.

Dan growled. He joined them.

***

Cobalt found himself in a giant concrete room. The machinery on all sides stretched as far as he could see. He'd have liked a closer look, but David walked fast, and the thought of Mr. Epic bumping into him and getting even more upset was something his processor refused to compute. David stopped the group in front of a metal monstrosity built of pistons, blades, and conveyor belts. Sheet metal littered the floor around it, each piece chewed to a varying degree. David pointed at a stack of untouched sheets. "I'm trying to turn those," he said, "into these." He pointed at one of the few perfect turbine rotors. "Can you do it?"

Cobalt picked up a sheet and examined it. With his robotic strength, he figured he could easily shape it into something, at least. "Let's see. If I fold it here…" He folded it there. "And I… can I tear it?" He could not tear it. He folded it in the opposite direction.

Cobalt took his attention off the sheet to examine the faces around him. David stood stiff, hiding his expression behind his hand. Mr. Epic stood with his hands on his hips, eyes drilling into Cobalt. The corners of his mouth twitched. Crimson folded her hands behind her back, giving him an encouraging smile. Silver shifted from one foot to the other, tapping his fingers together.

Cobalt returned to his project. Roughly 60 seconds had passed, and he now held a wadded-up ball of metal.

Dan Epic allowed himself a vindicated smile. "Not a coincidence, huh?" He glanced at his watch. "David, your mother and sister are expecting us. Let's find a place to put these robots for the night and we'll figure out where to send them in the morning."

David put his hands on Cobalt's shoulders. "Come on, Dad!" he implored. "What was I thinking? This isn't a fair test. Maybe we should let him try again after a little training." Cobalt tensed at the human touch, but gradually the warmth of David's hands permeated his metal skin. He shut his optics and slowed his processor. Throughout his life, he'd protected humans and other vulnerable beings from danger, people who were helpless until he came to save them. Now he knew how they felt.

Dan held up his hand. "We have wasted more than enough time on this."

Cobalt couldn't believe it. He'd failed. What happens when you fail? His brother and sister needed him, David trusted him, and he'd let them all down. He could fight robot armies and space monsters, but he couldn't make a simple tool out of a piece of metal! Why?

Cobalt held the wad of metal. The longer he looked at it, the more it shook, until it seemed a hundred chunks of worthless trash danced in his hand. The trembling spread through his hands and arms, down into his feet. It pulled the corners of his mouth into a vicious scowl. He tensed his arm, ready to launch the piece of garbage he'd made across the factory, but a pat on his shoulder stopped him. Everything stopped shaking, and once again only one piece of ruined metal mocked him.

Silver nudged his brother aside and picked up a fresh sheet of metal. "May I?"

Silver didn't wait for an answer. He mumbled to himself as he held the sheet in one hand and compared it to the sample rotor in the other. He flipped them over a couple of times and set the rotor down. He extended one of his blades and made several cuts in the sheet. "There, there, there, and there." He punched a section out of the middle and bent the other piece. "And then that should fit in there." He frowned, picked up the sample rotor for a second look, and raised his eyebrows. "Ah." He squeezed it until there was a satisfying click.

In roughly three minutes, Silver had produced a perfect copy of the sample.

David raised an eyebrow at his dad and twitched his chin. "Not a coincidence."

Dan's smile was gone, but he didn't look mad anymore.

Cobalt widened the space between Silver and himself. The two humans, fixated on Silver, paid him no attention as he went to Crimson's side, still carrying the chunk of bent metal. Crimson touched it and gave Cobalt a half smile. He twisted his mouth in response and looked around, trying to figure out what to do with the botched part. Crimson patted his back and tuned her attention to Silver and the humans. Cobalt set his wad of steel on one of the piles of other rejects.

"That was excellent," David told Silver. "Do you think you could possibly do it again?"

Silver flashed a cocky smile. "Of course! Now that I know how."

40 seconds later Silver had another perfect rotor.

David huddled in front of Cobalt's brother. "Here's the deal. I need roughly 900 more of these." Cobalt didn't consume air, but he could simulate the sound David made—holding his breath while talking. "If I brought you in here every day for the next couple of weeks, could you make them for me?"

Silver pointed one eye toward the ceiling and counted on his fingers. Then he folded his hands behind his back and smiled. "I could!" He stood on his toes and turned that eye toward David. "I trust there's something in it for me?"

The human knelt beside Silver and held his shoulders. "I will give you and your brother and sister someplace to stay for as long as you help me," David said. "In fact, if you can pull this off, it'll be worth more than that to me. You'll have a paycheck in addition to room and board."

Crimson gasped and clasped her hands together. She whispered into Cobalt's ear. "We have a home!"

Cobalt sidled closer to her and squirmed. He supposed he was glad, too. This resolved a lot of the uncertainties they were facing, but he couldn't return Crimson's smile. "Home" was the *Teacup*. And the *Teacup* was where he set the course and Silver pushed the buttons. In this cold gray room, and everywhere else on this planet so far, Silver set the course, pushed the buttons, received the applause, and delivered the speeches. And Cobalt stayed out of the way. Crimson wrapped her arm around his shoulder and squeezed. Her polymer hand wasn't as warm as David's, but it still felt good. He forced one of his cheeks into a half-smile to thank her and hugged her back.

Silver extended his hand. "I don't know what a paycheck is, but it sounds like something I want. You have a deal!"

David shook Silver's hand vigorously.

Dan pursed his lips. "David, wait. Where are you going to keep them? Not here in the factory. There's intellectual property here. They'd need constant supervision."

"Of course not, Dad. They can stay in my apartment."

Dan balked. "Absolutely not! I refuse to let them live in my basement!"

David threw his hands in the air. "You and Mom let me keep guests before. How is this different?"

"Your sister is home! You know how this is going to go over."

"They won't bother her. They'll stay in my apartment the whole time."

Dan ran his hands through his hair. "David, this is crazy."

David spoke in measured tones. "Dad, listen. We're up against the wall and the perfect solution just fell into our laps. We would be *crazy* not to do this. We only need two weeks. Let's just get the order filled. Once that's done, we re-evaluate. But for now, we do what's best for us, the robots, and the business."

Dan pressed his palm into his forehead and wandered in a circle. "I can't believe I'm considering this," he said. He snapped his arm back down to his side. "Alright, two weeks. But keep them away from me, your mother, and especially your sister."

David pumped his fist. "Yes! Thank you, Dad! You won't regret this!"

Silver danced around the piles of sheet metal. "This has been the most exciting day of my life!" He picked up another sheet of metal and folded it into an origami crane. He threw it. It hit the concrete three meters away, bounced, and knocked over a cart loaded with lubricants and cleaning products. "I did not think that through," he admitted.

David laughed heartily and threw his arms around Silver. "I love this guy!"

Dan growled and headed back to the elevator. Crimson buried her face in her hands. Cobalt folded his arms and shivered.

CHAPTER 8

Melinda checked the casserole one more time. She was glad to have finally heard from Dan. If it had to wait in the oven much longer, it might have dried out.

She stood at the bottom of the stairs. "Christine! Your father and David should be here any minute!"

Melinda had done and redone every task on her list at least twice today. She looked around the kitchen for something to occupy herself when a commotion started downstairs. Finally! She heaved a sigh. "They're here!" she yelled upstairs. Then down, "Dan? Why are you coming in through the basement?"

"Uh, just a minute," came the response. "I'm just, uh, we have to put something away."

Melinda wondered what that could be. Maybe a surprise for Christine? She headed to the top of the stairs and tried to make out what was happening. Strange, she was sure she heard more than two voices. A thump echoed up the corridor, followed by the clatter of something bouncing across the tile floor.

Dan's voice rose above the noise. "No! You! Sit!"

Crunch.

"No! On the couch! The *couch*! Now you... *this* way. Don't step on that!"

Melinda's curiosity got the best of her. When she got to the bottom of the stairs, she gasped so loudly that every eye in David's apartment was on her. "Oh, Dan! What were you thinking? Where did you get those?"

"Get them?" Dan echoed the words as if it was her crazy idea. "*Get them?* A life-size Cobalt Laser action figure? What makes you think I would want one?"

"Mom!" David waved at her. "I can explain! They're robots!"

"I know they're robots, David! Why are they in my house?"

"They're gonna save the business, Mom! I'll take care of them, I promise. You won't even know they're here! I'll take Silver to work with me every day, and Cobalt and Crimson will stay here and... I don't know... watch TV or something."

Dan sagged. His voice dripped with exhaustion. "It's only for two weeks. We'll get the order filled, and then they'll be out of our lives."

"Two weeks!" Melinda reeled with the news. "Of all the weeks in the year, why did it have to be this one? And of all the robots in the world, why did it have to be..." She struggled to find the right words. These robots represented the toughest challenge she ever faced as a wife and mother. She could write a novel on her effort to undo the chaos they unleashed on her family. She gave up. "...them?"

A new voice traveled down the stairs. "Hey, everybody! What's going on down here?" Christine got to the tiled landing and froze. "No!" She slapped her palm against the banister. "No! No! No!"

***

David poked at his casserole. "Dinner is great, Mom! You did it again."

Melinda swallowed, not looking up. "Thank you. I'm glad you like it," she said flatly.

David tried to engage his sister. "How's the world of finance?"

She gave him a look he hadn't seen since he was nine. He'd told Darlene that his sister still listened to a kids' album titled, "Uncle Chuckle's Railway Sing-Along" at full volume, more than once a week. She tucked her tongue into her cheek and dangled her fork from her fingers like a pendulum while she waited for the utter disdain to sink in.

"David," she said. "I am biting my tongue right now. I'd like to take a moment to enjoy this delicious meal before I obliterate you." She stuffed a bite of casserole in her mouth and spoke as she chewed, "Trust me, we're going to talk."

David set his fork down. "Okay, look. I was seven years old when *Cobalt Laser* happened. What problem do all of you have with these robots?"

"There's not much more to say than you already know," Dan said. "The show imploded and ended my career, and I handled it very poorly." He took a sip of water. "Thankfully, your mother was very gracious. She insisted we get counseling, and if it hadn't been for her..." He shifted in his seat as he glanced around the table. "Well, we wouldn't all be sitting here right now." He coughed uneasily.

Melinda blushed. She squeezed her husband's hand firmly, then dabbed her eyes with her napkin before poking at her meal once more.

Christine stabbed her plate with her fork. "You know very well what my problem with your robots is, David."

David set his fork down and shrugged. "But it was forever ago! You turned out okay."

Christine leaned across the table and gaped at him.

"I am not okay!" she cried, gesturing toward the stairwell. "Don't you understand? I am the real-life inspiration for Crimson Laser! Crimson Laser, David! One of the most egregious examples of discriminatory fictional characters in recent history!"

Dan set his elbows on the table and pressed his eyes into his palms. "How many times do I have to apologize for this?" he groaned.

Christine gritted her teeth and growled her frustration. "I'm not asking you to apologize, Dad!" She clenched her fingers like claws and pointed one at David. "I've forgiven you, okay? But this idiot son of yours just had to remind me I'll never live it down!"

Melinda raised her hands and shouted over the commotion, "Everyone, please!" She let the shocked silence linger before continuing in a shuddering voice. "Just one meal. Please."

Dan cleared his throat. "You're right," he whispered. "I shouldn't have taken it personally." He nodded at his daughter. "You have every reason to be upset right now."

Christine took a deep breath, ran her fingers through her hair, and picked up her fork. She almost got another bite to her lips before David spoke again.

"You should talk to her," he said. "She's a darling kid."

Clink. Christine's fork fell to her plate. Her hand still hovered close to her mouth. Her breathing quickened, and her lips puckered, twisting into a fearsome scowl. Her lungs inflated, then she slapped the table and bellowed.

"Daaaaa-viiiid!"

***

Crimson lay across the arms of a soft chair in David's basement, watching her brothers. Silver paced aimlessly around the room, burning nervous energy. Cobalt stood in one spot, jaw set as he followed his brother with his eyes. His expression grew sourer with every step Silver took.

When Cobalt's frown dropped as low as it could, he folded his arms and coughed. "Silver, sit down for a second."

"I can't." Silver walked through the room, weaving randomly around the furniture. "I'm too excited. I'm just remembering everything that happened today. Can you believe it?"

"No, I can't," Cobalt said.

"I rescued us from a mad scientist! Then I won the adoration of a crowd of strangers, saved a factory, and earned a roof over our heads! What a day!"

Cobalt shuddered and stomped his foot. "Yeah. You, you, you!" He swept his hand in Silver's direction. "It's all about you. Silver The Hero!"

Crimson straightened, kneeling in the middle of the chair. She'd never seen Cobalt fight with Silver. That was her job.

Silver seemed just as surprised. "What are you talking about? You've always been the hero, and have you ever heard me complain?"

"It's your attitude, Silver! You best me at every turn, and then you rub my nose in it!"

"That's not true!" Silver stopped pacing and pointed at his brother. "I'm just doing what it takes to keep us alive. I can't help it if that hurts your pride."

When she fought with Silver, it never felt like a big deal. He'd tease, she'd yell, and then it would end. This was nothing like those petty exchanges. Hearing her brothers' raised voices put a knot in her stomach like she'd never known possible, and she sprung to her feet atop the cushion. "Hey guys," she pleaded. "Don't do this! Why don't we all just sit down for a minute?"

Cobalt continued as if she hadn't spoken. "You can help being a jerk about it," he spat. He bobbed his head back and forth and waved his hands in the air. "It's all, hey Cobalt, look at what you can't do! Well, don't worry, I can! Stand back and watch this!"

Crimson curled up in the chair and hid behind the armrest. "Guys, please," she whined.

Silver folded his arms. "So, tell me exactly what you want." He stared Cobalt down. "Would you rather I left you with a behavior inhibitor? Would you rather still be in that laboratory? Would you rather be fending for yourself, wandering around outside somewhere?"

Cobalt looked at the floor. "Well, no." The tightness in his cheeks disappeared, and he worked his jaw in a slow circle. He shrugged. "Okay, thank you, Silver. Thank you for saving us, okay? But try to understand me. Think what it must be like to wake up in some strange place with no usable skills. Think what it's like to be totally helpless and useless!"

Crimson pulled her knees to her chest. Silver had a point, but listening to him recount all the danger they faced that morning only underscored all the reasons they needed to work together right now.

Cobalt swept his arms in a broad gesture. "And then everywhere you turn is this guy, your own brother, who can do everything!"

Silver stomped and clenched his fists. "Look, Cobalt. You were that guy in our cartoon world. Now in this world, it's my turn to shine." Silver pointed at himself. "*I'm* the hero here. You just need to come to grips with that."

Cobalt hid his face in his palms. "Argh! Silver."

Footsteps creaked on the stairs. Cobalt and Silver shut their mouths. Crimson wondered how they could jump at that tiny sound, yet not notice her shouting from a perch. She furrowed her brow at that thought, then also turned expectantly toward the opening in the ceiling.

David poked his head into the room. "Hey," he said. "Am I interrupting anything?"

A broad smile pulled Crimson's cheeks back. Yes, he was interrupting something. Thankfully.

"No, nothing important," Silver said.

Cobalt huffed.

Crimson considered contradicting Silver, but it felt too much like tattling. But weren't you supposed to tattle if it was really important? Crimson remembered that episode. That time, a bully was being mean, and it kept getting worse until someone told Cobalt, who put a stop to it. But here, Cobalt wasn't saying anything either. She mulled it over too long, and the moment passed.

David descended the rest of the way. He walked past the chair and stopped between Cobalt and Silver. "I just wanted to make sure you have everything you need," he said. "I'm probably going to be up late tonight talking to my sister. I haven't seen her all year."

Cobalt nodded back. "I think we're fine." He pointed at one of the wall outlets. "You showed us where to recharge."

"Great. And you guys do sleep, right?"

"We don't have to," Silver said. "But the only way to hit a full charge in a reasonable amount of time is to go into low-power sleep mode."

"Then you'd better do that." David pointed at Silver and flashed a broad smile. "Because I'm going to get you up pretty early tomorrow for your first shift."

Silver gave him a thumbs up. "Looking forward to it!"

Cobalt closed his eyes and massaged his forehead with a couple of fingers.

"You can use any of the couches, and that room back there has a spare bed in it." David started back up the stairs, then paused. "Oh! Do you need anything to eat?"

Cobalt rubbed his stomach. "No. It's kind of weird, really. I guess that didn't carry over from the cartoon world. Otherwise, I'd have asked Crimson to bake a pie by now!"

Pie. That got a little smile out of Crimson. Then she remembered her wiki article. She'd almost forgotten she was supposed to be ashamed. It was probably a good thing then, that they didn't need pie. She curled onto the chair cushion, draping her head on its armrest.

David nodded. "Alright. Hey, I know this didn't start out well, but I really appreciate you guys. I'm going to talk to my family. I promise it'll get better."

As he headed for the stairs, he passed Crimson's chair and flinched. "Oh! Hey, Crimson," he said. He patted her hand. "Have a good night!" He dashed up the stairs without waiting for a response. Crimson used to envy the Robot Ninja Clan's powers of stealth, but now that she was invisible, it wasn't as great as she expected.

"You heard the boss!" Silver marched toward the wall outlet. "I'd better get my sleep!"

Cobalt rolled his eyes. "There you go again."

"One more time, Cobalt. What do you want from me?"

"Some humility would be nice."

Silver waved his hands in the air. "Oh, this coming from the *Most Sophisticated Robot in the Galaxy!*"

Cobalt sneered and started toward the door. "I'm taking that spare room. I think I could use some time alone, specifically away from you."

"Likewise. Thanks for taking the initiative."

The door slammed.

***

David sat in the easy chair in his parents' living room. Across from him, on the other side of the coffee table, Christine sat with her legs crossed, twirling her toe in a circle.

David took a bite from one of the cookies their mother had set out before leaving them alone, buying himself a few more seconds before he'd have to address his sister. When she left home, she was seventeen and David was ten. And here she was, no less intimidating now than then. He wondered how Darlene managed all these years of working for her every day.

She pointed at the cookie and heaved an exasperated sigh. "You're going to make me lead this conversation, aren't you?" she asked. "That makes me doubt you know what you're apologizing for, if you plan on apologizing at all."

David set the cookie down. "Christine, these robots just fell in my lap! Dad told you the story, too! Why can't you let me have this? Surely you realize what this means to the business."

Christine's foot stopped twirling and she held her palms out to him. "Surely you realize what this means to me! Did you have to bring them here?"

David brushed the crumbs off his jeans. "Sort of. Dad didn't want to leave them at the factory. We made a hasty decision, but I guess I could've figured something else out. I just... I felt sorry for them."

"They're robots, David. They pour coffee, deliver packages, and scrub biohazards. They're not going to cry if you don't choose them from the showroom window."

David sat upright. Christine did know significantly more about robots. She owned several. Possibly thousands, if you counted the ones that belonged to her corporation. He, on the other hand, never bought even one out of respect for his dad. Was his nostalgia for the cute lifelike cartoons tricking him?

He re-ran the evening's events through his mind. The knock at the door. Shaking Cobalt's hand. Silver, Crimson, and the potted plant. The turbine rotor test. The excited chatter and repeated expressions of gratitude during the drive home.

He leaned close. "Christine," he said. "These are not ordinary robots."

Christine backed away. "David." She folded her arms across her chest. "Are you sorry or are you not?"

David hesitated. He poked the bitten cookie, rotating it around on its napkin. "Please be patient with me, but I guess you're right. I don't know what I'm apologizing for. I believe the show hurt you back then. I believe it devastated you. But if they're really just robots like you insist, why is it such a big deal, 24 years later, that I've got one dressed like Crimson Laser in the basement?"

Christine bristled. "David, Crimson Laser—that face, that unruly hair, that voice, that awkward teenage body in that red dress. I can't look at her and not remember. I just can't." She selected a cookie and chewed. "I mean, what if I went into the basement and hid a dozen rubber cockroaches in your kitchen cupboards? What's the big deal? They're fake."

David shuddered. Cockroaches. When his dad designed Heinous's character, he wanted the villain to be scary. He remembered David's hatred for the bugs and ran with it. A case of the creeps was nothing compared to the relentless humiliation his sister wound up facing, but now he understood, at least conceptually, why she was mad.

"I'm sorry for not listening to you," he said. "I am. I should've thought about what it would do to you before I brought them home. I promise to keep them out of your way from here on."

"Alright," she said. She smirked. "And I promise to go back to being the supportive big sister I've always been."

***

Crimson watched from her chair while Silver fiddled with the sofa.

"Well, that leaves this room for the two of us," he said over his shoulder. "Luckily, we're getting along really well for once. I don't think I could deal with both of you acting obnoxious at the same time. David said this couch unfolded into a bed. Oh, yeah. I see how that works. Nice! I'll take this one. You can do whatever. I'm going to start charging my power cell now. Cobalt was right about one thing, though. I do miss bedtime pie! Oh, well. This world makes up for it in other ways. Sleep well!"

Silver curled up on the bed, not giving Crimson a second look. She wasn't quite ready to go to sleep herself. She had a lot weighing on her mind. Before today, she'd just been living her life. She had Cobalt and Silver, and never really gave a thought to anyone else's opinion of her. She took inventory: useless, worthless, pathetic, weak, stupid... Even though she only heard a few of those specific words today, all of them were echoing in her mind now. Sure, she'd been insulted before. The few times Hex Ten or Heinous found it worthwhile to address her at all, it was always a curse of some kind, and Silver made an art form out of pushing her buttons. But today was different. Today, when the strangers in the parking lot and the anonymous voices on the internet labeled her, she believed them. A few people stood up for her, but those voices were impossible to hear right now, drowned in an ocean of negativity.

She'd been staring at the back of Silver's head for a while. He turned and looked at her in his peripheral vision. "Do you need something?"

"I'm sorry." She rubbed her elbow and looked away. "Do you think you could make room for me? Please?"

"Aw, Crimson. Gross!" Silver pointed across the room. "There's another couch over there. I don't think it unfolds, though."

"I know. I just…" Earlier, when she'd snuggled the chair, it didn't snuggle back. She just needed to know someone was there. "I don't want to be alone. Not right now."

Silver rolled over and glared at her, annoyed. This final display of disapproval tipped the balance. Crimson's world collapsed, and she sank under its weight. This was it. The night would never end, and even if morning did come, it wouldn't be any better.

Crimson had no idea how she looked, but it must've been terrible because Silver drew back as if he'd been ambushed. He reached out to touch her cheek but pulled his hand back before it got there. His expression softened, and he stammered, "Sure. Okay." He moved over.

Crimson crawled in beside him. The warmth of his back against hers gave her some comfort, even if it was her annoyed little brother.

Silver burrowed into the mattress. "It'll be okay," he told her. "Cobalt just has to adjust. Once he does, he'll stop acting like this. Don't worry."

Crimson hugged herself, weighing her words. Cobalt wasn't the only one who needed to adjust. "Silver, you know I love you, right? I mean, I know we fight a lot, but you're still my brother, and nothing will change that." She stared at the unfamiliar shapes in the darkness. "I'll always be right there beside you."

She waited for a response, but Silver was deep into sleep mode.

CHAPTER 9

"THEY'VE ESCAPED!" DR. SMALLS shook his fists at the ceiling.

Irk cowered by the computer terminal, watching his boss wear a circle in the tile floor.

The scientist took a break from his pacing to turn on him and yelled, "Irk, you imbecile! I left yesterday afternoon and came back first thing in the morning. That's less than 24 hours! How could you let this happen?"

"I'm sorry, Doc!" Irk said. He stuck his head out from behind the desk and whimpered. "I couldn't do anything to stop them!"

"This puts my whole plan in jeopardy!" Andrew took a broken keypad off the shelf beside him and threw it with all his strength at a battery shell on the other side of the lab.

It did not go very far.

Andrew ran after the keypad, snatched it from the floor, and flung it again. Now it was almost halfway across the room.

He screamed his frustration at the overhead lighting and slumped onto a nearby stool. He muttered to himself. "They were the first of their kind. A proof of concept. I was going to preserve them in a place of honor in my personal care. They would've had a life of perpetual ease, a living testament to my ultimate accomplishment."

Andrew caught his breath and stood. "But now they're out there, revealing my secrets to the world."

Irk grabbed the waist of Andrew's lab coat and smiled up at him. "At least I didn't leave! I'm right here beside you!"

Andrew brushed the little robot away. "Oh, please. Is that supposed to make me feel better? What makes you think I even want you around here?"

Irk's smile faded. His servos powered down as he released his grip, not just in his arms but in the rest of his body, too. "Oh. I thought because you made me first, you know, maybe you liked me best?"

"Are you kidding? I made you first precisely because you're my least favorite character on the show!"

Irk twitched as all of his servos jolted back to life. "What?"

Andrew broke away from Irk, waving his arms. "You're a prototype, you idiot! You thought I wanted to risk a bunch of failed experiments on my childhood hero? You thought I wanted to slap Cobalt Laser with a thousand prohibitions? No, that's what you're for!"

"Oh." Irk's servos sagged again. Time slowed down.

"And when things fell apart and it came time to wipe your memory and start over, do you think I could've hit that button when it was Cobalt Laser begging for one more chance?"

"That... happened?" Irk looked desperately for a crate to sit on. He slumped to the floor before he could find one.

Andrew looked over his shoulder, sneering. "More times than I could count. It's a good thing your pathetic sniveling made the job easier."

Irk tucked himself into the corner between the wall and desk and curled into a tiny ball.

Andrew groaned. "I have no choice but to go after them. I'm sure Dan Epic will be happy to hand them over. There's no way he wants them around. I'll be back, Irk. Try not to ruin anything else."

The door slammed. Irk uncurled, relieved to be alone. Still, he couldn't motivate himself to get off the floor. He had asked on multiple occasions, and every time Andrew insisted that he didn't have a stomach. Even so, though it was supposed to be impossible, Irk had a tummy ache.

***

"Hey buddy." David approached Silver's workstation. He admired the pallet of completed parts waiting beside his new friend. "It's already afternoon. You need a break?"

Silver put the finishing touches on one more turbine rotor. "Eh, it does get a little boring after a few dozen."

David raised an impressed eyebrow at the pallet behind him. "Well, at this rate you won't have any trouble making the deadline." He started toward the elevator and motioned Silver to follow. "No sense in burning you out."

"What do we do on break?" Silver's legs scampered to keep up with David's longer strides.

David noticed and slowed his pace. Silver was so eager to please, and he wanted to return that favor. "Most people get a snack," he said. "But since you don't eat, maybe we should watch something. Are there any shows you like?"

Silver stood by David as they waited on the elevator. "I never watched TV in the cartoon world," he said. "And I've only been in this world for about a day and a half."

"Yeah, a show within a show usually doesn't work too well," David said. "Let's find out what you like. That'll be fun in itself."

The elevator opened to reveal Dan Epic. He flinched. "Oh!" he said. "I was just coming to get you."

David's brow wrinkled. "Why?"

"We have a visitor in the conference room." Dan folded his arms and motioned his chin toward Silver. "One Dr. Andrew Smalls."

Silver cringed. "This better not count as my break."

***

Silver peeked into the conference room. Something sank inside him when he saw the occupied chair at the far end of the table. His insides turned to lead when that chair spun to reveal the grinning face of Dr. Smalls.

Andrew clapped his hands. "Ah, you do have him!" he said. He glanced between David and Dan before leaning back in his chair and addressing Silver. "Where are your brother and sister?"

Silver puckered his face and grabbed the chair on his end of the table, squeezing its armrest. "Not here."

Andrew winked at Dan. "Silver is the difficult one, isn't he?"

Silver planted his feet and jabbed his finger at the scientist. "Andrew, we'll let you know when we're ready to talk to you again. We're pretty happy with our current arrangements."

Dr. Smalls set his elbows on the table and leveled his gaze at Silver. "It's not that simple. You see, according to the law, you're my property. I've come to reclaim you and your siblings."

Silver flung the chair, sending it rolling across the floor. "I'm telling you we won't go with you!" He didn't know much about law or property, but he did know how to fight, and if that's what it took, he was ready! A sudden hand on his shoulder interrupted his battle stance.

He looked up to find the underside of Dan Epic's chin. Dan pulled Silver back gently and gave him a pat. "Dr. Smalls." He positioned himself in front of Silver. "Silver here is helping me out with a very important project. I'd like to borrow him for a while if it isn't too much trouble. I'd even be willing to pay rent."

Andrew pulled his face taut. "Really? I'm surprised you of all people would want replicas of the Laser siblings hanging around."

"You're right, but as I said, Silver has proven himself useful."

Andrew stood. "That's very generous of you, but I'm afraid it's impossible. These robots are part of a complicated experiment." He turned his head askance and curled his lip ominously. "They may even be dangerous."

Silver bristled. *Flashing Blades* unfolded slightly as he peeked out from behind Dan Epic. "There's only one dangerous person in this room, and I'm looking at him," he shot back.

Andrew wagged his head. "Silver Laser, I am very sorry to do this. This will severely limit you for the rest of your life, but you leave me no choice." He looked Silver in the eye. "I forbid you to disobey me."

A rush went through Silver's sensory network. This was going to be fun. He smiled broadly as he shot back, "I forbid you to forbid me to disobey me." Wait, no. He grimaced. "I mean, to disobey you." He stomped his foot. The perfect setup for a one-liner, and he botched it! "Aw! That would've been so cool if I hadn't messed it up!"

Silver's disappointment melted as the look on Andrew's face changed. His neural pathways tingled as he watched the scientist process what he'd just done. He forgot all about villain-hero banter and settled for the simple joy of watching Andrew seethe.

Andrew hissed at Dan Epic. "Give me my robots!"

"Dr. Smalls," Dan paused, feeling for the silk handkerchief in his pocket. "Having gotten to know your robots over the last several hours, there are some questions of personhood here that I'm not comfortable answering myself." He set his hands on his hips. "If you come back here with a warrant and the proper authorities, I will readily comply with the law. But I'm not willing to turn these robots over on your word alone."

Silver marveled at Dan Epic. The human could fight too, but words were his weapons. And unlike Silver's hacking and slashing approach, his creator measured each blow carefully and made every shot count. This was the most he'd ever admired anyone, himself included.

Andrew slammed his fist on the table. He winced and quickly snatched his hand back, cradling it. He choked back the pain as he roared at them. "You have no right to do this! I refuse to leave without my property!"

A low growl rumbled in Dan's throat. "Get out of my facility, Dr. Smalls, or I will be the one calling the authorities."

Andrew glared back. Frowning bitterly, he stormed out of the room. He sneered at David one last time as he passed by.

It took Silver a moment to believe that Dr. Smalls was really gone. He stood staring into the empty hallway, then spun to face Dan Epic. Silver gushed at his new hero.

"You were so cool! Those big words! So confident!" He threw his arms around Dan and squeezed. "Thank you so much! I'm sorry for wrecking your plant. I'll buy you a new one when I get my first paycheck!"

Dan patted Silver. "It's okay. No problem. You... you can let go now."

"He's right, Dad," David said. "You were pretty cool."

Dan waved his hand. "It was nothing. I've been in business a long time. He was obviously resorting to intimidation because he didn't have a leg to stand on." He crouched to Silver's eye level. Silver gaped back as his creator examined him.

"No, Dad," David said. "I mean it's cool that you want to keep Silver." He folded his arms and shifted his weight to one foot. "Thanks. It means a lot to me."

Dan reached for a water bottle, wetted a tissue, and rubbed at a grease smudge on Silver's cheek. "It didn't make sense, did it? The way I've been running the factory, I mean." Silver reflexively raised his hand to meet Dan's but stopped short. This was the sort of thing Crimson would do, and he'd wriggle away from her. Now he found himself hoping Dan would find a spot on his other cheek.

"Don't worry about it, Dad. We're in a good place now."

"We will be, now that I'm going to start listening to you," Dan said, withdrawing the tissue and admiring his handiwork. "I'm sorry for not starting sooner."

David switched to his other leg. "Never mind that, Dad." It was time to move on. Sure, his dad had been wrong. Sure, it gnawed at him for years. But to call it out? He'd rather forget it and forge ahead.

"David," Dan said, scrubbing at progressively tinier spots on Silver's eye shield, "I know it's awkward, but I'm asking for your forgiveness."

Hadn't he already done that? Why say it directly? That seemed like it would call out his dad's wrongs and cause more pain, not healing. Still, it's what he asked for.

David swallowed. "I forgive you, Dad." The moment the words came out, he realized how heavy they'd been. His next breaths came much easier without their added weight, and moving forward seemed a brighter prospect.

"Thank you, son," Dan said. He squeezed Silver's shoulder. "How about you?" he asked. "Are you going to be okay after all that?"

"Yeah," Silver said. He giggled. All that time searching the galaxy for his creator, Silver never knew what to expect. But this is where the journey led him. His lips pulled back, showing both rows of teeth. "I'm fine!"

"Good. Now take a nice, long break and have fun."

SERIES: Cobalt Laser
SEASON 1, EPISODE 1

"The First Step of the Journey"
TIMESTAMP: 06:15

"Ugh. It's dusty in here," Silver's voice echoed through the underground cavern. "This is no good for my allergies." He wiped a cobweb from his face.

Crimson wrapped her arms around herself and cast a worried look at her surroundings. "It's like a robot graveyard."

She was right. Hulks of robots and vehicles long past lay in wrecked heaps, illuminated by the intermittent blinking of electronics whose power cells were barely hanging on after ages of disuse.

Silver tapped her on the shoulder and whispered into her ear. "Boo!"

Crimson shrieked and jumped. She lost her footing and fell through a dust-covered cobweb on her way to the ground. "Sillll-ver-rr!"

Cobalt frowned at his siblings. "Get serious, guys." He pointed at some cryptic writing carved into the wall. "It's the creator's language! We must be getting close!"

Crimson glared at Silver before accepting his extended hand. She brushed off her dress. This sent up a cloud of dust, which drifted toward Silver and enveloped his head.

Silver sneezed violently into his hands. "Oh, my allergies!" he groaned. He pulled his hands away just enough to peek at them, then looked sheepishly at Crimson. "Uh, Crimson, do you have a tissue?"

Crimson nearly gagged. "Ew, Silver!" She pulled one from her pocket, tossed it at him, and followed Cobalt.

As he hurried after the others, Silver finished wiping and discarded his used tissue carelessly. It landed on an ancient computer console. Unseen by the Laser siblings, it arced with electricity and flashed a warning: "Virus!"

A tremor, too small for Cobalt and his siblings to notice, shook the nearby rubble as a figure rose from it. A pair of glowing eyes peered from the shadows and focused on the three robots heading down the corridor.

The next room opened into a huge underground cavern. Cobalt, Silver, and Crimson continued until the path ended at the edge of a lake. The water gave off a faint blue glow.

"Looks like a dead end," Silver said.

"I don't understand." Cobalt scanned the lake from one end to the other. "I was sure we were on the right track." He turned and flinched. "We have company!"

A hulking monstrosity blocked the path from which they came. Its translucent skin looked like a cross between glass and stone as it reflected the soft light cast by the water. The massive being projected its thundering voice to the stalactites above. "Cower, fools! Hex Ten lives again!"

"Hex Ten?" Silver said in a mocking tone. "What kind of name is that?"

A chipper little voice came from somewhere behind the terrifying creature. "Hex Ten, or Hexadecimal Ten." Out stepped a short copper-plated robot with a little round face. "Stylized 0x10. Shorthand for binary 00010000, equivalent to the number humans call 'sixteen'. As for me, my name is Irk!"

Silver pointed over his shoulder at the small robot. "What a nerd!"

Cobalt chuckled. "That's something, coming from you."

Another shape emerged from the darkness. A bug-like being with slender appendages slinked into the room and took its place beside Hex Ten. Its voice grated like sandpaper, but its words were smooth as butter. "A most auspicious number to binary-speaking beings. I pledge you my loyalty, Lord Hex. I am Heinous, at your service."

"What do you want with us?" Cobalt squared off with the intruders and prepared for the worst.

"The computer virus you released on us rings with an ancient power." In a dramatic motion, Hex curled his fingers into a fist. "We would like to find the source of this power."

Silver scrunched his face. "Virus? Power?" He lit up. "Wow! The snot in the tissue I threw away must have had a virus in it that spread our consciousness and intelligence to these ancient robots!"

Crimson fought her gag reflex again. "Oh, Silver! Please don't!"

Silver folded his arms and stuck his nose in the air. "You're just jealous," he said with a dismissive wave. "We can't all have magical snot."

Cobalt ignored the distraction and focused on the newcomers. "When you say you want to find the source, you must mean the creator. That's what we're searching for, too."

Hex Ten glowered at the siblings. "When I find this power, I will not share it with mere children. Your quest ends here!" He stamped the ground, and his cohorts took up positions beside him.

Crimson drew back, wringing her hands. "Cobalt, be careful!"

Cobalt smiled confidently. "Not a chance, Hex Ten! Prepare to meet your match!" He planted his feet. "*Perfect Punch*!"

It would be another 24 years before Cobalt understood the real meaning of a commercial break.

CHAPTER 10

"Oh, Ruffy. You're so silly! Diet cola doesn't come from cows. Scientists make it out of chemicals!"

Irk rolled his eyes and slid off his crate, slumping to the floor. Inspector Princess was a saint to have put up with Ruffy for this long. If Irk was her companion, every episode would be over in five minutes. He'd choose the right path every single time on the first try.

And maybe he could teach her something. He'd tell her they needed to build a flux manifold. Should they use the fabricator, the nanorefractor, or the molecular forge? She'd be so impressed when he told her the right answer was the fabricator!

"That's the device that built me!" he'd tell her.

Then she'd say they needed to go somewhere fun. Should they go to the playground, the toy store, or the movies? Irk would have to admit that he didn't know which one was the right answer.

"Irk," she'd say, looking into his eyes. "This time they're all the right answer."

Wooooow. He melted onto the floor.

Irk shook the fantasy from his head and wondered what he'd been missing. Ruffy was trying to figure out which end of a straw was which.

Irk slumped further onto the floor and glared at the dog. An idea formed in his head. The fabricator! He bolted upright. He could bring

Inspector Princess into this world! She could live here with him! In the laboratory. Locked away. Under the thumb of Dr. Smalls.

No. What a terrible, terrible thing to do to someone as wonderful as Inspector Princess.

Irk's musings ended abruptly when the door banged open, and Andrew charged into the room. Irk leaped half a meter into the air and scrabbled for the remote. He turned off the TV and meekly approached his boss. That uncomfortable feeling in his stomach returned.

Dr. Smalls ignored him. He rifled through his desk. He reached into his pocket and tossed a laser torch onto a pile of other forgotten tools. He huffed, turned, and made straight for the fabricator.

"The proper authorities," he mumbled. "You fool. I'm the only authority I recognize. And you will be sorry you invoked my wrath."

Cautiously, Irk approached the fabricator. When he was certain his boss was fully absorbed in his work, Irk peered carefully over his shoulder.

One glance at the screen, and the churning in his stomach increased tenfold. Even though nothing came out, Irk was certain he'd just learned how it felt to throw up.

On the screen were the schematics for Hex Ten and Heinous.

***

Hours later, empty soda cans and takeout containers littered the floor. Andrew rolled back and forth on his swivel chair, sending the cans rolling and griding stale leftovers into the cracks between the tile. He pushed away from the desk and set his chair into a slow spin. Now everything revolved around him: lab equipment, countless manuals, and other assorted reminders of his experiments over the years, all of them the work of pure genius. Let's see, what else existed here to serve him? There was Irk of course, his desk, those lamps, a couple of dried-up houseplants and... ah yes. The giant sapphire-encrusted monster robot stomping around on his fabricator platform, screaming at him.

"I am the great Hex Ten, and the day I bow to a pitiful human is the day the stars fall!"

Hex hadn't done much yet. He and Heinous had only been conscious for about a minute. Andrew spent the first part of that minute explaining his intent to boss them around. The twenty or so seconds after that consisted of raging and pacing on Hex's part, while Heinous waited patiently in the background for instructions. Andrew figured he should act before something got broken.

He grunted and lifted himself off the chair. It wasn't that comfortable anyway. "Yeah, yeah, yeah, Chuckles," he said. "It's a good thing I'm not pitiful, or it'd be a dark night." He paused to buff a rough spot out of one of his fingernails. "Look. I can tell you're going to be a tough nut to crack, so let's go straight to the nuclear option."

Andrew took his attention away from his fingernail and looked Hex in the eye. "Hex Ten, I forbid you to defy me."

Hex flinched. The look he gave Andrew said some mean things about the scientist's sanity.

That made this next part all the more delicious. Andrew smiled ominously. "Now bow."

Hex could only emit a few panicked shouts as his own body moved despite him. In seconds he found himself on one knee before the human.

"Lord Hex!" Heinous hissed. "What is the meaning of this?"

Andrew twisted his face into a manic grin and took a step toward Heinous, stabbing his finger at the startled minion. "You can forget Lord Hex," Andrew told him. "From now on, you only need to remember me." He pointed at himself. "Lord Andrew."

He turned his attention back to Hex. "Bow low. I want obeisance!"

Hex fell on his face. "What power is this?" His voice never went that high in the cartoon.

"I told you. The power of the creator! Now do you believe?"

"Yes! Yes! Forgive me, Lord Andrew!"

Seamlessly, Andrew stopped raving and became the picture of grace and majesty. "Very well, Hex. You may move freely." He turned to Heinous. "Now, can I count on your cooperation without resorting to such extreme measures?"

Heinous knelt voluntarily and extended his lower pair of arms with a flourish. "I live by a code of honor. I pledge my loyalty to the creator."

"Cute," Andrew said. "Speaking of..." He turned and shouted. "Irk!"

Hex and Heinous exchanged glances.

Irk peeked out from behind a stack of worn tires and waved. "Hi, Hex. Hi, Heinous."

"Irk!" Hex sounded almost glad to see him. "What is this place?"

Heinous focused both his compound eyes on Irk. "Is this the other side of the black hole?"

"Eh." Irk pulled up a crate. "Not exactly. Settle in. This will take a while to explain."

Andrew waved at them dismissively. "I've heard all this before. I'm going to attend to a few things while you do kindergarten story hour." He gestured at the disheveled mess of a lab around him and backed out of the room, flashing a generous smile. "Make yourselves at home."

***

Hex Ten spoke in a low voice. "Then this bug is not the creator."

It hadn't taken long for Irk to relate the story to him and Heinous. Childlike as he was, the big brain in his little copper head was mighty organized, and he distilled the events into a concise summary. Hex and Heinous listened with rapt attention, interrupting only a few times.

Hex turned his head, slowly scanning the disorganized laboratory. He knew Dr. Smalls had left, but this place was a maze. Paranoia didn't suit him, but even he wondered if the scientist could be lurking in the disarray. Hex bristled. How did a feeble human manage to unnerve him?

"Yet he did give us life," Heinous said. "We owe him our allegiance."

"Nonsense!" Hex struggled to keep his voice down. "If that's true, I owe him no more than the virus that revived us in our world."

Heinous stood tall and pointed one appendage at Hex. "That was an accident," he said. "This was an act of the Doctor's will. He awakened us for his purposes. My code of honor is clear."

Hex raised his chin and scanned past the tops of the surrounding equipment racks. "Suit yourself. He may force me to bow, but I am still my own master."

"Hold it!" Irk waved at them. "Remember what I said about prohibitions. I can't lie to the boss. Don't say anything to me that you don't want him to hear."

Hex eyed Irk suspiciously. A low rumble emanated from his throat. "Can I not trust my own minion?"

The little robot's animated eyes doubled in size. He hopped off his crate and backed away from Hex, holding up his hands. "It's not like that!" he insisted. "You can trust me!" He stood stock straight and saluted. "All hail Lord Hex Ten! Ah..." his voice trailed off.

Heinous crouched low. "Terror of..." he prompted. He fixed his segmented eyes on Irk, their multi-faceted surfaces reflecting hundreds of terrified little copper faces.

"Yes!" Irk yelped, his voice breaking into a squeak. "All hail Lord Hex Ten, Terror of the Galaxy!" He knelt and clasped his hands together. "Sorry, Hex! It's just been a long time since I've said it! It's been a long time since I've done a lot of things! Andrew is scary, Hex, and really powerful! I can't resist his control, but trust me, you're the master I want to follow! I promise!"

Hex ground his teeth. He detected pressure between the flat plates, with a bit of pain. The sensation surprised him, making him break his intimidating glare. Annoyed, he donned another surly expression and resumed his questioning. "How much of the galaxy does this scientist control?"

Irk wrinkled his eyes at Hex, as if the Terror of the Galaxy had asked for directions to the sky. "None," he said.

Hex's face contorted and his chest swelled.

Irk jumped again. "Whoa, Hex! I mean, it's just the planet! There's no interstellar travel here."

Hex's massive shoulders drooped. What sort of world was this? As far as he was concerned, it had been barely an hour since he was last on a starship. Now there were no interplanetary vessels, anywhere? He set his jaw. "Then I must rule this planet."

Irk fidgeted. "It's not that simple, Hex. Andrew isn't a warlord of this city, let alone the galaxy. But he owns every millimeter of this laboratory, and that includes us."

Heinous rubbed his clawed hands together in pairs. "Then we must obey," he said.

"Never!" Hex pledged through gritted teeth. He was starting to like the sensation.

Irk's voice squeaked once again. "Yes!" he shrieked. "Right now we have no choice! Until things change, we'd better tread carefully." He wrung his hands, trembling miserably. "Believe me."

Hex growled again. Until things change. Irk seemed to know a lot about this world, so he'd trust his judgement—for now. He relaxed his aggressive stance. He'd change things soon enough.

Irk shivered and looked away. The three villains settled back into their seats. Irk rocked on his crate and kicked his legs. "You know," he said. He cocked his head and smiled. "I really was missing you guys."

SERIES: Cobalt Laser SEASON 2, EPISODE 7

"Robots for Hire" TIMESTAMP: 15:33

SILVER STOOD AT THE front of the conference room. "Well, that didn't work out."

He approached the list of jobs on the marker board. Landscaping, Dog Walking, Small Engine Repair, Housesitting, Leaf Raking, and Car Wash were all crossed out. Taking a marker, Silver drew a line through "Telethon."

"That leaves Bake Sale!" Crimson jumped with excitement. "I told you we should've started with that!"

Cobalt stood tall. "Don't worry, Professor Squiggly! I promised we'd earn that scholarship money for Robot University, and I meant it!"

The stout little robot looked up at Cobalt and stroked the white titanium fiber beard that nearly reached his toes.

"Oh, thank you, Cobalt Laser! It means so much to our students!" He looked at the clock on the conference room wall through his round wire spectacles. "But we're almost out of time!"

Crimson knelt and wrapped her arms around the adorable teacher. "We'll make it, Professor!" She gave him a squeeze. "I'll stay up all night baking pies!"

She looked through the window into the hallway. "I see this office has a kitchenette. Mind if I put it to use?"

"Of course you may!" said Professor Squiggly. His red bowtie spun like a happy little propeller. "Thank you!"

Crimson scrutinized the kitchenette and examined the sink and counters. She slathered soap on a sponge. "I'd better clean all the surfaces. Foodborne pathogens are no laughing matter!"

With one quick swipe of the sponge, Crimson left behind a glistening, sparkling countertop. It was so pristine she could hear it shine.

Crimson proudly surveyed the results. "That's better!" she said. "Now to work!"

***

The next morning found Crimson sitting at a table in front of the main university building, surrounded by hundreds of pies. She grinned psychotically as her eye twitched. Her hair stood straight out on the left side, held firm with dried pie filling. A thin flour coating dusted her face and dress.

Silver looked her over with concern. "Wow, Crimson. Did you get any sleep last night?" He tried to smooth down some of her unruly hair with his fingers, but it sprung right back.

"Nope!" she yelped. She twitched one more time. Her head fell back, and her arms drooped. She snored like a diesel engine.

Cobalt put his hands on his hips and smiled at his sister. "Well, that's that," he said. A group of people emerged from behind a building and made their way toward the group. Cobalt perked up. "Here comes our first batch of customers!"

Silver squinted. "Something's not right, Cobalt."

Cobalt watched the crowd of university staff and students draw closer. They shambled and groaned incoherently as they walked.

"Oh, no!" Cobalt put his hands to his head. "They've been hit with that digital contagion that Hex Ten has been spreading around!"

Silver deployed *Flashing Blade*s. "I'm ready for 'em!"

"No, Silver!" Cobalt waved at him to stand down. "These people are innocent! We need a weapon that won't harm them. Something that will gum them up and stop them without causing injury."

Silver folded his blades and looked at the stacks of pies beside him. "Huh." He picked one up and grinned from ear to ear. "That's serendipitous."

Cobalt grabbed one of the pies and flung it at the nearest attacker. It slapped the student in the face, stopping him in his tracks. The student struggled for a moment before falling to his knees. The plate slid off, leaving his face covered in red sludge. "Mmm," he said in healing ecstasy. "Boysenberry."

"It's working!" Cobalt shouted.

"Lock and load!" Silver took a stack of five pies in each hand.

"Snnnnx," Crimson snored. She spoke to someone in her dreams. "The turtle can borrow my shoes."

Cobalt and Silver threw pie after pie at the approaching horde, leaving a wake of contented students and faculty in their path, licking their faces in unbridled joy.

"What... is... boysenberry?" Cobalt grunted each word in time with a pie thrown.

"Nobody... knows!" Silver said.

Finally, the nightmare was over. All around them in an ocean of broken crust and pie filling lay a crowd of exhausted robots, lazily snacking. Of all the pies they started with, only two remained on the table.

Cobalt picked them up and offered one to Silver. "Pie?"

"You know it!"

Silver was about to take a big bite when Crimson jolted awake. She looked around and blinked. Her face fell as she took in the destruction surrounding her. She caught sight of the pie on its way into Silver's mouth and clenched her fists.

"Sillll-verrrr!"

CHAPTER 11

CRIMSON SAT UPSIDE-DOWN ON the couch, her feet dangling over the backrest. Her head hovered a few centimeters from the floor, making her processor whir pleasantly. She hadn't decided whether it actually helped her think, but she liked it.

Silver left for work with David, and Cobalt had gone out. This world needs heroes too, he'd said, and he was as much a hero here as he was anywhere else. Crimson didn't like the idea. Why not take just one day off and figure things out when David got back? Cobalt wouldn't hear it. She grumbled an obligatory, "Cobalt, be careful," and he left without another word.

As for herself, Crimson decided it was time to finally start earning her keep. Today would be the day she stopped being useless. Unfortunately, she'd already spent the whole morning thinking about just how to do that, and she still drew a blank.

She somersaulted off the couch and took a fresh look at the apartment. Whatever she did, it would have to be in this room. She already promised she would not go upstairs. Earlier, she caught Mrs. Epic's gaze while staring into the upper living room and retreated in humiliated terror. Since then, she avoided the tiled landing at the base of the stairs as if it was electrified.

David was nice. He hadn't paid her much attention yet, but she hadn't given him any reason to. Maybe she should do something for him.

Her eyes landed on the partition that separated David's main living area from the kitchen. That was it! She and her brothers couldn't eat pie, but David could. It wasn't much, but she could work her way up from there. Crimson darted into the kitchen and had a look.

Okay. Now to bake a pie. First things first. You have to clean the surfaces. Good. She found a sponge and soap. Apply the soap to the sponge. Crimson hesitated. She expected the soapy sponge to feel fresh and clean, but this one felt foamy, squishy, and sticky. It oozed suds when she squeezed it. Oh, well. Surely it would still work out.

Next things next. Wipe the surface. She slopped the sponge on one end of the counter and swiped it across. She expected to see a gleaming countertop so pristine she could hear it sparkle. What she saw instead was a dirty countertop with a streak of soap slopped across it.

What could have gone wrong? She remembered something Dr. Smalls said about her cartoon world being more magic than science. Of course! She forgot the incantation. She scrunched her face, struggling to recall it. Then, starting with the sponge on one end of the counter she recited, "Foodborne pathogens are no laughing matter!"

She tried again, swiping the countertop twice as fast. Halfway across, she bumped the soap bottle and sent it flying. She let go of the sponge, which fell to the floor, and grabbed the bottle in midair with both hands, squeezing it. A jet of concentrated soap shot into her face and down the front of her dress. Blinded, she slipped on the sponge and fell to the floor.

By the time everything stopped moving, blue liquid soap dripped from the counter, the ceiling, the walls, and Crimson.

Lying flat on her back, she assessed the situation. If anything proved that Crimson Laser always was and never would be anything but useless, this was it. That's when she realized another terrible truth. She suspected it before, but now she knew. Her robot body could not cry, no matter how desperately she wanted to.

Careful not to slip again, Crimson picked herself up off the floor and considered her options. She had no idea when Cobalt would return. She could wait for David, but how many hours would that be?

The only other person in the house was Mrs. Epic. She could help, but Crimson guessed she wouldn't be happy about it. She could probably tolerate being covered in slime for quite a while, but she couldn't hide forever. And a lesson she'd observed many times in the cartoon world was, the longer you avoided consequences, the worse they got. Resigned, Crimson dragged herself to the stairwell.

Steeling herself, she looked up and called out, "Mrs. Epic?"

***

Cobalt stood on a street corner, watching the crowd shuffle past. He'd ventured twelve blocks from the house, but so far this planet lacked any form of adventure. The few people who recognized him didn't seem particularly impressed. They just pointed, said, "Huh! A Cobalt Laser! That's pretty neat," and moved on. He met a handful of robots, but they were all ordinary robots, interested in nothing except their assignments.

His enthusiasm waning, Cobalt rounded a corner and halted. A bright flash overloaded his optics, and it took them a split second to adjust. There, about two blocks down, red and blue strobes danced around a scene teeming with uniformed people, going about some urgent business.

Where Cobalt came from, this meant the Galactic Response Force was on the scene. And in Cobalt's experience, the Galactic Response Force was always relieved to see a hero, especially Cobalt Laser!

No time to lose! Cobalt routed all his power to his leg servos and dashed toward the commotion. Someone needed a hero!

***

Crimson stood sheepishly behind Mrs. Epic and waited for her reaction. She couldn't see Melinda's face, but from the back she looked plenty mad. She planted her hands on her hips and heaved her shoulders in an exhausted sigh. When she finally spoke, it reminded Crimson of her own tone after Silver did something especially little-brothery.

"Oh, Robot, what have you done?"

"I'm sorry," Crimson whispered. "I was only trying to help."

Melinda swept her arms, indicating the whole kitchen. "There's soap everywhere!" She groaned. "How did you manage to do this?"

Crimson looked away and toyed with her fingers. "I don't know." Her voice got even tinier. "I was just trying to clean the countertop. I think the sponge is broken."

Melinda spun on her heel. "Broken?" The incredulous look on her face scared Crimson worse than a Bloogsorbel.

Crimson crept past her and picked up the sponge. "Yes." She swiped the countertop again, flinging a huge glob of soap across the room.

Melinda threw her arms up and screamed. "Who programmed you to clean?" She snatched the sponge from Crimson.

Crimson stammered. "I... I... I don't know!" She clenched her eyes shut and grabbed her hair. "I just did what I used to do in the cartoon world! I just wanted to be useful! I just wanted to be nice to David! I just wanted everyone... anyone... to stop hating me! I... I..."

Crimson couldn't see straight. She searched for more words to throw at Melinda, but her processor couldn't find any. Just when she thought she would pass out, an overriding signal shut down the chaos in her brain.

Pressure. Warmth.

A hug.

Now Melinda whispered. "It's okay. I'm sorry. None of this is beyond repair. I shouldn't be so angry with you." She wrapped her hand around the back of Crimson's head and rested it on her shoulder. "We'll make it better."

Crimson built up the courage to return the hug. Humans were so much softer and warmer than robots. She melted in the reassuring arms and imagined that Melinda had taken all the broken pieces of her heart, glued them, and held them until she was sure it would stay together.

When she finally let go, Crimson noticed a blue splotch on Melinda's blouse. "Oh, no. Now I've gotten it on you, too."

"It's fine." Melinda picked up the sponge, rinsed it, and wiped a section of the counter.

Crimson watched curiously. It looked like a lot more work than she expected. "Where are the sparkles?" she asked. "And isn't it supposed to make a 'blll-ing' noise?"

Melinda looked at her, amused. "Not in this world, I'm afraid. So this really is your first encounter with a mess?"

Crimson thought for a moment. "The last time I washed something was..." She tapped her chin. "The bake sale. At Robot University."

"I remember," Melinda said. "We were raising money for scholarships!" She cupped Crimson's cheeks in her hands. "Crimson, it really is you in there, isn't it?"

Crimson didn't pull back, but she did glance away. "Yes, it's me. Who else would it be?" Glad as she was that Mrs. Epic wasn't angry, it did feel a little strange. She furrowed her brow. "And what do you mean, 'we?' You weren't there."

Melinda let go of Crimson and attempted to straighten her rumpled dress. "Oh, yes I was. In a way." She gave Crimson's hand a tug and headed toward the stairs. "Before we do anything else though, let's get you cleaned up."

Cautiously, Crimson followed. At the bottom of the stairs, she hesitated. The rest of the home still felt forbidden.

"It's fine, Crimson." Melinda beckoned to her. "Come on up, dear."

***

Cobalt surveyed the scene as he approached. Ten meters away, a man lay on the street. Kneeling in a circle, three people in white uniforms attended to him. They monitored equipment connected to the unconscious man and barked orders amongst themselves. By the time Cobalt got within five meters, one of them shined a light in the injured man's eye. Four meters out, one of them noticed Cobalt approaching. She barely had time to point at him before he skidded to a halt right in the middle of the spectacle.

"What's going on here?" Cobalt demanded.

The woman gave him a stern look. "You can't be here! This is an emergency scene!"

"It's okay," Cobalt said. "I'm a hero!"

The woman's jaw dropped, and her eyebrows disappeared into her hairline.

Someone shoved Cobalt aside. "Five cc's," he said, handing a syringe to the man on the woman's left. "What's this robot doing here?"

Cobalt regained his balance and planted his feet. He furrowed his brow at the person who shoved him. "I'm here to help," he said with an edge in his voice. "What can I do?"

"You can get out of the way!" someone else said as they shoved him in the other direction.

The responder jabbed the syringe into the unconscious man's arm, and he sputtered to life. He sat bolt upright, gasping for air.

The woman placed a hand on his shoulder.

"It's going to be okay, sir," she whispered. She eased him back into a lying position. "You had an episode, but it's over." She looked past Cobalt, pursing her lips. She waved at someone, then pointed emphatically at Cobalt.

Cobalt sank. He spent all morning trying to be a hero and here he missed his chance by seconds. He tried to match the energy of the relieved rescuers, cheering, "He's okay!" But he squirmed, shocked at the disappointment in his own tone. Hoping no-one else would notice, he pitched it up, holding out the last note of "okaaaaaay."

A gruff voice sent a jolt through Cobalt's neural net. "Yeah, no thanks to you!"

Cobalt whipped around to face an official-looking presence in a black and blue uniform. "Who's your owner, Robot?" the surly man demanded.

AMBULANCE

Cobalt stammered. "I'm—I'm a hero," he said. "If anyone else needs help—"

The officer cut him off. "Get out of here!" He pointed down the street. "Your owner is lucky I'm too busy for you today. I'd confiscate you in a heartbeat if I didn't already have a mountain of paperwork waiting for me at the office."

"I just—" Cobalt whimpered.

The radio on the officer's belt chattered. To Cobalt, it sounded like some sort of code. The officer pressed a button and spoke back to it. "Dispatch from 704. Copy, en route." He stabbed a finger at Cobalt. "Take this message back to your owner: If this is a joke, it could land them in prison. It better not happen again." He started for his car.

Cobalt shrank, small as a Neryllian sand flea. "I'm sorry," he squeaked.

"Go home, Robot."

***

Crimson examined herself in the bathroom mirror. "26 episodes, and I never once changed clothes." She pushed the button through its hole. "There, I got it!" she said, admiring the results. She was now dressed in a bright red pinafore over a white T-shirt with red trim. "Finally!" Her rumpled, soap-soaked dress sat in a laundry basket beside her.

Melinda smiled at her. "Most people spend the first few years of their lives figuring out buttons and zippers, so I'd say ten minutes is pretty impressive," she said, showing her a bundle of Crimson-sized outfits in various shades of red. "Let's take these downstairs and hang them up. Then we can finish mopping the kitchen."

Crimson followed Melinda. "Thank you for lending me your clothes," she said. She felt like a new robot.

Melinda led her to the closet and showed her how to hang the outfits. "These are Christine's from years ago," she said. "You can be sure she won't miss them. Now for the kitchen."

Crimson quickly mastered the art of wiping up a mess in the real world. While they worked, Mrs. Epic asked questions about her first day—how they escaped Andrew's lab, how they found the factory, whether she slept well last night, how her brothers were doing. The conversation was so pleasant and comfortable until Cobalt burst through the door. He came to a dead stop, staring at her and Mrs. Epic. Crimson tried a little humor to ease the awkwardness. She offered to teach him how to clean a kitchen, but her words bounced off him. He fidgeted, bashfully wished Mrs. Epic a good afternoon, and disappeared into his room.

Melinda put her hand on Crimson's shoulder. "Looks like you're not the only one who's struggling," she said.

"The rules that link us from the cartoon world to this one are hard to figure out," Crimson said. "Some things got left out, like me and changing clothes, and Cobalt and *Perfect Punch*." She boosted herself onto the kitchen table. "But then Silver is an expert in technology and building things just because the cartoon showed him pushing a few buttons. Cobalt feels like he got cheated."

Melinda swiped a towel over the damp countertop. "No one can control which advantages fall into whose laps," she said. "Still, it's pretty easy to be jealous of someone else's and proud of your own."

Crimson shrugged and watched her toes dangle. "Hm," she said. Gradually, her feet stopped swinging and she wrinkled her nose. "The one that really bothers me, though, is pie."

Melinda stopped wiping. "What do you mean?"

"In the cartoon, I made dozens... hundreds... of pies." Crimson spread her arms to encompass a room full of imaginary pies. "But the way it worked was, I'd say, 'I'm going to make a pie!' and I'd leave the room. Then a little later, I'd walk back in carrying a fresh pie. It never actually showed me making one."

"Well, yes," Melinda said. "People didn't tune in to *Cobalt Laser* to watch pies bake."

"But Mrs. Epic, I've been thinking about it and just figured it out. If you asked me to make a pie right now, I wouldn't know how to do it. Earlier, if I hadn't made that mess in the kitchen, I would've opened the cupboards and realized I had no idea what to do next."

"Oh, I see. But Crimson, you and your brothers don't eat in this world, anyway."

"That's not it. I'm Crimson Laser. I bake pies. At least, I'm supposed to. It's all I am. Or was. If Crimson Laser can't even bake a pie anymore, who is she?"

Melinda folded the towel and smiled gently. "Crimson, there is far, far more to you than pie."

Crimson kicked her legs and frowned. "Then you must not know me very well."

"Crimson, I know you better than anyone else in this world."

Crimson looked at her askance. "How?" This woman seemed to know more about her than she did herself. Sure, she was married to Crimson's creator, but there was a bond here that went beyond that. Did Melinda come from the cartoon world too?

"Let me show you something. It's been more than 20 years, though. Bear with me." Melinda cleared her throat. She pitched her voice up a step or so. "I'll always be right there beside you!"

A chill shot through Crimson's neural pathways. She needed to hear it again.

"Oh, wait! This one was always my favorite." Melinda drew a sharp breath, threw her head back, and bellowed, "Sillll-verrrr!"

Crimson whispered Silver's name to herself, to be sure. It was true! "You sound just like me!"

"It's probably more accurate to say you sound like me," Melinda said. "I was your voice, Crimson."

"It never occurred to me." Crimson's head swam. Despite coming from the cartoon world, she still had a lot to learn about how it worked.

Melinda gave Crimson's arm a squeeze and continued. "Here's what I'm getting at. Every time I stepped into that recording booth, I had to say those lines for Crimson Laser. To do that, I had to feel what Crimson Laser felt and think what Crimson Laser thought. I had to be Crimson Laser."

Crimson's jaw dropped. This was the most hopeful thing she'd heard since she woke in this world.

Melinda took her hands. "Do you want to know who Crimson Laser is? She is kind, thoughtful, and selfless. She has a strong sense of justice. She hates seeing people suffer. And even though she didn't really get a chance to show it in the cartoon, Crimson Laser would've done anything for the people she loves. Even her obnoxious little brother."

Crimson wished again that she could cry. She threw her arms around Melinda. "Thank you, Mrs. Epic! Thank you so much!"

"All that, and I'm still Mrs. Epic?" Melinda kissed her cheek. "Please dear, call me Melinda. Or, if you want, call me Mom." She held the trembling robot tightly. "I love you, Crimson."

SERIES: Cobalt Laser
SEASON 1, EPISODE 9

"Welcome to my Parlor"
TIMESTAMP: 09:51

A DISHEVELED BUNKER IN the middle of the desert served as a temporary base of operations on this planet for Hex Ten and his cohorts. Hex busied himself outside, stacking boulders to form a makeshift wall. Inside, Heinous stood watch over his prisoner, Prince Granite of the Royal Family of Mineralis.

"What do you want with me?" Prince Granite looked haughtily at his captor through the bars of the hastily constructed cell.

Heinous sneered at the proud royal. "Nothing, you pompous windbag. No harm will come to you if you do not agitate me." He was very close to being agitated.

Prince Granite turned away and sniffed. "Then why have you kidnapped me, heir to the throne of Mineralis?"

Heinous looked through the window at Hex's progress. "Your kingdom means nothing to me. You are nothing more than bait, you self-important honorless pebble."

Now it was Heinous's turn to boast. He outlined the plan in simple terms. "Lord Hex tasked me with preparing a diversion to lure Cobalt Laser into a trap." He put his face close to the prince's. "I, Heinous, general to the great Lord Hex, devised this plan of capturing and holding you hostage."

The prince curled his lip and held his head high. "Of course the great Cobalt Laser would come to the rescue of such a dignitary as myself."

"Don't flatter yourself," Heinous grumbled. "You are only a pawn, barely worth the attention of the local system constable. Cobalt Laser's interest in you is far more personal." His grating voice took on an unusually sweet quality as he revealed the juicy secret. "I understand his sister has taken quite a liking to you."

The prince recoiled as if he'd licked a Tartulian bitterfruit. "Ugh!" he exclaimed. "That tiresome commoner in the tasteless red dress? I'd rather be in this cell than in her vulgar arms!"

Heinous drew back and hissed. "This is most unexpected. It has been centuries since I've been a teenager, but had a pretty robot taken an interest in me, I might never have turned to villainy!"

Prince Granite folded his arms and stuck his nose in the air. "Ha!" he taunted. "That just goes to show your lack of refinement. My royal tastes are far more discriminating."

Heinous screeched, "You arrogant clod!" He grabbed the cell bars and pressed his insectoid jaws close, snarling. "Perhaps it would be honorable to prevent her from making a regrettable mistake."

CHAPTER 12

Hex Ten shifted irritably. Chairs didn't suit his long legs, so he'd chosen a spot on the floor to rest his considerable bulk while waiting for Dr. Smalls to finish pontificating. "If we're done with the noble questions of who we are and how we got here," the human said, leaning in close, "let's turn our attention to why we are here." Hex suppressed his urge to sneer, preferring to convey his contempt through utter boredom and indifference toward Andrew's confident enthusiasm.

To Hex's left, Heinous stood at rapt attention, one pair of claws folded behind his back and the other in front. On his other side, Irk sat on one of those plastic crates he was always finding around the place. The childish robot swung his legs lazily and gaped aimlessly around the room. Normally Hex would bark at him to sit still, but he left the little minion to his devices, hoping his inattention would insult Andrew.

Andrew didn't seem to notice. He continued prattling, enamored with the sound of his own voice. "I made three little robots. Irk already told you about them, and you are very familiar with them." He jammed his hands in his pockets and resumed pacing. "These three little robots ran away, and I need you to bring them back. I want them alive at all costs, but there's no obligation to bring them in intact." He stopped marching around the room and smiled at an image inside his head. "In fact, a little corporal punishment might help them see the error of their ways."

Appealing as it would be to capture Cobalt Laser, Hex fumed at the idea of doing it on someone else's agenda. He noticed his jaw setting and willed it to relax. He had to wait for his chance. He'd get Cobalt next time. There would always be a next time. For now, he consented to listen to the pompous human's lecture.

Andrew wheeled around and narrowed his eyes at his henchmen. "Now here's the part where you participate. How do we go about this? I'm looking for ideas!"

Free to express his passions on his own terms, Hex growled and pounded his fist into his hand. "I say we find Cobalt Laser, crush him, and bring him here in disgrace!"

Andrew blinked. "Yes, that's the general idea. Break it down for me."

Hex gave him a disgusted look. What did this blathering fool mean? It was a simple concept. He spoke slowly. "First, we find Cobalt Laser. Then, we crush him. Defeat him. After that, after he's been defeated, we bring him here. To the lab."

Andrew pursed his lips. "Brilliant. This is probably why your last line in every episode is, 'I'll get you next time, Cobalt Laser!'" He breathed into his hands. "A little help. First step, where do we stage our attack?"

Hex drew a blank. He'd never faced this problem before. Cobalt Laser was where Cobalt Laser was. Somewhere in space. And Hex Ten was always in the same place at the same time, never mind how they got there. He glanced at the floor. Now he was here, and Cobalt Laser was somewhere else. What to do? His electronic brain crunched the numbers for a few hundred nanoseconds. Of course, the answer was obvious! He scowled at the brainless human. "We go to where he is, you fool!"

"Mmmm. Okay," Andrew danced in place nervously. "This is only a minor setback. I can salvage this. Everything is going to be just fine." He stopped bouncing and drew a cleansing breath. "I think I see the issue. You cartoon villains are very one-dimensional personalities. If at first you don't succeed, you try, try again the same exact thing next episode. No problem! I just need to provide some direction."

He took a breath and motioned at Hex. "Nice try, Hex. Really," he said.

Hex knew sarcasm when he heard it. It was something the Laser siblings excelled at. He let it slide. *Next time*, he reminded himself.

Andrew continued. "But let's analyze the holes in your plan, starting with finding Cobalt Laser. Presumably, he and the others are at Dan Epic's private residence. That is, his house. If I raid a house with a robot kidnapping party in the middle of what is likely to be a neighborhood with manicured lawns and an HOA, I'm going to draw some unwanted attention and our plans will be cut very short."

Hex wondered why he hadn't considered that. He thought back on his previous schemes. Running in blindly, guns blazing never worked, yet he'd tried it again and again. He analyzed a couple of specific examples and realized that with just a little more forethought, he might have had the upper hand.

Irk leaned forward. "One thing we do know is that Silver Laser works with Dan Epic's son at Epic Manufacturing. They go there every morning and come home every evening."

Andrew snapped at him. "Think again, dimwit. That only gets us Silver."

Heinous hissed to himself quietly. Hex peeked at him out of the corner of his eye. His second-in-command was doing some cogitating of his own.

Andrew sneered. "I don't like that guy. In fact, of the three, he's the one I wouldn't complain about if you brought him back in pieces."

Heinous raised his hand. "Pardon me, Lord Andrew," He said raspily, yet politely.

"I hope this is good."

"It seems to me that we know how to find the one called Silver. Perhaps we could lie in wait and ambush him when he is outside the protection of the fortified HOA stronghold. We then leave a message with his human companion, ordering Cobalt and Crimson to surrender themselves in exchange for their brother's safety. We can then take all three of them into our custody."

Hex ran the pattern through his memory and found a match. It was very similar to the time they held Prince Granite hostage, but Heinous had shifted the variables a bit. This time, the hostage would be one of the Laser siblings, but the basic plan was the same. Capture who you can, and the people who care about them will come to you. Hex congratulated himself. He'd been wise to choose Heinous as his right-hand robot.

A smile spread across Andrew's face. "I like it." He slapped his hands together. "I like it! Guys?" He directed Hex's and Irk's attention to Heinous. "This guy. This guy right here. Employee of the month! This is what I want to see."

Andrew gave a wink and finger guns to his new favorite. Heinous looked at Hex and cocked his head, confused. Hex, not knowing either what to make of the human's bizarre behavior, shrugged back. Heinous couldn't wink his compound eyes, but he did choose two appendages and returned the hand gesture, best as he could with his long claws. Disgusting. Hex hoped they'd soon be finished playing sidekick to a human.

"Next up," Andrew said, "weapons. First you, Heinous."

Hex balled his fists. Did this human not understand the chain of command? A rumble rose from somewhere inside him. Heinous acknowledged him with one compound eye before returning his attention fully to Lord Andrew.

"That thing you do with your hands." Andrew pantomimed the weaving motions Heinous used to build his signature bomb orbs. "Unfortunately, that didn't transfer over to this world. You'll find you can't do it anymore. But don't worry, I've got a plan and I'm committed to making this work for you. I'll definitely get back to you, big guy."

Andrew turned his attention to Hex. "Now for you. You're known for those huge arms, right? That, and being the brains of the operation. Well, at least you've still got the smashing and punching thing going on. A ranged attack would be nice, but you know what? I think I'm good with what you've got. I'm not sure I want to put a gun in your hand right now."

Enough! Forget next time, he'd tear the puny creature in half now! Hex barely lifted his arms before his brain went numb. When his consciousness returned, he found himself obediently standing in place.

Hex caught the end of whatever Andrew was saying to him. "...behavior inhibitor, you might as well give up!"

Andrew straightened his lab coat. "So, weapons. Yes. Heinous, I'll get back to you."

Irk lifted his hands, making the left glow red hot, while a layer of frost formed on the right. "I've still got my ability!" he said proudly.

Andrew rolled his eyes. "That's not a weapon, idiot," he said, waving him away. "It's a plot device. Don't get in the way."

Irk's face fell along with his hands.

Andrew clapped, sending an echo through the room. "Okay, I'll take it from here. I have some planning to do. I'll be back in a bit."

Hex stood to his full titanic height and waited for Andrew to vanish among the lab furnishings. Heinous was hard to read, having no facial expressions, but Hex knew something had changed. He folded his arms behind his back and looked askance at his general. "Heinous," he said.

Heinous returned the stare. His compound eyes shifted about, reflecting Hex's face from dozens of angles. "Hex Ten," he said, matter-of-factly. Hex glowered at his reflection. Heinous's tone lacked its usual respect.

Hex turned his attention to Irk and rumbled. Not that the runt's loyalty really mattered, but he refused to lose any more ground, however small. Irk whimpered and ran away. He found a barrel to hide behind, far from the two massive beings. Good enough.

Hex locked eyes with Heinous a while longer. True, he was new to this world, but he was no fool despite whatever impression the cocky human had. "Lord Hex," he insisted.

"I live by honor, Hex Ten."

CHAPTER 13

MELINDA BUSIED HERSELF WITH a few last-minute chores. It was nearly bedtime, but she still had some nervous energy to burn off. She set about rearranging the flowers on the dining table. It was almost time to replace them, but she'd be happier if they lasted a couple more days.

A thump at the stairwell made her jump. There stood Crimson, scanning the room, wide-eyed. She looked ready to pounce.

Melinda's heart raced. Crimson knew to stay downstairs. Melinda took a peek at the upper railing, hoping Christine wouldn't pick that moment to say goodnight. "Crimson dear," she said, keeping her voice down. "What's wrong? Has something happened?"

Crimson rushed over to her. "Mom! Please help! Cobalt and Silver are fighting!"

Melinda held Crimson by the arms. "Fighting?" she repeated. She took another nervous glance toward Christine's room, then focused her undivided attention on Crimson. "With words, or are they hitting each other?" It had been decades since she'd broken up a sibling fight, but she still knew the drill.

Crimson slouched. "Just words," she said. She clenched her hands again. "But I'm scared."

"Say no more," Melinda said, waving her toward the stairs. "Get back down there and keep an eye on them. I'm going to fetch your father."

***

Dan Epic led the way downstairs. He'd seen siblings scuffle. And he'd watched these robots fold steel like paper. He wasn't ready for those facts to combine. As the room came into view he found Cobalt standing on his toes, shouting Silver down. Crimson clung to David's arm, and the two of them watched helplessly as the altercation unfolded.

"I've heard enough, Silver!" Cobalt raged. He stomped away, putting a couple meters between them, then wheeled around and roared. "You're not the only reason I'm alive right now!"

Silver shot back. "Alive? No," he said. "But think about where you would be!"

Dan halted halfway down the stairs. "Enough!" he bellowed.

Cobalt and Silver paused. They glared at him.

Dan, short of breath, pointed at the garage. "Melinda, hon. You and Crimson take Silver in there. David and I will talk to Cobalt."

Silver put his hands on his hips and opened his mouth.

Dan folded his arms and raised an eyebrow at Silver.

Silver stuck his nose in the air. "Fine," he said, and made for the door.

Cobalt fidgeted as he watched Silver retreat. After the door closed, he turned to his creator and toyed with his fingers. "I'm sorry," he said.

Dan sat on the couch and motioned to the recliner opposite him. "Let's get these emotions reigned in and talk like adults," he said. David sat beside him.

Cobalt burrowed into the cushion. "I'm trying to get along with Silver, really," he said. "It's true he's done a lot for me, but..." He threw his head against the back of the chair and groaned.

Dan rubbed his gold handkerchief between his fingers. "He's mighty proud, isn't he?" he said.

"Yeah," Cobalt said. "But I guess he's right." He slouched deep into the chair. "He makes me so mad, but I can't ever prove him wrong."

"Cobalt," Dan said. He set the handkerchief on his lap. "Your brother is a very gifted young man. It's true he's worked hard with those gifts and accomplished some impressive things, but he started with several advantages that you didn't have."

Cobalt pulled himself up and rested his head in his hands. "I guess it's true, then. He's the hero in this world, and I'm the sidekick."

Dan's throat constricted. It didn't seem so long since David's graduation party, where he'd had a similar conversation with his discouraged son about Christine's seemingly inexhaustible supply of talent. He didn't know what to say then either, so once again he leaned on his managerial experience. He brainstormed. "Not so fast," he said. "You're gifted as well, I know it. We just haven't discovered what those gifts are."

Cobalt winced.

Dan felt a prick in his heart. One more reminder that managing employees and raising kids were very different skills—not that he'd mastered either.

He turned to David. "I'm sure that over all your years of wanting to improve our factory, making parts isn't the only job for robots you've thought of. Maybe we should let Cobalt try a few of them and see what he takes a liking to?"

David jolted at his sudden inclusion in the conversation. "Uh, yeah," he stammered. "I can think of a few right now." He cleared his throat. "I'll make a list and we can set about it first thing in the morning." His expression softened. "Thanks, Dad."

"Good," Dan said. "Is that okay with you, Cobalt?"

Cobalt's mouth hung open. "Sure," he said, sputtering. He sat straight and set his jaw. "I mean, yes sir! Thank you! I won't let you down."

***

Melinda closed the door behind her and took a deep breath. Silver leaned against David's car.

Crimson wagged a finger at him. "You'll scratch the paint," she warned.

Silver pushed away from the car and scowled at his sister. "Get off me!" he yelled. "I can't even stand somewhere without getting criticized!" She recoiled and backed away.

Melinda rushed between them and knelt in front of Silver. "Silver, sweetie," she said, looking into his burning eyes. "Listen to me." She took his balled-up fists in her hands. "I love you. Very, very much."

Silver melted. He unrolled his fingers and let Melinda rub them. His cheeks sagged, and the anger in his eyes gave way to sadness. "Why is everyone so mean to me?" he asked.

Melinda massaged the metal knuckles. "I don't think they want to be mean," she said. "They only want you to respect them." She pulled his hands close and wrinkled her forehead. "And if I'm being honest, I don't see you doing that."

Silver snatched his hands away. "They aren't respecting me!" he huffed as he retreated to the other side of the garage. "I've done so much for them, and all they do is complain!"

Melinda rose gracefully. "And why have you done all these things for them?"

Silver stood with his back to her. "I dunno," he admitted. He shrugged. "I mean, I had to, I guess. There really wasn't a choice."

"You had to," Melinda said, "because you love your brother and sister, right?"

Silver shriveled. "I didn't really think about it," he said.

"That's okay. Let's think about it now."

"Yeah," Silver said. He turned partway around and acknowledged her through the corner of his eye. "I love them."

Crimson put her hand to her heart. "I love you too, Silver. Sorry for snapping at you."

"You see?" Melinda said. "Crimson just needed to hear you say that. Cobalt needs to hear it, too."

Silver cringed. "I don't want to say, 'I love you,' to Cobalt."

Melinda chuckled. "There's more than one way to tell someone you love them." She took a couple steps, and Silver turned the rest of the way around. "When Cobalt sees things going so well for you, so naturally, and then they fall apart for him despite his best efforts, what do you suppose happens?"

Silver shrugged. "He gets mad. But it's not my fault he's not as good at things as I am."

Melinda pushed her mouth to one side. "Sometimes we see people get mad, but that's not really what's happening under the surface. It often goes deeper than that." She knelt in front of Silver again. "I think Cobalt's hearing a voice in his head. Something that tells him he's not good enough. That sort of thing makes it harder and harder for a person to keep trying. They're afraid to invest their best effort if they already believe they're a failure, and before they know it, they've quit altogether."

Silver extended his hands to Melinda. "What do I do?" he asked.

She squeezed his fingers. "You need to be a different voice in his head. One that believes in him. One that tells him not to give up."

Crimson patted his arm. "We need to be right there beside him," she said.

Silver furrowed his brow and frowned. "I'll try," he said.

"It won't come naturally," Melinda admitted. "But don't give up." She wrapped him in a hug. "I..." She tapped him on the nose. "...believe in you!" She pecked him on the cheek.

"Ack!" Silver squealed. He giggled. "Gross!" He squirmed, but didn't really try to escape. That got him a kiss on the other cheek, then Melinda reached for Crimson and pulled them both into a tight, warm hug.

The door cracked and Dan peeked in. "Looks like things are going better in here," he said. He grinned at Melinda. "Your tactics haven't changed a bit!"

"I think everyone's ready to try again," she said.

"Glad to hear it," Dan said. "Sounds like we have a plan for tomorrow."

CHAPTER 14

Cobalt looked around curiously as the car took off. Crimson sat beside him, in the back seat. David occupied the driver's seat with Silver beside him. This was different from their taxi ride.

"Isn't it against the law to sit in the driver's seat?" Cobalt asked.

"Oh." David laughed. "The taxi, right. I had this conversation with your brother earlier. I own this car, so I can sit in the driver's seat. You can't do that in a taxi because it's not yours. And before you ask, no, I'm not driving. Humans haven't driven cars in ages. The controls are locked out and I honestly wouldn't know what to do with them anyway."

Cobalt scrunched his face. "But, why all the rules? It doesn't make sense."

David shook his head and chuckled. "It's the law, Cobalt. Sometimes there's no way to unravel how it got to where it is."

David choked on his laugh as the car screeched to a halt. "Sorry about that," its computer said. "There is an obstruction ahead."

Cobalt looked out the window. They were in an alleyway. Other than the high brick walls on either side and a dumpster, there was nothing to see except a box truck blocking their path.

"What's going on?" David asked. "Are we stuck behind a delivery?"

The car's dashboard lit up as several error indicators scrolled past. "More likely, the vehicle ahead of us is malfunctioning," it said. "It is not replying to standard queries."

David opened the door. "This doesn't feel right," he said. "Wait here." He stepped out of the car and walked toward the truck.

It felt like a bad idea to let David go alone, but Cobalt assumed he knew what he was doing. David only got a few steps away when the driver's door of the truck swung wide, and Dr. Smalls emerged to greet him.

Andrew rubbed his hands together. "Hello, hello, hello!" he said. "You still have something of mine, and I thought maybe it would be easier to reconcile the situation on neutral ground." He gestured at the foreboding surroundings. "Seems like a nice place for a little negotiation, doesn't it?"

"What's your problem?" David backed toward his car. "Leave us alone!"

Cobalt wrestled with his seatbelt and door latch. He should've trusted his own judgement!

Andrew wagged his head at David. "What's my problem? Really? What a stupid, stupid question." He gritted his teeth and marched toward David. "Give me my robots."

Cobalt prevailed against the seatbelt and stepped onto the pavement. Crimson followed, and Silver spilled out of the door in front of him.

Andrew's eyes widened ecstatically. "You brought me all three of them!" He projected his voice toward the truck. "Gentlemen, come on out. Our plans have just accelerated!"

The truck's passenger door opened, and Irk hopped out. A second figure followed him. Someone very tall and slender. With four arms.

Cobalt's whole system jolted. "It can't be!" he said. He scanned the image a dozen times, and every time it made a positive match. "Heinous!"

"Does that mean…" Silver began.

A screech interrupted him as the truck's cargo door slid open. A massive being with skin like sapphire leaped out. He landed on the pavement with a crunch that echoed off the brick walls.

Crimson brought her hands to her mouth. "Hex Ten!" she gasped. "Cobalt, be careful!"

David shook visibly. He fell on his hands and knees as he turned to flee. He scrabbled to his feet, then fell again after a few steps toward the car.

Hex Ten filled the alleyway with a villainous laugh. "Surrender, you pathetic fools, and we will take you with minimal damage!"

Cobalt's instincts took over. "Not a chance!" he yelled, charging at Hex.

David screamed at Cobalt as he passed. "Back to the car! Now!" He'd finally gotten control of his feet and broke into a run.

Silver yelled after him. "Cobalt, don't be stupid! You don't have *Perfect Punch*!"

Cobalt answered over his shoulder. "I don't need *Perfect Punch*!" he said. "Watch this!"

Hex drew his massive fist back as Cobalt approached. Cobalt doubled down and put on more speed. When he got within a few steps of the monstrous robot, Hex Ten threw his punch.

"Too slow!" Cobalt laughed as he jumped over the glimmering fist and landed on top of Hex's bulging forearm. He wrapped himself around it and hung on. This was Cobalt's moment! For the first time in this world, he had the situation under control. No more turbines, no more sheet metal. Just him, the villain, and the battlefield. Now he just needed to...

To... what? This was as far as he planned. He had to do something! He felt like he was back in the factory, with that chunk of bent metal in his hand, all eyes on him. He threw a few desperate punches, driving his fists into Hex's stony flesh.

Hex thrust his arm out, holding Cobalt at a distance. He watched him land a few harmless blows, then chuckled. He lifted Cobalt high and mocked him with his eyes. Cobalt tightened his grip as he rose above the monster's head. Hex laughed aloud and flicked his arm, flinging Cobalt onto the pavement.

Silver screamed across the distance. "Cobalt, you idiot!" He deployed *Flashing Blades* and charged at Hex, swinging the blades frantically at the hulking villain. Sparks flew as Silver chipped away at Hex's armor.

Crimson dashed over to Cobalt and knelt beside him. "Cobalt! Are you okay?"

Cobalt groaned as Crimson helped him back to his feet. "Do I look okay?"

"Come with me," she said.

"No!" Cobalt reached for his brother. "Silver!"

Crimson pulled his arm, and searing pain blasted through his sensory network. Cobalt was in no shape to resist. Limping, he followed his sister as she dragged him back to David's car.

***

Silver struck tirelessly, but it was useless. Hex absorbed every blow with virtually no effort. Silver sensed motion in his peripheral vision. He was being flanked.

A raspy voice confirmed Silver's fears. "Clear the path, Hex!" Each of Heinous's four hands unholstered what appeared to be pistols. "You are in the line of fire!" He took aim.

"These bugs are nothing to me!" Hex bellowed.

Hex blocked with his arms and waited. Silver struck his blades one more time against the glimmering skin. Hex grunted and stubbornly stood his ground. Silver couldn't handle being attacked on two fronts. He took his focus off Hex, just for a moment. Hex took advantage of the gap in Silver's assault, swinging his arms out and forcing Silver to somersault back and put some distance between them.

The somersault disoriented Silver. While the world spun around him, a loud crack split the air. The pavement near his foot splintered as something hit it. He jumped back and saw a glowing red object lodged in the concrete. Was that a bullet? Who gave Heinous bullets?

Heinous's voice echoed once more. "Get out of the way, Hex!"

"This is my fight!" Hex shouted back.

Andrew stood by the truck, shaking his fists. "Hex, you are jeopardizing the plan!"

Hex stomped and roared. "Do you dare insult the great Hex Ten?"

Apparently, Heinous dared.

The alleyway erupted with a buzzing sound as Heinous unleashed a rapid-fire barrage of glowing red projectiles from all four of his handguns. A few of these plasma bullets lodged in the pavement near and around Silver, sending him into a panic. A lot of them lodged in Hex Ten's back, sending him into a rage.

"Heinous!" Hex planted his foot and snapped to face his general. He charged.

"Hex!" Andrew banged his fist against the side of the truck. "I forbid you to fight Heinous!"

Hex barely flinched.

Andrew tried again. "I forbid..." He gasped as Heinous narrowly dodged Hex's fist.

Irk stood by the truck, smiling. "I think his emotions are running a little strong."

Andrew growled at Irk before running toward the quarreling robots. "I forbid you to..." He ducked as the dumpster sailed over his head.

Irk shouted after him. "Try using his name and yelling really loud!" He watched his boss get dangerously close to the brawl. "I'm gonna stay right here! Out of the way! Like you said!"

Silver stood in the middle of the alley, watching the scene unfold. A voice behind him snapped him out of the trance. "Silver! Silver!"

He turned around. David hung out of the back window, waving him back to the car.

Silver arrived to find Cobalt sitting in the front seat, arguing with the car's computer. "Get us out of here!"

The car responded calmly. "There is insufficient room to turn around."

"Then back down the alley!"

"That is ill-advised. Please wait for the proper authorities to clear the obstruction in accordance with safety protocols."

Silver nudged Cobalt. "I can drive this thing! Move over!"

"I can handle this. Just get in the car!"

"Cobalt! Move!"

"Shut up, Silver!"

David shouted from the back seat. "Guys, now is not the time for this!"

Silver glanced over the headrest. David and Crimson held each other in a bear hug.

"Just get inside!" Crimson screamed. She used her big-sister-knows-best voice.

Silver scowled at her. He ignored them and yelled at the car's dashboard. "Give me manual control!"

"Access denied. Manual controls may only be unlocked in the event of an emergency."

Silver pushed Cobalt harder. "Move!"

"Silver, you aren't the only one who can…"

A line of plasma bullets smashed into the car's open door and front bumper. Silver nearly jumped out of his armor. He looked where the shots came from and saw Heinous marching toward him. Screaming, Silver dove into the car, plowing into Cobalt and packing them both into the passenger side, with Silver on top of Cobalt.

The computer spoke pleasantly. "Immediate threat to life and health confirmed. Manual controls have been enabled."

"Get off me!" Cobalt shoved back, and Silver wound up in the driver's seat. Cobalt found himself curled up on the passenger's side with his feet pointed at the roof.

Silver shifted the car into reverse. "Here we go!" he said, hitting the accelerator. Through the windshield, Heinous receded from view.

Heinous glowered. He flicked the weapons in his two upper hands and ejected their spent magazines. At the same time, his lower hands holstered their guns, grabbed fresh magazines, and reloaded the drawn weapons as he aimed them. He let loose with another volley, shattering the windshield.

It was all Silver could do to keep the car from hitting the walls as it bolted in reverse out of the alleyway. "Go, go, go, go, go!" At last, they were out in the open, flying backward down the main thoroughfare.

The car cheerily intoned once more. "Open road ahead. Resuming automated control." Then, more urgently, "Warning! Rapid adjustment!" It hit the brakes and spun the front end around, skiing on two wheels.

Everyone screamed as the centrifugal force squeezed them against the doors and each other. The car screeched into the median, narrowly missing hitting another vehicle head-on. It landed back on four wheels with a lurch, pointed the right way again.

"Stupid robot," Silver muttered, rubbing his head.

The car scanned its surroundings, waited for an opening in traffic, and gently accelerated to the speed limit. "Route recalculated. We will arrive at our destination in seventeen minutes, twenty-three seconds."

***

David opened his eyes. Air rushed in and out of his lungs. He looked out the window and forced his racing mind to slow down. Trees and signposts swept by at a leisurely pace.

He released the last of his anxiety in a loud sigh. His arms were wrapped around something soft and warm. He gave it a big hug, and the fuzzy softness squeezed back. Looking up, he found himself eye-to-eye with Crimson.

Heat rose in his cheeks, and he released her from his grip. "Oh! Crimson!" he stammered. "Excuse me!" He scooted over to his side of the car.

Crimson smiled back, eyes sparkling. "It's okay! I really needed a hug after that, too!"

She settled into her seat and straightened her cap. Wait, a cap? David stared while Crimson smoothed the wrinkles out of the knee-length sweater dress she had chosen for the day. It was divided into three thick bands with different shades of red on the top, middle, and bottom. Since when had she gotten new clothes? What happened to her dress? He'd been so focused on Silver and Cobalt, she'd completely escaped his notice.

He caught Crimson's eye again. She stared back, head cocked. She squirmed a little.

"Is something wrong?" she asked.

David shook his head. "No, not at all." Not with her, anyway. He resolved to treat her better. "Crimson, when did you…"

Silver peered into the back seat. "Is everyone okay?"

The memory of their harrowing escape rushed back, pushing Crimson out of David's thoughts once more. "Yeah, we're alright back here," he said. He leaned over the backrest. "Cobalt, how about you?"

Cobalt's legs rested on the seat. His body was crammed into the compartment where his legs should've been. "Take me home," came the muffled reply.

SERIES: Cobalt Laser
SEASON 1, EPISODE 1

"The First Step of the Journey"
TIMESTAMP: 18:45

"WE'RE OUT!" COBALT HEAVED the metal door open.

The Laser siblings dashed into the sunlight, glad to be out of the underground labyrinth. A few hundred meters away, the *Teacup* waited in an open field, right where they'd parked it when they first arrived on this planet.

Silver looked behind him. "That Hex guy and his pals are still on our tail!"

"Then it ends here!" Cobalt stopped and spun around, staring intently at the labyrinth door. "You two keep running! I'll stop them!"

"No way!" Silver stood behind him. "I'm not leaving you behind!"

Cobalt stood his ground. "Don't worry about me! Taking risks is part of being a hero!"

Crimson pleaded with her brother. "Cobalt, be careful!" Silver grabbed her and dragged her toward the *Teacup*.

Hex, Heinous, and Irk emerged from the cavern. Hex paused to point at Cobalt as the other two caught up. "You will not escape!"

"Guess again, Hex!" Cobalt braced himself. "*Perfect Punch*!"

A powerful beam projected from his eyes and blasted the opening above Hex's head, causing the structure to collapse over Hex and his minions. Hex tried to jump through the opening as soon as the debris began to fall, but the rubble cascaded over his legs and back and pinned him to the ground.

The fearsome villain shook his fist. "You haven't seen the last of Hex Ten! I will pursue you across the galaxy! I will be the one to harness the creator's power!"

Cobalt ran, joining Silver and Crimson on the *Teacup's* boarding ramp. "If I do see you again, I'll be ready for you! Until then, so long!"

Hex twisted and clawed at the rubble like a cornered Volorian ratbeast. "I'll get you next time, Cobalt Laser!"

CHAPTER 15

Andrew leaned against the parked delivery truck and peevishly eyed the robots lined up in front of him. This garage was much smaller than the laboratory back home, but it was free of the stacks and shelves of junk he was accustomed to navigating around.

He gestured at the enclosing walls. "Excuse the tight quarters, but going all the way back to the lab is out of the question while we have outstanding objectives in this city."

He paced. "Let's review, shall we? Hex, would you like to tell me what happened out there?"

Hex stomped and thrust an accusing finger at Heinous. "I was unwilling to bear the affront of Heinous's insubordination!"

"I see." Andrew rubbed his chin. Things had certainly gone in a different direction than he'd expected. When he fabricated these two, Heinous was an afterthought. Andrew only included him to invest Hex in this reality and ensure his cooperation. He hadn't considered what an asset the henchman's unquestioning loyalty could be—or the liability of Hex's competing ambitions with his own. "Heinous, what's your version of the story?"

Heinous cast a sideways glance at Hex. "I mean no dishonor." He turned back to Andrew. "I only wish to represent the facts."

"Of course," Andrew said.

"I saw our window of opportunity closing. Seeing Silver Laser nearby, I thought it prudent to achieve our original objective of capturing him, even if the others escaped. Unfortunately, Hex Ten did not heed my warning to exit the line of fire. Judging that he was largely impervious to my weaponry, I decided to risk going ahead with the attack."

Andrew put one hand to his face and feigned indecision. "Mmm-hmm, mmm-hmm," he mused. Time to arrange his pawns. "So, piecing your testimony together, I think I can conclude what happened. One, Hex got angry, and then two, Hex screwed up." He knelt in front of Irk. He needed to knock all the supports out from under Hex—down to the tiniest and least significant. "Does that sound about right to you?" he asked the little robot.

Irk backed frantically against the wall. "Oh, please. I did what you wanted! I stayed out of the way! Please don't make me answer that!"

"I think you just did." Andrew winked at Irk. "You might want to be judicious about scheduling your sleep cycles."

Irk cowered in front of Hex, wringing his hands. Hex responded with a menacing glare. Andrew had landed his first punch. Now for the knockout.

He stood and slapped his hands together. "Well, I think I have a solution. Hex, this whole thing started because you felt Heinous was defying the chain of command. That won't happen again." He folded his hands and pointed two fingers at Hex. "Because from now on, you are subordinate to Heinous."

Hex clenched his fists and struck the floor. "Outrage!"

Heinous bowed low. "Your confidence honors me, Lord Andrew." He straightened and nodded at Hex. "I promise to execute my new role graciously, Hex Ten. You will continue to have my respect."

"Bah!" Hex drove his fist through the wall.

Andrew rolled his eyes. "So much for my deposit," he said. He straightened his lab coat, exhaled sharply, and nodded at the row of robots. "Now that the unpleasant business is out of the way, can we set aside our differences long enough to have a little meeting?"

Heinous inclined his head. "Certainly, Lord Andrew."

Hex glared at Heinous and seethed.

Irk glanced nervously at the two of them before focusing his attention on Andrew.

"First item of business," Andrew said. "This is home for the foreseeable future. We're going to let things cool for now, but when the time is right to strike again, I want to be local."

Irk sat on the concrete floor. "Is there a TV here?"

Andrew closed his eyes and counted to ten. The little brat irritated him to no end. Every day he considered resetting him, but that had its own issues. He needed Irk's expertise. And starting over, making a capable lab assistant from a freshly immigrated cartoon world villain, was out of the question. One, he didn't have the time. And two, it always turned out like this eventually. Fine. The kid needed his silly TV show to preserve his sanity, and the kid's sanity was in Andrew's best interest—for a few more days, anyway.

Andrew pressed his fingers into his brow and composed himself before continuing. "I'll furnish the place later today. The Organization has acknowledged the importance of what we're doing here and is in the process of transferring the funds now." He pointed at a door on the other side of the garage. "There's a common area through there. The upper level is mine and off limits."

He folded his arms and stared daggers at Irk. "Now, are there any other questions totally unrelated to what I'm actually trying to talk about?"

Irk shrank against the wall and hugged his knees.

Andrew turned his attention back to Hex and Heinous. "While we're waiting for our next chance at Cobalt Laser, The Organization has given us a little assignment."

Heinous raised one of his hands. "Pardon, Lord Andrew. The Organization?"

Andrew pointed at Heinous and bounced on his heels. "Of course!" He hoped someone would ask, and he was glad it was Heinous who did.

Now that he had to describe The Organization, Andrew found himself at a loss. He grasped for an example these cartoon villains could relate to. Where they came from, Hex was the top of the food chain, and Andrew already had enough difficulty disabusing them from that woefully inaccurate notion.

The silence lingered long enough for Irk to volunteer an explanation. "That's Andrew's bosses!" he blurted.

Andrew clicked his tongue. The time would soon come when he didn't need the little nuisance any longer, and he'd take out all his accumulated frustration in one terrible, satisfying moment.

Heinous cocked his head. "Your bosses, Lord Andrew?"

Andrew swept up the pieces of his broken ego and molded them into a swagger, which was very nearly bulky enough to cover his embarrassment. "If you want to hopelessly oversimplify it, yes," he said. He lolled his head at Irk and made air quotes. "My 'bosses', who happen to be some of the most powerful people on the planet, hide in the shadows. They pull the strings in virtually every government and industry in the world, enabling me to act as their hands and feet."

He sniffed. "You might more accurately describe the relationship as a partnership." Irk huddled against the wall.

Andrew started pacing. "The Organization has plans. We have a vision for the future of all humankind, and robots play a major role in that plan. Phase One is to get our robots into every home on every continent of the planet. My Adaptive Personality technology aims to do that. Robots are no longer mere tools to get jobs done. They're friends. Members of the family. I chose Cobalt Laser to be my personal robot and gave him his siblings for company."

Hex Ten squinted. "I take exception to your worship of my nemesis."

Andrew shrugged. "Take it how you may. Anyway, Cobalt Laser is immaterial to the plan. The point is to get lots of robots into lots of homes."

Andrew stuck his hands in his pockets. "Once that's done, we need a method of communicating with all those robots to inform them of little errands The Organization might have for them. That brings me back to our assignment. The key ingredient is a material called refractium. Its molecules resonate over long distances, making it ideal for a widespread communication net such as we need. Now, it's possible to get refractium legally, but most of the time it's used to build mundane things like unblockable tracking devices for pets, or to coordinate search and rescue efforts.

"For such applications, less than a microgram will suffice. Our vision is not so..." he waved his hand in search of an appropriate word, "uninspired. To accomplish our goals, we'll need something in the neighborhood of half a ton. Fortunately for us, a shipment of roughly that size is scheduled to arrive in this city in two days, and I'm relying on you to get it for me."

Hex planted his fist in his palm. "Tell me where to find it!" he insisted. "And I will march in, take this refractium, defying anyone who dares oppose me, and bring it here!"

Andrew laughed. "I appreciate the enthusiasm, Hex. Really." It felt so good to deflate the lummox. He put a hand on Heinous's nearest arm. "But our plan needs a little more attention to detail. I'll be heading up this operation with Heinous. Don't worry! We'll tell you what to punch and stomp on when the time comes."

Hex flexed and bellowed. "I am Hex Ten!" He lifted his voice to the ceiling. "Armies on a thousand stars cower at my name! I will not be mocked!"

"Yeah. Okay." Andrew closed his eyes and sighed irritably. "I know I said the upper level was off limits, but there's a room at the top of the stairs to the left, and I'm thinking that can be Hex's special bad mood corner. Would you like that, big guy? Why don't you try it out now?"

Hex roared and stormed out of the room. Andrew savored a liberating breath as the brute exited. His ego healed, prompting a craving for a large cup of tea and a soft chair. Yes, that sounded very nice. He'd find a café and wait there for the fund transfer.

***

Irk peeked cautiously into the room. Although Hex faced the single broken window with his back to the door, Irk knew he was aware of his presence. Nobody sneaks up on Hex Ten. Ever. He stopped in the doorway and waited for Hex to acknowledge him.

A light breeze filtered through the shattered glass. Irk was just about to announce himself when Hex spoke up. "Well? What do you want, insect?"

Irk took a cautious step inside. "I want to know if you're okay."

Hex turned and furrowed his brow. He regarded Irk as if the little robot had asked if a plastic fork would make a good weapon. "Am I okay?" he echoed.

"Yeah." Irk took another step. "Your whole world has turned upside down. I mean, it has for all of us, but it seems especially hard for you right now."

"Not all of us." Hex looked out the window again. "Heinous is rising above me." He clenched his fist. "And against me. The traitor."

Hex leaned against the wall and slid his massive body to the floor. Irk sauntered over and sat beside him. "I don't think it's really Heinous's fault," he said. "I blame Andrew. Oh, excuse me," Irk changed his voice to imitate Heinous's raspy hiss. "Lord Andrew."

That got a chuckle out of Hex. A happy feeling tickled Irk's tummy, and he thought about snuggling the titan. Just then, the shadow settled over Hex once more, and Irk reconsidered.

Hex's chest rumbled. "Heinous made his choice. And he will suffer for it along with his new master, if I can ever free myself from these burdensome prohibitions."

"So," Irk looked up at the giant robot beside him. "Are you okay?"

"I have no use for your pity."

"It's not pity, Hex. It's being a good friend. Andrew has humiliated and tormented me too. I know how you feel."

Hex jolted. His features contorted as he towered over his tiny companion. "You, a child's plaything, knows how Hex Ten, the Terror of the Galaxy, feels? Can a Voxian space slug know the mind of a Ytrrian Flying Neton?"

Irk tapped the side of his head. "Voxian," he mused. "Are those the big ones covered in prickles, or..."

Hex stood and roared. "They are tiny, insignificant specks! Like you!"

Something broke inside the little robot. How did the conversation turn so drastically? He knew he should be terrified, but instead he hurt.

"You could never know how I feel!" Hex bellowed. "When I came into this world, I fell from the height of the stars! You, you were never anything to begin with!"

Hex crept closer to Irk, until their eyes almost touched. Irk scrambled to keep his distance, but he merely backed into the wall.

"You cannot possibly know what it is like to lose the mantle of greatness, to have been the pinnacle of existence, only to awaken one day in the pathetic station of..." His eyes bore through Irk's soul. "Something as loathsome as you."

Hex withdrew and made for the door. Irk, still clinging to the wall, watched him go. He replayed the conversation in his head, but he couldn't figure out where it went wrong.

"I will regain my standing. I will prove that Hex Ten is no fool. And then," Hex said, glaring at Irk, "we will both be right back where we belong." He left.

Irk's mind reeled from the verbal beating, and he wasn't sure what was happening anymore. In desperation, he chased after Hex. Out of the room, down the stairs, and into the garage. He watched Hex exit onto the street. Along the line, they caught the attention of Heinous, who followed out of curiosity.

Irk stared at the door, trying to think of a response even after Hex was gone. His stomach churned. A new feeling swallowed his sadness and left behind an empty burning. He clenched his fists and ground his teeth.

Irk shouted at the featureless door. "I am not pathetic!" A compressed air tank stood in the corner of the garage, just in front of Andrew's truck. He ran over and punched it. He left a tiny dent.

"I am not pathetic!" he repeated. He kicked the tank. Now the dent was a little bigger.

Heinous watched patiently.

"I am not pathetic!" He pressed his left hand into the dent. After a few seconds, it glowed red hot. He prepared his right hand, bringing it to a sub-freezing temperature.

Heinous silently retreated to a spot behind the truck's cab.

Irk's voice reached a squealing pitch. "I am not pathetic!" He switched hands.

The metal popped and cracked as Irk's cold hand abruptly dropped its temperature a few hundred degrees. Then, with a deafening explosion, it burst. Irk flew through the air. His insides rattled as he hit something hard. The motion stopped, and his skull rang. When his eyes focused, he found himself lying on the floor, looking up at the truck. There in the side of the truck's box was a dent about the size and shape of a grade schooler.

Irk rolled his head to the side, and Heinous came into view.

"That was extremely foolish." Heinous knelt beside the little robot and looked him over. "You were lucky to survive this experience. You would be wise to learn from it."

"I am not pathetic," Irk said in an insistent whisper.

Heinous stood without touching him. "I will refrain from comment." He left.

***

Hex clung to the shadows. No one could sneak up on him, ever, and his unparalleled vigilance ensured they'd never see him coming, either. The imposing giant was improbably stealthy, even in the middle of the city. He divided his attention between navigation, avoiding detection, and brooding.

Hex wanted to punch the human. He wanted to squeeze the human, then punch it. He wanted to throw the human across the room, run over, pick it up, squeeze it with both hands, and then punch it. Twice. But he knew what the behavior inhibitor would do to him if he tried.

Just yesterday, Andrew called him a simple cartoon villain, but it only took a couple of hints for Hex to unlock the potential of his electronic brain. True to his cartoon persona, he was very smart, and insidiously clever. In mere seconds, he'd analyzed his entire cartoon life and all its mistakes. From there, he found his way onto the internet and consulted this new world for its wisdom. He read about great warriors and their conquests. He learned logic and deduction. He even set up a chess simulation to constantly run in one corner of his mind.

He'd show them. They had no idea who he had become, but they would find out soon enough.

CHAPTER 16

COBALT HID IN AN isolated corner of the factory with David, Silver, and Crimson. Toolboxes and maintenance equipment walled them in. He tried to stand still while David buffed the scratches out of his armor. "That thing tickles!" he grumbled.

David withdrew the rotary polisher and turned it off. "Sorry. We can't risk letting my dad know what happened this morning. We're lucky we haven't seen him yet. If he finds us all the way back here, he'll have questions. Then he'll call the police, and then who knows what will happen to you guys!"

Silver examined himself. There were still a few dents here and there from his scuffle with Hex, but a lot of them were gone already.

"It's a good thing we have self-repair systems," he explained. "It's nanoscopic and not very fast, but we do heal."

Cobalt groused. Was there anything his brother didn't know?

Crimson brushed herself off and scanned the other faces. "I'm just glad we're all safe."

"Yeah," Silver said. "Good thing I was able to distract Hex from Cobalt. And create an opening for the rest of you to escape. And drive the car to actually make the escape. And... Help me out here. Feels like I'm forgetting something."

David started another pass with the polisher. Cobalt pushed him away and unleashed on Silver. "What is wrong with you, Silver? Don't you ever stop?"

Silver narrowed his eyes. "If I did, you'd be dead."

Cobalt seethed. He planted his elbows on a workbench and buried his face in his hands. Silver was right, and that made him madder. Why couldn't he one-up Silver, just once?

Crimson panicked. "Guys, don't do this!"

Guys. Was she saying he was part of the problem, too? Cobalt turned around, ready to protest.

David stepped between them. "She's right. Look, Silver. Why don't you get to work and I'll take care of Crimson and Cobalt?"

"Right." Silver jutted his chin at Cobalt. "I need to make revenue. You know, save the factory. See you later!"

Silver hung around a split second. Cobalt considered saying something, but he wanted Silver to leave more than he wanted to make his point. Silver probably wouldn't get it anyway, no matter how much Cobalt said. He let his brother win the stare-down. Silver harrumphed and marched away.

David put a hand on Cobalt's back. "Hey, if you just want to go home today, I'll understand."

Cobalt shrugged him off. "No. If I give up, it's just another thing he can rub in my face. I can do anything. Just keep him out of my way."

"You got it." David led him and Crimson onto the bustling factory floor. The morning shift was well underway.

***

Cobalt straightened the steering wheel. His turns were much smoother. Confident in his newly acquired driving skills, he took his eyes off the paved path long enough to admire the immaculate landscaping that separated the main factory from the warehouse. He couldn't wait to see the look on Silver's face when he came to pick up the finished turbine parts.

Cobalt's sturdy metal body could lift and load far more weight than the humans who were originally on this task. They seemed happy enough to be assigned to something else, and he was thrilled to be at the helm of a vehicle. Dents and scratches on Cobalt's delivery cart betrayed its age, having come from a time before everything with wheels could drive itself.

Cobalt drove through the loading dock past several workstations. He followed the winding path of fluorescent tape to Silver's position and craned his neck to see his brother's reaction.

He was right. The look Silver gave him was everything he hoped it would be.

Silver looked up from the turbine he was working on, mid-stroke. "Hey!" he said. "You're uh... you're driving."

"Yep!" Cobalt patted the steering wheel. "It really wasn't that hard to learn. I could probably build parts too, if I just gave it a little time."

"Maybe." Silver set the part down and walked over to the vehicle. He pointed over his shoulder at his work in progress. "Of course, you'd need blades to do this." Cobalt picked up a stack of finished turbines and set them on his cart.

Silver took a closer look at the driving controls. "I mean, it's not a car, but I see how it could remind you of one."

Cobalt stopped loading and faced Silver. "Nobody's ever as good as you, are they Silver?"

Silver looked away, stammering. "Don't get me wrong, Cobalt. It's still cool." He shrugged. "Just smaller."

Cobalt scowled. "I may have been the center of attention in the cartoon world, but did I ever act like this? Because if I did, I was a pretty awful guy."

For once, Silver didn't have a comeback. Cobalt thought he saw a hint of shame in his eyes. Silver picked up the part he had dropped and tried to continue where he left off.

"Later, Silver." Cobalt returned to the driver's seat. "I've got a job to do."

Cobalt struck the steering wheel with his palm once Silver was out of sight. He finally climbed one step closer to Silver's level, only for the jerk to turn it into an insult! His cart took the next curve a little too fast. He forced himself to slow his speed as well as his rapidly ticking processor. *He's your brother*, Cobalt reminded himself. He wished Silver would remember that. As much as Silver's words stung, Cobalt resolved to be patient. He could be mature, even if Silver wouldn't.

***

There wasn't much room under the desk in Christine's temporary cubicle, but she tried to stretch her legs anyway. A tap on the aluminum frame interrupted her. She looked up from her computer. "Oh, hi David."

David leaned against the fabric-covered wall. "How's it going?"

"Not bad. You guys had a strong year, and if you can pull off this order of turbine parts, you'll be in excellent shape." She leaned back. "Since I've got all the numbers I need, I'll probably finish this at the house tomorrow where everything's quiet. What's up?"

"Just seeing if you needed anything," he said. He shrugged. "But if not, do you want to get lunch somewhere?"

Christine livened at the suggestion. She felt closer to David since their conversation about the robots, and the chance to have another talk appealed to her. They might never have discussed their childhood if he hadn't brought those robots home, so while she still begrudged him for the decision, at least something good came from it.

She thought about nearby restaurants. There was a sandwich place she remembered from her teen years. It used to make her feel grown up, taking her little brother there and treating him with her own money. She was about to suggest it when a figure approaching from down the hall caught her attention. Someone tall, thin, and dressed in red.

David pushed away from the wall to see what she was looking at, but Crimson's chipper voice made that unnecessary.

"Hi, David!" she sang. Her smile came through in her voice. Christine nearly gagged on its syrupy sweetness. "I've been looking for you!"

"Oh! Crimson!" he said, turning around. "Hey, now's not a good time. Can I catch up with you later, please?"

The smile went away. "Oh. Okay," she said. The robot's disappointment response piqued Christine's interest. All the robots she was used to would have politely excused themselves and exited. She wondered how realistic its personality might be.

David ran his fingers through his hair and winced. "Sorry, Christine. I forgot to tell her to leave you alone."

Crimson gasped. She stepped halfway into Christine's lair and bowed her head politely. "I didn't mean to intrude," she said, then turned to David. "I was just checking if you found a job for me. I think Cobalt likes his. But I'll go back to your office and wait."

Christine decided to push a little harder. She cast a skeptical eye at the robot. "A job, huh? I don't know, David. You make machine parts here. Not pie."

Crimson flinched. She regained her composure and emitted a good-natured chuckle. "I'd like to find something else I'm good at, Ms. Epic."

Christine gave her a cold stare. "That might be difficult." She folded her hands and leaned forward. "As I recall, you're good at nothing."

Crimson recoiled. A rush went through Christine. That last jab wasn't even calculated. She'd only blurted it out of reflex.

David stepped between them. "Christine, please! It's my fault she's here. Be mad at me if you're going to be mad at anyone!"

Christine leaned to one side, maintaining line-of-sight with her target. "Nothing, that is, except screaming, complaining, whining, and needing rescuing."

Crimson stood, mouth agape. Such an incredible simulation! Over the years, Christine spent a small fortune on counseling, but none of those therapy sessions provided her an outlet so effective as this, and it was completely free!

The experiment was over. Crimson bolted out of the cubicle, pushing David aside. Christine frowned. She'd broken her toy before she was really done playing with it.

David regained his balance and stuck his head into the hall. "Crimson! Wait!" He dug his fingers into his hair. "Christine! How could you?" She looked back at him with a satisfied smile. He ran after Crimson, shouting over his shoulder, "She's just a kid!"

"It's just a robot," Christine yelled back. She stepped out of the cubicle and shouted after him, "Now keep your toys out of my room!"

***

Crimson hadn't gone far. David found her a couple doors down in the smaller conference room. She sat at the table with her head buried in her arms.

David peeked into the windowless room. "Crimson?" He sat beside her and put his hand on her back. "I am so, so sorry. I know Christine has something against you, but I had no idea she'd be so cruel. I would never have put you through that on purpose."

"I want Mom," Crimson whispered.

"Did you say Mom?" David was at a loss. "I'm sorry, I'm not sure who you mean. The only "mom" I know is my own."

"Yes." She kept her face hidden. "I want Mrs. Epic. I want Mom. Please."

"Okay." David reached into the center of the table and pulled the conference phone toward him. "I can get her for you, if you want." Why did Crimson call her "Mom"? Did she think that was her name? Surely not. He suddenly remembered her change of clothes and realized where she likely got them. He meant to ask her about that. Why hadn't he?

Melinda's voice came over the speaker. "Hello, is that you, Dan?"

"No Mom, it's David. I'm here in the conference room with Crimson Laser. She says she wants to talk to you."

David switched the call to video, and his mother appeared on the opposite wall.

Crimson lifted her head. "Mom?" Her face was the picture of anguish.

David's heart raced. He'd never forgive himself if Crimson was broken beyond repair.

Melinda tensed at the sight of the miserable girl. "Crimson? What's wrong, dear? Are you okay?"

"No!" Crimson wailed.

"David, what happened?"

"She had a run-in with Christine. It was terrible. I wasn't expecting it. It's all my fault!"

"Don't be too hard on yourself, David," Melinda said. "Would you leave us alone, please? Now that she has a mom, she needs me."

"Thanks, Mom." David gave Crimson's arm a gentle squeeze and left, closing the door behind him.

CHAPTER 17

David followed close on Cobalt's heels as the agitated robot flung the door open and stomped out of David's garage into the apartment.

Crimson followed directly behind the two. "Cobalt, let's talk about it," she said.

"No!" Cobalt marched through the apartment, heading for his room.

Silver emerged from the garage, rolling his eyes. He stayed by the door.

Cobalt pointed at him. "I'm never getting into a car with him again! Silver doesn't know when to shut up!"

Silver shrugged, leaned against the wall, and spread his hands. "Okay, look. I'm sorry!" he said. "Your job is important, too!"

Cobalt slammed the bedroom door, shutting himself in.

Silver mumbled. "It just doesn't save the factory directly. That's all I was trying to say."

David projected his voice through the door. "Cobalt, this won't help things. We need to talk it through."

"Ugh," Silver said. "He's so sensitive."

David drew a deep breath. He was tired, so tired. "Silver, buddy. Take a seat."

Silver watched expectantly while David fetched a chair from the kitchen.

David set the chair backward and straddled it. He rested his forehead on the backrest and gathered his thoughts. When he first wished for robots, he never imagined they'd need so much emotional guidance. "I'm your friend, Silver, and sometimes friends have to say things we don't want to hear."

Silver sat across from him and narrowed his eyes.

"I have a sister that's always doing things better than me. For as long as I can remember, all her achievements cast a shadow over everything I did. Her grades were better. She did sports and I didn't. She got a scholarship to a prestigious university, and I took a few business and engineering courses at the local community college. Fast forward to today. She runs one of the largest investment firms in the world, managing thousands of employees. I still cobble together machinery on the production floor of my dad's factory."

Silver made a face like he'd bitten a Flovian Tartfruit. "Are you comparing me to your sister?"

"I'm saying, I can kind of identify with Cobalt here. He feels like you're against him."

Silver's whole body tensed. "Then I'll ask you what I asked him. What do you want from me?" He jumped up and stuck his nose in David's face. "Am I supposed to fail so everyone else can feel better about themselves? Am I supposed to let us all get killed?"

David put his hands on Silver's shoulders and made him step back. "Listen to me, Silver. And remember, I'm your friend. More than that. I love you, little buddy." He gave Silver a gentle squeeze and withdrew his hands. "In those moments when we're counting on you, we need you to do what it takes to save the day."

"Exactly!" Silver threw his arms in the air.

David took a breath. Here came the hard part. "But before those moments come, we need to trust you. Cobalt needs to trust you. He doesn't right now because in the other moments—those moments when our lives aren't on the line—you haven't shown him that you have his best interest at heart."

Silver shook his head, exasperated. "Well, how do I do that?"

David hoped Silver was listening. Even though he was clearly not taking these words seriously at the moment, maybe they'd sink in later. "Try to keep others in mind. These little moments we're talking about? Try to make them about someone other than yourself."

David's eyes drifted around the room... of course!

"Here's the perfect example." He reached for Crimson's hand and pulled her closer. "Crimson's been sitting here this whole time and we've been completely ignoring her. How do you think she feels?"

"I don't know," Silver said. "If she wants to be noticed, why doesn't she speak up?"

Crimson squirmed.

David blew through his lips. It was hard to stay patient with Silver being so obtuse, but keeping his own cool was critical right now. "If you blame it on her, you're only sidestepping the problem. Good friends figure out what's important to the people they care about and draw it out. Something has changed about Crimson. There's probably a story behind it that's important to her."

Silver glanced at his sister, shrugged, and looked back at David. He wasn't trying.

David closed his eyes and sighed. He turned his attention to Crimson. "You changed your outfit, Crimson. What happened?"

Crimson sparkled to life. She pulled at her sweater dress. She wasn't quite sure where to begin. "Mom... Mrs. Epic... gave it to me. I made a mess, and I was really scared at first. And she started out upset, but it turned out..."

Silver cut her off. "How was I supposed to notice that?" He stormed out of the room.

"Silver!" David shouted after him. "Don't get mad. Let's talk..."

Silver retreated into the garage and slammed the door behind him.

David sighed and shook his head. His track record as a robot counselor was off to a pretty poor start. He returned to his chair to find Crimson staring dejectedly at the floor. By now, she probably thought of him as the guy who always got her yelled at.

"I'm sorry," he confessed. "I really am."

She shrugged and forced a half smile.

He wondered which would hurt her less: leaving her to contemplate alone or sitting with her in miserable silence. He very nearly got up when he remembered—they did have one thing in common. He asked with genuine curiosity, "So, what's going on between you and my mom... our mom?"

Crimson straightened. A contented glow settled over her.

"Yeah," she mused. "How did it all start?" She pieced the memory together slowly at first, but soon picked up steam. She talked for over an hour, beaming the entire time.

***

The following morning, Cobalt returned to work. It wasn't as thrilling as saving the galaxy, but at least it occupied him. He determined not to let Silver get him down.

He stopped his cart in the courtyard and took in the scenery. He'd been to several cartoon planets, but his memories of solid-color animated plants and animals were nothing like the detail and variety he enjoyed here. Frequently while driving through, he'd seen people working on the landscaping. It looked like a job he would enjoy, being surrounded by such pleasant things all the time. And he wouldn't have to talk to or even see Silver all day.

No-one was out here now, though. So it seemed odd to him when a shadow moved out of the corner of his eye.

A voice spoke up behind him, sending a chill down his spine. "I'm calling a truce, Cobalt Laser. Do not panic."

That was a lot for Hex Ten to expect, but then again, he was not known for being a reasonable person. Luckily for Hex, Cobalt forgot how to scream and wasted a couple of seconds trying to remember.

Hex clapped his hand over Cobalt's mouth and squeezed harder than necessary. "I said do not panic! Why am I continually surrounded by fools?"

The fuzz cleared from Cobalt's brain, downgrading his status from absolutely petrified to extremely concerned. If Hex was planning to crush his head, he'd have done it by now. He relaxed his jaw.

"Are you done?" Hex asked.

Cobalt attempted to nod, but Hex's grip immobilized his head. To Cobalt's relief, Hex felt the gesture and released him. Hex backed into the shadows and sat on a retaining wall near a flower bed. He almost blended in with the stack of boulders.

"I observed during our last battle that you and I have something in common." Hex bent the limb of a decorative tree with his finger and watched it spring back. "We both have lost, and are striving to regain, our former glory."

Cobalt glanced around for a means of escape. "There's no way I'm going to help you!" He wasn't sure if the cart was fast enough to outrun Hex.

"I'm not asking you to help me." Hex lowered his voice and beckoned. "At least, not directly. I want you to help yourself. I will benefit passively."

Cobalt stepped closer and cast him a sidelong glance. "I don't understand."

"Tomorrow afternoon, a shipment will arrive. Heinous, Irk, and I will be there. Our goal will be to steal it."

"A shipment of what?"

"That is none of your concern. Your only business is to ensure that Heinous fails. You will be the hero, and Heinous will be the fool."

Hero? Cobalt squinted. There had to be a catch. "What are you going to get out of this?"

"I have a plan. I have told you what you need to know. Do you want to be a hero?"

Of course he did. He just knew it was a bad idea. Unless, of course, he could manage the consequences.

"I have so many questions," Cobalt said. "How do you expect me to stop Heinous? I don't have *Perfect Punch*, and he almost killed me in the alley!"

Hex grinned. "I will loan you a weapon. And while I must not help you defeat Heinous directly, neither will I do anything to stop you. You will succeed. I promise that."

Success! A promise! Whatever the risks were, Cobalt felt sure the benefit was worth them.

He hesitated. A promise from Hex Ten. It occurred to him that he shouldn't even be entertaining this conversation. Once more he scanned for an escape. He didn't realize how far Hex had lured him away from the cart.

Hex plucked an orange tulip from the landscaping. "An interesting world we find ourselves in. I try to think of it as the other side of the black hole you banished me to. I wonder sometimes if our actions here are just as scripted as they were before, but as far as I can tell I have a choice." His eyes bore into Cobalt's soul. "And the possibilities are endless."

Hex crushed the flower between his fingers. "What possibilities have you harnessed since you arrived here, Cobalt Laser?" He nodded toward the delivery cart and produced a sly smile. "Do the results of your choices satisfy you?"

Cobalt trembled. The urge to escape was still there, but Hex was starting to make sense. This was a new world. Things were different here. Hex was different. He was different. If he wanted to be a hero, he would have to make the right choices. Epic Manufacturing was a great choice for Silver, but Cobalt wasn't convinced it would work out so well for him.

Cobalt made his decision. "What do you need from me?" A surge of anxiety shot through his neural net, but he shook it off. Taking risks is part of being a hero.

A satisfied smile spread across Hex's face. "We will talk again in a few hours." He motioned toward the warehouse with his chin. "I have detained you from your human keepers long enough. They will wonder what is delaying you."

***

Inspector Princess waved her magnifying glass at the children on the other side of the screen. "We had so much fun together," she said. "But it's time for me to go."

The moment Irk had been dreading for weeks finally arrived. There were so many episodes of *Inspector Princess* when he first met her, but now he was at the end of the list. And this was the final minute of that episode.

Ruffy scratched his head. "Where will we go, Inspector Princess?"

"I don't know for sure, but on to new adventures!" She looked out of the screen, into Irk's eyes. "Do you remember when we learned about ants? The time we fed the koi? How about the time we made the sun feel better?"

Irk looked away, focusing on the remote he'd left beside the TV. "Yeah. That was my favorite." He swung his feet.

"You learned so much! Here, you earned this." Inspector Princess reached behind her back and produced a badge that filled the screen. "Congratulations, you're a Junior Detective now! You can help other people all by yourself!"

The badge dissolved, revealing a smiling Inspector Princess. Irk walked to the screen and touched her cheek just before the scene cut away.

Inspector Princess and Ruffy climbed onto her scooter. She waved at Irk. "Thank you so much for all your help! I'm glad you came along. I'll always remember you!"

Irk took his hand off the screen. "Yeah, me too." He watched the credits to the end, determined to memorize every last image of his only friend before she left for good. Finally, the screen went black. It presented him with the option to restart at episode one or begin another recommended series.

Irk turned the TV off. It didn't feel right to relive all her memories. He would know everything she was going to say before she said it, while he would be a complete stranger to her. Neither was he ready to make a new friend. He needed more time to grieve the one he just lost. He tossed the remote onto the coffee table and sat beside it.

Irk barely started collecting his thoughts when someone entered the room.

Oh, no. Not now.

Hex looked at Irk and cocked his head. Irk scowled and retreated to the opposite corner of the room. He curled into a ball and sat with his back to the intruder.

"If your intent is to hide, you have chosen an ineffective approach," Hex said. "Don't be a coward. Stand your ground and face your adversary."

Realizing this was the closest he'd ever get to hearing Hex Ten dispense friendly advice, Irk decided to heed it. He stood and glared at the monster. "What do you want?"

"This morning, I made an assessment of your value. That assessment was inaccurate."

Irk eyed Hex cautiously. Was this an apology?

"I was blinded by my fury and spoke hastily. The truth is, there are things I cannot do without you." Hex sat on the floor. "I believe the creator knew that, and that is why you were given to me as an assistant." He leaned toward the little robot. "I need you."

This was more than Irk could process. He sat facing Hex. Was that kindness? On the face of Hex Ten? This warranted further investigation. "What do you need me to do?"

A smile formed on Hex's face. "I was hoping you would ask," he said. "Of course you are so perceptive." He glanced around the room and lowered his voice. "I need you to fabricate something. An armored exo-suit."

Irk flinched. "But Hex, you are practically already a walking exo-suit!"

Hex motioned for Irk to keep his voice low. "It is not for me. It needs to accommodate a human-sized pilot. With defensive and offensive capabilities. Strong enough to withstand…" He waved his hand in a circle, pretending to conjure some options. "For example, someone as powerful as Heinous."

Irk shrugged. "That wouldn't be too hard, except Prohibition 351 prevents me from using the fabricator without permission."

Hex tensed.

Irk grinned slyly. "But it doesn't have to be Andrew's permission."

Hex smiled back. "You have my endorsement to proceed. One more thing. You must do this without Heinous and Dr. Smalls finding out. I am trying to prove my worth, so it is imperative that this endeavor remains secret. Later tonight, they will want to rehearse the plan for the refractium theft with me. Can you complete the project during that time?"

"Sure," Irk said cheerfully. "Andrew will want me to stay out of the way, anyway. Our little secret will be waiting for you on the roof before you return."

Hex rested his hand on Irk's back. He could almost enclose the tiny robot in his fist if he wanted to. He smiled. "Such a faithful associate! I hope you don't hold this morning's misguided rantings against me."

"Forget about it," Irk said. "I'm just glad I can finally help someone else all by myself!"

SERIES: Cobalt Laser
SEASON 1, EPISODE 6

"Parting is Such Sweet Sorrow"
TIMESTAMP: 14:44

A VESSEL LOOMED SEVERAL kilometers off the bow of the *Teacup*. Vanessa, a robot girl in blue ninja garb watched it anxiously through the porthole. "My people won't stop until they get the module back."

Cobalt looked up from the navigation console. "But the module is a part of you."

Silver bristled *Flashing Blades*. "And I'm not going to let them have you back!"

Vanessa beamed. "Thank you, Silver." She returned to the porthole and spoke with conviction. "But I would never go back. I refuse to participate in the Robot Ninja Clan's plans any longer."

Silver took Vanessa's hands in his. "Then stay with us. We'll keep you from them."

Vanessa pulled him close. "Oh, Silver. You're wonderful!" A cloud settled over her. "But my people are relentless. You're already on the run from Hex Ten. You would never get a moment's rest!"

Vanessa's and Silver's noses nearly touched. Crimson nearly gagged.

"Silver? Wonderful?" Crimson sputtered. "I'd like a moment's rest from that."

Vanessa jabbed a finger at Crimson. "Your brother is wonderful! He's the sweetest boy in the whole galaxy! You should show him some respect!"

Crimson put her hands on her hips and wagged her head at the delusional little girl. "You should have your optics checked!" she sassed. "I thought you ninjas were supposed to have highly tuned senses."

"Someone should teach you some manners!"

"Me? Ha! I've been trying to teach Silver manners for years, but he refuses to learn!"

"That's enough!" Vanessa drew her hand back. "Servo Interruption Pulse!" She jabbed two fingers into the side of Crimson's neck.

Crimson trembled, then collapsed into a heap. "Hey!" She strained, but couldn't move so much as a finger. "I'm all numb!"

Vanessa turned her back on Crimson and took Silver's hands again. "I'm afraid there's no other way."

Silver's voice trembled. "What do you mean, no other way?"

An explosion rocked the *Teacup*. Cobalt switched to the tactical monitor. "They're gaining on us!"

Vanessa went to the other side of the *Teacup* and looked out the porthole in that direction. "I have to destroy the module." The star they orbited shone brightly through the glass.

Silver panicked. "But the module is a part of you! And we can't separate it!"

Vanessa held Silver at arm's length. "The only solution is for me to fly into that star, taking the module with me. I won't be back."

"No!" Silver shook her hands off him. "I won't let you do it!"

"Please, Silver." Vanessa reached out again and pulled him close. "I'm afraid. I need your courage."

"My courage? I don't have any courage! Don't talk like this! I'm terrified!"

Vanessa intertwined her fingers with Silver's and showed him their clasped hands. "See this? When two people with no courage join hands, something special happens. Out of nowhere, courage flows and fills them both."

Silver squeezed her hand tighter. "Alright," he said. All the emotion drained from his voice. "But I'm still sad."

"Me too."

The *Teacup* shuddered under the force of another blast.

Vanessa released Silver's hand and opened the hatch to the *Teacup's* escape pod.

"I'll never forget you," Silver said.

Vanessa looked at the star again and put one foot into the escape pod. "When I get to the next world, I'll remember you there."

The hatch closed and the pod launched. Silver ran to the porthole as the pod came into view.

The pursuing vessel turned away from the *Teacup* to chase the escape pod, but it was a hopeless endeavor. It got smaller and smaller, then disappeared into the brilliance of the star's surface. The other ship stopped and turned to face the *Teacup* once more.

Cobalt flipped some switches. "We've got an incoming transmission!"

A grim voice echoed through the intercom. "Our precious module is destroyed. Our people will never be the same, but it is no use trying to change the outcome now. We have no quarrel with you, Cobalt Laser. We leave you in peace."

The ship left the *Teacup* alone in orbit around Vanessa's final resting place. Silver collapsed on his knees and cried.

Crimson lifted herself off the floor and limped over to her brother. "I'm sorry, Silver. She was very brave." She knelt beside him and wrapped him in her arms.

Cobalt looked through the porthole at the searing surface of the white dwarf. "She truly was a hero."

CHAPTER 18

Crimson stared at the ceiling with her knees draped over the arm of David's couch. It was so quiet in the apartment by herself. This morning, she told David she wasn't up to going back to the factory yet, but now she regretted that decision. Running errands and taking orders would've at least been a distraction. Alone here, all she could do was relive yesterday in her mind over and over. Worse, Christine was in the house. Crimson avoided seeing her by staying in the basement, but not long ago, she heard that dreaded voice upstairs, cementing her resolve to stay put.

Melinda came down the stairs, interrupting her thoughts. She propped herself on her elbows and smiled brightly. "Hi, Mom!"

"Hello, dear." Melinda sat opposite Crimson and put her hands in her lap. "I think it's time for you to have a very difficult conversation with Christine."

Crimson bolted upright. "I can't."

"It needs to happen," Melinda said. "She needs to realize that you're a person with feelings, and she can't just step on you to make herself feel better. And she needs to hear it from you."

"I'm too scared."

"So am I. But do you remember Vanessa, the robot ninja girl, and what she said to your brother?"

Crimson narrowed her eyes. "Yes." It was not one of her more cherished memories.

Melinda gave Crimson a nudge. "Hey, she was a good girl! I was her voice too, you know. That conversation between you and her was challenging to record."

Crimson grimaced. She'd rather not know that.

"Anyway, her advice was good." Melinda took Crimson's hand into her own. "You take my courage, and I'll take yours."

Crimson examined their clasped hands. "Will you go with me?"

"I can't. This is your battle."

"Then how will you hold my hand?"

Melinda looked around the apartment. She went into the kitchen and came back out holding the sponge. She put it in Crimson's hand. "When you get scared, squeeze this. Imagine it's my hand, squeezing back. I'll be down here the whole time, waiting for you."

Crimson closed her eyes and felt the sponge. She could imagine Melinda standing beside her now, but would it work when she was facing Christine? "What if I can't do it?"

"Come back here and tell me. I will still love you, even if you run away."

"Okay."

***

The door stood ajar. Crimson tapped on it.

"What." It was not a question.

Christine sat in front of a desk, hands still on her laptop. The rest of the room looked as if a tornado hit it. Her suitcase lay open on the floor, its contents scattered all over the room.

Christine curled her lip when she noticed Crimson.

"Oh, it's you." She looked as if she'd just laid eyes on a Strobian toxworm, right after shedding its slime coat. "What are you doing here?"

Crimson surveyed the disarray. "Would you like me to help you clean up?"

Christine bristled. "What do you think I am? Some kind of baby? I know how to clean a room!" She gestured at the computer. "I'm just a little busy right now!" She leaned toward Crimson and sneered. "You know, working. Being useful!"

Crimson winced. Christine knew exactly what her weakness was, and she struck without mercy. "Actually, I only came here to talk. I thought maybe offering to do something for you would help open things up."

Christine's face flushed. "Get out. I have nothing to say to you!"

Crimson couldn't bear the vicious glare any longer. Her eyes went to Christine's feet. "You had plenty to say to me yesterday."

"Do you want me to say it again? It got you out of my hair last time."

Crimson closed her eyes and squeezed the sponge. "Why do you hate me so much? I try so hard to be nice."

"Oh, you're nice all right." Christine rose from her chair and advanced on Crimson. "That's the problem." Christine was just a bit taller than her. As she drew closer, it forced Crimson to look up.

She continued, "Crimson Laser is nice, cute, friendly..." She stared straight down at Crimson. Christine's breath fogged her eye visor, clearing just as she delivered the crushing blow, "And weak."

She spun on her heel and put space between them, granting Crimson some relief. "Do you want to know what you did to me?" She didn't wait for an answer. "You destroyed my childhood!"

This was the part Crimson couldn't understand. "How is that possible?" she said. "I didn't even know you!"

"My dad told me he was making a character in his cartoon just for me. He told me I was the inspiration for Crimson Laser, and she was going to be just like me. And I bought it!"

Crimson continued to puzzle over what she could've done to change any of this as Christine paced, waving her arms. "She already had my curly blonde hair, so I bugged my parents to get me an all-red wardrobe so I could complete the look. I was so proud of you, and I told everyone at school. It was all I talked about. For a whole year I built up the anticipation of this amazing thing that was supposed to represent me."

Crimson recalled the wiki's article about herself, all too clearly. "And I disappointed you." She withered.

"Disappointed?" Christine practically roared the word at her. "I wish that was all! You humiliated me! You devastated me!"

Crimson closed her eyes again and squeezed the sponge. "I wasn't there."

"Oh, it was fun at first. I was a real character in a cool cartoon! But it didn't take long for the kids to catch on to what you really were, and let me tell you, there's nothing crueler than a middle school bully. You spent that season running from Hex Ten and hiding behind your brothers. I spent it out in the open, getting my heart shredded by people too cool for me."

Christine's voice went higher and louder. "I worked relentlessly to break away from that little cartoon girl. I got good grades. I excelled at sports. I even dyed my hair! But people remembered, and I'd still get teased about being useless Crimson Laser. Eventually, I graduated, moved away, and remade myself. That's what it took to become a success. Christine Epic is nothing like Crimson Laser. I am strong, successful, independent, and above all…" She got into Crimson's face and snarled. "I fight my own battles!"

Christine stood unmoving, staring down her nose at Crimson. Crimson backed away. Nothing was more important than escaping the cruelty. She groped for the door. Christine glared triumphantly as she watched the frightened robot withdraw.

Crimson could only think of retreating to the basement and back into Melinda's arms, but when she reached for the doorknob, she remembered the sponge in her hand. She closed her eyes and gave it a squeeze. She knew Christine was still in front of her, but in the blackness, she tried to imagine her light years away, while Melinda was right there beside her. She clocked her buzzing processor down and tried to recall some of Christine's words.

She let go of the doorknob and stood tall. "You mentioned having to break away from that little cartoon girl. I think we have something in common." She opened her eyes. Christine was still there, angry as before, but Crimson was no longer scared. Her processor continued to pulse fast, but she'd evened its pace. "Right now, I'm trying to figure out where she ends and I begin."

Christine shoved an accusing finger at Crimson. "My mom is convinced you are that little girl! She didn't end. She's one hundred percent you!"

Crimson narrowed her eyes at Christine's finger. "Mom loves me. If she believes I'm still that cartoon girl, there must be something there worth loving."

That wasn't enough. Christine lectured, "She only loves you because she thinks she's your mom, and that's what moms do. You can be a total disappointment and complete failure and still go running back to your mom. She'll take you even when you don't deserve anything from anyone else in the world!"

She seemed to have an answer for every point Crimson made. Clearly, Christine had spent a lot of time thinking about this, and it dawned on Crimson why that might be. She cocked her head. "Is that how you feel?"

Christine doubled in height. "How dare you!" She shook her hands at Crimson, brandishing them like claws. "Do you have any idea who I am? Where I've been? What I've accomplished?"

Crimson closed her eyes. She squeezed the sponge. "Yes." She opened her eyes. "I do." A few steps away, a blouse lay draped across the back of a chair with one of its sleeves inside out. Crimson retrieved it. "You're an amazing person, and I respect you." She dropped the blouse in a hamper by the door.

Christine seethed, spinning to face the window on the opposite side of the room. She ran her hands through her straight brown hair. "You need to get out of here right now!"

Crimson flicked at the hamper's contents and shrugged. "Just last week, I was standing on the deck of the *Teacup* on the greatest day of my life. But then I woke up. I woke to a world that hates me, brothers that don't need me, a creator that doesn't want me..." She turned toward Christine. "And you."

Christine locked eyes with Crimson's reflection in the window. "I'd leave you alone if you'd just stay out of my way!" Her voice reached a crescendo. "You've caused enough damage! Get out of my room and get out of my life!"

It seemed Christine was finally out of answers. Unfortunately, that didn't seem to change her mind. Anger was the only thing she had left, and she clung to it. Crimson's shoulders sagged. "You don't have to be my friend if you don't want to. Just please stop hurting me."

Christine pounded the window frame. "Stop asking for it!" On the carpet, her shadow heaved in time with her labored breathing.

Crimson toyed with her fingers, then wrinkled her eyes at Christine's reflection. "You know what it's like to be bullied. Why are you doing it to me?"

Christine flinched like she'd been slapped. She slumped, taking a seat on the windowsill. Her angry expression morphed into befuddlement. Finally, Crimson found a question Christine couldn't answer.

Crimson stepped into the column of sunlight beaming into the room. "Maybe I was there after all," she said. The carpet was so warm in that spot. "When those kids made fun of you, they were also making fun of me. I was there the whole time. Right there beside you."

Christine opened her mouth, but no words formed. Those eyes—the ones that pierced Crimson so mercilessly moments before—could no longer lift themselves to her level. She breathed a couple more times, then said, "Mom was right."

It was like escaping an asteroid field. One moment, sirens are blaring, warning lights are blinking everywhere, debris is crashing against the hull of your ship, you can't stay on your feet, and everything's flying off the shelves. The next moment, it's not. You're cruising peacefully through empty space, the danger behind you.

Crimson took a tentative step into the quietness.

"She was right. You are real, aren't you?" Christine said quietly.

Crimson's processor halted, cycling through several conflicting ideas. A few days ago, she'd have said yes, she was real, without hesitation. But she learned so much since then. Now she was no longer sure she knew what the word meant.

Christine crept forward, tears welling up. She touched Crimson's hair. "I'm sorry, Crimson. I'm so, so sorry." Her hand moved to Crimson's cheek. "I was using you as a punching bag. My dad and his writers are the ones that hurt me, not you."

Crimson tensed. The warning lights in her mind flashed again. "I don't want to make you mad at your dad!" she said.

Christine withdrew her hand. She admired Crimson for a moment, then chuckled. "Mom was right about another thing. You are an absolute sweetheart." She took Crimson's hands into her own. "Don't worry. I took care of that long ago. The feelings were just fresh. I'm done hurting people now, I promise." The tears returned. "But there's no excuse for what I did to you. I was very, very wrong. Please forgive me."

Leaving an asteroid field behind never felt so good! Crimson threw her arms around Christine and held tight.

Christine rocked Crimson gently. "I need to take back what I told you about mom. Mom will love you no matter what, but her arms aren't just a place to hide. They're where anything can grow, no matter how badly it's been hurt or how much love it needs." She touched her nose to Crimson's. "And the same is true for sisters."

A warm, fluttering sensation filled Crimson's belly. A sister! All her life, she'd been an orphan, the oldest, and surrounded by boys. Now she had not only a mom, but a sister too! An older sister, even! If life could get better than this, she couldn't imagine how.

Maybe this is what "real" meant. Being something, not only to yourself, but to someone else. Assuring someone they're more than a character in someone else's script, and they return the kindness. Crimson thought about her brothers. Cobalt especially needed to know he was real to her.

Suddenly, Christine pushed away from Crimson and held her at arm's length. The alarms went off in Crimson's mind again. Had she done something wrong?

"I just remembered," Christine said, wide-eyed. "I need to show you something!" She bolted for the door, tugging Crimson along by the hand. "Follow me!"

***

"Everything's red." Crimson's eyes swelled at the forgotten bedroom.

"Of course!" Christine said. "When I was fourteen, I didn't believe in any other color." She scanned her old room. "It's just like I remember it. Mom put it all back exactly after I moved out."

The walls were red. The carpet and bedspread were red. And lined up on red shelves were more than a hundred red toys—all of them Crimson Laser in various forms: action figures, plushies, bobble heads, and products of every kind bearing her image. The only thing that wasn't completely red was the carefully arranged display of action figures, featuring the main characters of *Cobalt Laser*, huddling around and admiring Crimson Laser.

Crimson browsed the shelves from one end of the room to the other. "It's... It's..." She couldn't take it all in at once. "It's me."

"It certainly is," Christine said proudly. "This has to be the largest collection of Crimson Laser merchandise in the world."

"Girls?" Melinda's voice made them turn around.

"Hi, Mom," Christine said. A cloud settled over her. "I'm sorry."

"No, no." Melinda put her hands on Christine's shoulders. "I'm just happy for both of you."

Crimson's hand hovered in front of the shelf as she fought the temptation to touch the toys. She cocked her head curiously and pointed at an action figure in its package. "Why is that one in a containment field?"

Christine chuckled when she figured out what Crimson meant. "These toys are worth more when they're in their original packaging." She plucked it off the shelf.

Crimson ran her fingers over it. There was so much to read and look at. It was embarrassing to see what amounted to an advertisement for herself. The action figure in the bubble stared straight ahead, arms to its sides. It was boring in contrast to the nonstop action that the card behind it promised.

Christine took the toy back and gave it a long look. "You know, twenty-four years is a long time to be stuck in the same pose." She dug her fingernails into the plastic and peeled it away from the card.

Crimson reached for the toy, alarmed. "Wait, are you sure?"

"Absolutely. What do I care about the collector's value? Even if I did, there's no way I could ever bring myself to sell this!"

She extracted the doll from its prison and exercised its joints. She found a small plastic block and set it on the shelf. She posed the toy victoriously on top, as if it had scaled the imaginary mountain.

"She's free," Crimson said.

"Yes," Christine said. She wrapped her arm around her sister. "We are."

CHAPTER 19

"You're ahead of schedule this morning, sir!" Tad stood by as Cobalt parked the delivery cart beside a stack of new conduit.

"Oh, uh... yeah." Cobalt hastily loaded the conduit onto the cart. "I'm trying to get my rounds finished early today. I've got, uh, a special project today."

"Oh?" Tad raised his eyebrows. "Well, good for you! You're a good kid, Cobalt."

Cobalt's cheeks warmed up. He looked away. "Thanks, Tad. I just want to do my best."

"Yes, sir," Tad said. "Super reliable, altogether trustworthy. A guy can count on you, Cobalt."

Cobalt set the last armload of conduit on the cart. He stammered. "I'm glad you think so." He jumped into the driver's seat without looking back. "Well, gotta go!"

***

Cobalt dropped his last delivery off with no time to spare and parked the cart behind a tree in the courtyard. Abandoning it, he ran north as fast as he could. If Hex Ten was telling the truth, he'd be gone for just over an hour. With the work he did ahead of time, he'd be back before anyone missed him.

Stealthily, Cobalt crept into an abandoned apartment building. He looked across the street through a broken window at the warehouse Hex told him about.

"There you are," came the low, smooth voice Cobalt had come to dread. He whirled around to find Hex leaning against the opposite wall.

"Right on time." Hex took a step forward. "You're reliable, Cobalt. Good to know I can count on you." He gestured through an empty doorframe into an adjacent room. "Your new weapon awaits."

Cobalt froze when he saw the shiny exo-suit. "Wow."

"It's not *Perfect Punch*," Hex said. "But I think you'll come to like it far better."

The person-shaped machine stood just a little taller than Hex Ten. Someone the size of Cobalt Laser could fit into its body cavity and close the cockpit. Just looking at it, Cobalt could tell it had adjustable shielding and some sort of projectile weapon. And by the complexity of the controls, he could tell there were several less obvious things it could also do. He ran his fingers across its coal black finish. So smooth.

"I can see that you are pleased," Hex said, smiling. "Irk tells me the controls should be intuitive to anyone who operated machinery in our world."

"Oh, yeah," Cobalt said. "No problem."

Hex got down to business. "One more time, here's what to expect. You will prepare the exo-suit and wait for Heinous, Irk, and me to enter the warehouse. Give us 70 seconds, then follow. Then stop Heinous at all costs. Irk will offer you no resistance. If you are forced to engage me, simply make a show, push me away, and re-engage

Heinous. Remember, your only goal is to neutralize him. After that, I will give you instructions on securing the refractium."

Cobalt nodded. "Got it." His brow furrowed. "But how will anyone recognize me in this?"

Hex raised an eyebrow. "Ideally, they won't."

"How will I get my reputation as a hero back if no-one recognizes me?"

"Ah." Hex grasped for a thought, then appeared to catch one. "Erm, I am told that in this world, heroes keep their identities secret."

Cobalt didn't remember signing up for that. "Oh."

"Rest easy." Hex spread his hands in a magnanimous gesture. "When you have won the praise and admiration of the people, you may reveal yourself as their beloved hero!"

Before Cobalt could protest, Hex held up a finger and looked out the window. An armored car pulled up to the warehouse and backed into the receiving dock. A heavy metal door rolled down, sealing it inside. "It is time. Prepare yourself!" he said.

Once again, Cobalt was left to marvel at how quickly and quietly someone the size of Hex Ten could vanish. He climbed into the cockpit of the exo-suit, enclosed himself inside it, and ran it through its paces. He'd never experienced such power! The strength of the walking tank dwarfed that of his own arms and legs. As much as he wanted to test its weaponry, he knew he shouldn't risk alerting anyone nearby.

He caught a glimpse of his reflection in one of the few still-intact windows and stepped closer. His armor was clearly a villain's design, and that unnerved him. He reassured himself. Deep inside the exo-suit was still the same hero, and as long as he held the controls, the suit would do good no matter what it looked like on the outside. Likewise, his actions, while hard to explain on the surface, made a lot more sense when you understood the bright blue intentions at their core. So, he'd just keep his hands on the controls, and everything would be fine.

Besides, that gleaming black finish was super cool.

***

The box of Andrew's delivery truck lurched as Hex entered, joining Heinous and Irk. Hex intoned, "The way is clear. Now is the time to strike!"

Heinous pointed a clawed finger at him. "I did not need you to tell me that!" he hissed. "You were supposed to stay here!"

"I prefer to make my own assessment."

Heinous stomped his foot and clenched all four fists. "Do not jeopardize this mission with your foolish displays of envy and paranoia!"

Hex glared at Heinous and rumbled. "I said, now is the time to strike. Will we go, or would you prefer to argue?"

From the driver's seat, Andrew poked his head into the compartment. "Come on, kids— put your differences aside and get along. We've got a robbery to commit! Go!"

Heinous hissed. He pushed past Hex and jumped out of the truck. Hex and Irk followed.

Moving quickly, the three robots approached the loading dock and headed straight toward the rolled-down metal door that separated them from the refractium shipment. As they walked, Heinous drew a pistol with one hand, a magazine with another, and snapped them together. He repeated this with alternating pairs of hands until all four held a loaded weapon. As he executed this little ritual, he allowed Hex to overtake him. "Open the door," he commanded.

Without a stutter in his momentum, Hex wound up his fist and plowed it into the loading dock door. It ripped like foil, and whatever shreds remained, Hex pushed aside like a curtain. He marched into the open receiving area past the armored car.

At the back of the loading dock, two industrial robots were setting a large mass of crystalline material onto a wheeled cart. Hex made note of its location, then turned his attention to the dozen or so guard robots that were just now reacting to their presence. Some were quicker than others and had already armed their weapons.

"I will say this once," said a raspy voice directly behind Hex. "Get out of the line of fire!"

Hex dropped to the ground and rolled toward the armored car. A buzzing sound echoed off the concrete walls as glowing red projectiles flew past him. The guards were armored, but the impact of the plasma bullets against their shielding knocked them over and sent them sprawling. They lay on the floor, seemingly inoperable.

Hex jumped back to his feet and watched Heinous walk past him. Irk toddled behind, taking everything in with an oblivious grin.

Heinous aimed at the back of the dock and unleashed another hail of bullets. The industrial robots flew apart in a magnificent spray of molten metal and debris. The refractium fell to the floor, emitting a high-pitched ring that reverberated for several seconds before finally dying out.

Heinous holstered two of his pistols and pointed at the refractium. "Hex, collect the objective." He turned around. "Let's..." His voice trailed off. His compound eyes shifted about, focusing several of their surfaces in turn on something at the front of the dock.

Hex suppressed a smile. If only Heinous had a more expressive face! Even so, he savored the moment. As his gaze swept past, he glimpsed Irk, his mouth agape.

A shiny, jet-black presence hovered menacingly over the wreckage of the ruined entry door. It was huge, just a bit larger than Hex Ten. Before anyone could react, it stretched its arms toward them and emitted what sounded like a series of high-pitched whistles.

Heinous flew backward as an unseen force tossed him like a rag doll. Cracks spiderwebbed across the wall behind him as a barrage of ammunition pummeled it. The pieces that ricocheted or embedded themselves in the walls looked like tiny beads. Hex marveled at the superhard nanoceramic bullets. They were still unmarred spheres, even after tearing through Heinous's metal flesh and bouncing off solid concrete. He avoided looking directly at his former general, concerned that the satisfaction on his face would give him away.

Heinous lay on the floor, screaming in a combination of agony and rage. "Destroy it!" His voice was more raspy than usual. "Destroy the intruder!"

Hex caught Irk's gaze. The little robot stared back, eyes wide. Almost imperceptibly, he shook his head. "No," he whispered. "No, no!"

Hex knelt in front of Irk and whispered. "Keep silent if you hope to live." He stepped back and faced the exo-suit down.

Hex dashed toward the enemy. The enemy ran too, closing the distance. As they approached each other, the mysterious robot stretched out its arm and Hex ran into it. He fell to the ground in mock defeat.

With the tall black entity distracted, Heinous struggled back to his feet and reloaded his weapons. He took aim and fired. Armor plating closed over his opponent's body like a shell and deflected the glowing plasma bullets, making them ricochet into the walls.

The rain of bullets ended, and the enemy leaned in Heinous's direction. Rockets on its back propelled it toward him. Heinous stood paralyzed as the unidentified warrior collided with him and crushed him in a bear hug.

Heinous's already compromised body could take no more punishment. He offered no resistance as his opponent threw him at the loading dock exit. He landed at Hex's feet.

Hex propped Heinous up and shoved him toward Irk. "Get him back to the truck," he said. "I will take the refractium."

Speaking took all the effort Heinous could muster. "You... can't." Irk dragged him to the door. It was a struggle, but he made steady progress thanks to Heinous's relatively light frame.

Hex stood tall and looked purposefully at the interloper in the walking tank. He marched toward Cobalt.

***

Cobalt waited for Hex to approach. He struck a menacing pose and aimed his nanoceramic blasters. Their power shocked him. Hex had compared them to *Perfect Punch*, so he shouldn't have been surprised. But truth be told, they scared Cobalt. His battles in the cartoon world had been marked with playful banter and mock violence with no lasting consequences. Now, Heinous lay a few meters away, actually wounded. The villain's screams triggered a prickly sensation under Cobalt's armor, but it would be okay. Heinous could be repaired because Cobalt was in control, and he'd stopped before it got past that point.

Cobalt adjusted his aim, forgetting the exo-suit's mass. His heavy arms chugged, throwing his balance off for a moment. By the time he recovered, Hex was in earshot. Cobalt addressed him in a low voice. "Now what do we..."

Hex interrupted him with a sharp punch to the chest that knocked the exo-suit onto its back.

"What was that?" Cobalt demanded.

Before he could get back up, Hex jumped on top of him, pinning him with one gigantic hand. Cobalt felt certain he could take Hex on, or at least draw him into a stalemate, but he wasn't sure if this was all part of the scheme.

Hex whispered to Cobalt through the exo-suit's face shield. "We are being recorded. This needs to be convincing. I will now take the refractium."

A burst of radio static erupted from the building's intercom. "Multiple intruders, armed and hostile," an urgent voice said. "Loading dock 12."

Cobalt grunted, struggling against Hex's grip. "This wasn't the plan! I was supposed to defeat Heinous and stop the theft!" he said. "I can't let you do this!" Pinned to the ground, he couldn't muster the leverage to break free.

Hex produced the grin of a villain whose plan had come to fruition. "You will. And you will say nothing of this to anyone, unless you want to explain to the rest of your family how you came to be in league with Hex Ten!"

Normally, this would be the part where Cobalt reminded Hex of one crucial detail he'd missed—one brilliant quip that would turn the tide. But that would've required Cobalt to have studied the details and anticipated Hex's plan, and he'd skipped that part. It usually happened offscreen.

Commotion echoed through a nearby corridor. Reinforcements made their way to the loading dock.

Hex looked threateningly at Cobalt. "I will now make my escape. I suggest you do the same." Still gripping the exo-suit, he lifted its cockpit several centimeters and forced it back down, smashing it into the floor. "I will meet you tomorrow in the usual place for a debriefing."

Hex rose, hefted the crystal ingot onto his shoulder, and ran for the door. Cobalt, out of time, made a break for it as well. Dashing back into the ruins of the retired warehouse district, Cobalt shed the handsome black armor and slipped back to the factory.

***

Back in the truck, Andrew hovered over Heinous's wrecked body.

"What do you mean, you were attacked by an intruder?" he screamed. "You were supposed to be the intruder!"

This was supposed to be simple. It was all muscle—go in, take what you came for, and get out. Everything hinged on this. They wouldn't get a second chance, and these incompetent robots fumbled a perfectly aligned opportunity! His future with The Organization, bright and promising as of this morning, suddenly felt cold and ominous.

Heinous lay in a broken heap on the floor of the truck's cargo box. Irk knelt beside him, gently patting the one spot on his upper left arm that didn't have a hole in it.

"A powerful warrior." Those were the only words Heinous could force out.

Andrew grabbed Irk and shook him. "What is he talking about? Did you see it?"

Irk fidgeted and stammered. "An exo-suit! With someone in it! I assume! I mean, I assume someone was in it. I know it was an exo-suit. But I don't know who was in it!"

Andrew clawed at his hair. "Shut up!"

The truck lurched. Hex entered, carrying an enormous glittering mass. He set it on the floor and looked Andrew in the eye. "Go."

Andrew beheld the refractium. So the mission was a success after all, but there had apparently been a side objective no-one bothered to inform him about. He gazed back at Hex and cocked his head. A smile tugged at the corner of his mouth. "What did you…"

"Go!" Hex repeated.

Andrew snapped out of his daze and hopped into the driver's seat.

CHAPTER 20

Silver stretched across the couch, his feet in Cobalt's lap. Cobalt stared into space, not seeming to notice. Crimson sprawled on the floor in front of them, conducting an imaginary battle with action figures.

Silver massaged his temples. He wanted time to himself, to retreat into his own head and collect his thoughts, but that was impossible with his sister rolling around on the floor, making explosion noises with her mouth.

"Crimson, can you stop that?" he scolded. "I built almost 200 turbines today, and I just can't deal with all your energy."

Crimson held a plush doll of herself, making a sound effect as it danced on the coffee table.

"Bloop, bloop, bloop." Plush Crimson blooped across the table to talk to the Silver Laser action figure in her other hand.

"Whatsa matter, Silver?" Plush Crimson asked. Real Crimson made no effort to conceal her moving lips.

"Oh, Crimson," Action Figure Silver said in the dopiest voice Crimson could muster. "I had a tough day and I'm tired and grumpy like a big dumb baby."

Silver gritted his teeth. "Stop it," he hissed. She was always treating him like the immature one, but wasn't she too old to be playing with toys? He wished he could be alone. Cobalt had his own room, but he'd gotten stuck with the living room. He could retreat to the garage again, but there was no comfortable place to rest. He redoubled his efforts to rein Crimson in.

"What's gotten into you? You're the one acting like a baby! Why?"

Crimson froze, holding the tiny Silver at arm's length.

"Sorry," she said. She pulled her knees to her chest and ran her fingers through her hair. "I just had a really good day." She tickled her plush replica and let out a small chuckle. "I'm happy," she said wistfully.

Silver rolled his eyes. "Well, good for you," he said. He yanked his feet out of Cobalt's lap. "Not all of us are feeling so chipper right now, so could you dial it back a bit?"

Silver's sudden movement jolted Cobalt into the present. "Hey, come on, Silver. Don't take it so seriously." He pointed at Crimson's toy collection. "Where did you get those?"

"Christine let me have some of them!" Crimson handed him a Cobalt toy. "Back when the show was on TV, there were toys of all of us!" Cobalt turned the likeness of himself over in his hand. Silver leaned in, examining its facial features. It looked so confident and heroic.

David emerged from his room in time to hear her explanation. "Christine gave them to you? That's great!" He knelt beside the coffee table and examined a few of the figurines. "I haven't seen these in years!"

He was in the middle of helping Crimson arrange the toys when Dan, Melinda, and Christine rushed down the stairs. Dan pointed at the TV and barked at him. "Turn on the news."

David complied. A reporter described the scene as security camera footage showed Hex Ten and Heinous battling a mysterious black robot.

"The thieves, who seized 500 kilograms of refractium earlier today, were disguised as characters from *Cobalt Laser*, a cartoon series that hasn't been in circulation for decades."

Dan dug his fingers into the back of the couch. "Don't tell me that mad scientist built Hex Ten and Heinous, too!"

"Yeah," David said. "And they're not just content to try to kidnap me and the Lasers anymore. They're committing robberies now!"

Dan's head spun so fast his neck cracked. "Wait a minute, what did you just say? How much do you know about this?"

"Uh, nothing." David busied himself, picking the toys off the floor.

Silver kicked his feet onto the coffee table and leaned back. "No use trying to hide it anymore," he said. "Dr. Smalls sent Hex, Heinous, and Irk to attack us a couple days ago. But it was no big deal. I handled the situation, no problem."

Dan and Melinda locked onto Silver. Dan puffed up, ready to burst. Melinda held her hands over her mouth.

Cobalt drew his arms and legs together, trying to disappear into the couch cushions.

Dan held his temples and made a few trips around the room. He stopped, shuddered, then towered over David and his toys, rubbing his silk handkerchief.

"Okay, let me get this straight. Sometime in the last week or so, this nutcase built Hex, Heinous, and Irk, you knew about it, they tried to kill you, and you didn't say anything?"

Silver couldn't understand why Dan was so upset. He said he'd handled the situation.

Cobalt sat stock still, confining himself to a tiny corner of the couch. Silver stretched out, occupying the rest of it. Crimson curled up on the floor and hugged Plush Crimson.

David held his hands up. "We think they were trying to kidnap us, not kill us, but…"

Dan glared at him.

David dropped his hands. "Yes."

Crimson locked eyes with Plush Crimson as she spoke. "Actually, he would've just built Hex and Heinous. Irk was Dr. Smalls's first experiment. He was already in the lab when we were brought to life."

David reeled. "What?" He looked at his dad, wide-eyed. "I swear, this is the first I'm hearing of this!"

Silver's stomach turned. He still didn't understand what the big deal was, but David's fear was contagious. Like he said, he could handle the villains. That made it okay, right?

Dan shook his hands over his head. "Okay, great," he said. He snapped them against his sides. "Before we go any further, does anyone else have any secrets that need to come out?"

Silver looked at Crimson. Crimson looked at Silver. Crimson and Silver looked at Cobalt. Cobalt looked at the TV, unblinking. Silver wished he'd speak up. When people started panicking, Cobalt was supposed to say something heroic and confident and quell all the fear.

Christine put her hand to her chin and scrutinized the footage. "Who's the huge black robot, though? It looks like it fights Hex and Heinous in the beginning."

Dan furrowed his brow. "I don't recognize it. It's not one of my characters, not even from a discarded draft." He took a breath and scanned the room. "There's no other option. I'm calling the police."

David jumped to his feet. "Dad! No!"

The toys fell out of his lap and scattered across the floor. He folded his hands, pleading with his father. "They'll take Cobalt, Crimson, and Silver away! That's why I didn't tell you about Hex Ten!"

Silver's processor began to race. He'd fight Hex Ten and Heinous again tomorrow if he had to, but *Flashing Blades* wouldn't give him his home and family back. If two hundred turbines today weren't enough, he'd make three hundred tomorrow. But his life was out of his hands now, and no amount of hard work would change that.

Dan swallowed. "What do you suggest we do, then?"

Christine spoke up. "Well, they've made their presence known. The police will be hunting for them. Is there anything we could really add to the investigation?"

"I could leave an anonymous tip about Dr. Smalls," David said. "That's who they need to be looking for anyway, not us or the Lasers!"

Dan knelt in front of the couch. His mouth drooped as he studied the robots. "You're right. I can't risk turning them in, but we're getting in over our heads. They'll connect us sooner or later, and what's to stop someone from the factory from putting two and two together?"

Melinda ran her hand through Crimson's hair. "Maybe we deal with that if it happens," she said. Her other hand reached out, patting Cobalt on the knee. "I can't bear the thought of what might happen to these innocent kids."

David pointed at himself. "I'll bear the blame if anyone does report us."

Christine put a hand on David's shoulder. "You're also forgetting that I have access to one of the best legal teams in the world. Let me get their input before you do anything, Dad."

Dan sat on the edge of the coffee table. His features softened. "That sounds like our best option."

Silver still didn't fully understand, but things seemed more hopeful now. He jumped off the couch and wrapped his arms around his creator.

"Don't worry," Dan told him, patting the back of his head. "We're here. Right here beside you."

SERIES: Cobalt Laser SEASON 1, EPISODE 11

"A Stitch in Time" TIMESTAMP: 19:22

COBALT SMILED CONFIDENTLY, DESPITE being cornered against the wall of a weapons factory on Nebimus III. Hex Ten took one more menacing step toward him.

"You almost got me this time, Hex!" Cobalt said.

"Almost?" Hex laughed confidently. "There is no escape for you, now!"

"Almost, Hex. You forgot one thing." Cobalt pointed at something over Hex's head. "Next time, watch where you're standing."

Hex glanced around, then up. He stood directly underneath a load of depleted uranium, suspended from the ceiling by chains. His eyes widened.

Cobalt planted his feet. "*Perfect Punch*!" He blasted the chains, and the pallet broke free. The stack of metal rods rained down, burying Hex under their weight.

Hex clawed at the pile of dense matter on top of him. "I'll get you next time, Cobalt Laser!"

SEASON 1 EPISODE 12

"This Won't Hurt... Much"
TIMESTAMP: 19:51

"*Perfect Punch*!" Cobalt shouted.

He blasted the missile before Hex could launch it.

Furious, Hex screamed from inside the fireball. "I'll get you next time, Cobalt Laser!"

SEASON 1, EPISODE 13

"Who Needs Enemies?"
TIMESTAMP: 18:44

"*Perfect Punch*!"

SEASON 1, EPISODE 14

"Coffee, Anyone?"
TIMESTAMP: 19:15

"*Perfect Punch*!"

SEASON 1, EPISODE 15

"For Such a Time as This"
TIMESTAMP: 21:19

"I'll get you next time, Cobalt Laser!"

CHAPTER 21

Back in the garage, Irk waited. He desperately needed to talk to Hex, but he'd been in his private room ever since they returned to the hideout. At long last, Hex came down the stairs and walked through the room as if it was another routine day.

Irk dashed over to him.

"Hex! What have you done?" He struggled to keep his voice down. He looked around the room, ensuring they were alone. Andrew was upstairs, running tests on the refractium specimen. Heinous was in the fabricator, undergoing extensive repairs.

The side of Hex's mouth curled in a sadistic grin. He whispered back. "What does it appear that I've done?"

"It looks like you tricked me into building a weapon to clobber Heinous so you could swoop in and save the mission!"

"You are a perceptive little bug, then."

Irk held his head in his hands and bounced nervously. "Do you realize how much trouble I'll be in if the boss finds out? He and Heinous will both want to kill me!"

Hex chuckled and nodded. "Of course. Do you realize how much incentive you now have to keep this between us?"

Irk wrapped his arms around his stomach. "I thought you were trying to be my friend." He turned away from the monster, hunching over.

Hex gave Irk a condescending smile. "Friendship is a concept I find hard to grasp," he said. "But if it makes you feel better, I can honestly say that I appreciate your effort."

Hex turned toward the door. He sensed someone approaching several seconds before Irk heard anything. Heinous entered, looking like he had a lot to say. Ninety minutes in the fabricator had him looking good as new. It had also given him time to contemplate the day's events.

Irk huffed. He needed more time with Hex, but the big jerk kept him waiting and now it was too late. It was on purpose, Irk knew it. He stamped his foot. He tried to growl, but it came out more like a squeak. No one noticed.

Heinous marched up to Hex and stuck one compound eye in his face. Hex watched his own reflection in several of the glimmering surfaces as they took turns focusing on him.

Heinous hissed. "What did you do out there?"

Hex chose one of the eye surfaces and addressed it. "Against all odds, I neutralized the unexpected threat and retrieved the refractium." His features twisted into a hateful scowl. "I succeeded where you failed."

"Against all odds!" Heinous tensed all four arms. "You manipulated the odds! Who was in that walking tank, and how did you recruit them, you honorless traitor?"

Hex folded his arms and grunted. Then, with a swift motion, he reached for the bulbous eye stalk and caught it between his fingers. Heinous emitted a shout and clawed futilely at Hex's enormous hand. Hex gave the eye assembly a slight twist, and Heinous dropped to his knees. His voice trailed off into a high-pitched whine.

A low rumble emanated from Hex's throat. "I could make you spend the rest of the day in the fabricator."

Andrew came breezing into the room.

"Hey, hey, hey, no!" He held a pebble-sized chunk of refractium. "Bad robot! Bad! Don't make me get the spray bottle!" He walked past the quarreling giants without another glance and chose a scanning tool from a shelf on the other side of the room.

Hex released his grip. Heinous held his sore eye with two of his hands and crawled away, still on his knees.

"Good work out there, Hex," Andrew said. "I tend to agree with Heinous, though. There's something a little off about this morning's proceedings, but I'm not going to argue with results."

He put the crystal into the scanner and turned it on. He hit his forehead. "I forgot the entanglement generator."

That was apparently in the other corner of the room, in a drawer under a mess of cables. Irk rolled his eyes. He barely had a day to enjoy the clean new space before Andrew's organizational habits infiltrated it.

Andrew snapped the two pieces of the device together and watched the screen. "And while I'll warn you against taking actions that jeopardize future missions, I will admit this proves you are more resourceful than I initially gave you credit for."

Hex stood over Heinous and smiled haughtily. Heinous rose to his feet. His eye was apparently feeling well enough to glare back.

Andrew focused on the device as it took measurements. "Now that we've completed this little errand, The Organization has ordered us to return our attention to addressing the flaws in the Adaptive Personality."

The scanner beeped, prompting a smile from Andrew.

"Perfect." He turned his attention to the robots. "I would like to understand just how Cobalt and his little pals were able to override the behavior inhibitor. For that, I want a diagnostic dump from all three of them. Do you think you can handle that?"

Heinous touched his tender eye again. "We'll have to obtain the data by force. I would recommend we make a renewed attempt to capture them and bring them back here." He cast a suspicious glance at Hex. "Unless there's a reason to suspect that the mysterious fighter in the walking tank will interfere."

Hex waved his hand dismissively. "How would I know?"

"Indeed." Heinous's voice dripped with sarcasm.

Hex cocked his head and smiled. "You are wise to be cautious. But we needn't expose ourselves to unnecessary risk. I can obtain the data by stealth."

Heinous tensed his arms and thrust his head at Hex. "How?"

"You don't need to know. Give me two days. You will have the data."

Heinous stomped. "I will not stand for this!"

"Heinous, Heinous!" Andrew waved off the gangly cockroach. "Hey, listen. You're still my buddy. Let's see what Hex can do. If he doesn't deliver, you're up."

Heinous stepped back, glaring at Hex.

Andrew motioned for Heinous to follow him. "Come on. Help me out with this refractium sample. I don't want the fabricator occupied all day, reattaching pieces of you that shouldn't come off."

Heinous kept his eye on Hex a few more seconds before following Andrew out of the room.

Alone at last, Irk determined not to let Hex get away. He wrapped his hand around one of the giant's fingers and tugged.

"Hex?" he whispered.

Hex turned his attention to the little robot with a gaze that was less cold than the one he reserved for Heinous. He took his hand back, not abruptly, but not quite gently either.

Irk toyed with his fingers and looked at the floor. "One thing I don't understand. That exo-suit isn't autonomous. Who was driving it?"

"An old friend," Hex said. "Now if you want to survive, stop asking questions."

***

Hex Ten waited for Cobalt in his hiding place atop the stonework in the Epic Manufacturing courtyard. Although Hex was not one to appreciate beauty, he had to admit that if he was to lie in wait somewhere, he'd rather be here than in any of the places that wretched human, Dr. Smalls, had taken him.

Immediately to his left was a shallow pool of water. In this, several colorful creatures swam aimlessly around the edges. Hex tried to guess their purpose. They were ineffectively camouflaged for being confined to such a limited space. Their movements were random as far as he could tell, and they did not seem to be accomplishing any useful work. He decided to call them, "Pathetic Creatures that are no Match for Hex Ten."

Hex realized he used that name for a lot of things and wondered if he should start dividing the list into subcategories. He put this thought on hold when Cobalt approached.

Cobalt jumped off the cart and paced in front of it.

"Okay, Hex. You used me, and now the game's over." His eyes darted everywhere, and he couldn't decide what to do with his hands.

"I left the exo-suit where I found it. Take it back and leave me out of your plans from now on!"

Hex laughed. "Oh, no. Keep the exo-suit for now. I like this game. I'm not done playing, and neither are you."

"Forget it. I won't cooperate." Cobalt had kept his distance this time. He headed back to the cart.

Hex raised his voice in a haunting sing-song tone. "And what will Dan Epic say when he finds you willingly helped me?" He dipped a fingertip into the pool, and to his delight, the colorful creatures scattered in terror. "More importantly, what will your brother and sister think?"

Cobalt stopped, mid-step. Hex chuckled.

Cobalt sliced the air with his hand. "They'll never find out!" His voice cracked. "I don't have to tell them!"

Hex shrugged. "It's your secret, not mine." He shook the water from his finger. "I could broadcast it at any time. Better yet, I could grab you right now, drag you into that building, and announce you have a confession to make." He smiled broadly at Cobalt. "I would love that."

Cobalt balled his fists. "You got what you wanted. Just leave me alone!"

Hex rolled over and planted his feet on the grass.

"I got some of what I wanted. I want more." He leaned toward Cobalt and beckoned to him. "Out among the stars, you defeated me again and again, but in this world the rules are different. It's your turn to experience the humiliation. You will be stuck in an endless cycle, betraying your family to keep your secret, again and again."

Cobalt fell to his knees and pleaded. "Please."

Hex's eyes nearly sparkled. "Ha! I like that! Let's make it a regular part of these meetings." He transformed the joyful expression into a cold stare, which he drilled into Cobalt's soul. "No, Cobalt Laser. I will not let you escape. This is my *Perfect Punch*."

Cobalt dug into the grass and twisted off handfuls of the green blades.

Hex tossed a small electronic device in front of him. "And this is my next assignment for you. It should be much easier than the last one. Pick it up."

Woodenly, Cobalt complied. He looked to Hex for further instructions.

"It is a data collection module. It will give the good Doctor some insight as to what is happening in that head of yours. Hold it to your temple and activate it."

Cobalt looked into the scanning end of the device and hesitated.

Hex scanned the courtyard, shifting impatiently. "I just told you I have long term plans to torment you. This will not grant you the relief of a premature end."

Cobalt closed his eyes and did as he was told. It caused a fluttering sensation in his head that lasted a couple of seconds. Cobalt waited a bit longer before opening his eyes. He presented the device to Hex.

Hex held up his hand. "Ah, no. You need to repeat this procedure on your siblings. It should be simple if you wait until they're asleep."

Cobalt's eyes swelled. "What are you going to do to my brother and sister?"

Hex smiled. "Tell them your secret if you don't cooperate."

Cobalt dropped to his knees and begged. "Please don't make me do this," he whined.

"That's the best part of all this," Hex said. "I'm not making you do anything. I'm merely presenting you with a choice. It's up to you to determine which is harder: keeping up this double life, or admitting to it and facing the consequences."

Cobalt clutched the device and thrust it at Hex. "That's not a choice!" he said.

"Yes, it is," Hex insisted, stepping back. "I'm not going to release you. That's up to you."

Cobalt opened his hand and examined the device once more. He heaved a sigh and hung onto the dreaded object. He addressed Hex, no longer shuddering. "Fine," he said.

Hex had never played with a toy, but after pulling this puppet's strings he understood the appeal.

"I knew you'd make the sensible decision." He stood and surveyed the courtyard one more time. "I am done here. Complete the task tonight and bring the device here tomorrow. I will return." He headed toward his usual exit.

"Again and again."

"Watch out for those asteroids!" Cobalt pointed at the giant space rocks looming in the cockpit window.

Silver motioned at the viewport and rolled his eyes. "We're in an asteroid field. Did you think I was going to overlook them?"

Cobalt jumped into the seat on the opposite end of the cockpit. "Just keeping you on your toes!" He flipped a few switches and grabbed the joystick below the targeting viewscreen. "I'll handle the guns. Are those space pirates following us in?"

"Yep!" Silver hit some buttons on his console. "If they think they can outmaneuver me, they're about to be disappointed!"

A burst of static came through the intercom, followed by Crimson's voice. "Silver, what are you doing up there? The galley is shaking apart!"

"I'm trying to keep us from getting sliced up by space pirates, Crimson! I've got bigger concerns than apple pie right now!"

The camera cut to Crimson in the galley. As the *Teacup* pitched back and forth, plates and utensils fell from the shelves. Crimson darted around the ship's kitchen, catching the falling items and putting them back in place.

She ran back to the intercom panel and jammed the button. "Well, if you don't fly a little smoother, you'll have to replace all our dishes again!" A casserole pot threatened to slide off the countertop. Crimson lunged just in time to nudge it back into place. "And besides," she yelled back at the microphone, "it's not apple, it's boysenberry!"

"Ugh!" came the response. "What is boysenberry, anyway?"

Crimson spun on her heel and exploded into the intercom. "Nobody knows! You know that!"

CHAPTER 22

Christine descended the basement steps to find Crimson in front of the TV, watching herself hold the *Teacup's* galley together. She lay on her back with her feet in the air. Her head hung from the edge of the cushions, giving her an upside-down view of the screen.

"Mind if I sit with you?" Christine asked.

Crimson smiled back, paused the video, and set the remote on her belly. "Hi, Christine. Sure!" She patted the cushion beside her.

Christine hesitated to accept the invitation. They'd shared a very sweet moment, but some time had passed. While Crimson seemed eager to forgive and embrace her, Christine wasn't convinced she'd earned her place yet in that little silicon heart. She pointed at the screen. "I see you're watching... yourself?"

"I'm just getting some perspective."

"Does being upside-down help?" Christine sat beside her, right-side up, leaving one cushion between them.

"Maybe a little." Crimson somersaulted onto her feet. She hopped back onto the couch, this time planting her feet on the floor. "I only remember these episodes from my own point of view. It's helpful to see myself from the outside."

The impromptu acrobatic display teleported Christine to her teenage years. The little robot—she corrected herself—the quite tall, nearly adult robot had so much personality. How could she have ever mistaken this girl—her sister—for anything less? She fought a tear forming at the corner of her eye. "I imagine that feels pretty strange," she said.

"Yeah," Crimson said. "I also get to see what everyone else was doing at the time." She turned her attention to the screen. The paused image showed her sprawled on the floor, holding a coffee cup aloft that she narrowly saved from destruction. "I remember this. Those dishes were a real emergency to me at the time. I was genuinely furious at Silver for making it difficult. Now I realize I was just a clown for someone else's joke."

Christine set her hand on Crimson's. "This isn't your fault." She gave the polymer-coated fingers a pat. They were warm. "That was all scripted."

Crimson flipped her hand over and squeezed Christine's. "Still, it's like I said. I don't know where that girl ends and I begin." She pointed at the screen. "In my memories, this actually happened to me. This moment you see here helped make me who I am today."

Christine wondered what that must be like. Crimson actually remembered flying on a spaceship, and now she sat on a couch in her brother's living room. Sure, she spent most of her time in that ship's kitchen, but even so, she was on a space adventure! Surely that experience taught Crimson more than how to look after her brothers. They just had to discover how it manifested in this world.

She pressed, "And the system that made you pulled whatever it could from these cartoons and put it into you, right?"

"Exactly. Whatever it could." Crimson sank into the couch. "And in my case, that wasn't much. Silver became an expert at just about everything. Cobalt at least got strength and a confident attitude. All I got was the ability to annoy my brother."

Christine gave Crimson's hand a squeeze. "Hey, don't underestimate that! I've heard some of your comebacks. You have a quick wit."

That prompted a giggle from the depressed robot, and the smile stuck. Her mess of curly blonde hair draped over her eyes. That hair, which used to annoy Christine to no end, now warmed her heart. She tucked a few of the unruly curls behind Crimson's ears.

She handed Crimson the remote. "Can we see where this goes? It's been a long time, and I'm not sure I remember."

Crimson groaned. "This is so embarrassing." She resumed the video.

***

The camera cut back to Silver at the helm. He shouted into the intercom. "You wanna come up here and drive, Crimson?"

Cobalt paused from blasting asteroids to check the rear-view camera. Red text appeared under the image of a pirate starship, flashing the warning, "Approaching High Velocity!" He shouted across the cockpit. "They're on our tail!"

"Gotta go, Crimson!" Silver cut the intercom and took a long slurp from the juice box he'd left on the console. He grabbed the steering control and pulled back.

Outside the ship, the camera followed the *Teacup* as it pitched steeply, narrowly missing an asteroid. The pirates in pursuit were not so nimble and crashed into the giant space rock. The *Teacup* continued its path, executing a tight vertical loop.

Back inside the *Teacup*, Silver's juice box started to levitate. "Hey, come back here!" He grabbed at it and missed. He jabbed the intercom with his finger. "Better hang onto those dishes, Crimson! The artificial gravity can't keep up with the ship's movements!"

Back in the galley, Crimson watched in horror as every piece of diningware in the ship hovered overhead. One by one, they began to wiggle and fall. Crimson dashed from one end of the galley to the other, catching plates, cups, dishes, pots, pans, forks, spoons, and knives. In the end, she lay on her belly on the floor, with a plate between every pair of fingers, coffee mugs dangling from her pinkies, silverware between her teeth, and everything else stacked neatly on the floor around her.

Back in the cockpit, Silver pumped his fists in the air. "We made it!" Swiftly jerking the steering control, he pulled the *Teacup* out of the looping maneuver and returned the ship to its original course.

This last sudden lurch shifted the galley one more time, causing the cookie jar on top of the cupboard to wobble. It rolled to the edge, and then off. On its way down, it smacked the top of Crimson's head. There was a horrible clatter as everything in her hands hit the floor and shattered.

"Sillll-verrrr!"

***

Back on the couch, Crimson stopped the video. She curled into a ball and hid her face in Christine's shoulder.

"Oh, please." Her muffled voice groaned her embarrassment. "No more."

Christine nearly jumped. Had she been in Crimson's position, she might never be able to show such affection to someone who had been so cruel to her. She felt as if Crimson were giving something up and nearly pushed her away. But she took another look at the screen and realized—the two of them had taken very different paths to this point. Even if it didn't make sense to her, Crimson needed to forgive her. And if Christine wanted her sister to be happy, she'd have to let her. She took Crimson into her arms and squeezed tight.

The tears flowed, and as she blinked them away, she got a fresh view of the paused image of Crimson and the wrecked kitchen. Then, like a cookie jar to the head, it hit her.

Before she could say anything, a ringtone interrupted. This was one call she didn't want to miss. "Hello!"

***

Darlene scolded Christine from the other end of the call. "You are supposed to be on vacation."

Normally, she could see a mountain range through the glass wall in her private office, but today's rainy haze cut the view short. She pushed away from her desk and stretched her legs.

"So you can come back relaxed and refreshed. So I can keep my sanity."

Christine's voice projected from the phone on her desk. "I am on vacation! It's one of the happiest weeks of my life!"

Darlene set her feet on the floor. "People on vacation buy outfits, souvenirs, and fudge. In your case, maybe even a chateau or a small island. But no-one has ever relaxed while making large capital purchases of industrial machinery."

"It's a gift."

Darlene took another look at the price of the robotic fabricator advertised on her computer. "It looks more like a majority shareholder investment in a factory you swore you'd never tie yourself to, because going into business with your dad and brother was the last thing you ever wanted to do with your life." She paused for a breath. "Do I still have that memorized right?"

Christine's voice took a serious tone. "Darlene, something very big, very important has happened here, and you are the only person in the world I would ever trust with it."

"Okay, Christine. I'm listening."

"That file folder I sent you earlier. It's full of photos and videos. I want you to open it now."

Darlene scrolled through her messages. "Okay, here it is. I'm looking." She went through the photos first. They were certainly confusing. "Are you hanging out with *Cobalt Laser* cosplayers? That doesn't sound like the happiest week of your life."

"No. It's hard to explain, but these are the real Laser siblings, brought to life in robot form. One of the videos I sent makes it clearer. In fact, look at this." She switched the call to video.

Darlene pushed her glasses up her nose and shoved her face into the tiny screen. "Are you... cuddling with Crimson Laser?"

"Yes! Can you believe it?" Christine nudged Crimson. "Say hi to Darlene. She's my best friend and she helps me run my business."

Crimson waved. "Hi, Darlene!"

"Uh, hi... Crimson." Darlene shook her head. "What is going on over there?"

Christine nodded impatiently. "The video will explain. Right now, I need to focus on that fabricator."

"Ah, yes. The machine that costs twice as much as your personal residence. Which costs five times as much as my personal residence. And you want it delivered to Epic Manufacturing ASAP."

"Yes," Christine said. "How S is P?"

"I've been in touch with the people who build these things, and there is a working unit available two cities over. They say they can deliver the day after the funds are secured."

"Secure the funds today."

"Christine." Darlene closed her eyes, leaned back in her chair, and breathed into her hands. "It's my duty as your assistant to do what you ask. But it's my duty as your friend to point out that this sounds crazy. Ever since we were in school, the mere mention of Crimson Laser sent you into a raging fit."

Crimson squirmed.

Darlene noticed. "Oh, I'm sorry."

Crimson smiled bashfully. "It's okay. I know all about it."

Darlene collected herself and continued. "And now, in a matter of a week, you want to buy her a machine worth almost twice that factory's annual revenue so you can..." Her brow furrowed. "That's my other point. What is this machine for?"

"It's not just for Crimson," Christine said. "She, Cobalt, and Silver all need it. They're in danger. This fabricator will allow us to repair them and build the tools we need to defend them."

"Tools?" Darlene's eyebrows shot up. "As in, weapons?"

Christine cleared her throat. "Well, when you put it like that, yes."

"What have you gotten yourself into?"

"Darlene, thank you for being a good friend. Your concern convinces me that I'm in good hands. I don't blame you for thinking I'm crazy, and I thank you for being cautious."

"But?"

"Darlene, do you remember after high school, when we went our separate ways to college, what we said to each other?"

"Of course. We made a joke about you going on an Epic Adventure. Then we swore to each other that, if either of us was faced with an

Epic Adventure, we wouldn't take a single step without first inviting the other along. That's how I wound up here." Darlene motioned to the extravagant office around her.

Christine nodded. "That's right. Darlene, I'm letting you know that I am on the cusp of another adventure. The adventure of a life-time, and I am inviting you to join me."

Darlene swallowed. It was crazy, no doubt. But joining Christine on her business venture sounded crazy when they first talked about it years ago. Everything, ever, that changed the world sounded crazy the first time anyone dreamed it. She made her decision. "That day, we also agreed what we'd say when the other person accepted the invitation."

"And?"

"I'll be right there beside you."

"Thank you."

"There are only three hours left before close of business." Darlene set her phone down and put her hands on her keyboard. "I'd better get those funds secured."

CHAPTER 23

"Cobalt? Cobalt!"

"Huh?" Cobalt's daydreams dissolved, replaced by the image of Crimson's hand waving in his face.

"I said, did you have a good day?"

Cobalt's mind joined his body in David's apartment. Crimson withdrew her hand. He sat on the couch, staring into space. Crimson stood in front of him, with her smiling face in the center of that space.

Cobalt shook the cobwebs from his head. "Oh, yeah," he said. "Good enough."

It was only sort of a lie. Technically, considering he'd helped his nemesis commit a crime, it went as well as he could reasonably expect.

He tried to push the day's events out of his mind. If he let Crimson do the talking, he wouldn't have to think about it. "How about you?"

"Good enough," she echoed. She sat on the coffee table, opposite him. "I watched a whole bunch of episodes of our show. Christine watched with me. She taught me the word, 'surreal'. That's how it feels to see your life played out on a TV screen."

Cobalt chuckled. "I'll have to remember that, too. Things really changed between you and Christine, huh?"

"Yeah. I told her how it felt, the way I was being treated, and she realized we had a lot more in common than she thought." A cloud passed over her. "It hurt. Everything inside me wanted to run away, but I'm so glad I didn't. We needed to be honest with each other and push through the hurt. That's what made it better."

Cobalt squirmed. All this talk about honesty and facing difficulties made him uncomfortable. He forced a smile. "I'm so glad for you."

Crimson looked around the room. "Do you wanna do something? There are board games, video games, TV shows."

Cobalt thought about it. Seeing his sister emerge from her shell brightened his world. But the more he thought about how happy she was making him, the guiltier he felt. He didn't deserve to be happy.

"I think I need to get some rest," he said. "Maybe on the weekend?"

Crimson's face fell. Now Cobalt felt guilty about that, too.

"I'm sorry, Crimson." He looked in time to see David and Silver coming down the stairs. "Maybe Silver would like to do something?"

The look in Crimson's eyes told him that idea wasn't as appealing.

Silver planted his feet on the tile landing and strutted toward the couch. "I've already done plenty of somethings today," he crowed. "I'm ready to crash and do it all again tomorrow."

Cobalt buried his face in his hands. "Please, Silver," he whispered to himself.

David playfully scratched the back of Silver's head. "Aw, Silver, that's no fun," he said. "Work isn't everything." He sat beside Cobalt, opposite Crimson. "Would you like me to play a game with you?"

Cobalt watched his sister's reaction. That lifted her spirits. Cobalt silently thanked David in his heart.

David reached under the coffee table and pulled out a box. "This one works for two players. Let's take it into the kitchen so we don't disturb Sleeping Beauty over there."

"Yeah, yeah." Silver unwound his charging cable. "I appreciate your consideration."

David showed Cobalt the game box. "Last call, Cobalt. Want to join us?"

Cobalt was already halfway to his room. He shook his head and smiled weakly. "No. Thank you, though."

Cobalt went into his room and closed the door. His memory pathways buzzed contentedly as he recalled the day he claimed this room. It had been nice having his own private space. It was sparse, with minimal furniture, but he really didn't need much, and it allowed him to retreat from the others. Had that been a good thing? He imagined being around Silver all day. Yes, he made the right choice. Aboard the *Teacup*, they shared a room. How did they last so long without one of them blowing the other out an airlock?

He reached under the mattress and retrieved the device Hex gave him. He shut off the light and sat on the bed, examining it in the darkness. Now he had to wait for the house to get quiet. That would give him plenty of time to convince himself he wasn't hurting his siblings. The device didn't hurt him. It only pulled some data. And as long as he was around, he could ensure that Hex didn't use that data to hurt Crimson and Silver. Yes, it was going to be fine. He just needed to play Hex's game a little longer.

***

A little over an hour passed. Several times, Cobalt heard Crimson and David talking and laughing. He couldn't make out what they were saying, but they were usually interrupted by a bark from Silver, demanding quiet. Finally, the last cheerful word was spoken, the light under his door disappeared, and footsteps receded.

Cobalt waited a few more minutes before venturing into the living room. Silver lay in his usual spot on the fold-out bed, sound asleep. Carefully, Cobalt approached, wielding the data collector. Squinting in the darkness, he confirmed David's door was closed. He swept his eyes slowly across the room and sensed no other motion.

He stood by the bed and looked at Silver. Cobalt expected this to be easy, almost a revenge for Silver's behavior these last several days. But seeing his brother so vulnerable, Cobalt admitted what a terrible thought that was.

He grasped for another way out. He could lie to Hex. He could run away. He could fight. But every scenario turned out the same. His secret would be revealed and he'd have to bear the shame of everyone knowing what he did.

Just get it over with.

He held the device to Silver's temple and tapped the button. It blinked softly for a few seconds and stopped. Silver didn't seem to be affected at all.

No harm done. Hopefully. Oh, just forget it. It was done. No going back.

He turned his attention to the stairs. Crimson was up there, having claimed the bright red room that housed Christine's childhood. He navigated the darkness carefully.

No light or sound came from Crimson's room. Cobalt waited another minute to be sure, then cracked the door open. Sure enough, there she was, deep into sleep mode on top of the red sheets. Melinda had explained that her daytime clothes would stay nicer if she didn't wear them to bed, so she was dressed in something called a "nightie". If he thought Silver looked innocent in his sleep, this was going to kill him.

Cobalt ensured once again there was no other motion in Crimson's bedroom and crept close enough to collect the data. He tried to keep his eyes on the device, but he caught a glimpse of her peaceful expression and his stomach sank. Just minutes ago, she'd been laughing and enjoying herself. He could've been part of that. And right now, instead of facing this grim task, he could've been asleep with nothing on his conscience except the commitment to do a good job tomorrow.

But no, he had to be a hero.

He collected the data and closed the door behind him.

It was a sleepless night.

***

Yes. It was definitely a koi pond. Irk knelt at the edge of the stone pool. The rising sun glinted off the rippling water, and he leaned in close for a clearer view of the graceful creatures.

The koi that Inspector Princess showed him were crayon drawings, but the resemblance was unmistakable. The bright colors and the way they moved left no doubt in Irk's mind that these were real live koi.

The fish mesmerized Irk. They moved slowly, letting him view them from every angle. He wondered if they knew how nice they looked, and if they realized they were giving him a much-needed break from his troubles. "Good job, fishies," he whispered.

"Where's Hex?"

Irk jumped and snapped in the direction of the voice. The fish had done too good of a job.

"Um, hi, Cobalt," Irk said, stammering. "Hex, he... he sent me because he was busy. I actually wanted to talk to you, so I made him busy. That is, I made him busy so he would send me. I tricked Heinous into thinking Hex was… He needed to talk to Hex…"

The details disinterested Cobalt. He tossed the data collector, and it landed at Irk's feet. "Tell him I got what he wanted." He turned to leave.

Irk shouted after him. "Wait! Please!"

Cobalt stopped. "What?"

"Please take me with you!" Irk knelt by the edge of the pond and reached for Cobalt. "I promise I'll be good. You can lock me up like a prisoner if you want to. Just please take me away. I don't want to do this anymore."

Irk rehearsed this moment in his mind all morning. He expected Cobalt to gloat and make unreasonable demands, and Irk was prepared to agree to all of it. He'd imagined the worst names Cobalt could call him and the most humiliating punishments the Lasers could inflict on him, and all of them sounded like a warm hug compared to his life in the lab. However, Cobalt just stood there, unwilling to look him in the eye.

At last, Cobalt spoke. "I can't."

Of all the scenarios Irk predicted, this was not what he expected from the hero. "Why?" he asked.

Cobalt shrugged. "If I bring you home, my family is going to ask questions. I'll have to give answers. They'll find out about me and Hex."

"We'll come up with a story! I won't tell them anything!"

"No good," Cobalt muttered. "If you don't bring the data back to Hex, he'll tell on me."

Irk picked the data collector out of the grass and showed it to Cobalt. "This is only going to make it worse."

Cobalt pressed his hands to his head and paced. "Yeah, that's how traps work. I just need a little more time to figure a way out of this."

Irk begged. "Please. I won't ask anything from you. I just... I need things to change."

Cobalt was running out of patience. "You're a villain! You belong with Hex Ten and Heinous! Why do you want to leave?"

Irk slammed his tiny fists on the retaining wall. "It's not that simple in this world, Cobalt!" he squealed. "You know that by now! Good guys, bad guys... Here, everyone thinks they're the good guy!"

"I am a good guy!" Cobalt roared.

"Then be a hero!" Irk shot back. He sank to his knees. He'd drained his capacitors, and it would take a moment for them to recharge. He whispered, "Be my hero. Please."

Cobalt gripped the sides of his head and let out an agonized groan. "I want to!"

Now it was his turn to bottom out. His arms sagged. "But I can't," he said, wrinkling his eyes. "I can't be your hero and my family's hero at the same time."

Irk held the data collector, turning it over. It blinked at him. He could reason with it for hours if he wanted to, but no matter what he said to it or how hard he tried, it would only ever blink, blink, blink in return. Just like this conversation. "Huh," he mused. "I guess we all have good reasons for doing bad things."

Gritting his teeth, Cobalt spun around. He clenched his fists and trembled.

Irk flinched and clutched the device to his chest. A gust of wind played through the grass, causing the tender blades to flutter around Cobalt's feet.

The breeze relented, and everything seemed to drain from Cobalt. Still refusing to look Irk in the eye, he whispered over his shoulder, "I'm sorry."

Irk's stomach somersaulted. Time was up. He'd never get another chance like this. He scanned everything around him for ideas. Grass, trees, flowers. He scanned himself. Just a terrified little metal boy, carrying nothing but Cobalt's data collector and a tablet device hanging from his waist. He'd used it to navigate here. Of course! He pulled out the tablet.

"Wait, one last thing!" he said as he fiddled with it. "Here's where to find me." He showed a map to Cobalt. It highlighted a building, not far from Epic Manufacturing. "This is where Dr. Smalls and the rest of us are hiding."

Cobalt nodded. "I have to go now."

Irk watched his only hope leave. He slumped beside the koi pond. He put the tablet away and toyed with the data collector. After a bit, he turned his attention back to the fish. Timidly, he crawled toward the pond and dipped his fingers into the water. The fish retreated to the other side.

Irk frowned. Of course. His only friend in the world slept in the limbo of a canceled TV show, and his prospects of ever finding another, even a fish, were hopeless.

As he dwelt on that, the koi relaxed and decided that the fingers in the water were no threat. They widened their circles, drawing gradually closer. It wasn't long before they had the courage to nibble at the strange copper intrusions.

Irk giggled. "Thanks, guys. That makes me feel a little better."

Now it was Irk's turn to panic. He suddenly wondered how long he'd been out here. Hex warned him sternly to arrive moments before the transaction, complete it, and leave. He looked up, and to his horror, someone in the courtyard was watching him: A tall man, with swept-back gray hair, excellent posture, and hands tucked into the pockets of perfectly pressed slacks.

The fish retreated once more as Irk snatched his hand from the water. Holding the data collector close, he jumped off the other side of the retaining wall and ran as fast as his legs would go.

CHAPTER 24

Christine leaned on the back of the couch and looked down at Crimson. "Can I talk to you for a minute?"

Crimson tipped her head back and returned the gaze curiously. "Sure."

Christine beckoned to Silver. "Silver, you too. In the kitchen."

Silver narrowed his eyes. He hurried to follow. "Hey, if this is about that stupid plush toy, I didn't do anything to it. If she promises to stop teasing me, I'll give it back."

Christine raised her eyebrows. "You took her limited edition, Super Choco Flakes promotion, Crimson Laser doll?"

Silver froze. "No."

The mischievous little robot reminded Christine a lot of herself at that age. Now she understood why her parents often turned away, choking back laughter when they really should be angry with her. Christine fought the smile pulling at her own lips. Hard as it was, she needed to be stern out of fairness to Crimson. She folded her arms and waited for a confession.

He looked at the floor. "Well, when you put it like that, yes." He pointed at the cupboard. "It's in the blue casserole dish."

Christine stopped fighting her smile. "Thank you, Silver." She retrieved the doll and set it on the table. "Crimson, let's ease up on the teasing, okay?"

Crimson rolled her eyes and nodded.

"And Silver," Christine said, "if you can't take it, don't dish it out."

Silver folded his arms and huffed.

Christine gave him a pat on the head. "Now that the serious business is out of the way, here's what I really wanted to talk about. Do you two like science?"

Silver brightened. "Of course! That's what I'm all about!"

Crimson shrugged. "I suppose. I never really thought about it before."

Christine nodded. "Well, please give it some thought." She held the lid of the casserole in one hand and the dish in the other. "Because we're going to conduct a little experiment here that will require you to... Think fast!"

Christine threw the lid of the casserole like a frisbee, aiming for a point just above Crimson's right shoulder. Faster than Christine could see, Crimson's hand shot up to meet the projectile and snatched it out of the air. Christine smiled ecstatically.

Crimson clutched the plate, shaking all over. "What was that about?"

Christine felt bad upsetting her little sister like that, but she had to take her by complete surprise. "It worked!" she said, cheering. "Don't you see? You got that ability from your cartoon personality! You have the reflexes of a cat!"

Crimson frowned. "Okay, so I can catch dishes. So what?"

"I don't think you realize how unique this is!" Christine hefted the dish of the blue casserole and transferred it to her other hand. "Let me show you." She spun and flung it at Silver. "Catch!" It struck his armored chest plate and shattered. The pieces littered the tile around his feet.

Silver lifted his foot, avoiding the blue ceramic shards on the floor. "Oh. I see. When you said, 'catch,' you meant, 'right now.'"

Christine knew Silver would take it in stride, but she made a mental note that she owed him an apology. For now, this next part would make it up to him.

She took a stack of plates out of the cupboard and set them on the table in front of him. "Silver, I have a very important job for you, but there are a couple of rules." She put her hands on Silver's shoulders and got his undivided attention. "This is the only time I'm going to give you permission to do this, in the interests of science. I want you to throw these plates and try as hard as you can to hit your sister."

Crimson emitted a squeak and backed away, eyes wide.

"All right!" Silver yelled, snatching a plate off the stack. "This is the second-best day of my life!"

"Wait, wait, wait!" Christine said. "If you hit her... though I'm betting you won't... even once, we stop immediately, okay?"

"Okay!" he agreed enthusiastically. Christine was pretty sure he didn't absorb her instructions.

Silver wasted no time. The dishes were already flying before Christine managed to duck behind him. When she looked, Crimson had three dishes between the fingers of her right hand, one in her left hand, and a look of terror in her eyes.

"You're doing it, Crimson! You're doing it!"

A smile flashed briefly on her lips. It disappeared when another plate came flying. She caught that one too and set her face in determined concentration.

Silver exhausted the stack of plates in seconds. Christine was about to coach him into the next phase, but he was way ahead of her. Displaying a tremendous sense of initiative, he flung the cupboards open and unleashed the kitchen's full arsenal.

Christine directed her instructions to Crimson instead. "Don't worry about catching anything else. Just don't get hit!"

Cups, glasses, silverware, plastic, ceramic, glass, and metal bounced, bent, and shattered against every surface in the kitchen as Crimson dodged, flipped, and somersaulted, successfully avoiding every piece of ammunition Silver sent her way.

Silver bubbled with joy. "I love learning!" He was down to his last weapon. He showed it to Christine. "What's this thing?"

"A colander," she said, reflecting his contagious grin. She couldn't remember the last time she'd had so much fun.

"Neat!" He threw it.

Crimson flattened herself against the countertop. The perforated metal bowl missed her and struck the tile above the sink, cracking it and sending a piece flying. That piece landed on the floor, at the feet of a thoroughly distressed and dumbstruck David. Like another asteroid storm, the activity screeched to a halt. David, however, looked ready to unleash a new one.

He stretched his mouth taut and spread his arms to encompass the destruction. "What... what is this?"

The cupboards lay wide open, the entirety of their contents strewn across the floor, in the sink, on the counters, under the stove, on top of the refrigerator, and in the case of a hopelessly misshapen wire whisk, hanging from the light fixture. Most of the breakable items had pieces in multiple locations.

Silence reigned until Crimson sat up and something under her made a loud crunch. She addressed David cautiously. "Um... Science?" She smiled sweetly and swung her dangling feet.

David shook the cobwebs from his head. He pointed at his sister. "Are you the responsible adult here?"

Christine rolled her eyes. Kid siblings were so much more fun than adult ones. "Oh, come on David. I'll replace everything. Besides, when was the last time you used any of this? Mom feeds you every meal."

"That's not the point!" David ran his hand through his hair and twirled the other one aimlessly at the kitchen floor. "Who's going to clean this up?"

"We'll get it later. Don't ruin the mood." Christine gathered Crimson and Silver to her. "Experiment successful, you two! Bring it in!" Debris crunched under Crimson's and Silver's feet as they made their way across the floor. Christine planted a kiss on each of their foreheads. "Big kisses for good robots!"

"What? No!" David wagged his finger at them. "Bad... naughty robots! Very naughty robots, and naughty..." He bugged his eyes wildly at his sister. "...irresponsible adult!"

Christine handed Crimson her plush toy and stuck her nose in the air. "We don't need this kind of negativity right now. Let's go upstairs." She motioned to the two robots and led them out of the kitchen.

David grabbed his hair with both hands and blew through his lips. He took one final look at the destruction before following.

***

Cobalt squirmed in his chair and smiled back at Dan and Melinda Epic from across the kitchen table. His language module churned, searching for something to say, but so far it kept returning zero. On the other hand, his mood analyzer churned out nonstop responses to awkwardness. This was the third time he'd tried to stop kicking his legs.

Dan broke the silence for him. "Well, you're doing a good job," he said. "I just want you to know that your hard work is appreciated."

Cobalt nodded. "Thank you, sir."

He tried to remember just what got him into this conversation. He'd followed Crimson into the living room, who had something to say to Melinda. Then Melinda started talking to him, and Crimson disappeared without him noticing. Next thing he knew, he was alone with Melinda and Dan, being interrogated.

Well, not interrogated, really. It was a friendly conversation. Just very uncomfortable.

"You don't have to call me sir," Dan said.

Melinda patted Cobalt's hand. "Your sister calls me Mom. I would be very happy if you and Silver did the same."

Dan shifted uncomfortably. "You don't have to call me Dad either," he stammered. "I mean, you could. That would be fine. More than fine. But I expect you're not ready for that. No pressure."

Cobalt felt embarrassed for him. He'd rather have a frozen language module than a babbling one like Mr. Epic's.

Dan stopped talking and focused on something behind Cobalt. He breathed a sigh of relief and waved. "Hello!" He seemed to appreciate the interruption. Cobalt knew he did.

Cobalt turned around. Christine came up the stairs with Silver and Crimson in tow. A few seconds later, David joined them, in a daze.

Dan rebooted the conversation. "I'm glad you're here! I was just about to show Cobalt something, and it involves the two of you as well." He went into the other room.

Cobalt sat up. What could it be? He looked to Melinda, but she only smiled back pleasantly. He scanned the other faces in the room but received only shrugs in response.

Dan returned carrying a framed picture. "This has been hidden in a drawer for many, many years." He set it on the table.

The siblings huddled around the image. It was a pencil drawing of four cartoon robots, preserved under glass. Three mischievous looking boys, and a taller girl with an annoyed expression on her face.

"It's us!" Silver said.

He was right, of course. Someone had to say it, even if it was obvious. They didn't look exactly like their real counterparts, but it was readily apparent which one was Cobalt, Crimson, and Silver. A fourth, very familiar-looking, robot stood at the end of the line.

Dan pointed at the drawing. "This is the first concept sketch I ever did of the Laser siblings," he explained. "You popped into my mind, and I dropped what I was doing to put you on paper." He picked it up and headed toward the far wall.

"Melinda and I thought it would be appropriate to hang it here." He held it against the wall, positioning it beside two portraits of Christine and David as babies. He blinked back tears. "It's basically your baby picture, and we're..." The words caught in his throat.

Melinda put her hands on her husband's shoulders. "We want you to know that you're welcome here. This is your home, and from now on, we're going to be right there beside you."

Dan regained his composure. "I realize I've been very distant and unapproachable. I promise to change that. I don't expect you to warm up to me right away, and I don't blame you for taking your time. But please believe me when I say that I finally realize you are mine. You are all so special to me. And I..." He sighed deeply. "I love you."

Crimson wrapped her arms around Dan and Melinda and held them. "We love you too, Dad."

Cobalt's stomach dropped. He knew he should be happy. He'd have to pretend. They just agreed to love him without knowing what he'd done. When they found out, they'd surely take it back. He couldn't blame them. They thought they'd adopted a hero, but they got a villain instead. Now more than ever, he had to break Hex's hold on him and erase the evidence before it was too late.

Silver cleared his throat. "So, do you need hugs from us too?" He squirmed uneasily. "Because I kind of feel like Crimson covered it pretty well."

Cobalt shook his head at Silver and nudged him. How could he be so unappreciative? Unlike Cobalt, he had every reason to celebrate this moment. Silver shot back with a scowl and a shrug.

Melinda put a hand on each of their shoulders. "It's okay," she whispered, drawing them in. Cobalt wished people would stop giving him kindness he didn't deserve.

Crimson still held Dan's hand. He returned her smile.

Cobalt needed to change the subject. "So," he said, pointing at the pencil sketch, "who is the fourth one?"

It wasn't the right question. Cobalt knew who the fourth robot was, and he was sure Silver and Crimson did too. What he really wanted to know was why Irk was there.

Dan took the picture back. "Well, believe it or not, there were originally four Laser siblings: Blue, Red, Silver, and Gold." He pointed at each one in turn. "They would travel the galaxy, helping people in need and getting into the kinds of trouble only four unsupervised children with a spaceship and futuristic weapons could. But as we started writing the episodes, we decided it was too difficult to develop four protagonists. We moved Gold over to the villains' side to even things out. That's where Irk came from, and that's why he's so different from Hex Ten and Heinous."

Cobalt, Crimson, and Silver exchanged guilty looks. Though he didn't show it, Cobalt felt a gnawing pain inside, where his stomach would be if he had one. His siblings wouldn't know, but he was the guiltiest one of all.

SERIES: Cobalt Laser SEASON 1, EPISODE 3

"Green Thumb" TIMESTAMP: 7:19

THE HEAT AND HUMIDITY of the jungle planet was uncomfortable, even to a robot. Kneeling behind a curtain of vines, Cobalt stealthily pulled the vegetation aside. Peering into the valley below, he spied as Hex Ten carried out his plan to steal the rare flowering Philadodecahedron. Crimson and Silver crouched behind him, sharing the view.

At Hex's direction, Irk carefully used his right hand to freeze the flower.

Silver kept a wary eye on the villains. "Do you think he sees us?"

Cobalt crawled toward the edge of the drop-off. "Not a chance," he said. "Just stay quiet. I'm going to get a closer look." He grabbed a vine and started rappelling down the cliff.

Crimson reached toward him, whisper-yelling. "Cobalt, be careful!"

Cobalt winked at her. "Don't worry about me! Taking risks is part of being a hero!"

Hex clawed his gigantic fingers into the soil like a power shovel and pulled the frozen specimen out of the ground. He examined the stunning flower. Its petals gathered in a 12-sided figure nearly the size of his fist. Even through its ice coating, it glimmered in iridescent shades of red and blue.

Hex turned the frozen flower in his hand.

"Ah, yes," he crooned. "The Philadodecahedron is the galaxy's only source of Hypercube Nectar. Once I've refined it into Epicycloid Vapor, I'll have the fastest starship in the quadrant! No-one will be able to stop me!"

Hex spun and pointed at the dense foliage across the valley. "Not even you, Cobalt Laser!" He nodded at Heinous. "There! Attack!"

Heinous began weaving a bomb. Cobalt jumped out of his hiding place, growling. "How did you see me, Hex?"

Irk laughed, wiping his icy hand on the grass. "Hex Ten's translucent skin refracts light over a huge radius. He can sense motion and make out shapes in every direction, even around obstacles!"

Hex handed the flower to Irk and prepared to fight. "Nobody sneaks up on Hex Ten. Ever."

CHAPTER 25

Hex handed the data collector to Andrew. His plan had come together beautifully. "The diagnostics you requested, Doctor."

He'd done it entirely by the sharpness of his wit, without firing a single shot. As Andrew's fingers touched the device, Hex took a bow. Such a flawless performance demanded it.

Irk knelt on the table near Andrew's workstation. He moved out of the way as Andrew reached across.

Andrew raised an eyebrow. "Let's have a look."

He plugged the device into his terminal and downloaded its files. "This is it," he said as the readout scrolled across the screen. He threw his arms up and laughed. "This is the real thing!" He spun his chair to face Hex, giving him a congratulatory grin. "How did you do it?"

"I have a friend on the inside." Hex grinned back and spread his arms generously. The secret was too good to keep. He allowed a wicked smile to creep across his lips. "I have compromised Cobalt Laser himself."

Andrew leaned back in his chair, nearly lying flat. "Impressive. Very, very impressive."

Heinous clenched his claws. "Your dishonorable ways cannot prevail! When you finally fall, I will be the one who leads us to victory." His whole body shook.

Hex waved him off. Honor! Did Heinous even know what it meant? As far as Hex could tell, it was nothing more than some vague principle for him to appeal to when he was losing. "I have shown you my results. Show me yours."

Irk retreated to the other end of the table, away from the brewing conflict.

Heinous seethed. "You have only succeeded by sabotaging me!"

"I have succeeded by doing what you cannot."

Andrew paid no heed to the exchange. "I need one more thing." He tapped the data collector on the table. "I want to analyze the hardware that produces this data. That means getting one of the Laser siblings here in the lab." He brought the device to his mouth and addressed Hex slyly. "Do you think you could convince your friend to offer up his brother?"

Hex put one enormous hand to his chin. "I am uncertain. It may be a step too far. I could more likely bring Cobalt himself."

Andrew jumped off his chair and paced in an orbit around it. "You may not understand this, but I still think of Cobalt as a childhood hero. The thought of harming him just feels..." He twisted his arms in an exaggerated shrug. "...Distasteful. Silver Laser on the other hand, well, I think I'd enjoy seeing him regret a few of his choices."

He put his hands on the chair and cast a sideways glance at Hex. "If it helps, this doesn't need to be a stealthy operation. When I examine Silver Laser, it will be a postmortem analysis."

"Ah." That was much more to Hex's liking. He gave the doctor a broad smile as the concrete walls echoed with the cracking of his knuckles. "Then perhaps I can arrange something."

***

Dan Epic focused squarely ahead on the main building as he strolled through the sunlit courtyard. *Eyes forward, even pace. Don't let him suspect anything.*

It was just a bit earlier than when he walked through yesterday. If their meetings were regular, this would be his chance to find out what was going on between Irk and Cobalt.

The koi pond should be in view now. Don't turn your head. Just your eyes.

He thought he caught a glimpse of something, but it didn't seem to be Irk. He risked a longer glance. No Irk, but something was off about the retaining wall. It glistened. Like sapphire.

Something caught in Dan's chest, and he stopped.

Did he see you? Of course he saw you! Nobody sneaks up on Hex Ten. Ever.

Relax. He can sense motion, but he can't read your mind. Recover. Pretend to tie your shoe. Don't look. Whatever you do, don't look. Stand. Walk. Even pace. Eyes forward. Just keep going.

Dan got to the shadow of the main building before realizing he'd been holding his breath.

What has Cobalt gotten into?

***

Hex Ten would never have considered himself a patient person in the cartoon world, but this place had taught him the benefits of waiting. He spent so much time fruitlessly pursuing Cobalt Laser, armed only with the ideas that scriptwriters gave him—ideas that were doomed to fail. But now, after only a week to develop his own thoughts and actions, he proved he had been capable all along of defeating the hero.

He wondered what more time would teach him, and what possibilities lie ahead.

He sensed someone approaching. Keeping still, he pointed his eyes at the motion. It was not Cobalt. The time was still a few minutes early, and the vehicle that normally carried Cobalt was absent. Hex risked a closer look.

It was the human, Dan Epic. That fool was responsible for the cartoon prison of cyclical failure that defined Hex's past. Hex would love to have just a moment to tell the human what he thought of that silly little children's show before crushing the terrified creature into oblivion. But now was not the time. *Patience*, he reminded himself. *I'll get him next time*. And then he would savor the experience.

The human paused. Did it detect his presence? No. It did not look in his direction. It knelt and did something to its foot. These weak beings were always performing some self-maintenance of one kind or another. Hex sneered at its stupidity as it continued along its way, oblivious to the magnitude of power and intelligence that had allowed it to pass unharmed, not out of mercy, but out of convenience.

Shortly after the human left, Cobalt appeared as expected. Hex watched Cobalt dismount his vehicle and drag himself to the meeting place. Cobalt's young face bore the dread and anxiety, not only of what he had already done, but of discovering what new thing Hex had in store for him. Hex knew that his former tormentor would do anything to end these meetings. Anything, except reveal his secret. And that made Hex Ten feel wonderful.

"You did very well," Hex told Cobalt. "We have almost all the information we need. I have just one more favor to ask, and you can perform it now."

Cobalt drooped. "What? What do you want now?"

"Bring your brother Silver here."

Cobalt flinched. "What? Are you crazy? Do you know what will happen the moment he sees you?"

"He won't see me," Hex said. "I'll be perfectly hidden. He'll walk right past without noticing I'm even here." He smiled reassuringly. "He won't suspect a thing."

"Why do you need to see him?"

"Don't concern yourself with that."

Cobalt cringed. "Look Hex, I'm feeling... I don't know... dirty. If you wanted to humiliate me and make me miserable, you've done it. Okay? You won. I'll never be the same." He glanced back at Hex, winced, then dug his toe in the grass. His voice squeaked. "You defeated Cobalt Laser, and I have no will left to fight back ever again. Please just let me go."

Hex's chest swelled. Triumph! He wished he had time to gloat, but there was work to do. He towered over the miserable blue robot.

"I am very pleased to hear you say that, but I have made a commitment. I need your brother. Complete this one final task, and I will consider your debt forgiven."

Cobalt locked eyes with Hex. "One last time. You promise?" A glimmer of hope brightened his tired expression.

Hex couldn't wait to crush it. "After this, I will have taken all I want from you."

"And I just have to walk him past here? Nothing else?"

"That's all I ask."

Cobalt set his gaze across the courtyard. "Okay." He looked at Hex and nodded. "I'll be right back."

Hex waited for Cobalt to drive away, then crouched behind the retaining wall and growled contentedly to himself.

***

Cobalt approached Silver's workstation. "Hey, Silver! You got a minute?"

"Hang on." Silver put his thumb in the middle of a turbine blade and pushed until it made a satisfying click. "Alright! Fifty more and that makes a thousand!" He set it with the other completed pieces. "Yeah, now's the perfect time for a break. What's up?"

"There's something I want to show you. I..." Cobalt hesitated. Summoning his will, he feigned enthusiasm. "It's outside."

Silver shrugged. "Okay."

"Can I come too?"

Cobalt turned around. Crimson! She wore her original cartoon dress, the one from the day she entered this world. Cobalt stammered. "Oh, uh. Hi, Crimson. What are you doing here?"

"Christine brought me. We were bored at home, and she thought a trip to the factory would be educational." She shrugged. "So now I'm bored here. She's talking to David about that fabricator she bought."

Cobalt grasped for an excuse. "Sorry, Crimson. This was going to be just me and Silver."

Crimson's shoulders sagged. "Really? Come on, Cobalt."

Silver patted Cobalt on the shoulder. "Let me handle this." He faced Crimson and pressed his hands together. "Here's the thing, Crimson. This is boys only, because girls are gross."

Crimson folded her arms. "Christine says you shouldn't say things like that."

"Well, Christine isn't here, and even if she was, I'm not scared of her."

"She's right over there in David's office. I could tell her what you just said."

Silver palmed the side of his head. "Oh! Did I accidentally say girls are gross? I keep mixing that up. I thought we were talking about grills.

Grills are gross. Disgusting. Hard to clean. Girls are awesome, please don't say anything to Christine, and of course you can come along!"

He turned to Cobalt and shrugged. "Well, I tried."

Cobalt forced a smile. "It's fine, Crimson. No problem at all." His head buzzed. He hoped his nerves weren't showing. He thought Crimson and Silver were looking at him suspiciously, but hopefully that was in his head, too. "We're just going on a quick trip to see something interesting. Hop on the cart!"

CHAPTER 26

The moment Dan Epic entered the building, he broke into a run. Halfway to the elevator, one of his employees tried to flag him down.

"Hey, boss!"

"Excuse me, sorry," Dan said. "I can't right now. I've got... something."

The elevator moved far too slowly. As soon as the door opened enough, he turned sideways, forced himself into the hallway, and ran to his office.

Slamming the door behind him, he rushed to his window overlooking the courtyard and caught his breath. He got there just in time to see Cobalt arrive in the cart. He took note of the heaviness in Cobalt's steps as he approached the koi pond.

"What are you doing, Cobalt?" he whispered.

He weighed his options as Cobalt and Hex talked. He could confront Cobalt, but he might be accused of spying. He could plant a microphone in the spot and wait for their next conversation, but then he would actually be spying.

"If only I'd been reasonable," Dan said through the window. "If only I'd realized sooner what I was doing to you, this wouldn't have happened."

He needed to have a frank conversation with Cobalt. He only hoped Cobalt would trust him enough to believe Dan would forgive whatever he'd done. If only it would get him away from that monster, Dan would stand by him through anything.

Right now, Cobalt's safety was his primary concern. He watched for several tense minutes and heaved a sigh of relief when Cobalt finally withdrew and drove away. Hex Ten got back on his feet.

"That's right," Dan said. "Get away from my family and my factory."

To his dismay, though, the monstrous robot did not leave. Instead, Hex walked around the retaining wall and crouched.

Dan's flesh crawled. "What are you up to?"

He knew he had to do something. He wanted to intercept Cobalt now, but that meant letting this deadly intruder out of his sight. He could call the police, but would they arrive in time? What would he tell them? How could he prepare them to face a monster like Hex Ten?

Dan cursed himself, rubbing the handkerchief in his pocket. He knew he'd already wasted far too much time deciding. Finally, it occurred to him to call David and tell him to stop Cobalt, now. Keeping an eye on Hex, he reached for his phone.

But he was already too late. The cart returned with all three of the Lasers to the courtyard. It stopped just short of the koi pond, and they dismounted. Cobalt walked a few steps and motioned for Silver and Crimson to follow.

Dan tried to make sense of what he saw. Were all three of them in conversation with Hex Ten? No. If that was true, why was Hex hiding? That could only mean... oh, no.

The events unfolded a split second after Dan predicted them. Hex stayed hidden as Cobalt walked past, but the moment Silver stepped in front of the retaining wall, everything exploded.

Dan could only watch as Hex launched himself into the air. Two tons of metal, carbon, and raw hatred hung over Silver Laser, threatening to crush him into powder. Dan screamed. "No!" He threw himself at Silver to protect him, but the window stopped him more than 50 meters short.

To his astonishment, Crimson must have seen the incoming threat. She moved like lightning. Wrapping her arms around Silver, she spun on one foot and heaved the two of them out of the way. Hex landed where they had been standing, making a small crater in the grassy soil.

"Oh!" Dan held his hand to his chest. "Thank you, Crimson!"

Hex Ten struggled to his feet and howled with rage. Dan tried again to reach them through the glass. Finally coming to his senses, he pushed away from the window and bolted for the door.

***

Silver rolled Crimson off him. "What was that?" He turned and found himself staring into the eyes of Hex Ten. "Oh, boy." He scrambled, trying to get to his feet. *Flashing Blades* bristled around him.

Starting with the momentum from Silver's push, Crimson continued rolling to the side, kicked her legs into the air, and then flipped into a standing position, facing her enemy. Hex regarded her curiously, clearly surprised by this display of agility and confidence. He saw that confidence falter under his withering stare, and it made him smirk.

Cobalt's voice came from somewhere behind Silver. "Hex! What are you doing?"

"Taking what I came for!" He swung a massive fist at Silver.

Seeing the blow coming, Silver jumped back and brought his blades down on the stone-encrusted fingers. Sparks flew as he carved a shallow trough through one of Hex's knuckles.

Hex winced and withdrew his hand. "You'll pay for that!"

Immediately, Silver concocted the perfect comeback. He opened his mouth, but before he got the first word out, Crimson tackled him again.

He and his sister rolled across the grass. When they stopped this time, he ended on top of her. No sooner had he lifted his head, than the ground in front of him erupted in a blaze of glowing red shrapnel and flying dirt. He squeezed Crimson tightly and rolled her with him, away from the danger.

"Heinous!" Hex screamed in unbridled fury. "What are you doing here?"

Heinous sneered at Hex as he reloaded. "Ensuring you don't fail again!"

Silver scanned the courtyard. "Where's Cobalt?" he said.

Crimson flipped to her feet and searched. "I don't know!" She winced and held her arm. "Your blades are sharp!"

"Sorry, but that's kind of the idea." Silver tried to copy Crimson's flipping maneuver, but he just flopped into an even less dignified position on the ground. Embarrassed, he rose to his feet like an ordinary armored battle robot. "Did Cobalt abandon us?"

Crimson watched Hex and Heinous, wide-eyed. "I just hope he's safe." She tensed like a loaded spring. "What do we do?"

Hex Ten and Heinous seemed to have set their differences aside for the moment. Each of them turned a threatening glare toward the two frightened robots.

A shout echoed across the courtyard.

"Hey, you! Hands off my kids!"

The authoritative voice made even Hex Ten jump. All four robots looked in the direction of the echo to find Dan Epic bearing down on them like a homing torpedo.

Hex and Heinous looked at each other, stupefied at first, then amused. Hex let out a chuckle, which developed into a laugh. Heinous cocked his head. He aimed his weapons.

Crimson saw it coming. She bolted across the lawn, wrapped her body around Dan Epic, and tuck-and-rolled as the buzz of Heinous's bullets filled the air. Another shower of glowing plasma shredded the ground behind her.

Silver stood frozen as the scene unfolded. He watched Crimson pluck their dad out of the line of fire and narrowly escape the danger. It suddenly dawned on him how absolutely cool his big sister was, and this was the second time Dan—his dad—came to his rescue. He began to understand what it meant to be proud of someone other than himself.

Then, he understood how it felt to be hit by a train. Rather, he was pretty sure, because he guessed it felt a lot like taking the full force of Hex Ten's fist to the side of your body.

Silver was still busy figuring out what happened as he watched the scenery fly and spin around him. He felt himself hit the ground and bounce two, maybe three, times. When everything stopped moving, he thought he was waking from a nap. He was suddenly aware of a ringing in his ears. He heard Crimson shout his name, but it sounded like she was on the other side of a tunnel. He tried to move, but his right arm and leg wouldn't work. He looked to see what was wrong, and the view of his crushed side set his mind reeling.

That's when the pain registered. His eyes squeezed shut.

"Criiiim-sooon!" he wailed.

A shadow passed over him. In his still-confused mind, he thought it was Crimson coming to make everything better. He forced his eyes open.

It was not Crimson.

Hex Ten towered over him. Wearing a sadistic grin, he drew back one of his massive fists, aiming for the center of Silver's face.

Silver clawed frantically at the grass with his good arm, trying to drag his broken body away from the danger.

"It will stop hurting momentarily," Hex said in mock comfort.

Silver clenched his eyes to shut out the hovering fist and waited for it to crush him.

Right when he expected to die, the ground throbbed under him with the echo of an earth-shattering crash. When he dared to look, Hex was gone, replaced by the presence of a shining black robot.

"Crimson, get Silver out of here!"

It was Cobalt's voice, but where was it coming from? The huge black robot knelt and scooped Silver off the ground. Silver shrieked in agony as the movement shuffled his damaged parts.

"Sorry, buddy. No time to be gentle!"

The next thing Silver knew, he lay in the back of Cobalt's transport cart. Crimson ran to meet him.

Crimson gaped at the stranger. "Cobalt! Is that you?" she said. "How?"

The shiny robot spoke again with Cobalt's voice. "Yes, I'll explain later! Just go!"

In the distance, Hex lifted himself off the ground and rubbed his head. He zeroed in on Silver and raged. "He's getting away!"

Crimson gripped the steering wheel. Her eyes danced over the controls. "How do you make it go?"

Silver's head still swam, but he finally caught up with his surroundings. "Your foot." He groaned and pointed at the floorboard. "Use it to push that pedal."

Hex Ten scrambled to his feet. Crimson stomped on the brake.

Silver rolled over and let out an agonized groan. "The other pedal!"

Hex Ten ran toward them. Crimson lifted her foot and stomped again. The little cart lurched and launched itself across the lawn. Crimson screamed and reflexively removed her foot from the pedal. They stopped again, a few meters from where they started.

"No, no!" Silver shouted. "Keep going!"

He looked behind them. Hex was closing the distance. He got unsettlingly close before he fell to the ground, tackled by the black robot. The fog lifted from Silver's mind enough for him to realize Cobalt had the exo-suit from the news story, and he was fighting Hex with it. Silver was still too fuzzy to understand how that could be possible.

The cart lurched two more times before Crimson kept it moving. It took off toward the factory.

***

Cobalt pinned Hex to the ground. Hex roared as the cart got away with Silver. He thrashed like a madman and threw Cobalt off him.

Cobalt leapt to his feet and squared off with Hex.

Hex pulled his fists back. "I will annihilate you!" He threw them at Cobalt, one after the other.

Leveraging the protection of the exo-suit, Cobalt deflected every blow with his arms, then wrapped his own augmented hands around Hex's, holding him back.

The sudden hiss of Heinous's voice froze them both. "Enough!"

Cobalt faced him. Heinous held Dan Epic in his grip, with a pistol to his head.

"I have your human," Heinous said. "You will stop resisting, or it will die. I will take it with me. You will not follow, or it will die. Later, we will convey to you the terms of its release. You will comply with those terms, or it will die. Do you understand?"

Heinous's grip on Dan made it difficult to speak. "Cobalt, buddy," he gasped. "Go to your brother and sister. Go to David, Christine, and Melinda. They need you. Don't do what these guys say, no matter what they tell you they'll do to me!"

Heinous squeezed the human harder to stop more words from coming out of it.

Cobalt turned his attention from Heinous to Hex Ten, with whom he was still locked in a stalemate. "Hex, stop struggling and I'll let go."

Heinous grumbled. "Hex," he ordered. "Disengage."

Hex's eyes blazed. "This is my battle!" His voice was desperate, almost unhinged. "I will not be denied!"

"Disengage!"

With a roar, Hex swung his arms and broke Cobalt's grip. He backed away, keeping an intense eye on his adversary.

Heinous watched Hex warily for a moment before addressing Cobalt.

"We will leave now. We will contact you soon with the terms of your surrender. On my honor, the human will remain safe as long as you do not defy me. Come, Hex Ten."

Hex took another step back, keeping an eye on Cobalt. "I defeated you! Remember, you said it yourself!"

Agitated, Heinous scanned the courtyard. "Hex, come!"

Hex thumped his chest. "You are broken, Cobalt Laser! You are destroyed! Your secret is laid bare, and you have revealed yourself! Your family knows you betrayed them!"

Heinous hissed. "Fool! Gloat if you must, but I will not jeopardize what little success I have managed to salvage from your failure! Time is up!" He clutched Dan Epic to himself and ran.

Hex seethed. Throwing his head back, he sent up a tremendous roar. He leveled his gaze at Cobalt, delivering one last vicious glare before moving off in pursuit of Heinous.

Cobalt watched until they were gone, then he surveyed the courtyard. He used to come here to escape his troubles, but now every rut, every tear in the once pristine turf told the story of his downfall. He had good reasons for the things he did. He'd tried so hard.

The koi cowered in a corner of their pool, slithering over each other in a cyclical struggle to be the one furthest from danger. One of the trees had fallen into the water. Cobalt tried to set it upright, but his weaponized hands only succeeded in severing the last couple roots it still had in the soil. Giving up, he tossed it aside.

All his hard work, all those sleepless nights, all the hiding and sneaking, and here he was. He wanted to be a hero. That left him with a secret. Protecting that put his family in danger, so he had to protect them too. But it was more than he could handle. Now Silver and Mr. Epic were in terrible danger, and the secret he'd buried under so many layers of deception shined like a beacon. All his good reasons abandoned him, leaving him alone with the bad things he'd done.

He turned toward the main factory and started walking. He went slowly. He was in no hurry to face the truth.

SERIES: Cobalt Laser SEASON 1, EPISODE 4

"Looking for Trouble" TIMESTAMP: 10:16

SILVER KICKED A PEBBLE. It bounced off the wall of the massive crater the Laser siblings found themselves in. "Hex Ten is always one step ahead of us!" he fussed.

Cobalt put his hand to his chin and swept his eyes back and forth. He scanned the floor of the freshly drilled hole on the isolated asteroid. "No doubt about it. Hex found another piece of the Epsilon Crystal here."

Crimson eyed the rim of the crater. "You don't suppose there's a Bloogsorbel here, do you?"

Silver rolled his eyes. "I swear, Crimson. You'll fall for anything! Bloogsorbels are a myth created by corporations to sell Bloogsorbel poison."

Crimson put her hands on her hips and retorted, "Then how do you explain that video?"

Silver gave her a condescending look. "That grainy footage of a guy in a rubber costume stomping on a cardboard city? Gee, I dunno."

"Guys!" Cobalt waved at his siblings. "Can we save this for later? We need to figure out where Hex is going to strike next."

"How?" Silver said. "He's holding all the cards!"

Cobalt picked a piece of paper off the ground. "Maybe not all the cards," he said.

Silver took it from Cobalt. "A punch card!" He read it aloud. "One starship wash and wax at Zed's, in the Fromax Nebula. Get five punches, and the sixth one's free!"

Crimson scrunched her face. "How will stealing a wash and wax from Hex Ten help us get the Epsilon Crystal?"

Cobalt pointed at the card. "Not that! Look, there are three punches in it! That means they spend a lot of time in the Fromax Nebula. That must be where their hideout is!"

Silver waved the card above his head. "So that's where we can find Hex Ten!"

Cobalt nodded at his brother. "Exactly!"

A deep roar echoed off the walls of the crater. The siblings trembled as the head of a giant lizard peeked over the rim.

Crimson screamed. "A Bloogsorbel!"

"To the *Teacup*!" Cobalt said, leading the way.

Silver looked over his shoulder as he chased Cobalt. "That's not a Bloogsorbel!"

Crimson hiked her skirt and ran faster. "Oh, yeah? Then what is it?"

Silver waved his arms. "I don't know! Some kind of giant monster! That doesn't automatically make it a Bloogsorbel!"

"You should've let me buy that poison on the last planet!"

"Yeah, right. You're gonna just put it in its mouth? It's not even a Bloogsorbel, anyway!"

"It is, too!"

Silver reached the *Teacup's* boarding ramp. "You can't just call every random giant lizard monster a Bloogsorbel!" He grabbed Crimson's wrist and pulled her into the ship. "That's not the way life works!"

***

In less than a minute, the *Teacup* was safely in orbit. Crimson set a slice of pie for each of her brothers on the bridge console.

Cobalt smiled at her. "Thanks, Crimson."

Silver punched a few commands into the guidance computer. "So, plot a course for the Fromax Nebula?"

"You know it!" Cobalt flicked the edge of the laminated card. "No more waiting and guessing! It's time to take the fight to Hex Ten!"

CHAPTER 27

CRIMSON ROCKETED THE CART through the garage door, narrowly missing a pylon as she swerved a little far to the left. Safe inside, she slammed on the brakes, eager to relinquish the driver's seat and forget she ever occupied it.

David waved at her from the fabricator platform. "Quick, get him up here!"

A high arch, a little taller than a person, rose from the low table where they were trying to put Silver. At the crest of this arch, four many-jointed arms radiated, each ending in a different tool. It looked like a robot octopus handyman. Well, half an octopus, really. A control console stood at about chest height, mounted at a corner of the fabricator.

Between Crimson, David, and Christine, and Silver helping as much as he could with his good leg, they got him into place. "He's heavy!" David grunted.

Christine carefully tucked Silver's mangled arm beside him. "That looks really bad," she said, fitting it into the fabricator's work area. Silver whimpered. Christine fought tears as she kissed his forehead. "I'm so sorry, little guy!"

David worked the control panel. "Unfortunately, Silver's the expert on this thing. It does have an auto-repair mode, though. Hopefully it's smart enough to figure out how to put him back together."

"It better be," Christine said, "or the people who sold it to us are going to need reassembling."

A schematic of Silver's body appeared on the screen as the fabricator's arms passed over, scanning. The arms withdrew, and parts of the schematic changed colors as it analyzed the pieces and determined which ones belonged where. Eventually, the colors stopped shifting and a timer appeared with an estimate of three hours, eighteen minutes. The arms set in motion once more.

One of the arms poked deep into the wreckage of Silver's right side. He yelped and twitched, wide-eyed.

Crimson's face mirrored his agony. "Oh, no!" She knelt by him and cradled his head in her arms. David and Christine rushed to her side.

"It's okay," Silver said. "I think it just numbed me." His eyes relaxed. "Yeah. That's a lot better." He smiled at her. "Thank you for saving my life. I love you. I'm sorry for all the mean things I said."

"It's alright." Crimson cupped his cheeks. "I love you too. Very much."

Silver closed his eyes and went into sleep mode while the fabricator got to work.

David brushed his hand through Crimson's hair, knocking loose a few clods of dirt. "Wow, look at you," he said. Her cartoon dress hung from her, tattered and covered in grass and dirt stains. Melinda had just washed it for her, but it was unlikely she'd ever wear it again.

Christine gripped David's shoulder and pointed at the door. "What about Hex Ten and Heinous?"

A chill shot through Crimson's network. She had been so focused on helping Silver, she completely forgot about the danger outside.

Just then, the delivery door opened to reveal the silhouette of something very big. Crimson, David, and Christine crowded together in front of Silver as it took a step toward them.

Crimson's shoulders loosened as she recognized the exo-suit. "It's Cobalt."

The front of the exo-suit opened and Cobalt stepped out. Crimson felt another chill as David and Christine left her side to join him. She gathered the ruined dress tighter around herself.

Christine pulled Cobalt into her arms. "Are they gone?" she asked. "We stopped watching once Crimson got Silver inside."

Cobalt looked away and blinked.

David stepped outside the door. "Wait a minute," he said, scanning the courtyard. "Where's Dad?"

Cobalt stared at the floor and whispered. "They got him. They took him hostage."

David grabbed Cobalt by the shoulders. "Hostage? Where?" He chased Cobalt's eyes until they stopped trying to escape. "What do they want?"

Cobalt squirmed in David's grip. "Heinous took him." He hid his hands behind his back and looked at the floor again. "He said he'd call soon to tell us."

Christine eased David's hands off Cobalt and wrapped her arms around him.

"Thank you for trying." She motioned to the exo-suit. "If you hadn't showed up, I don't think any of us would've survived this."

Cobalt set his chin on Christine's shoulder. He noticed Silver asleep on the fabricator bed and reached for him. "Silver."

Crimson stepped in front of him. "He's healing. It'll take some time." She wrapped her hand around Cobalt's and steeled herself. They all needed answers, though she was sure they wouldn't like them. "Cobalt, what happened out there?" She nodded toward the exo-suit. "And how did you get that?"

Cobalt followed her gaze to the walking tank. "I..." He turned back, looking up into his big sister's eyes once more. He trembled. "I have to tell you something."

***

"Bloop, bloop, bloop."

Plush Crimson hopped across the fabricator bed and planted a kiss on Silver's cheek. Silver looked back with sleepy eyes and smiled weakly.

Crimson pulled the doll away and set it in her lap. She'd cleaned up and changed into an oversized red shirt and leggings, which Melinda brought when Christine called to tell her what happened. She craned her neck, glimpsing the control panel. "Almost done. How are you feeling?"

"Exhausted," Silver said. "But I think everything's going to be okay."

"Good." Crimson ran her fingers over the top of his head. "Hey, Silver. I did a lot of thinking while you were out, and I want to apologize."

Silver would've leapt to his feet if his body weren't anesthetized. "You? Apologize?" he sputtered. "Whatever for? You saved my life out there! Three times!"

Crimson put her hand back in her lap. "We can be pretty mean to each other. I know it seems like it's all in fun, but I want it to change. If anything should happen to one of us, I don't want my last conversation with you to be a name-calling contest. I'm sorry for my part in it."

Silver groaned. "Oh, Crimson. You're killing me." He looked away. "I started that. And just about every other argument we've had. I don't really think girls are gross, by the way. I said that because I knew it would make Cobalt bring you along." He smiled bashfully. "And I'm so glad you were there."

Crimson petted her brother's cheek.

Silver pressed his face against her hand. "I know I need to change. You and everyone else have been telling me for days, but it's hard. How do I do it?"

"Well…" She sat Plush Crimson on the floor and put Action Figure Silver in the doll's lap. "I figured maybe the next time one of us says something unkind, the other could say something to call out the behavior. Then we both agree to stop without getting defensive or trying to even the score."

"Oh, yeah!" Silver looked into space, his imagination in high gear. "Like a code word. I always thought 'chartreuse' would make a good one. Can we use that?"

Crimson shrugged, smiling. "Maybe, but I was thinking more along the lines of saying, 'That wasn't a very nice thing to say,' and then the other person says, 'You're right, I'm sorry,' and comes up with something kind to say instead."

Silver gave it some thought. "Huh. The direct approach. Yeah, I suppose that works too."

The fabricator chimed and retracted its arms.

Silver groaned and stretched. It took some coaxing to get his rebuilt body parts to respond, but within a minute he was sitting on the edge of the fabricator and flexing his knees back and forth.

David entered the room, followed by Christine and Melinda. "Looks like the timer was right on!" Silver was the glad recipient of many hugs and kisses.

Once he had his personal space back, he waved across the room. "Hey, Cobalt. Come on over."

Cobalt sat with his back to everyone. Silver hadn't seen him move since he woke, and that wasn't changing now. Silver tried again. "Please? I want to talk. We need to."

Cobalt moved, but only to shrink even further.

Silver turned to Crimson. Cobalt might have locked him out, but she stood a chance of getting through.

Crimson sat with her hand to her mouth. Then with a decisive nod, she picked up her doll and the Cobalt action figure and rushed across the room.

"Whatsa matter, Cobalt?" Plush Crimson said to her toy counterpart.

"I think I'm scared," the Cobalt toy said in a slightly deeper version of Crimson's voice. "I did something I really regret, and I don't think you could ever forgive me."

"I love you," Plush Crimson said. "And so does everyone else here. Yes, we were hurt, but we know you were, too. It's going to take all of us to make it better."

Silver joined Crimson, his limp improving with each step. "I was awful to you, Cobalt. You tried to tell me, but I kept ignoring you. If I had listened, maybe I could've been a better brother and friend. Instead, I pushed you toward Hex Ten."

Cobalt stirred, but he didn't turn around. "I made that decision myself." He slouched again. "It was stupid. He said this was a different world with different rules, and I fell for it."

Silver groaned. "It is a different world!" He put his hand on his brother's back. "And I helped stack it against you. And Cobalt, even after that you saved my life! Please forgive me."

"What about Mr. Epic?" Cobalt said. "He's in danger, thanks to me."

Melinda sat beside Cobalt and put an arm around him. "Wherever he is right now, I guarantee you he blames himself, not you. He knows he should have started to build a relationship with you sooner."

Cobalt turned his head. He pulled away from her just a little, but not enough to make her let go.

"I guarantee you right now, he loves you. And I love you." She took Cobalt's face in her hands. "The fact is, you're ours now. Nothing anyone does—including you—will ever change that."

Cobalt wrapped his arms around her. "Thank you... Mom."

Christine sat beside Melinda and put a reassuring hand on him. "We love you too, Cobalt. Don't we, David?" She craned her neck, looking for him. He stood by the fabricator, distractedly toying with its controls.

At the sound of his name, David's hand stopped and hovered over the interface panel. He drew a ragged breath and turned to face her. He set his mouth in a frown.

Christine's face fell. "David." She locked eyes with him and lowered her voice to a whisper. "Please."

David licked his lips and looked at the floor. He filled his lungs again and stood frozen with his mouth hanging open.

A ringtone interrupted the moment. "It's a call from Dad's phone," he said, forcing the lump out of his throat. He moved urgently, fumbling with his phone.

The ringtone abruptly stopped. No other sound took its place as David slowly lifted the speaker to his ear. "Hello? Dad?"

Silver listened intently. He couldn't make out any words, but the voice on the other end was unmistakably Dr. Smalls.

David gasped. He raised his voice. "What have you done with him?" Apparently the response touched a nerve. He gritted his teeth. "You can stop with the jokes! We won't..." He stopped and listened.

A barrage of words came from the other side of the conversation. The surprise in David's face gave way to anger again. "I..." The phone beeped. The call was over.

Melinda ran to David and grabbed him. "What did he say?"

"He's demanding an exchange." David jammed his phone back into his pocket. "Dad for Cobalt, Crimson, and Silver. He's going to send me a location, and we're supposed to meet there the day after tomorrow."

Melinda seethed. "Your father would never want us to agree to that."

Christine spoke up. "Even if we did, I wouldn't count on that creep to hold up his end of the deal. The day after tomorrow? He's obviously making preparations."

David clenched his fists. "What do we do about it?" His voice broke. "He's holding all the cards!"

Silver didn't know. He turned to the knot of people gathered around Cobalt, and wished one of them had stayed near enough to hold him.

A glimmer entered Cobalt's eye. Metal clunked against concrete as he leapt to his feet. Everyone jumped back, and a contagious energy crackled through the room. "No more waiting and guessing," he said, punching his fist into his palm. "It's time to take the fight to him! I know where their hideout is!"

This was the Cobalt Silver remembered. Now they were getting somewhere!

"Wow!" he said. "Don't tell me Hex was dumb enough to tell you!"

Cobalt bristled with determination. "No. I found out when I was talking to Irk. He..."

He stopped abruptly, deflating before their eyes. He continued, his voice heavy. "He wanted me to rescue him. And I told him no."

A loud slap made everyone jump. David had struck his palm against the side of the fabricator.

"More suffering." He put one hand on his hip and rubbed his eyes with the other. "You had to be a hero, didn't you, Cobalt? Was it worth it?"

Melinda shook. "David! Please! That's not fair!"

David turned on her. "Fair? Tell that to Dad! He's your husband! Don't you even care?"

His mother stood tall. "How dare you say such a thing! You know how much I love your father!"

David waved her off. "Sorry, sorry. I know. I shouldn't have said that. But Cobalt..." He looked up and groaned.

Cobalt cowered, tapping his fingertips together. His voice squeaked. "I'm sorry."

David hit the fabricator again and shouted. "Sorry won't..." He interrupted himself and turned his back. "Aagh!"

Christine fought tears. "David!"

Silver couldn't decide whether to watch David or Cobalt. David couldn't really be mad, could he? They could solve this, couldn't they? Crimson. Crimson could fix this. He turned to her, expectantly. She stood staring at David, mouth agape. Silver clutched his hands to himself, then ran to her and hid his eyes in her shirt.

Melinda pleaded with her son. "David, look what you're doing to them!"

David turned away from the astonished faces. "I..." He hit the fabricator one more time, not quite as hard. "I need some time." He spoke over his shoulder as he walked away. "I hope you realize what you've done, Cobalt. I hope... I hope you've learned something."

Silver reeled. Hopelessness hung like a dark curtain, but for a brief moment, Cobalt had ripped it open and filled the room with light. He'd barely gotten to taste that familiar feeling before the curtain snapped shut again, reminding him that such triumphs, though commonplace in his cartoon world, could only be wished for here.

Crimson led Cobalt to a crate against the wall. She sat on it and took him into her lap. "Cobalt, listen to me. Things are done getting worse. As of today, as of now, we start making them better, okay?"

Cobalt leaned his head against her shoulder. "I was so scared of letting you find out the truth. I was afraid it would hurt, and the only way to keep that from happening was to hide it. Hex Ten helped me keep the secret, but only so he could hurt me more. And then I wound up hurting other people."

Silver crept over and sat on the floor beside Crimson. She rested a hand on his head and spoke gently to her brothers.

"This is a scary world. Much scarier and more dangerous than the one we came from. I've spent a lot of time thinking about what we brought with us, and what we left behind. But there's one thing that no-one could ever take away from us, no matter how many worlds we travel through."

Silver snuggled tight against her, eager to know what bit of cartoon magic could survive in this place.

Crimson squeezed his hand. "And that's our promise to each other," she whispered.

The curtain opened. Just a crack, but the magic of this world is that it only takes a little light to wipe out a lot of darkness. "I'll be right there beside you," the three siblings said together.

Cobalt settled once more against his sister's shoulder. "Crimson?"

"Yes, Cobalt?"

"I can't cry."

"I know." Crimson held him, rocking on the crate. "It's okay."

CHAPTER 28

Andrew snatched a heavy wrench off a nearby table and hurled it at Hex Ten. "I wanted Silver Laser!"

The wrench traveled about a third of the distance and clattered harmlessly on the floor. Hex studied the spot where it landed. He considered handing it back to Andrew for a second try but decided against it, electing instead to keep a loose hand on Dan Epic. His former creator was now his prisoner. He grumbled at Andrew instead. "There were unforeseen circumstances."

Andrew let out an exasperated groan. "That is merely a symptom of poor planning! Even if you'd managed to get your hands on his pathetic sister, I could've done the analysis." He motioned at Dan Epic. "Instead, you brought me this!"

Heinous bowed slightly. "That was the result of my effort to salvage the situation," he said. "We have a hostage. We finally have something with which to negotiate."

Andrew sighed. "Alright. Good work, Heinous." He sneered at Hex as he stressed Heinous's name.

Hex growled back. Heinous was no genius. He only ever had one idea: to capture a hostage. He used the same formula over and over, just swapping the variables. Still, Hex had to admit, that formula worked for Heinous every time so far. And it drove him mad. Tension rippled through his servos, and he had to consciously reset them. *Next time*, he told himself. He wasn't really failing if he learned from every failure. He let the wave pass through and out of his body. All his planning and hard work would pay off soon.

Andrew plopped in front of his workstation. "We need to make the plan work this time, though. We can't afford another failed attempt."

He spun to face his hostage. "So, Mr. Epic. Welcome." He stared into Dan's steely eyes and waited for a response. His prisoner just stood there, staring him down and rubbing the gold-colored silk handkerchief in his pocket between his thumb and forefinger.

Andrew noticed. "That is a quality piece of silk."

Dan dropped his hand to his side. "It'll take more than a little small talk to make me let my guard down."

Andrew shrugged. "It's my understanding that you waltzed into the middle of a robot battle in slacks and loafers." He kicked his feet up onto a nearby console. "What exactly was the plan there? To get splattered on the ground and hope they slip in the puddle?"

Dan tensed, unblinking. "I don't expect you to understand what lengths a parent's love will drive them to."

Andrew rolled his eyes. "Oh, please. What I hear you saying right now is, 'I'm stupid, but I feel good about it.'"

Dan Epic ignored the insult. "How about you? What exactly is your plan in all this? Why bring my robots to life?"

Andrew leaned back. "Your robots specifically? Because I like them. I'm a huge fan."

"You'll excuse me if I don't accept the compliment."

Andrew smiled wryly and shook his head. "Robots in general? That's probably the answer you're looking for."

He eased himself into a standing position and paced. "A group of friends and I have big plans for humanity. But to accomplish that, we need to establish a world presence. With this technology, I can bring to life any character, fictional or otherwise, for anyone who wants it. Theoretically, with enough information, I could even bring back a deceased relative or famous ancestor."

Dan grimaced. "Do you and your friends ever consider the ethics of your actions?"

Andrew threw his hands up defensively. "Hey, I didn't say I wanted it myself! I'm merely willing to provide it." He snapped his arms to his sides, annoyed. "Look, can you save the questions and comments for the end of the presentation?"

Dan glared. Andrew resumed his pacing. "Anyway, this is just a means to an end. It's a unique service that only my organization and I can provide, and it's a sure inroad to all the living rooms in all the cities in all the nations all over the whole planet."

"I think I see where this is going," Dan said.

Hex recognized what was happening. Dr. Smalls was succumbing to the temptation to reveal his plan. He hid his interest, listening intently. The foolish scientist made two mistakes. Not only would the heroes know his plan, but his rival would as well.

Andrew raised a finger.

"Don't be too sure," he said. "That refractium specimen I acquired will ensure that no matter where on this planet my robots end up, I will have a direct line of communication with them. The nature of refractium ensures that no-one will be able to intercept or interfere with my commands, and each robot will contain such a minute amount that I'm confident we'll escape detection."

Dan's lip curled. "And when the time is right, you'll issue the command to enslave humanity."

Andrew smirked and rolled his eyes. "And, no. See, this is why I asked you to save the questions until the end." He returned to his chair and gave Dan a condescending look. "Why would I want a bunch of human slaves when I already have an army of robot ones? The idea here is to serve humanity, not enslave them."

Dan's brow furrowed.

Hex tensed. He composed himself, hopefully before he betrayed his surprise. He didn't think Andrew noticed. He had his attention fixed on his prisoner.

Andrew continued. "Over the ages, mankind has pursued world peace. It's a noble goal, but it's really dumb. People won't get along. Ever. No matter how hard they try. Read any history book. My organization is pursuing a more realistic goal: World order. When everyone has a robot babysitter, we can ensure they all play nicely. If you're willing to behave, you can hang out with your human friends. On the other hand, if you're a little grumpy today, you can stay inside and think about what it means to be a good citizen."

"It sounds like you're planning to keep everyone in a human zoo."

Andrew rested his chin on his hands.

"A human zoo. I hadn't thought of it that way before. I honestly hadn't." He pounded his armrest and perked up. "I'm bringing that up at the next meeting! They'll love it!"

Hex watched the prisoner's reaction. The creator pulled back, contorting its face. Human motives were still largely a mystery to him, but he did grasp Dan's apprehension about being on display, like the colorful creatures in the rock pool.

Andrew jumped off his chair and lectured with renewed vigor. "It's the perfect analogy! See, we're giving people the benefits of world peace, but in a sustainable package. They will live comfortably, in controlled environments, even when they're insufferable jerks. We'll still feed the wolves, tigers, alligators, and cobras of the world. We'll keep them healthy and safe. We'll just make sure they're behind glass and unable to touch the, I don't know, squirrels, and..." He waved his hands, trying to conjure words. "I can't think of any harmless things right now... whales and pandas."

Dan glowered. "And which category do you fall under?"

Andrew chuckled to himself. "Admittedly, it's a lot easier to be a good citizen when you're the one writing the definition, but such are the perks of being the salvation of the human race."

He turned his attention to Heinous. "Heinous, do me a favor. Put this exhibit in a controlled, comfortable environment. I'm thinking one of the windowless rooms in the basement."

Heinous rested a claw on Dan's other shoulder and guided him away from Hex. The pair headed to the stairwell in the garage.

Andrew shouted after them. "I'll feed you in an hour or so. You like sushi? I hope so. I've been in the mood for it all day, and I'd rather only order from one place."

Once they were out of sight, Andrew slapped his hands together and spun on his heel to address Hex and Irk. "And now for you two. That little stunt with the exo-suit backfired on you, didn't it?"

Irk darted behind a table leg and peeked out. "How did you know about that?"

Andrew knelt and pinched Irk's cheek. "You really are a child, aren't you?" Still looking at Irk, he yelled aside to Hex. "It's obvious whose idea that was." He leaned in close, prompting Irk to retreat to a further corner of the table. "And it's obvious he didn't build it himself."

Hex rumbled. He wanted Andrew to face him. Instead, the coward picked on a defenseless child. Not that Hex cared for Irk, but the more Andrew blamed Irk for the plan, the less credit it left for Hex. It was his plan, all his. And it was genius.

At last, Andrew stood and pointed at Hex. "Heinous was right about your fixation on short term solutions."

Hex sneered. The human knew what it was doing. Intimidate the child, insult him. He defended his actions. "That strategy put Cobalt Laser under my thumb. Without that, you never would have acquired the data you needed."

Andrew wagged his head and thew up his arms. "We could've taken it by force!" He hissed through his teeth. "Without gifting them a heavy weapons platform!"

"And then I would not have proven myself to Heinous!"

"Argh!" Andrew swung his arms and walked in a circle. "As if I care about that! And besides, how is that working out for you right now? You had Cobalt Laser in your clutches, and you fumbled your advantage completely!"

Hex's servos rippled again, and this time he did not reset them. He drew back his fist, roared, and surged toward Andrew. He knew what would happen, but he wanted to make a point. His rage-blinded brain went numb. He stopped, mid-step. His arm dropped to his side.

Andrew chuckled under his breath. "As long as you have those prohibitions, you can't lift a finger against me."

Andrew walked back to the table where Irk was cowering and knelt in front of him. He put a finger under the little robot's chin and forced him to meet his gaze. "As for you, you're going to hop back on that fabricator and make another exo-suit. One that stands a chance against the one you built for Cobalt Laser." The little robot trembled.

Without bothering to turn around, Andrew waved Hex off. "Get out of my hair for a while. I don't require anything from you right now beyond contemplating where you went wrong."

Hex pounded the floor with his fist. Fuming, he stomped up the stairs.

***

Irk knelt on the swivel chair and stretched his arm to reach the screen. He named each component as he pointed to it on the exo-suit schematic. "Booster rockets, shielding, and nanoenforced ceramic projectiles."

Andrew looked over the diagram. "The boosters are just a toy," he mused. "But the nanoceramic is a nice touch. If you could turn it against itself, could it crack its own shield?"

Irk nodded thoughtfully. He had to make this look good. "It would take a sustained burst, but yes. Not many materials can stand up to that type of ceramic, especially at those speeds."

"I want Cobalt's firepower to be useless against me. How would you accomplish that?"

Irk squinted at the screen. "I could angle the armor so it deflects the beads. He'd run out of ammunition before he could make a hole in it." Something pricked at his insides. He only wanted Andrew to believe he was doing his best, but at this rate, Cobalt Laser might actually not stand a chance.

Andrew spun Irk's chair to face him. "Suppose you were to do that." He stuck his nose in Irk's face. "Would Cobalt Laser still have any advantage over the improved version?"

The scientist's gaze intimidated Irk, but he steadily and confidently returned it. "No." He hoped all the questions were this easy. He could not lie to Andrew.

Andrew smirked. "Good boy." He raised his eyebrows and focused one eye on him. "Now tell me, Irk. You've been surprisingly cooperative. Do you intend to sabotage this exo-suit?"

Irk blinked. Of course Andrew saw right through him. Since Cobalt wasn't coming to his rescue, he'd hoped to rescue himself by ensuring his master's defeat when Cobalt came for Mr. Epic. But now he'd have to abandon his plan. He averted his eyes. "No." He sank into the chair. His prohibitions forced him to add, "Not anymore."

Andrew laughed and pushed the chair away. "You really do hate me now, don't you?"

Irk burrowed into the backrest and hugged himself. Inspector Princess taught him that hate was a strong word, but he wondered what she would say if she could see him now. Maybe she still wouldn't want him to hate Andrew, but she wouldn't stand for Andrew hating him, either. Andrew treated Irk like a tool—one that would produce just a little more work if he twisted that much harder. And it didn't stop there. Irk was also Andrew's toy. Ever since the cruel scientist discovered that his tool could experience pain, he found it immensely amusing. His favorite game became this balancing act, keeping Irk just across the line from a mental break.

It had been nearly a year since that game started, and Irk wished desperately for it to stop.

"Anything would be better than this," he said. "Why don't you just lock me in the basement with Mr. Epic?" Irk wasn't sure what his creator thought of him. He'd made Irk a villain, after all. Even so, Irk heard the man speak of his love for his children. Maybe mixed in with that love, there was some mercy in his heart for bad guys. Especially for one who would've given anything to join the good guys.

Andrew huffed. "Because I need you to finish this. I can put up with your whining as long as your prohibitions and directives force you to give me what I want." He stood over Irk and smiled maliciously. "But don't worry. I will get sick of it, and I'll be looking for a way to put you out of your misery, and mine. When this is done, I can wipe your memory once more, and you can start all over again."

Irk waved the scientist away. "You're a monster, Andrew." He twisted in the chair, making it spin to face the console. "Just let me get back to work."

The mysterious forces in his brain would compel him to complete the work no matter how much he hated it, so his own desires drove him to finish as quickly as possible.

Andrew patted Irk's cheek. Irk shook him off bitterly.

"Aw, you're growing up so fast."

CHAPTER 29

Melinda tiptoed into the office, where Crimson lay recovering on the couch.

"Hi, dear. How are you doing?" she asked.

Crimson rolled over to face her and lit up. "Better, I think." She stretched her hands and massaged her knuckles.

Melinda held out her hand and motioned to Crimson. "It's Silver's turn again. Guess what he's getting?"

Crimson placed her hand in Melinda's. "Those booster rockets. What a goofball." She winced as Melinda pressed her fingers against the palm of her own hand and stretched them back.

"Yep." Melinda relaxed Crimson's fingers for a moment before stretching them again. "It's just like him. He keeps saying that with those rockets, plus his blades, he'll basically be a living bullet."

Crimson laughed to herself. The conversation with Mom was refreshing. In the cartoon world, she only had Cobalt to confide in, and he would've egged Silver on. "Well, as long as it's not up to me to pull him loose if he gets himself stuck in something." Crimson wiggled her fingers. "Oh, that's much better." She gave Melinda her other hand.

"Cobalt's been practicing with the nanoceramic blaster. He calls it his new *Perfect Punch*."

Crimson tensed as the pain shot through her hand. A couple knuckles popped, and she relaxed. Silver exasperated her, but Cobalt made her worry. "I wish he could just use the exo-suit with its armor." She presented her right hand to Melinda again and asked bashfully, "Would you do that again, please? It feels really good."

Melinda smiled warmly and took Crimson's hand. "It's better not to trust it, considering who built it. Besides, it's awfully big and noisy to be using in a stealth mission." She chuckled. "Just listen to me! I guess I learned a thing or two working on those cartoons! I'll have dinner ready when you come back from your invasion, dear."

Crimson giggled. The door cracked and Christine poked her head in. "How are you doing?"

"Better!" Crimson sat up and smiled brightly.

"Good. Because I have a little surprise for you." Christine opened the door wide and lugged in a set of armor. "I snuck onto the fabricator between Cobalt's and Silver's upgrades. It's my own design."

Crimson knelt beside it and admired the brilliant red finish. "Wow!" She ran her finger over the crest on the breastplate. It depicted a golden lightning bolt superimposed on a dark red shield. "It's beautiful!"

Christine squatted on the floor beside her. "I have to admit, this gives me a whole new appreciation for the color red."

She set her hand beside Crimson's on the ruby-colored metal. "As adorable as that outfit looks on you, I don't think it's going to hold up in a firefight."

Crimson smiled. She pointed at the crest. "You gave me a superhero symbol!"

"Yeah, I actually commissioned that," Christine said. "Now, I'm not ready to claim I'm an artist, but my intent is for the shield to represent your desire to protect your family and other people in need. The lightning represents the little surprise you have in store."

Melinda joined her daughters on the floor and put her arms around them.

"When your father sees you in this, he's going to be so proud of both of you." She smiled at Crimson, then furrowed her brow. She turned to Christine. "While we're on the subject of battle readiness, what do we do about this?" She took a lock of Crimson's hair and stretched it over her eyes.

Crimson looked back at her through the strands and frowned. "Hmm. That's no good. I guess we should cut it?"

Christine bolted to her feet. "Over my dead body!" She marched out the door. "Give me five minutes!"

***

Silver walked around Crimson, viewing her from every angle. "What did you do to my sister?"

His mouth gaped. "You're pretty," he said in awe. "Like in the same way Vanessa was pretty."

Christine snapped a picture. "Darlene needs to see this."

"I like the hairstyle," Cobalt said. "What do you call it?"

"Pigtails!" Crimson shook her head, whipping them back and forth. "With titanium bands! It'll take a low-grade explosive to knock these loose!"

Silver pointed at the shiny accessories. "Ha! A blast to the side of your head might knock some sense into you!"

Crimson tensed and glared at her brother. She opened her mouth but caught herself before firing back. "Silver," she said, calmly but firmly. "That wasn't a very nice thing to say."

Silver squirmed sheepishly. "Sorry." He put on a grandiose air. "Please forgive me for slipping into old habits." He took a deep bow. "Your golden strands are as lovely as they are blast-resistant."

Crimson nodded graciously at her brother. "Thank you for saying so, Silver."

David spoke up. "Alright, it's time to get serious, everyone. You haven't had much time to practice with your new tools, but you know how they work, right?"

"Yep." Silver said. Crimson and Cobalt nodded.

Christine stepped up. "If this goes according to plan, you won't even need your weapons. Cobalt, you'll use your new millimeter radio vision to figure out which room they're keeping Dad in."

Her phone pinged. "Oh. By the way, Crimson, Darlene says you're the cutest thing she's ever seen." Ping. "And the way Silver was admiring you is super sweet."

David rolled his eyes. "Since we're coming at night and they're not expecting us until tomorrow, we're counting on everyone to be asleep, including Hex Ten. We're hoping and betting that his motion detection doesn't work while he's unconscious. That means you get in, find Dad, and get out."

Cobalt stepped forward. He spoke in a hoarse whisper. "What about Irk?"

David blinked at Cobalt and cleared his throat. His eyes shifted, and he locked them on Crimson instead. "If you find him, you can bring him with you."

Crimson shifted uncomfortably and glanced at Cobalt. David looked at the floor and hesitated. He composed himself and addressed Silver. "But remember, he still has those prohibitions and other rules you told us about. He might be forced to resist you."

Silver frowned and tried to direct the attention to Cobalt, too. David looked away uneasily.

Christine stepped forward. "Once we get Dad back, Dr. Smalls won't have anything to bargain with. At that point we can call in the authorities and force him to surrender." She looked Cobalt in the eye. "Then, we can make him turn Irk over too."

Cobalt allowed himself a half-smile and glanced away.

Melinda took Cobalt's, Silver's, and Crimson's hands into her own. "Thank you all so much for doing this. I love you so much, and I know Dan does, too." She brought their hands to her lips and kissed. "I believe in you. Now, bring your father home!"

David swiped on his phone. "Well, if there are any other questions, you have an hour and twenty-three minutes to ask them." He looked around the room.

"Six people," he said thoughtfully. "It'll be tight, but I guess we can take my car."

CHAPTER 30

Cobalt and David stood outside a poorly maintained garage deep in the city's industrial district. Melinda, Christine, Silver, and Crimson waited in the car behind them on the curb. Occasionally, headlights pierced the blackness and swept past, but so far everyone seemed to be ignoring them.

Cobalt's eyes glowed green as he used his new visual ability.

"It's taking me a minute to figure out exactly what I'm looking at," he said. "So far, this millimeter radio mode just looks like a bunch of shapes and colors dancing around." His brow furrowed. "I'm making out objects, but it's hard to tell exactly which ones are people. There's junk everywhere inside this building."

David stood beside him, hands in his pockets. "Hmm. Well, all I see is a blank wall." Another car passed. David glanced after it, watching until it disappeared. "As long as none of them are moving, I guess that means they're asleep."

Cobalt stared intently through the windowless wall. "Still, I want to know where everyone is. Asleep or not, I don't want to stumble into Hex Ten's lap." He took a step closer and looked down the inside of the wall, into the basement. Suddenly, out of the jumble of shapes and colors, one figure stood out. He pointed, bouncing on his toes. "There's a person in the basement, alone! That's got to be Dad..."

He caught himself. "Dan... Epic." He stopped bouncing. Hopefully David wasn't offended.

David bristled. He cleared his throat and drew a breath. "Good work."

On second thought, Cobalt wished David would speak his mind.

"I'm sorry, David." He toyed with his fingers and stared at his feet. "I promise I'll bring him back."

David put up a hand. "Not now, Cobalt. I don't want you distracted. Let's just get this done and we can talk later."

Cobalt's eyes returned to their normal blue color. "But it's distracting to know you're so upset with me. Please, David. I'm sorry." Even if David yelled at him, at least they could talk it through.

David pressed his lips together. He took Cobalt by the shoulders and turned him to face the building. "Not now."

Cobalt squirmed. Fine. If David wanted him to focus on the work, he'd do the best job he possibly could. He switched on the green glow and scanned the wall. "I think I'm getting the hang of this." He pointed at the upper story. "That's another human! It has to be Dr. Smalls." He turned his head to the right. "And in the next room, a huge robot!"

"Must be Hex Ten."

"And there's Heinous, and there's Irk. They're in the same room." Cobalt walked around the corner of the building and pointed at a spot two-thirds of the way down the next wall. "If Silver cuts a hole here, we'll be right next to the stairwell, and it'll be a clear shot to... um... Mr. Epic."

David nodded. "Alright. Keep an eye out for any movement and let the rest of us know if anything changes." He turned toward the car, addressing Cobalt over his shoulder. "I'm going to get the others now."

Cobalt dutifully watched the motionless shapes through the building's walls as he waited. He focused on Irk, in a room on the other side of the building, curled up in a tiny ball on the floor. Cobalt scanned the surrounding rooms, looking desperately for a way to snatch the little robot up and bring him to safety. Heinous rested less than three meters away. It looked impossible. Cobalt sank.

If only he hadn't turned his little brother away! Hex could make Cobalt's whole life miserable with just a few minutes a day. What could he do to Irk in the hours they spent confined in this building?

The appearance of Silver and Crimson at his side woke him from his thoughts.

David pointed at the wall. "Here, right?"

Cobalt's mind was still on Irk. It took a moment to remember the stairwell. At last he stuttered, "Yes, that's it." He shook his head and scanned the building again. No motion. "It's all clear. Go for it."

A wide grin spread across Silver's face as he deployed *Flashing Blades*. "I gotta admit, it feels good using these to wreck something again." He spun the wrist blades alternately on his left and right arms, cutting slices in the metal wall. In seconds he cut a portal, as quietly as tearing foil.

Cobalt stepped through the hole and scanned the interior of the building. Everything and everyone remained in place. He poked his head back through. "Okay, Silver and Crimson, come on. David, we'll meet you back at the car."

David looked past Cobalt into the darkness. "I wish I could come along."

Silver folded his blades and wedged himself between David and the hole. "You know the plan," he said. "The squishy people wait in the car while the bulletproof ones do the breaking and entering."

David tapped him on the nose. "Yeah, but all the bulletproof people are children. I don't want to let you guys out of my sight."

Crimson hugged him. "We'll be back."

Silver joined the hug. "Promise," he said.

Cobalt hugged himself. The thought of David being angry at him forever was too much to bear. Then another terrible thought occurred to him. What if Dan Epic was mad at him? Mom said he wouldn't be, but what if she was wrong? He hoped he could do this. He needed to. He had to set right what he'd put wrong.

Crimson and Silver ducked into the building, joining him. Their smiles shone at him in the green-tinted light. They waited—right there beside him. They kept their promise. Cobalt had broken his, but he swore on the spot it would never happen again. He still didn't know if he could do this, but maybe that wasn't the idea. They were going to do this—together. His smile stretched so much his cheeks hurt.

"Well?" Silver said, motioning to the stairs. "Lead the way, Cobalt."

***

Silently, Cobalt, Crimson, and Silver descended the stairs.

"It's so dark down here," Silver said, whispering.

Cobalt swept his gaze back and forth. "Don't worry. I can see everything plain as day." He scrunched his face. "I mean, if day was in clashing rainbow colors and walls looked like dirty glass."

"I want that too!" Silver said, whispering less quietly. "Next time, I'll get X-ray vision and you get booster rockets!"

"Millimeter radio, not X-ray," Cobalt said. "X-rays are dangerous."

"I love danger!" Silver said, coming unnervingly close to not whispering anymore.

Crimson hissed through her teeth. "Will you stop it! We'll all be in danger if you don't reroute the power from your mouth to your brain!"

Silver stuck his lip out at his sister. "Sounds like someone is slipping into old habits again," he teased. "It's okay. When you're ready to apologize, I'm ready to accept."

Crimson clenched her fists. Silver was beyond taxing her patience. His account was accruing interest charges and late fees. She hissed again. "Sillll-verrrr."

Silver smiled at her through half-closed eyes. He reduced his voice back to a whisper. "I'm kidding." He turned to Cobalt. "This is the door?" Cobalt nodded.

Silver slid a blade between the door and frame, slicing the deadbolt. He turned toward Crimson as he worked. "I love you." He mouthed the words silently.

Crimson folded her arms and rolled her eyes.

Silver opened the door and Cobalt and Crimson crept inside. The room appeared to have been a storage area at one time, but all it held now were a couple of shelving units. Dan Epic had made himself as comfortable as possible on one of the shelves and managed to fall asleep.

Gently, Cobalt put a hand over Dan's mouth. That was enough to stir him awake, and he began to struggle.

"Dad, it's us!" Crimson whispered. She and Cobalt put their faces in front of his.

Dan stopped struggling and stared back. It took him a moment to process what was happening, and another couple moments to believe it. He touched Cobalt's hand, and Cobalt removed it from his mouth. "How did you get here? How did you ever find me?"

"Never mind that now," Cobalt said. "Let's just get you out of here."

Silver pointed back the way they came. "I cut a hole in the wall. Just right up the stairs and we're out!"

Dan rose stiffly from the shelf. "We can't." He grimaced as he stretched his neck and arched his back. "There's no time to explain, but we need to find the refractium Hex stole. There's a big scheme going on here. If Dr. Smalls escapes with that specimen, nobody is safe."

Cobalt turned and scanned. "Let's see if I can find it," he mused. "A half-ton crystal, probably upstairs somewhere, and... Oh no."

Cobalt saw it through the wall moments before everyone else saw it darken the doorway.

Hex Ten stepped into the room, grinning maliciously. "What have we here?" He also kept his voice to a whisper.

"But you were asleep!" Cobalt said. "You can't sense motion while you're sleeping, can you?"

Hex chuckled. "Nobody sneaks up on Hex Ten. Ever." He blocked the exit with his massive body. "And I've added a new rule in this world. Hex Ten never sleeps. Ever. He lies very still, charges slowly, and never misses an opportunity." He rubbed his hands together. "I see you didn't bring the exo-suit I gave you. Very foolish. You might have stood a chance against me, but not now. It will be effortless to capture you all single-handedly and present you as my prisoners."

Hex knelt in front of the doorway and levelled his gaze at Cobalt. "By your own admission, I've already defeated you. You said you didn't have it in you to fight back, but here you are."

"Yes," Cobalt said, "but I'm not here to fight for myself." He put a hand to his chest. "I'm here to fight for the people I love."

Hex sneered. "I see."

Cobalt kept his eyes on his adversary while metal feet tapped the floor behind him. Silver and Crimson filed into position, backing him up.

Hex looked very satisfied with himself. "I've already shown that the villain can defeat the hero mentally. Now I get the pleasure of defeating the hero physically, as well." He cracked his knuckles. "I assure you the pain will be commensurate."

Cobalt flashed a cocky smile. "But you haven't defeated the hero."

Hex raised his eyebrows. "Your memory is short. Did you not just agree with me that I defeated you?"

"Oh, you defeated me all right." Cobalt pointed at himself. "I'll never be the same after betraying my family and giving in to your blackmail. That's going to stick with me for the rest of my life." He paused, holding up a single dramatic finger. "But you missed one crucial detail."

He stepped aside, revealing Crimson. She stood, feet planted firmly, hands extended, her index fingers pointing at Hex.

Cobalt motioned as if introducing her. "I'm not the only hero of this story."

"Hey, Hex," Crimson said.

Hex shifted his attention from Cobalt to her. He cocked his head, perplexed.

"Be careful."

Her fingertips lit up and a blue-white arc of electricity connected her to the metal monster. Lightning cascaded through and across Hex's body, seizing him. The strike lasted a few seconds. When it ended, Hex stood frozen, his face contorted in pain and astonishment. It seemed he'd stay that way, but then his massive body tipped ever so slightly. Like a felled tree he collapsed, hitting the floor face down with a thud.

Cobalt stared at the motionless villain and blinked.

Silver waved away a plume of smoke rising from the center of Hex's back. "Wow." He turned to his sister. "I'd just like to reiterate. I'm only kidding when I tease you. It's done out of love. I consider us to be on very good terms, and I hope you do too."

Dan stepped out from behind the shelves and admired the scene. "That was incredible, Crimson!" He glanced around the room. "And all of you! Let's find that refractium. Hopefully we haven't raised any more alarms."

Cobalt shook his head, returning to the task at hand. "Right." He scanned the floors above him. "No other movement. I guess they didn't hear that, surprisingly enough."

Meanwhile, Crimson stood quietly, staring at her hands. Smoke poured from her index fingers. The polymer skin had vaporized, revealing the underlying structure. A coating of soot covered that, along with dots here and there of metal that had melted, flowed, and re-solidified. Her eyes widened, big as old-fashioned data discs, and a scream worked its way through her chest and into her throat. It came out.

"Ooooooooooowwwwwwww!"

Cobalt saw three figures jolt and sit up. "Okay. That got their attention."

Silver put his hands on his hips and pouted at his sister. "Now who needs to reroute the power from their mouth to their brain?"

Crimson slapped him. Unfortunately, that hurt her hand more than his cheek. She reeled, struggling to suppress another scream. She tucked her injured hands under her arms and groaned.

Dan rushed to her side and put a hand on her shoulder. He gave Silver a stern look.

"Enough out of you, mister!" He pointed at Cobalt. "Go help your brother!" Returning his attention to Crimson, he held out his hand to her. Grimacing, she showed him her burned fingers. Dan took a deep breath. Pressing his lips together, he pulled the silk handkerchief out of his pocket. He rubbed it one last time before gritting his teeth and snagging it on the edge of the metal shelf, ripping it in two.

Silver backed away, rubbing his cheek and scowling. Turning around, he noticed the intensity in Cobalt's expression and bristled with vigilance.

Cobalt's eyes tracked across the ceiling as he watched something the rest of them couldn't see.

"Heinous is coming down the stairs!" He flexed his arms and they unfolded, revealing a cylindrical blaster on each forearm. He jumped over Hex's motionless body and out the door to meet the approaching threat. "*Perfect Punch!*"

Silver joined him in the hallway just in time to see Cobalt take aim and unleash a volley of nanoceramic scattershot in Heinous's direction.

Heinous saw him coming. Milliseconds before Cobalt fired, he folded in on himself, forming a shield over his body to absorb the shot. Some of it bounced off, leaving pinholes in the walls. Many of the beads embedded themselves in the thick metal plate protecting Heinous, but none of them penetrated it.

Heinous kept coming. He didn't dare to emerge from behind the shield, so he poked his guns at them from around the edges. Heinous couldn't see them, but if he sent enough bullets flying, he wouldn't need to aim accurately.

Cobalt looked at Silver, out of ideas. Silver's eyes darted all over Heinous, taking in the terrifying sight. Just as Cobalt was about to turn and run, Silver hunched over and closed his eyes. Blades bristled all over his body. He leaned in Heinous's direction, and the booster rockets on his back spun up.

"Aaaaaaaaaahhhh!" Silver let out a high-pitched squeal as he blasted down the hallway like a rocket-propelled pincushion. Heinous managed to get off a few shots before Silver plowed into him, but his bullets planted themselves harmlessly into the walls, ceiling, and floor. Silver, on the other hand, planted himself quite harmfully into Heinous. His blades lodged themselves into Heinous's shield, and Silver's rockets carried the two of them the rest of the way down the hall until a wall prevented them from going further. The building echoed with a crunch as cracks radiated from the point where Heinous made contact. The rockets shut down, and Heinous slumped to the floor with Silver still firmly attached.

Cobalt ran to check on his brother. "Silver! Are you okay?"

Silver had passed out. Carefully, Cobalt threaded his hand through the maze of blades and patted Silver's face. "Silver! Wake up!"

"Hmmm?" Silver opened his eyes. "Aaaaaahhh!" He struggled to get loose, but his blades were still firmly embedded in Heinous's shield.

"Fold your blades, Silver," Cobalt said. "Hey!" He squeezed Silver's cheeks. "Calm down. Fold your blades."

Silver snapped out of it and stopped struggling. Three forward-facing blades stuck in the shield. Silver folded the rest of them, and when it was apparent he wouldn't be able to dislodge those three, he detached them.

Cobalt lifted Silver off Heinous and held him until he got his legs back under him.

Silver looked at Heinous's motionless form. "I think I smooshed him," he said in a hoarse voice. The two halves of the shield parted. Heinous lay sprawled beneath it, but there was surprisingly little external damage. And, though a few centimeters of blade protruded through the interior of the shell, they did not seem to have touched the robot inside. That said, Heinous's jaw lay slack, and his compound eyes pointed in very different directions.

"He's probably okay," Cobalt said. "Maybe."

Crimson and Dan joined them. Crimson held her hands in front of her. Two tightly wrapped gold-colored bandages protected her injured fingers.

Cobalt looked at Crimson's hands and winced. "I won't ask you to do that again, but it was amazing!"

"Thanks," she said. "It's not just the burns, though. That really took a load out of my power cell. If I had to do it again, I don't think I'd have enough energy left to stay standing."

Seeing Dan made Cobalt remember the refractium. He turned on his millimeter vision and scanned again. "The refractium is upstairs, opposite the wall we came in."

He stood on his toes and evaluated something invisible to the rest of them. "Dr. Smalls is waiting for us. Irk is with him."

Crimson clenched her fists, at least as much as she could with the sore fingers. "Let's take the refractium and rescue Irk!"

Cobalt kept his eyes fixed on the far side of the building. "That's not all," he warned. "Andrew has an exo-suit. Similar to the one I had. Maybe bigger. He's ready for us."

"Let's face him together, then," Dan Epic said.

"Oh, no." Cobalt shook his head emphatically. "This is robots only."

"I won't leave you kids to do this alone!"

Cobalt tensed. "And I won't risk losing you! I spent my whole life searching for our creator, and I only just met you!" He looked at Dan through cloudy eyes. He blinked and a tear formed. It rolled down his cheek. "And then…" He choked. "And then, I almost got you killed!"

His body heaved with sobbing. "It was my fault! All of this was my fault!"

Dan clutched his hand to his chest. He rushed over to Cobalt, tears flowing down his cheeks. He wrapped his arms around the heartbroken young robot.

Crimson gaped at the scene. She turned to Silver. "How?"

Silver shrugged. "I don't know. When the fabricator worked on his eyes…" He shook his head. "Maybe something happened then?"

Dan held Cobalt and rocked him. "Listen to me, buddy. This is not your fault. You were bearing a load that many adults couldn't handle." He squeezed tighter. "You aren't just young, you're brand new in a strange place. And of all people, I should've been there for you. No, Cobalt. I'm the one who's sorry. And from now on, I will always, always be right there beside you. I love you, son."

Cobalt buried his face in Dan's chest. "I love you too, dad."

Crimson put her arms around Dan and Cobalt, and Silver joined her. "We can't wait any longer," she said. "Dad, at the top of the stairs, there's a hole in the wall. Go through that and to the right. You'll find the car with Mom, Christine, and David. Tell them what's going on and get help!"

SERIES: Cobalt Laser SEASON 1, EPISODE 5

"Out of Our Mind" TIMESTAMP: 12:17

THE BATTLE IN DEVULON City, whose skyline stretched into its planet's orbit, had taken a sinister turn. Cobalt Laser dashed across the roof of the skyscraper, ignoring Hex Ten and his accomplices. He skidded to a stop at the edge, where Crimson dangled precariously, high above the city. He extended a desperate hand to his sister. "Crimson!"

Too late. Crimson lost her grip and fell to the street below.

Heinous laughed. "That's one." He held up a claw. "Two remain."

Cobalt clenched his fists and screamed at the aggressors. "You'll pay for that!"

Silver peered over the ledge. "I think she's hurt, Cobalt!"

Cobalt set his jaw and planted his feet. "Go help her!" He focused his glowing eyes on the villains. "I'll take care of this."

Silver wrapped his arms around the building's outer structure and slid to the ground. Overhead, the zap of *Perfect Punch* told him Heinous was paying for his treachery.

It was a long ride to the street below. When he got there, he found Crimson on the sidewalk. Her impact left a dent in the pavement almost as deep as her body. She lay very still.

Silver fought back tears.

"Crimson!" She didn't respond. Cringing, he untucked the bottom of her blouse and opened a panel, exposing her internals. Sparks popped from a breach in one of her metallic organs. "Oh, no! Your power cell is cracked."

Crimson groaned weakly as Silver opened a panel on his chest and stretched a cable from it. He plugged the other end of the cable into Crimson's belly. With a jolt, she came back to life.

"What happened?" Moving only her eyes, she examined the crater she made.

Silver smiled and relaxed. "Your power cell was damaged. I'm sharing mine with you," he said. "I thought we were going to lose you, but..." He stopped. Something suddenly occurred to him. "Wait a minute. I'm sharing a power cell with my sister. Gross!"

Crimson scrunched her nose. "Yuck. Well, at least I'm still alive. Thank you." A puzzled look crossed her face. "Wait a minute. We're talking, but our lips aren't moving."

"Oh." Silver's voice was audible even though his mouth remained closed. "This connection not only shares power, but data. Our minds are linked, too."

"So," Crimson said carefully. "We're also sharing our thoughts?"

Silver and Crimson stared into each other's eyes. Simultaneously, they turned away from each other, sticking their tongues out. Their voices echoed in unison within their combined mind.

"Grooooosss!"

CHAPTER 31

Davɪᴅ sᴀᴛ sɪʟᴇɴᴛʟʏ ɪɴ the front seat of the car, alternately cursing Cobalt and praying for him. Occasionally, guilt crept in for the way he'd handled things. But who could blame him? His dad was in danger, and it was Cobalt's fault!

Still, as he'd reminded Christine, the robots were only kids. Then again, unlike Cobalt, Crimson was innocent. Well, mostly innocent. His kitchen suddenly didn't seem like such a big deal. He'd even laugh at it now, if the situation wasn't so dire.

Christine shared the back seat with their mother. She shifted, stretching her legs. "Any idea how long they should be?"

David impatiently studied his reflection in the windshield. "I'm giving them ten minutes before we give up and call the authorities."

Melinda's reflection smiled back. She folded her hands in her lap. "It's going to work out. You'll see."

David gripped the steering wheel. His chest tightened, but whatever thoughtless words he had ready to erupt, he cut them off. He closed his eyes and exhaled. How could she be so calm? "Aren't you the least bit nervous about what will happen to Dad?"

Melinda narrowed her eyes. "Of course. But it doesn't do to worry. Cobalt, Crimson, and Silver love your father. And you and Christine have equipped them for the job."

David sputtered. "This isn't a cartoon, Mom!"

Her voice remained level. "Dr. Smalls seems to think it is. And that's what makes your little brothers and sister perfect for the task at hand."

David grumbled. "If only Cobalt hadn't been so stupid. I really expected more from him."

Christine reached into the front seat. "David, remember. He's just a kid."

David remembered, all right. "That doesn't excuse him. He made a decision that impacted lives. A foolish decision."

Melinda's voice came from the shadows. "Like another scared little boy I love," she said. "How long ago was that day I had to pick you up from the police station? Eighteen years ago? Nineteen?"

"I didn't get anyone kidnapped or sabotage my family!"

"You broke an old woman's leg. It took her a month to recover, and then she walked with a limp for the rest of her life."

David turned to face his mother. "That's not fair! Jerry Hatchet was so convincing! He told us Mrs. Simmons was a cruel old woman, and it was only supposed to be a harmless prank."

Christine's face wrinkled. "Harmless prank? You dug a trap in the poor lady's front yard! What did you expect to happen?"

David twitched. "I was only thirteen!"

How could they bring this up again? He thought he'd finally lived down this humiliating chapter of his life. It was one moment of bad judgment from an otherwise very good kid. Okay, one moment of terrible judgment. But he was sorry! Very sorry!

Melinda leaned forward. "Almost Cobalt's age." The streetlight partially illuminated her face. "Hex Ten was very convincing, and a lot less innocent than Jerry Hatchet. And it was only supposed to be a harmless shot at being a hero."

David faced forward and cleared his throat. It was one moment of bad judgment from an otherwise very good kid. Cobalt was an extremely good kid. But if David didn't let him out from under the burden of his mistakes, he wouldn't stay that way.

Melinda leaned back into the shadows. "Thankfully, Mrs. Simmons was the exact opposite of the horrible person Jerry said she was. She told the judge that she couldn't bear the thought of ruining a bunch of young lives for one lapse of judgement. She joked that she was done running marathons anyway. She said she could live with the consequences, and she believed you and your friends regretted your actions and would learn from them."

David sighed and tapped his fingers on the dashboard. "It was awful. I'll never forget her screaming for help, and all I could do was say, 'I'm sorry,' over and over."

The passenger door opened. Everyone jumped.

David squinted into the darkness. "Dad!"

Dan Epic slid into the passenger seat. "Give me a phone! Now!"

***

Cobalt's own face stared back at him from the mirror-like surface of Andrew's exo-suit. Ensconced in the safety of his armor, Andrew took one step toward the siblings. His voice projected from a loudspeaker, bouncing around the room at a painful volume.

"Nice of you to finally join me!" he said. "Another minute, and I would've come looking."

Cobalt, Crimson, and Silver had taken cover on the other side of the room. Looking through the maze of shelves, furniture, and assorted junk, they watched Andrew warily, not daring to venture any closer. Cobalt ducked behind a heavy shelf, while Crimson and Silver hid behind the wide base of a particle analyzer.

Silver patted the machine. "The steel casing on this thing should protect us from anything he throws at us," he told Crimson. "At least for a while."

Cobalt unfolded his arms, preparing *Perfect Punch*. "Hand over the refractium! And we want Irk, too."

Irk took a step toward Cobalt. "You came for me! I knew you would!"

Andrew laughed through the exo-suit's loudspeaker. "Don't be a fool! They want the refractium. You just happen to be conveniently nearby."

Before the little robot could react, Andrew snatched him around the torso with the robot tank's massive hand and hoisted him into the air.

He held Irk in front of the exo-suit's cockpit. "You three I need, and I also need the specimen, but him?" Irk struggled against the machine's grip, casting a pleading look where Andrew's face would be. "I think I've used him up. You can have him."

Andrew laughed cruelly. The exo-suit wound up its arm. With a mighty pitch, it flung Irk across the room. A tiny scream flew over Crimson's and Silver's heads. It ended abruptly when Irk smacked the wall behind them with a sickening crunch. A spiderweb-shaped crack spread from the point of impact. Irk's limp body dropped to the floor.

And there he lay—very, very still.

"That," Andrew said, "was cathartic."

Cobalt stared at the tiny body. His eyes drifted and settled on Crimson. She sat motionless, fixing her gaze on their little brother. Gradually, her head began to shake: no, no no! Finally, she clenched her fists, tensed her body, and let out a horrified scream.

Crimson's cry shocked Cobalt out of his daze. She spoke for both of them. A boiling sensation shot through his network as he bolted to his feet, pointing his weapons at Andrew.

"You'll pay for that!" A series of high-pitched whistles drowned all other sound as he unleashed a barrage of ceramic shot.

Andrew stood unyielding as the bullets pelted his robot armor. Everything around him disintegrated as the armor deflected the nanoceramic into his surroundings, but the shiny surface remained unscathed, mocking Cobalt's anger.

Cobalt wouldn't stop. Roaring at Andrew, he kept up the flow of projectiles as everything around his target shattered. Parts of the exo-suit lost their reflective quality as scratches appeared, but for all his firepower, that was the only progress Cobalt made. Scratches.

"Enough!" Andrew commanded.

Snapping out of his delirium, Cobalt relented. He dropped his arms and glared at Andrew, daring him to make a move.

"You know," Andrew said, "I really didn't want to hurt you, Cobalt. I was very attached to you. I wanted to give you a life of comfort and ease. Your every need would've been met, and your only responsibility would've been to serve as a conversation piece for people who came to admire me." He took a step forward. "They say to never meet your heroes. I should've listened. You proved to be ungrateful, rebellious, and a general obstacle to my plans. You can be sure that you are no longer a hero to me."

The exo-suit took aim at Cobalt's half of the room as Andrew continued speaking. "I no longer have any reservations about wiping you out and starting over with a new hero." The giant robot braced itself. "I think it's time for me to choose a new favorite show."

Cobalt dove for cover just before the whistling sound came back at him. His surroundings exploded before his belly hit the floor. A stinging sensation burned the top of his head. Touching it, he could make out a few lacerations where the bullets grazed him.

Silver yelled over the noise, a short distance away. "We'll never be able to touch him as long as he keeps this up!"

***

Crimson couldn't contain herself any longer. Sprinting from her hiding place, she charged at the motionless little form sprawled on the floor. Out of the corner of her eye, she watched the giant polished robot sweep its arms back and forth, spraying destruction. She never really found words to express the instinct she had for dodging projectiles. It was just an indescribable sense that told her where she needed to be and what steps she needed to dance to get through unscathed.

The floor shattered around her feet as she kicked and flipped. One last cartwheel brought her close enough to pounce on Irk, hug him to her chest, and roll behind the cover of a thick-walled storage unit. She leaned against it, clutching the little robot. The cabinet vibrated against her back as it rang from the pelting.

Relatively safe again, she relaxed her grip on Irk and examined him. His body lay limp across her lap.

"No," she whispered, brushing his cheek with the back of her hand. His eyes fluttered. "Oh!"

Moving quickly, she opened the panel on his chest. Crimson was no expert in robot anatomy, but she knew a cracked power cell when she saw one, and she knew she had to act fast. Opening the front panel on her own armor, she found her coupling cable and plugged it into Irk.

Irk stiffened violently as power flowed into him. Crimson's head buzzed as her own power cell struggled to support the two of them on her already diminished resources. The power load leveled, and her vision cleared. She'd barely adjusted when their minds merged. Irk's terrified thoughts flooded into her own, overwhelming her.

"It hurts!"

Crimson's mind floated above her body in a pool of panic. She punched it down, forcing it back into its rational box. She whispered telepathically. "It's okay. I'm here now. I've got you."

"You shouldn't," came Irk's thoughts. "I'm obligated to fight you. Just let me go. I can die knowing that you cared about me."

Irk wriggled, struggling to get free. Crimson now fought a battle on two fronts—one mental, one physical. She pinned the weakened little robot's arms to his sides and confined him in a tight hug.

"I will not!" Crimson's thoughts echoed assertively through their shared mental space. "I'll wrestle you for hours if that's what it takes, until Silver can get in here and release your prohibitions!"

Crimson sensed the glimmer of an idea, but it came from Irk, not her. His voice filled her mind. "Wait, we might not need to do that. I can't modify my own code, but you can."

"I don't know how. That's Silver's thing."

"I can help. Think back on the moment when Silver released your prohibitions."

Crimson recalled the memory. In her mind's eye, she saw Silver plug the cable into her temple and felt him poke information into her brain. They didn't share words. It was more like a picture, or an abstract shape.

Irk reached into the memory, latching onto that thought. He suggested something to her. Another wordless sensation formed, and she recognized it as the code Silver had pushed to her. The moment it took shape, she felt Irk's presence invade her mind. The image almost disintegrated from the interruption, but Crimson hung onto it and let it rematerialize. Irk approached again, more carefully this time. She hung on, counting the milliseconds. When she got to 1,837, she sensed Irk's relief. It was over.

She'd been so absorbed in the operation that she'd nearly forgotten about the physical world around her. The awareness came rushing back when she felt Irk twisting combatively in her arms. Terrified he'd injure himself, she hugged him against her chest.

Irk squealed audibly in pain. Telepathically he said, "You'd think I'd already have the emotional catalyst! What would it take to shock me more than this?"

Crimson recalled an image. A framed pencil drawing of four robot children.

"You're my sister!"

Just as abruptly as it came, Irk's presence disappeared completely from her head. He lay catatonic in her arms. Although the details of his thoughts were gone, their emotions lingered. Overcome with pity, she cuddled her little brother.

How long would it take? Crimson forgot to keep track of the time. Worried, she counted milliseconds again. She only got to 381 when Irk's mind came back to life. She watched nervously as he stirred.

His thoughts echoed in her head once more. "I'm free! For the first time in my life, I'm not anyone's puppet!" He caught Crimson's eye and his smile faded. He shrank, embarrassed. "I'm so sorry. That was very invasive."

She gave him a squeeze. "It was worth it," she assured him. Her thoughts took on a wry tone. "Now, if I had to let Silver do that, I think I'd be sick."

They laughed together in their shared mind.

Irk snuggled deeper into her arms. "Wow! My first hug!"

A sense of awestruck wonder overcame Crimson. Irk was coming to terms with his newfound freedom, and the mental link allowed her to experience his emotions as her own. For a whole year, he'd been prohibited from even the simplest things. Once, he'd been just a little too enthusiastic about a team of ants carrying crumbs back to their colony. Andrew, in a bad mood at the time, prohibited him from uttering the word "cool" or studying ants from that moment forward.

For Crimson, it was as if curiosity, excitement, and joy were three colors of putty, and a generous portion of each had been rolled into a ball and placed into her arms.

"Yes!" she practically screamed. Yes, as soon as they got home, they'd look up everything they could learn about ants. Yes, of course he was coming home with her! He could leave the lab now, whenever he wanted—he just realized. That seemed a little scary, being able to go wherever you want, whenever you want. The world is a big place. He didn't have to worry, though. He had siblings and parents now, and they'd go with him to make sure he didn't get lost or lonely. Yes, it was all very "cool!"

The moment ended abruptly when the rain of bullets stopped. Irk and Crimson had been so adjusted to the constant devastation raging around them that the sudden silence made them both jump.

"What's happening?" Crimson asked.

Irk peeked over her shoulder. Crimson felt his terror as she heard heavy footsteps and the crunching of debris.

"He's coming."

***

Irk trembled as Andrew's voice echoed off the crumbling walls.

"This is no fun! The Cobalt Laser I know was never afraid to take a chance. Taking risks is part of being a hero, after all!" He laughed. "This world changed you, Cobalt. Your experience with Hex Ten broke you."

Thunderous footsteps paced at the front of the room.

"Too much of a coward to stand and face the challenge when victory isn't scripted for you? Fine, I'll come over there and finish you off."

Cobalt yelled back. "Maybe I'm finally learning to rely on someone other than myself!"

Irk craned his neck in the direction of Cobalt's voice. There he huddled, bunkered behind what was left of Andrew's fabricator. Cobalt looked back at him and Crimson. "What do we do?"

"I don't know!" Crimson answered.

Irk clung tighter to his sister. He only just met his family, and here he was, about to lose them! In the cartoon world, Cobalt always had the answer. What would they do now if he didn't?

Silver's voice rose above the approaching footsteps. "Is anyone going to ask me?"

Cobalt yelled back. "Do you have any ideas?"

"No."

In the cartoon world, Cobalt was always a step ahead of Irk and the other villains, but the rules were different here. Irk had designed this machine specifically to defeat Cobalt, and so far it seemed he'd done a very good job.

Wait a minute. That's right. He designed this machine. If it was up to him, how would he take it down?

His own voice surprised him as much as anyone else in the room.

"Hey, everybody! Listen to me!" The words came out in a shrill squeak, and the heavy footsteps halted at the sound. Irk reinitialized his voice box. Funny how even at a time like this, he could embarrass himself. "His arms! His blasters are on the ends of his arms! If you get close, less than two meters, he can't aim at you!"

Footfalls shook the floor as Andrew retreated a few steps.

"You imbecile!" Cruel laughter came from the loudspeaker. "You should've waited to reveal that until I was closer!"

"Oh, no," Irk muttered.

"Don't listen to him, Irk!" Cobalt yelled. "You just put him on the run! Who's the coward now, Doc?"

"Yeah!" Silver peeked from behind his cover to taunt Andrew. "Not feeling so invincible anymore, are ya?" He locked eyes with Irk. "Any more ideas, you just shout 'em out!"

Irk smiled bashfully and snuggled Crimson.

Crimson patted his head. "Good job," she told him telepathically.

Dust rained from the ruined ceiling as Andrew screamed with rage. "I'll show you who's the coward! Every last one of you will tremble, just before I crush you under my feet!" He stomped his armor to punctuate the point, resulting in another rain of debris. "Prepare to..." Andrew stopped mid-tantrum.

Irk had buried his eyes in his sister's armor. When he dared to peek, Andrew stared past him, fixed on something behind them. Andrew pounded his metal fist onto his old workstation table, snapping its heavy wooden legs and flattening it to the floor.

"What do you think you're doing here?" he screeched.

Crimson tensed. Irk sensed her astonishment in their shared mind. He followed her gaze to the door where she, Cobalt, and Silver had entered. Standing there were Hex Ten and Heinous.

Heinous stepped forward with a pronounced limp. "We have come to render assistance." His hoarse voice came out in a stutter. He fumbled with his weapons as he drew them and aimed. One of them fell out of his hand, and the other three shook.

Burns covered Hex's body. He moved more cautiously than usual, but other than that he appeared to be as formidable as ever. Cracks were apparent in his armored skin as he flexed his powerful arms. He produced a low growl that, over a few seconds, developed into a vengeful roar.

Cobalt scrambled backward away from Hex, but the remains of the fabricator blocked his escape. He searched frantically for another opening.

Hex advanced, cracking his knuckles. "You were foolish to forget me, Cobalt," he said. "You left yourselves fully exposed from the rear."

Andrew pounded the floor with his robotic fists. "Crush them!"

Irk didn't want to watch, but he couldn't look away either. He dug his fingers into Crimson's arms, overcome by the fear in their shared mind.

Cobalt's eyes stopped dancing around the room and landed on Hex. Irk was just about to scream, when he thought he saw his brother relax. A smile pulled at the corners of Cobalt's mouth. "You almost got me this time, Hex!"

"Almost?" Hex said, laughing. "There is no escape for you now!"

Hex raged at the ceiling with a maniacal cackle. It echoed off the walls, and then, as gradually as it built up, it trailed off. The confidence drained from his face. He stood frozen, staring straight at the building's air conditioning unit directly overhead.

Cobalt shook his head and let his smile shine. *"Perfect Punch!"*

His ceramic shot knocked the heavy machinery loose, and Hex and Heinous found themselves pinned to the floor under a mass of twisted metal.

"I think I've seen this episode," Cobalt said, dusting his hands, "Next time, watch where you're standing."

Crimson piped up. "Season 1, Episode 11." She scrunched her face. "Somewhere toward the end."

Irk giggled far more passionately than the joke deserved and squeezed her.

Silver rolled his eyes. He groaned, also louder than the joke deserved.

Andrew came fully unhinged. Swinging his arms and stomping his feet, he bellowed in unfettered rage. "I have no use for any of you anymore! I will destroy you all and start over!"

Cobalt motioned to Silver. "He's distracted!" The two of them rushed the flailing exo-suit. Cobalt clung to one of its arms, and Silver climbed onto its back.

Crimson spoke telepathically to Irk. "If I try another lightning bolt, I'll hit the boys!"

"It wouldn't work anyway," Irk said. "That armor would just direct the charge away from all the vital components."

"Then I guess all we can do is help Cobalt and Silver!"

Crimson crouched, ready to spring into the fight, but Irk interrupted her thoughts. "Wait! I have an idea."

An image flashed in Crimson's mind. She froze. "Oh boy. Are you sure?"

Cautiously, Crimson peeked out from behind the cabinet to check on her brothers. She watched the exo-suit stagger aimlessly, trying to dislodge the two pests. "Now's our chance," she told Irk. "I hope you're right about this." She dashed toward Hex and Heinous.

"There's no other option," came the reply. "That rubble won't hold him long. If we don't do this, we're his next target."

CHAPTER 32

Hex Ten strained against the weight on his back. Pouring all his strength into a determined push, he lifted the pile. Some of the debris spilled off the top, reducing the burden. He made a little more headway. Just a few more centimeters, and he'd get his knees under him.

He nearly succeeded when something landed forcefully on top of him and erased his progress. His arms slipped out in front of him, and he landed flat on his chest once more with a pile of debris on his back.

He roared his frustration and twisted his neck to see what added itself to the heap.

That girl again. That irritating, obnoxious girl. He still didn't know exactly what she had done to him in the basement, but it was clear that after twenty-six episodes of ignoring her, he could afford to do so no longer. No more was she a simple piece of the background, a forgettable bit of minutiae that made noise while he focused on important matters. It was time to pay attention. If he heard her name again today, he would commit it to memory.

"Fool!" He fought against the load on his back. "You have only angered me! Your destruction is sure!"

"We have a proposition for you, Hex." He knew that voice. Why was Irk with the girl?

Something poked the side of his head. "Irk! You treacherous little imp! What are you doing?"

"Helping you, if you'll hold still a moment."

There was a click, and Hex felt a presence intruding on his thoughts. "What is this?" he demanded.

"Ugh. This is a disgusting place. I feel dirty already."

Hex knew enough to recognize a mind link. "The girl!"

"My name is Crimson Laser."

Irk's annoying little voice echoed in his head. "We don't have time! Hex, we have nothing to lose, so I'm releasing your prohibitions right now. We hope you'll be grateful enough, or at least motivated, to help us defeat Andrew."

"Yes! Give this to me! Now!"

"Well, that sounds like a strong enough emotional catalyst..." Hex didn't hear the rest of Irk's sentence. The chatter stopped abruptly as he blanked out of consciousness.

When he came to, Irk started babbling again. "Okay, you're back! Here's the plan, just like the Ferusian Crown Jewel." An image of a safe appeared in their shared mind. "Got it?"

"Understood. Go. I will free myself and join you in time to execute my part."

***

Crimson winced when the link broke between her mind and Hex's. There was a mild electric jolt, followed by a wave of calm. Hex's abrupt absence from her head underscored what a burden he'd been. Now she felt like a fresh, clean robot. How could someone survive with a heart so full of rage, and fury motivating every action? She might've even convinced herself to feel sorry for the brute if she'd had time to ruminate on the experience. She jumped off the pile of debris and took cover once again behind the battered cabinet. Eyeing the exo-suit, she gave Irk a little boost and leaned him against her shoulder. Andrew was still occupied with Cobalt and Silver, swatting at them like mosquitoes.

"This is it," she told Irk. "If they can do it, I know we can. Are you ready?"

"I'm scared." Irk clung to his sister's neck.

"So am I. We'll have to lend each other our courage."

"I don't have any courage!"

"Our mom taught me something about that." Crimson intertwined her fingers with Irk's. She raised their clasped hands and showed them to him. "Now, are you ready?"

A sense of wonder flooded their shared mind, and Crimson felt she could take on the world. She knew she'd succeed. She had to. Her new little brother adored her and letting him down was not an option. Not wasting another second, Crimson darted out from behind cover and made straight for Andrew. He saw her coming and got off a few shots, but between her reflexes and Cobalt's and Silver's interference, they didn't come anywhere close to hitting her.

She closed the distance quickly. Leaping, she caught hold of the shiny robot's chest plate and wrapped her legs around its waist. Letting go of Irk, she grappled with the other hand and sandwiched him securely between herself and the exo-suit.

Irk wriggled under her. "Gotta get my hand out from under..." He worked his arm loose. "There!" He now faced the exo-suit's armor plating, pushing away to maintain a small gap between it and himself.

Andrew's voice bellowed from the loudspeaker. "You!" he roared. "I thought I'd smashed you!" The booming echo took on a sinister tone. "Seems I built you a little sturdier than I thought. Well, you're about to regret that. This time I'll step on you, nice and slow. That alloy makes a real satisfying crunch under pressure."

Crimson shut her optics and tightened her grip as Andrew tried to pluck her off his chest, but it was just as Irk predicted. Like a spot he couldn't itch, she was tantalizingly out of reach of the claws' grasp.

Andrew continued taunting. "Fine. The more challenging you make this, the more I'm determined to enjoy it!" He scanned the room. "If I crush you against the wall, I can watch the life drain from those ridiculous cartoon eyes. I wonder what hilarious expression they're programmed to make under those conditions?"

Andrew's monstrous form lurched as he tried to take a step. Cobalt had wrapped himself firmly around the left knee joint, and refused to let it bend. "Good luck getting anywhere!" he grunted.

This whole time, Andrew's amplified voice had been a mix of confidence and rage. Now the ratio shifted, and his words carried only unhinged fury.

"I call this little move the 'Trash Compactor!'" he shrieked. He leaned on his right leg and poured all his effort into folding Cobalt with his left knee.

Cobalt strained. He opened his mouth to scream, but the whine of rocket boosters drowned him out. Silver thudded into the side of the massive weapon, and it began to tip.

"Surprise hug!" Silver announced. Inarticulate noises came from the cockpit as Andrew swung his arms to maintain his balance. He landed back on both feet and froze.

A little red hand glowed in the corner of Crimson's vision.

"Things are gonna heat up!" Irk said. Shutting out all distractions, she focused on keeping Irk in contact with the reflective metal.

"You absolute idiot!" Andrew screamed. "Stop wasting my time! This armor has a higher melting point than you do!"

Irk spoke through gritted teeth. "I know that, Doctor!" He held up his right hand. Vapor curled around it, rising from the layer of ice that had already formed. "I'm the one who made it!" He pulled away his hot hand and slapped the cold one in its place.

Irk's hand hissed as a cloud of steam enveloped them. The temperature shift conducted through to Crimson, straining her further. She counted the milliseconds.

3,128.

The reflective metal blackened as it popped and pinged, filling the crumbling room with an echo that increased in frequency and pitch. Like the safe he cracked in the cartoon world, the rapid temperature shift sapped the strength out of the armor under Irk's hand.

5,219.

Crimson's low battery had already taken a toll. Hanging onto the walking tank as it pitched and rolled took everything she had left. Darkness crept around the edges of her field of vision. She fought to stay alert.

5,328... 5,329... 5,330.

Her power cell scraped at its last reserves, struggling to support both Irk's and her efforts.

Just when she thought she couldn't hold on any longer, a familiar roar reverberated against her back. Any other time, the screams of Hex Ten approaching from behind would've sunk her stomach into her feet, but right now it meant she could stop counting.

7,112.

"Everybody! Cobalt! Silver!" The words felt like marbles in her mouth. She blinked hard to restore her blurry vision. "Let go! Get clear!"

Leaning back, she wrapped her arms around Irk once more and kicked herself away from the exo-suit. As she fell backward, she saw Silver and Cobalt still hanging on. They watched her, apparently unsure whether they had heard her correctly. She almost yelled again, but at the last moment they followed suit. They were barely clear when rapid, massive footfalls passed by her, accompanied by the steadily increasing roar. The noise seemed to come from the far end of a tunnel.

The exo-suit took aim with its blasters and fired. The roar turned into a furious howl, and Crimson saw a shadow pass over her. Blinking again, she made out the form of Hex Ten, braving the rain of bullets with one enormous fist cocked. Sheer momentum carried him the rest of the distance, and the sapphire-encrusted fist connected with the tarnished spot on the exo-suit. A sound like breaking glass accompanied a spray of metal shards. The fist kept moving, pushing Andrew's robot aside and opening a gaping hole in the supposedly impenetrable armor.

Andrew's high-pitched scream drowned out Hex's howling. Hex's legs stopped, but his momentum carried his upper body forward, tipping him off balance. Andrew took advantage of his opponent's blunder and delivered a punch of his own. Hex went sprawling, landing on his head and rolling in an awkward somersault away from his target.

Crimson blinked again, but her vision remained blurry. Even so, she could tell that Andrew was setting up one more shot at Hex.

"Hey, Andrew!" she yelled. She couldn't tell for sure if she even heard her own voice, but apparently it worked. Andrew's armor appeared only as a silvery blur, but she saw it turn toward her. She saw no detail except for one discolored spot—the hole Hex had opened. She pointed at that patch with one index finger and squinted against her shrinking field of vision. She covered her target with the gold-colored blob that told her where her finger was and held steady.

"Be careful!"

Everything went dark and silent for a moment, then she jolted as if she'd just woken from a nightmare about falling out of a starship. She stuttered in and out of consciousness. She couldn't see anything, but sounds faded in and out in bursts.

Crashing noises.

Cheering.

Silver speaking. "Tacky, Crimson! Never use the same catchphrase twice in one fight!"

Cobalt shouting, "No, Hex! Don't!"

Sirens.

"Crimson? Crimson!"

And then she was done.

***

"Tacky, Crimson! Never use the same catchphrase twice in one fight!"

Silver knew his sister was amazing, but not letting it get to her head was important work. He knew firsthand what pride could do to a person, and he wasn't about to let her fall into the same trap.

He looked at the exo-suit lying limp on the ground and pumped his fists in the air. "Wow!"

He wished he could watch it all over again. Crimson and Irk clinging like daredevils, jumping away just in time for Hex Ten to show up and smash a hole in the armor, and then that final bolt of lightning, spraying sparks everywhere and trapping Andrew inside an immobilized husk of metal. He and Cobalt raised a victorious cheer when the invincible robot tank toppled over, finally harmless.

He wanted a closer look at the menace. As he approached, he racked his brain for something appropriately scathing to say to Andrew. He wasn't halfway there before Hex Ten pounced on the prone machine, screaming furiously and tearing at the cockpit with his fingers. Silver let out an embarrassing squeak and jumped back.

"Vengeance!" Hex tore the cover off the cockpit and flung it violently across the room. It smashed a hole through the wall and landed in the alley beyond. He glared at Andrew, now exposed. "I am no longer subject to you!"

Andrew squirmed helplessly in the open cavity. "Hex, please!" He pleaded with the metal monster. "There's so much more for us to do! You're great, Hex! You've proven yourself! With you leading the team, the possibilities are endless!"

Hex set his face. He folded his hands together, raised them high over his head, and prepared to bring them crashing down on the unprotected human body.

"No, please!"

Silver couldn't watch. No sooner did he hide his eyes than a high-pitched whistle blasted across the room, ending in a dull thud. Cautiously, Silver took his hands away. The exhausted giant lay collapsed in front of the exo-suit. Several meters away, Cobalt stood, brandishing *Perfect Punch*.

Hex began the arduous process of picking himself up. Cobalt closed the distance between Hex and himself, stopping beside the downed exo-suit.

"No, Hex! Don't!" he said, maintaining his aim. "I won't let you stoop to that!"

Andrew propped himself on the edge of the open cockpit. "Oh, Cobalt Laser! You saved my life!" he gushed. "Thank you so much! You truly are my hero!"

Cobalt kicked the frame of the exo-suit and Andrew fell back inside with a grunt. "Shut up."

He returned his attention to Hex. "It's over, Hex. We'll let the authorities take it from here."

Silver stood at the ready in case Hex retaliated, but the fight was clearly over. Eyeing Cobalt resentfully, Hex walked to the other side of the room, pointedly keeping his distance from Andrew. Cobalt tracked his movements, keeping *Perfect Punch* trained on the fuming robot. Hex made his way to Heinous, who had nearly extricated himself from under the wrecked air conditioning unit. Hex finished clearing the rubble with a mighty heave and hefted Heinous to his feet.

"We," Heinous said haltingly, "we are defeated."

"Yes, once again." Hex's voice dripped with bitterness. He addressed Cobalt. "I wish to release the prohibitions on Heinous. Grant me that. Our fight today is done."

Silver relaxed as Cobalt withdrew *Perfect Punch* and folded it back into his arms.

Hex pulled a cable from his temple and performed the procedure.

Silver smiled. Even if it was Heinous, that was the final robot to be released. None of them remained under the authority of Dr. Smalls. He walked over to Cobalt and put a hand on his shoulder.

The wail of distant sirens approached. As they got louder, blue and red lights shone through the cracks in the walls.

"Police!" Silver said. "I guess it's finally over."

Hex propped Heinous over his forearm. "I take my leave."

Cobalt jerked away from Silver. "What?" He tensed. "You can't just go!"

Hex chuckled. "No, I can't just stay." He jostled Heinous. The former general hung limp. "I am prepared to forgive you, Heinous, if you will recommit yourself to my leadership."

Heinous's voice stuttered. "Dr. Smalls has no honor," he rasped. "I align with you, Lord Hex. I will seek to atone for my error."

Hex gripped Heinous firmly. His lip curled, and he raised an eyebrow at Cobalt.

"I'll get you next time, Cobalt Laser." He didn't shout it this time. In fact, Silver thought he heard a trace of respect in the farewell.

The hole in the wall, made when Hex threw the cockpit hatch, gaped nearby, and Hex made a run for it. Cobalt prepared *Perfect Punch* again, almost halfheartedly, but Hex and Heinous disappeared into the early morning darkness before he could aim.

"Don't move!"

Armored police spread through the building, weapons at the ready. Cobalt and Silver raised their hands.

A welcome voice shouted above the chaos.

"Where are they? Are they okay?" Melinda entered the room close behind a commanding officer. David, Christine, and Dan followed her.

"Mom!" Cobalt and Silver said in unison.

Melinda put her hands to her face and gasped. "Oh, boys!" The relief didn't last long. She dropped her hands and scanned the room desperately. "Where's your sister?"

Christine pointed to a heap of shiny red metal on the floor, huddled over a tiny lump of copper. "There!"

CHAPTER 33

"Crimson? Crimson!"

Everything faded.

"I think it worked." Irk's voice echoed in her mind, far, far away.

"I can't move," Crimson replied. "I think that's the end of my energy reserve. Are... Are we going to die?"

"No!" Irk assured her. "Sorry, it didn't occur to me to say anything. In this world we can survive a complete shutdown. Of course, waking from one takes hours, and it feels terrible."

"I can't imagine feeling much worse," Crimson said. Everything hurt. She was suddenly aware of parts she didn't know she had.

Irk giggled. "I love you!" he said. "I love you so, so, so, so much!"

A warm glow bathed Crimson's disembodied mind, soothing her pain.

"I can't wait to get you home," she said. "You can share my room for a while. It's probably going to take them a month to pry you out of my arms, anyway."

Irk disappeared from her mind. That was it, then. She nearly fell asleep when a pinprick of light appeared in the distance. It glimmered there for a moment, dancing. There was a click, and it rushed into her eyes and flooded her skull.

The world seemed close again, right outside her head. An ocean of bright light inundated her, and noise. Lots of noise. People everywhere, shouting, moving things, throwing things.

Her head throbbed, and her stomach turned inside out.

The light took shape, and she came face-to-face with Silver. He almost touched noses with her.

"Are you okay?" His eyes looked monstrous at this angle.

"Aaaaaaah!" Her arms and legs went rigid. "Sillll-verrrr!"

Silver recoiled, falling on his rear end. "Huh. You're welcome, I guess."

He picked himself up and knelt beside her. An interface cable ran from his power cell to hers. She traced the cables, and to her relief found Irk still daisy-chained to her. She brushed his cheek, and he stretched languidly in response.

His eyes opened. The mental link returned. "What happened? Did we win?" His words echoed in her head.

Silver's voice dominated their thoughts. "Did you win? You more than won! You should've seen it! It was amazing! You're both incredible!"

Crimson put her hand to her head. "Whoa, slow down." She could not fathom how someone could yell a thought, but if anyone could do it, it made sense that Silver would be the one to figure it out. She felt the intensity recede in their shared mind as Silver took control of his emotions.

"Sorry. Hey, come here." He slid her onto his lap and leaned against a chunk of bullet-riddled debris, cradling her and Irk. Crimson wished she could see this gentler side of her brother more often.

Silver broke the silence again.

"Hey Irk, you remember back in the lab when I said I was nothing like you? It's bothering me."

Irk curled up and smiled warmly. "Don't worry about it. You didn't know. None of us did."

Silver hugged his little brother as carefully as he could. "No, that's not it," he said. "I wish I was more like you."

A voice came from outside. "She's okay!" Crimson recognized it as Christine's.

Another voice, Melinda's. "Oh, Crimson!"

Crimson reached for Melinda.

"Mom," she said. The word carried her exhaustion with it. Melinda squeezed her hand. Christine, David, and Dan followed a few steps behind her.

She heard Silver's mind. "I'm sharing a power cell with my sister and brother. Gross."

"Worse than that, we're sharing our thoughts."

"Grooooooosss," they thought in unison. They laughed together, audibly.

Crimson looked into the faces around her and caught them staring back curiously.

Silver noticed too. "Oh, excuse us. We're doing a little telepathic thing over here." He shrugged. "It was an inside joke anyway."

Irk giggled too. It was the first audible sound he made since they connected, and it came out distorted. Crimson snapped to attention. She hadn't taken the time to really look at him until now. Cracks and dents covered his body. She ran her fingers down his back and realized he'd been flattened when Andrew dashed him against the wall.

Irk winced and squirmed in response to her examination. She withdrew her hand. "Oh, I'm sorry!" she said.

In the process, she noticed that her own right index finger was completely missing. Her knuckle ended in an ugly lump. The rest of her finger was probably a puddle of metal somewhere on the floor, and

Dad's handkerchief was likely vapor. She still had the other half of it, at least. She glanced around, searching for something that might work as a mirror. The exo-suit lay on the other side of the room, too far away for her to make out any detail. She decided it was for the best.

"It's okay," Irk said with his staticky voice. His right eye drooped dark and lifeless over a caved-in cheek. "It hurts, but that's all. For the first time in my life, I feel…" His left eye scanned the faces around him, taking each one in. "Wonderful."

Crimson looked past her family at the scene around her. Police led Dr. Smalls away in handcuffs while others tagged evidence and snapped pictures.

"Where's Hex?" she said aloud.

Cobalt answered. "He took Heinous and got away."

"Just like in the cartoon," Irk said. "I'm glad I didn't have to go with them this time."

Cobalt patted Irk gently.

"Me too, buddy," he whispered. "I only wish I had taken you with me when you asked the first time. I promise with all my heart, from now on I'll always be right there beside you."

"You were already there," Irk said, "from the moment you decided to come for me."

Crimson squeezed Irk's hand. "We couldn't have done it without you, Irk. You're a hero!"

Irk drew back, astonished. "Me? No, you're the hero, Crimson. Without you, we never would've made it."

"Thank you, but it wasn't just me." Crimson poked the stub of her missing finger at her youngest brother. "Irk, you are a hero. Don't argue with your big sister. Cobalt, Silver, we needed you and you came through. David, you were the first one to have faith in us. Christine, you gave us and taught us so much. Dad, you risked your life for us.

And Mom..." Crimson looked deep into Melinda's eyes. "Mom, thank you."

Melinda put her hand on Crimson's shoulder. "Do you know who Crimson Laser is? She is kind, thoughtful, and selfless. She has a strong sense of justice. She hates seeing people suffer. And she will do anything for the people she loves."

Tears rolled down Christine's cheeks. "Crimson Laser..." She drew a stuttering breath. "You are very, very strong."

Dan took Cobalt's hand and knelt beside Silver. "I've been a grumpy old man for a very long time, and I'm afraid I haven't been a lot of fun to be around."

He looked tenderly into Melinda's eyes. She brushed his cheek.

"And then a bunch of robot children came looking for me and wouldn't take no for an answer." One by one, his steely gray eyes took in Cobalt, Silver, and Crimson, then he gently set his hand on Irk's head. "I am so proud of what you've become." Tears filled his eyes as he turned to David and Christine. "All of you."

He looked away, smiling. "It's been a long time since I've been excited to see what the future holds. I think I'm ready for a fresh start."

The officer in charge tapped Dan Epic on the shoulder. "Excuse me, sir. I need to take a statement." Dan wiped his eyes before walking away.

Silver squirmed uncomfortably.

"Hey, guys." He shifted Crimson and Irk in his arms. "I might not have been throwing lightning bolts around today, but I haven't exactly been slacking either. I've got less than half a power cell left, and three robots to feed with it. I know it's a little intense right now, but do you think you could get some sleep?"

The mere suggestion made Crimson's head droop. She took another look at Irk through heavy eyelids. He was already out. She smiled, nodding her head. "I think..."

She didn't finish the sentence.

***

Cobalt watched his sister drift off to sleep. A moment later, Silver's eyes grew heavy, and he began to slump. Melinda and Christine propped him, Crimson, and Irk into more comfortable positions.

He felt a tap on his shoulder.

"Hey, buddy."

He turned around. "David!" He fidgeted. "I... I'm..."

David wrapped his arms around him. "You'll never have to say it again. I forgive you. Can you forgive me? The blame I put on you was very unfair."

Cobalt shuddered. Tears streamed down his cheeks, and he buried his face in David's chest.

David patted his back. "Let's go for a walk." He took Cobalt by the hand and led him out of the miserable building.

Two minutes later, they sat on the hood of David's car, watching emergency crews dart in and out of the building while police taped off perimeters and reported to each other. The sun peeked over the horizon. In its light, the garage looked like something from a war zone. With all the cracks and holes in the walls, Cobalt wondered that the building still stood.

"Everyone okay here?" A stocky, gray-haired woman in a paramedic's uniform approached them.

David sat straight and cleared his throat. "Yes, I'm fine."

The medic nodded pleasantly at him. She turned her attention to Cobalt. "How about you?" She touched the top of her head while looking at Cobalt's. "You have a little something going on up there."

Cobalt had completely forgotten his injuries. "Oh, yeah. I'm fine. It doesn't even hurt anymore." He touched the place where the nanoceramic shot grazed him. He winced and snapped his hand back, then chuckled. "Well, as long as I don't touch it."

The medic held a finger in front of Cobalt's face. "I loved your show when I was in school. I was so sad when it got cancelled." She moved the finger left, right, up, and down while Cobalt tracked it with his eyes.

"Thank you." Cobalt sidled up to David and looked at her bashfully.

She pulled out a tablet device and made some notes. "They're taking good care of your brothers and sister. They've set up a generator. That should hold them over until we get this whole mess sorted out." She winked at him. "It was very special to meet you, Cobalt. If anything changes, let anybody here know and we'll be there to help."

"How about that," David said. "She's a hero, and you're her hero." He put his arm around Cobalt. "I'm lucky. My own brother is my hero."

Cobalt smiled back. "Mine too."

Dan Epic emerged from the building. Blinking in the sunlight, he noticed David and Cobalt and headed over.

"May I sit here?" he asked. Cobalt made room, and Dan sat on his other side.

Dan wrapped his arm around Cobalt's shoulder. "Thank you for saving my life," he said.

Cobalt didn't know what to say. He leaned against his creator and thought about who the man was to him.

"Thank you for creating mine," he said. The words felt off the cuff, but he meant them.

"Son," Dan said. He paused, squinting at the sunrise. "You did so much more than pluck me from danger today. I'll live to see tomorrow, but that wouldn't have meant much to the man I was just over a week ago. That man would've put on his shoes tomorrow morning, gone to work, and then home in the evening, still wondering why it was worth the trouble. The man I am today..." He choked. "Thanks to you..."

He stopped and blinked at the sun again. Tears streamed down his cheeks. He let go of Cobalt's shoulder and tugged on David's sleeve.

"I wasn't what I should've been," he said. His voice croaked. "I'm so sorry. But I can be that to him. I can be that to Cobalt, Silver, Crimson, and Irk. Hopefully you can see that and know what I could've been to you."

Dan bowed his head of gray hair. The wiry strands sprawled in every direction, and his rumpled clothes heaved with his sobs. Tears fell from his eyes, leaving shiny spots on his scuffed loafers. "I'm sorry, David."

David wrapped his arms around his dad, squeezing Cobalt between them. "It's not too late, Dad," he said. "I'm here. Christine is too, and Mom."

Cobalt scrunched himself into the diminishing space and waited patiently. The embrace went on for a while, and he couldn't help himself anymore. He giggled at the humans squishing him flat.

Dan and David parted. "Sorry, buddy!" Dan said, chuckling and wiping his eyes. He rested his hand on Cobalt's back.

Cobalt beamed at him. "I searched the galaxy for you," he said. "I wanted a creator to tell me who I am, my place in the universe." He took his dad's and brother's hands in his own. "But I got a dad. And a family. And we're the universe to each other."

They watched together, side by side, as the sun rose over the city. Dan forced the lump from his throat. "From now on…"

Cobalt finished the sentence with him. "I'll always be right there beside you."

SERIES: Cobalt Laser SEASON 3, EPISODE 2

"A Fresh Start" TIMESTAMP: 00:00

HI, I'M COBALT LASER, the most interviewed robot on the planet!

It's not as impressive as it sounds. All told, I'm a pretty ordinary guy.

As you can imagine, our story made headlines all over the world. A lot of people supported us when they learned about the orphan robots that finally found a family after searching a cartoon galaxy and a real-world city. Ultimately, the courts ruled that the law defines robots as property, and we were turned over to Dan Epic, our rightful owner, as Dr. Smalls had stolen the source of our personalities from him. The judge told us we could count on robot law changing very soon, but for now we're just glad it worked out in our favor.

Dr. Smalls challenged the ruling and swore to appeal, but we've been told not to worry about him. He's got his hands full appealing his prison sentence.

A lot of people are excited about the Adaptive Personality technology. Researchers at the university are trying to reverse engineer Dr. Smalls's work. There's still that little matter of it being part of a world domination scheme, but all the professors seem nice so far, so we feel pretty good about it. They ask for a lot of cooperation from me, Crimson, Silver, and Irk.

Speaking of my brothers and sisters, they're doing great. Silver loves the factory. He and David have taken ownership and are using the latest technology to expand it. David hasn't quite reached Christine's level of fame, but he says he has enough success to keep him busy. Epic Manufacturing has gone far beyond turbine blades and is now one of the leading producers of robot systems in the world.

In his spare time, Silver has also uncovered many of the mysteries behind the symbiosis between us and the fabricator. He figured out what made it possible for me to cry, and that opened the door to a multitude of possibilities. The first priority on the list? Let robots eat pie.

And we eat a lot of it now that Mom helped Crimson open her bakery. That's right. Crimson is making pie, and this time no-one is laughing. Thanks to Christine's business advice, Crimson's name is on grocery shelves everywhere, and she has her own line of bakeware. There's even talk of her getting her own cooking show.

Oh, and it turns out that boysenberry is a real thing. I personally hate it. Dad says that's good, otherwise it would've ruined the joke.

Dad retired, from both the manufacturing and entertainment industries. He just wants to spend time with Mom and us kids, human and robot. He took Irk to meet the people who created Inspector Princess. Irk had the chance to tell them what Inspector Princess meant to him, and that gave him some closure. He's excited now about creating his own cartoon. He spends all his time drawing and writing, and Dad is teaching him everything he learned from creating our show.

Hex Ten and Heinous are still at large. Investigators caught wind of robots working with an underground group, most likely the organization that Dr. Smalls belonged to. It's only a matter of time before they resurface. With that in mind, Christine stepped back from her controlling interest in Epic Investments and devoted herself to our development and training. With help from Silver and Irk, she worked out the bugs in Crimson's lightning bolts and improved the rest of us as well. Now it's practice, practice, practice. We can all cry now, and training is usually when it happens. Christine is a good sister, though. Like Crimson, you can count on her to make it better when it hurts. And we love it when Aunt Darlene takes a break from running the investment firm and comes to visit. We can count on her to spoil us when Christine is expecting too much.

As for me? Well, I wanted to be a hero, so I joined emergency services. Now I go around helping people in need. A lot of people call me a hero, because of that and because of my story. But I don't know. I've seen a lot of heroes, and I think I have a lot to learn. Often, I think back to when I faced Hex Ten and told him I wasn't the only hero of the story. I don't think any one of us is a hero on our own. In an emergency situation, every member of the crew has a job. And facing Dr. Smalls, I needed all my brothers and sisters, metal and organic, and I needed my mom and dad. And they needed me.

And you know what? Day-to-day living in this world isn't easy, either. There are times when I would rather fight Hex Ten and Heinous again than get up for work, improve myself, or fix a relationship. But I face those challenges anyway, because taking risks is part of being a hero. So it's going to be okay. A lot of people love me, and they've promised that they'll be right there beside me.

So, am I a hero? I suppose it's possible. But if it is true, then I'll bet you're one too.

The End.

Acknowledgements

First off, I want to thank my children. You guys—whether I witnessed your birth or met you later by marriage—are my best friends and the heart of this story. I could never have written *Cobalt* if I hadn't been a parent. Whether you personally enjoy the book or not, I hope these pages serve as a reminder of my love for you.

And Mom and Dad, I couldn't have been a parent if you hadn't shown me how. It's a hard job, but you stuck with it, and I am forever grateful. Thank you for all the lessons and support, and for giving me the freedom to chase my dreams and opportunities.

F, thank you for your art. Without you, I still wouldn't have a mental image of Cobalt. It was so much fun to work with you, both here and with Fountain's Pen. I wish you tremendous success, and I hope we get to do this again soon.

My editors: Stephen, Lucy, and Kate. I can't recommend you enough, and I hope you get all the fun and exciting projects you can handle. Lucy, your developmental notes in particular made this book ten times better than the manuscript I gave you.

I had a few beta readers at various stages of development and I appreciated all of them, but I especially want to thank Belén Ou Yang. Your glowing review of a very early draft kept me going whenever I felt like giving up. Cobalt owes his existence to you, and you are a hero in his world.

I also deeply appreciate Joshua Pruett and his storytelling course. You opened my eyes to a world of possibilities in just a few short sessions. Also, thank you forever for suggesting that a certain amateurish fanfic screenplay just might be better retold as a novel with original characters. Whether this sells ten copies or a million, it's my own.

And call me crazy, but I'd like to thank Cobalt, Crimson, Silver, and Irk. I know you guys only exist in my heart, but during a very difficult life season, I treasured our time together. You were right there beside me, and I love each of you very much.

About the author

Jeremy A. Freed has loved cartoons as far back as he can remember, and all that time has wished he could visit the cartoon world. Acknowledging the impossibility, he decided learning to make cartoons would be almost as good. That pursuit led him to the art of video game programming. He chased that dream briefly before it parked him firmly in a career of software engineering in the "sensible" fields of business, logistics, and manufacturing.

That treated him well. He has had four children, and they bring him much delight. He is immensely grateful for a career that kept everyone fed, clothed, and housed, and he describes himself as inexplicably blessed. But unexpressed creativity is a heavy burden, and he often wondered, "What if?"

Cobalt Laser is his attempt to satisfy that question. And in that process, for a few hours here and there stolen from late nights and quiet weekends, he did get to visit the cartoon world. And it was just as much fun as he hoped it would be. Today, he lives in the real world in Illinois with his two youngest kids and a couple stray cats that somehow got in here.

You can find him on Twitter/X @JeremyAFreed.

About the illustrator

When I asked F what he'd like to say on this page he said, "Just make something up for me."

I will try. I've been working with F for over a year now, and in that time I've come to like and appreciate him. And I love his art.

I wanted someone who could 1) design characters and 2) draw robots. He's drawn XJ-9 tens of thousands of times, so that's box 2) checked. As for 1), like all artists F has his own unique style, but he usually has to bend it for his employers. I'm glad he could be himself for *Cobalt*. I teared up when I finally saw the Laser siblings for the first time.

Like me, F grew up in the Midwest, where careers are "professional" when they're "practical." He left for Hollywood in time to contribute to Nickelodeon's Golden Age, where he built an influential career making things you have surely seen and are likely posting memes of today.

He now lives in North Carolina with his wife, two dogs, and a delightful daughter whose artistic skills he is carefully cultivating. He runs Fountain's Pen Productions, his independent animation studio where he helps undiscovered talent connect with opportunity.

I'm glad our paths crossed, F.

You can find him on Twitter/X @FountainCartoon.